About the Author

Charlotte Gilbertson is a veterinary surgeon and author of the new novel *A Witch's Deceit*, the first instalment of an intricate three-part series.

When she's not imagining new worlds in a land of fantasy fiction, Charlotte is working full-time as a small animal veterinary surgeon. She loves to run, write and brunch, and started writing her debut novel during her first year studying at Nottingham Vet School. Through her childhood, Charlotte was enthralled by the bittersweet stories of authors like Michael Morpurgo, and only hopes to enhearten a new audience with the story of her own perfectly imperfect character.

Dear Alice,

Hope you enjoy this first edition!

Love Charlotte xx

C.R. GILBERTSON

A Witch's Deceit

C R Gilbertson

A Witch's Deceit

Olympia Publishers
London

www.olympiapublishers.com
OLYMPIA PAPERBACK EDITION

A CIP catalogue record for this title is
available from the British Library.

ISBN: 978-1-80074-155-3

This is a work of fiction.
Names, characters, places and incidents originate from the writer's
imagination. Any resemblance to actual persons, living or dead, is
purely coincidental.

First Published in 2022

Olympia Publishers
Tallis House
2 Tallis Street
London
EC4Y 0AB

Printed in Great Britain

Dedication

For my family, who always support me through every endeavour I choose and, particularly, for my nan, who has kept the countless pages of hand-written, unfinished stories I've written throughout the years.

Acknowledgements

Thank you to my family who have shaped me into the person I am today, for encouraging my creativity and passion, and giving me a drive without which I wouldn't be where I am today.

Thank you to all my friends, old and new, who not only inspired some of the friendships between my characters, but also to those special few who have listened to me talking through the fictitious storylines running through my head. Special mention to Jade Smith, my novel's number one fan, who invested her time and patience in reading all of my first drafts.

And, finally, thank you to all the authors through my childhood, and even now, whose imagination and skill create characters I can believe are real. You inspired me to create my own and I only hope my work can do for someone else what yours did for me.

CHAPTER 1

The hallowed halls of Vistaldors were alive once again with the chorus of students ready for the start of a fresh school year, all raring for what the year would bring. The corridors radiated with life as the castle brushed off its cobwebs and cleared the dust that had gathered over the long summer. Flame torches lit each hallway igniting every morning as the dawn broke across the horizon.

Students flocked from far and wide to attend Vistaldors, the most renowned school for magical creatures in all the regions. The school had an outstanding reputation for nurturing the students' budding talents. Many creatures of the graduating classes went on to become leaders, scholars and pioneers, and many went on to join the Guard, a peacekeeping order vital to the preservation of the magical world. A magical world that had Vistaldors at its very heart.

Vistaldors was more than just a school, it was a home. A home to many and all magical creatures. Griffins, shapeshifters, witches and warlocks were all made to feel welcome and treated as equals, no matter their species or their talents. Every student had one thing in common, and that was their immeasurable potential. They all journeyed from Hirtshelm, Alsek, Lagen and Pelion to attend Vistaldors, the school that stood firm and strong in Curo, the core region of the magical world.

Though most creatures of the magical world had at least heard tales of Vistaldors, the accepted students were never quite prepared for its grandeur. To most, the school was a sight nothing like they'd ever seen before. The school grounds stretched on for miles along the shallow edges of the Perimere Lake and its surrounding woodland. The grass never grew higher than a brick and it never lost its emerald green gloss. Bunches of flowers bloomed across the well-tended grounds of Vistaldors almost all year round, enlivening the monotonous brick of the buildings that formed the school.

The grey brick of the school's infrastructure, though dark, towered tall and strong. Each individual brick held together by more than just cement and mortar. A potent protective enchantment ran strongly through each and every brick and had done since the school's inception. Even the most powerful magic user would struggle to break it.

The Grand Hall stood at the very heart of the school, comprised of rising stone walls and an arched ceiling that made up the blank canvas for the flickering of the overhead lanterns. The ceiling and its wonders distracted most from the secret room masterly hidden overhead by the convincing cover of ordinary-looking wooden beams, very few were even aware of the room's existence. Even fewer were aware of its purpose.

Magnificent mahogany doors towered at the entrance to the hall, a series of intricately carved patterns whirled through the wood as the doors remained open for all that were welcome. Three winding wooden tables stretched across the marble floor, long enough to make room for every member of each house. A single circular table was perfectly placed in the very centre of the hall, encompassed by the house tables, where the professors of Vistaldors would sit.

At each formal meal time, students would eat with fellow members of their house. Though friendships across houses were certainly encouraged at Vistaldors, the rule was one laid out by their founder, Professor Vistalus, in order to strengthen the unity of a single house. It was a vital aspect to the house system their founder had put in place. The house system, though imperfect, served as a binding agent between the different species that attended Vistaldors since segregation of species was more common in other schools across the magical regions.

Hundreds of years ago, great divides existed between species, so much so that colonies of magical creatures would remain separate, their paths only crossing in conflict. In a time of civil unrest, Professor Vistalus instead chose to build a school that welcomed all creatures, but only if they viewed one another as equals.

The professor implemented his house system to unify those apprehensive about truly mixing and he showed the rest of the magical world that no species was greater than another. Upon their arrival, each student was handed a key. That key would allocate the student to a house and they would become a part of either House Solonious, Armungus or Vistalus. Each house aptly named in honour of a distinguished figure in the magical world's history.

Septimius Solonious was a well-known shapeshifter who lived hundreds of years ago. His tale was told to many young creatures. A cautionary tale for those who tried to manipulate others for their own selfish needs.

According to the stories, Septimius was born in the human world to a farmer and his wife, two humans with no magic of their own. As a toddler, a stranger passing through, unbeknownst to Septimius' parents, gifted him the power of shapeshifting. At first, he could only take the form of the livestock he was surrounded by on their farm, but as he grew older, his power grew stronger and he learnt to control it. He'd pose as influential people to help his parents gain stature in their community and improve the worth of their farm. Before long, his parents were able to sell their farming business for a great deal of money, never having to work a day of hard labour again for the remainder of their lives. Septimius and his family could live comfortably in the estate house he'd procured for them.

Eventually, word had spread of his incredible talents and, in their lust for power, a group of humans tried to use him. They offered him whatever his heart desired in order to get him to do their bidding; to kill people that got in their way and pose as them in their place. When Septimius refused their offers, the humans resorted to blackmail, threatening to destroy the life of comfort he had made for his parents. So, he pretended to go along with their plans. He bided his time patiently. He fooled them into believing he was doing their bidding, and then, when they thought they were secure, he picked each member of the group off, one by one, until they were all dead. After that, no one tried to manipulate him again and he was left to live as he wished, peacefully with his parents.

The tale of Aeliana Armungus was a particular favourite bedtime story for many young witches. She was one of the early witches of the magical world, a member of the sacred sisterhood of witches formed at the dawn of magic itself.

In the beginning, magic was just a raw force lying dormant in chosen people or objects, but it was untested and unknown. The sacred sisterhood, all gifted with a powerful magic, appointed themselves as protectors of magic and its entities. They studied its workings and crafted how witches and warlocks could use it, but the sisterhood weren't the only creatures this force had awoken in.

A great demon Magnus, born to the magical world in a crash of earth and fire, possessed such a power. He saw the magical world as his possession and all those who lived in it as his subjects. He spread fear across the magical world, reigning terror on all in his way and extinguishing anyone that was a threat to his reign. Aeliana was the last remaining witch of the sacred sisterhood and it was her alone who defeated the demon Magnus, banishing him and his demon underlings to the land in between the living and the dead. A limbo inaccessible to anyone where he would remain until the eventual day when the sun sets on magic.

The final house was Vistalus, named appropriately after the school's founder Professor Lionel Vistalus. Lionel began his life as a warlock some five hundred years ago originally residing hidden in the human world until the humans shunned him, running him out of their towns for fear of his power. Lionel was forced from his home to live a life of isolation, a hermit amongst the hills of the Scottish Highlands with just the wildlife for company.

After years of seclusion, Lionel stumbled upon the ruins of what was once a great fortress hidden amongst the hills overlooking the loch. Whilst Lionel was exploring the ruins, he spotted a wild creature, a species that he'd never seen before. The creature had the body of a lion but the head and wings of an eagle, he'd read about such creatures in a book his father had left him before he passed. The creature was a griffin, it was alien to this world, like him.

Intrigued, Lionel followed the creature through the ruins, but when he reached what remained of the guard tower, the griffin walked off the cliff's edge and disappeared. Lionel quickly followed and looked off the edge to see if the creature had fallen, but there was no sign it had even been there. He took a leap of faith and stepped off the edge expecting to experience the rush of free falling and be greeted by the sharp rocks that lay below. Instead, he found he'd wandered through a portal and into another world, the grass soft beneath his feet. The world looked so similar to the one he'd just left, but the differences very quickly became apparent. Lionel looked up and saw a flock of griffins soaring through the sky in a tight formation. A herd of strange looking creatures cantered from the forest in the distance and across the rolling hills. He certainly wasn't in the human world any longer.

From there, Lionel explored all regions of the magical world where people like himself had built settlements full of unique creatures. He met other warlocks and witches, shapeshifters and elves, and he didn't feel quite so alone any more.

After a couple of years exploring, Lionel returned to the hills where he'd come through a portal that should never have been there and had since sealed itself. It was there where he'd found his home and so it would be there that he'd build a school, a school that would later be home for hundreds more creatures. Using the stones of the ancient castle ruins he rebuilt it with his own design and opened Vistaldors School for Magical Creatures.

The ancient castle from which Vistaldors was made, was originally an impenetrable fortress. Now, it was a place of learning. Classrooms equipped for all species' needs surrounded the Grand Hall connected by open arched corridors and underground passages. A student could easily get lost in the maze of underground passageways; they spanned as far as the grounds' boundaries and all the way to the Shacklebolt stadium where students would have the chance to represent their house at their quarterly games.

Three stone towers stood at pivotal points around the main castle. Having once been used as guard towers, Professor Vistalus bewitched each tower to serve as separate dormitories for each house. Inside each tower a spiralling staircase led to two dormitories. The tower of Solonious was decorated with emerald green, velvet curtains that loosely hung across the stain glass windows. Each bed had pillows and blankets made from a soft green silk. The grey stone walls were decorated with portraits of the many forms of Solonious and photos of the house's Shacklebolt teams throughout the numerous generations. The tower of Armungus housed only deep red coloured décor and everything in the tower of Vistalus was royal blue.

It was a start to a new year and the corridors were already ringing with the muttering of students trying to make their way to their first class. The new selected students were getting themselves muddled trying to figure out which underground passage took them where. The older students stood out of the way, waiting for the congestion to disperse. They'd been caught too many times in the morning mayhem rush that always happened on the first day. Trolls used their advantageous size to plough through the bustling crowds, pushing students aside with their trunk like arms. They led the way for the small group of popular witches who often employed their services for the first day rush.

The popular witches were an elite group idolised by the younger students and envied by the older students. There were only ever five witches in the group at one time, each descendent from a rich and powerful family, and possessing a name that gave them superiority over everyone else.

The position of leader of the group had originally gone to the witch with the most power but had since become the witch with the most family money. Sapphire Frinton-Smith was their current leader, only because her father was the richest out of them all. She strutted down the corridors with such disdain for anyone not in her group. She flicked her perfectly quaffed auburn hair away from the eagle-shaped badge she wore over her robes as she looked down her nose at the other students with her shrewd teal eyes. It was the badge of the five popular witches, passed down from generation to generation, and Sapphire ensured it was on show at all times.

One witch looked on from the crowd of students, and scoffed at Sapphire's pomposity. Sapphire paused for a second to pick out the disrespectful witch with an icy glare, but the witch glared back with her deep violet eyes, bearing a disdainful look of her own. Astrid could feel Sapphire cower at her glare and she tucked a strand of her glossy brown hair behind her ear. The blonde witch that had been walking closely behind Sapphire whispered something in her ear and urged her to walk on. Astrid smiled smugly and then slunk back into the crowd of students, keeping to herself and not stopping to speak with anyone. Not many students knew who she was, bar Sapphire and the blonde witch Astrid had recognised as Hesper O'Connor.

Hesper and Astrid had once been best friends, many years ago. They'd been placed in the same house at Vistaldors and bonded fast. They'd shared practically everything. The two had been inseparable until Astrid was taken out of school for two years, leaving without so much as a goodbye. This was Astrid's first term back and a lot had changed. She was once popular and bubbling with personality, now she was reserved and concentrated more on her studies than making friends. She barely spoke to anyone. She hadn't spoken a word to Hesper since she'd come back and Astrid could see the hurt in Hesper's soft brown eyes.

Hesper had only become a member of the popular witches in Astrid's absence. She'd always come from a wealthy family and she'd always been talented, but her ideals were very different to that of Sapphire and the rest of the empty-headed witches. Hesper had a heart of gold that fitted perfectly inside her petite chest underneath her black and red V-neck jumper. She had power far beyond that of Sapphire's and her charismatic, caring personality made her much more likeable to other students. She was a threat in every way to Sapphire but was too nice to use any of that to her advantage, which Sapphire intended to exploit, keeping Hesper firmly under the thumb.

The school bell sounded, and the passages were instantly cleared. That's when Astrid chose to make her way to class. Her first class was Witch Transportation.

At the end of Year 11, every witch and warlock blindly picked out a unique figurine, typically of either a dragon or a griffin. Each figurine was carefully carved using the trimmings of an ancient yew tree and a knife containing extracts of unicorn horn. They were all unique to their owner with one incomparable detail that could only be recognised by the rightful owner.

The selection of a figurine was a rite of passage for any young witch soon to embark on the world. A witch would click her fingers and the figurine would come to life, growing in size and breathing its first breath. When a witch or warlock graduated from Vistaldors, their figurine was gifted to them and the student was presented with a choice: to become their figurine's true master and call upon it when they were needed or to set them free.

Astrid's dragon was named Ender. He'd been a gift to her before she found out she'd be returning to the school. She'd already practised with him in full form several times, although none of them were supposed to have done that yet. She kept that quiet and pretended to go collect her figurine with the rest of the witches from the box their professor kept locked in her office.

Their first lesson would be practical. The students had spent enough time reading about their figurines and writing essays on ancient dragon law, it was about time they got to grips with powering and communicating with their figurine. Some students needed as much practice as they could get.

Their teacher, Professor Rhea Munroe, had been teaching Witch Transportation for years, though you wouldn't have thought it from looking at her. Her dark-skinned face was free from any wrinkles and her forehead pulled taut where she scraped back her thick hazel locks. Her youthful looks and petite frame made her age difficult to place and that was how she liked it. She was a patient witch, but she had no time for troublemakers or time wasters. Students who tested her patience quickly found out how she earnt her reputation as the drill sergeant. The professor commanded respect, the same respect that she expected her students to show their figurines. A dragon was not a witch's plaything and anyone who thought otherwise didn't belong in her classroom.

Before the professor even spoke a word, the witches spaced themselves out across the blank stone wall, each witch looking as nervous as the next, clutching to their figurines. The witches fell silent, not even a whisper to be heard. Professor Munroe paced along the line of students, making a mental note of those she saw with a bead of sweat careening down their flushed cheeks. She stopped at Astrid who stood calm and collected at the very end of the row, unmoving beneath Professor Munroe's dissecting stare. A rumble of creatures overhead echoed off the walls and a cloud of dust fell from the ceiling. The professor sighed and impatiently tapped her foot as she waited for the stampede of students to pass before she spoke.

"Well, witches, you're going to need your figurines if we're going to get anywhere today," barked the drill sergeant. They promptly placed the figurines a good few paces in front of them, and returned to their positions against the wall.

"Right, now we can actually get somewhere. On the count of three everyone will summon their figurine with their finest pronunciation and finger clicking. One... two... three."

"Figuration!" chorused the witches as they clicked their fingers and focused on their figurines.

Professor Munroe looked upon the chaos that ensued and found herself sorely disappointed. Some witches were still furiously clicking at their figurines that sat immobile and wooden in front of them. Others had conjured haphazard creatures with a head for a tail or too many legs for them to even stand. The haphazard creatures were stumbling and fumbling, crashing into the mirrors causing a great commotion whilst some of the dragons unintentionally propelled balls of fire from every orifice. Only a small handful of the class had managed to execute the spell perfectly; a couple of the popular witches, Sapphire and Hesper, and of course Astrid.

Ender towered 12ft off the ground with majestic coarse wings and emerald green eyes. A unique pattern of violet swirls danced beneath his tar black scales and his lavish spikes glistened in the fire light as his clumsy tail swung from side to side. Every time he turned, the professor had to tuck and roll as she tried to take some control of the chaos throughout the room.

When Ender was in full form, he shared an intimate connection with Astrid; the two could feel each other's emotions, pain and every thought that went through one mind would pass to the other. Even without riding on Ender's back, Astrid had total control — a power that most witches take years to develop over their figurine.

"Very impressive, Astrid. Take note girls of what your tragic attempts should actually look like," said Professor Munroe, blowing her cheeks out with a heavy sigh. She looked at the mess around her, finding herself profoundly discontented by their failure. "Girls. Take control of your figurines. Please. Let's try not to burn the classroom down."

The witches were trying to restrain their figurines, but it seemed their attempts were only making matters worse. The creatures were sprouting fire with every stomp as they ran across the classroom, setting the banners hanging from the ceiling ablaze. Professor Munroe clicked her fingers and quickly extinguished the fire before it spread. She ducked as another makeshift dragon sprinted past her and the second tail sprouting from his back swung inches from her head.

"Enough!" she bellowed, clicking her fingers.

There was an almighty crash of thunder and the room tremored with the shockwave as all, but one, of the figurines shrank to its original size each disappearing in a puff of smoke. Professor Munroe had confiscated the figurines of the entire class to keep until the witches could improve their control. She glowered at Ender who, despite her best efforts, still stood tall and calm by the side of his rider. Her brows knitted, and she felt the rest of the class begin to doubt her authority.

With a small smile, Astrid calmly faced her dragon and stroked his nose shrinking him back to normal size. She then picked up her figurine and returned him to the professor's hand before she could even say a word. Astrid's conceited smirk had said enough.

Professor Munroe went to say something, but she snapped her mouth closed as the bell rang out for the end of their lesson. She heard the mocking murmurs of her class and shot them all a fierce glare, which quickly silenced their conversations.

"I expect a two-thousand-word essay detailing the importance of controlling your figurines by tomorrow's lesson if any of you wish to have them returned to you," barked the professor. A chorus of whining irradiated from the witches and the professor sharpened her glare. "What an absolute shambles. Go on. Off you go." She threw her hands out to the side as she dismissed her class and the students swiftly dispersed.

Sapphire barged her way past Astrid, scowling at her as she did so, and then clicked her fingers, flashing to their next class. Sapphire had always disliked Astrid, even more so since Astrid had returned more powerful than ever. Astrid paid no attention to the entitled little princess and grinned as her Ender figurine appeared in her hands. Unbeknownst to the professor, Astrid had used an illusion to trick her teacher, as if she would give up her figurine so easily. The professor would likely be impressed, she had an acquired appreciation for gifted students. Astrid clicked her fingers and flashed to her next class.

The second lesson of the day was Advanced Potions, a class that only the most gifted witches were selected for and yet another class that Astrid shared with Sapphire, much to their mutual disdain. She quickly arrived in the Potions classroom and was the first to arrive, once again. Of course, the perks of getting to potions class first was being able to pick the freshest ingredients and the seat furthest towards the back, away from other people, a place where Astrid felt most comfortable.

A few moments later, Sapphire and Hesper arrived complaining about the loss of their figurines and then began to whisper in hushed tones as soon as they noticed they weren't entirely alone. Not that the change in volume affected Astrid's ability to eavesdrop. Astrid could easily read their lips, a talent she'd picked up when she was six years old and would watch from the staircase as her social workers discussed which home she'd be sent to next.

The other walking witches soon arrived and promptly took their seats muttering amongst themselves.

"Okay, okay, that's quite enough now thank you. Quiet." Professor Teagan Towinni clicked her fingers and the blinds dropped, stamping out all the natural light from the classroom. She caressed her bony, slender fingers along her desk and raked her long raven hair behind her flat shoulders. With a drilling glare of her coffee ground eyes, the witches went quiet and the professor had their attention.

"Today class, we'll be creating the elixir of life." The mutters returned and Professor Towinni fell into her chair with an exuberant sigh, she rubbed her temples and waited for the students to be quiet again. "I'm assuming by the frankly *rude* clucking that you've all made this potion before and will have no problem doing it again now." The chatters stopped, and every eye remained on the professor. Her thin lips twitched. "No? Shame. Well, I do hope you've all got your textbooks with you since this will be a formal assessment. If you're not up to my challenge, then you simply don't belong in my classroom. Don't let the door hit you on the way out." The witches remained still, glancing at one another and pondering whether the professor was being serious, she was. "Well. Get on with it then."

The witches quickly grabbed their textbook from their bags and furiously flicked through for the recipe, their faces stricken with panic when they couldn't find it. Professor Towinni couldn't help the laugh that escaped her lips as she watched the unnerved witches flap about. She'd forgotten to mention that the textbook only listed the potions by their Latin name. She took a long sip from her cup of tea and continued to watch her students, closely observing the ones most likely to crack first under the pressure.

None of the witches were lucky enough to be fluent in Latin. Apart from recognising the odd word, they had no idea what the potion translated to. Everyone looked around at one another waiting for someone to figure it out, so they could catch a glimpse of the page number and follow their lead.

Astrid couldn't help but smirk from her counter at the back of the classroom. She'd been trained meticulously in all aspects of magic, including potion making and had been studying potion books for as long as she could remember. Astrid had practically all potions memorised to heart, so the textbook wasn't really necessary, though she had picked up a few Latin phrases along the way. Not that she'd be sharing that with anyone else in the class. She moved her unopened textbook to the side and lay each ingredient neatly across her desk. She could feel the gaze of other witches nearby who'd noticed she seemed to know what she was doing, and they quickly followed her lead, sourcing the exact same ingredients.

Sapphire peered at Astrid's work, but refused to follow her example. She passed her hands over her book and the letters rearranged themselves on the pages, translating every Latin word to English. She smiled smugly and glared over her shoulder to check that Astrid had seen her handiwork. She had. Though Astrid couldn't help but scoff as she watched Sapphire attempt to extract the spinesickle scorpion's venom. *That's one way to lose a finger.*

Astrid returned her attention to her own work and removed the spinesickle's head allowing his venom to drain into a flask. She snatched the female maurodious beetlebug from her nest and proceeded to chop and dice, making sure it was a female first. Using a male in the elixir of life could result in some pretty spectacular adverse effects. Astrid wondered if Sapphire's tutor had taught her that, smiling as the wicked thought crossed her mind.

Astrid took her small cauldron out from under her desk and filled it with a cupful of yew tree sap. She clicked her fingers and hovered the cauldron over a roaring flame allowing it to slowly simmer. She brought the sap to boil and cautiously added the venom and then the finely diced beetlebug, stirring slowly between the addition of each ingredient. Astrid threw in the juice of three rhubarb stalks and just a sprinkle of jajoomal sand, too much and the broth would sour. A puff of purple smoke lifted from the cauldron and the liquid slowly cooled to a purple molten substance. "I've finished, Professor," she said.

The rest of the class stopped what they were doing and Professor Towinni rose from her chair, her face scrunched in intrigue as she looked for the student who spoke. She wandered to the back of the classroom and found Astrid Harper standing confidently next to her concoction. Astrid wiggled her sample flask and gestured for the professor to give it a try. Professor Towinni pursed her lips. She'd heard many stories in the staffroom of this witch's potential. It appeared she'd been a favourite amongst the professors prior to her unexplained absence. Professor Towinni hadn't been able to fault her written work over the summer, it was that which had earnt her a place in her class, but her true abilities were yet to be tested.

Professor Towinni took the flask and studied its appearance beneath the candlelight. "Hmm." She removed a recently deceased crow from beneath her cloak and trickled a few drops of the elixir into the bird's mouth. The rest of the students had already gathered to watch. Nothing happened. The professor rolled her eyes and opened her mouth ready with a witty remark, but a sharp squawk interrupted her. The crow clumsily stumbled to its feet before taking flight, it flapped gracelessly around the classroom until it found a high cabinet to perch on. Some of the other students proceeded to congratulate Astrid, looking on with admiration before returning to their own assignment. Astrid's cheeks flushed. She appreciated the recognition, but she could do without the sudden attention.

"Not bad, Miss Harper," remarked Professor Towinni, willing to show praise when it was earnt. She spotted the untouched textbook and knitted her brows. "Though arrogance is better left outside of my classroom." The professor looked over to her desk as the dead crow hit the wood with a heavy thud. She smirked and pushed the textbook back in front of Astrid. "You forgot the hawthorn bark. It tends to prolong the elixir's effects for a few extra minutes."

"Thanks, Professor," Astrid replied flatly. She always forgot the hawthorn.

"Let's see if you girls do any better with a spot test," announced Professor Towinni to the entire class, her grin grew larger with the groans that sounded throughout the classroom. She clicked her fingers and distributed the papers she'd written to each student. The mess the other witches had created, vanished in a flash, before any more beetlebugs went walkabouts.

The witches welcomed the sudden chime of the school bell, ringing for their third and last lesson before lunch, Duelling with Professor Phelonius. Duelling was a lesson that most witches and warlocks actually looked forward to; it was the perfect opportunity to put their true power to the test and rivalry between classmates only made things more interesting.

Year 12 was the time when both witches and warlocks would begin to practise the more difficult duelling spells; spells reserved only for when the students were deemed to be in full control of their power. In the hands of inexperienced magic users, the spells could be unpredictable and dangerous, which made the class all that bit more exciting.

The students handed their papers in to Professor Towinni on their way out and quickly made their way to their duelling skills classroom. They didn't want to miss a minute of their new duelling class, especially with what they'd all heard of their dashingly handsome teacher, his reputation preceded him.

Now that the witches were starting a different level of duelling, they'd been relocated to a better equipped classroom. In the centre of the room, an enchanted orb hovered about a metre or so above the wooden floorboards, sharp bursts of blue sparks seeped from its pearl-like surface diffusing across the room. Parchment posters unfurled across the tall stone walls detailing the laws of magic, rules of duelling and step-by-step guides of various spells and offensive moves. Life sized, dark wooden dummies were lined up against the far wall, their paint was beginning to peel away, and the wood had started to splinter. They'd clearly seen a lot of use.

Professor Phelonius' office overlooked his classroom. A marble balustraded balcony led from his office door to the set of spiralled steps that emerged from the bricks of the stone wall. An ancient text lay open, carefully displayed on a beautifully hand-crafted stand next to the wall. Astrid took a step closer, the need to brush her hands against the fragile, stained pages was overwhelming. The pages were bound with strands of gold and the cover was carved from an Elvish wilmore tree. Astrid stole a look at the first page and saw the inked symbol of the sacred sisterhood, it must have been the original text the sisterhood wrote when documenting the birth of magic. How it came to be in Professor Phelonius' possession was another story entirely.

"Quite something isn't it," remarked Professor Phelonius, strutting his boots confidently along the thin edge of his balcony.

Astrid could feel his glare focused on her. She stepped away from the book and looked up to study the professor she'd heard so much about. His eyes were still fixed closely on her. They were like nothing she'd ever seen before, both an enthralling mix of flecks of violet, blue and green, entwining like some astronomical phenomenon. He ran a hand through his voluminous, coal coloured quiff and scratched at his stubbled cheeks.

"Not that you'll have much time for reading it in my class," muttered Professor Phelonius. The professor continued down the steps, each brick emerging from the wall at the very right moment to meet his foot.

The witches watched him intently, swooning with every fluid motion he made. Astrid noticed how he repeatedly rubbed the old scar across his eye as he walked.

"This is an exciting day for you all I'm sure, taking your duelling skills to the next level can be challenging, but that's why

I'm here. I'm Professor Alexander Phelonius. We'll be spending a lot of time together over the next couple of years working on your spells and I look forward to getting to know each and every one of you." His gaze fell on Astrid again. She immediately slunk back amongst her peers. Astrid frowned as she looked around; the other witches seemed to hang on the professor's every word, his voice like smooth honey.

"He can get to know me over a bottle of wine any time," said Sapphire to Hesper, loud enough so the professor could hear her. He didn't acknowledge her invitation, but Astrid noticed the arrogant grin he was trying to hide. She rolled her eyes.

"You might want to wipe that bit of drool off your chin first, Sapphire," remarked Astrid. Sapphire's eyes narrowed.

"All right, that's enough girls," interjected Professor Phelonius, attempting to diffuse the tension before it became anything more.

Astrid turned her attention to the egotistical professor. "And exactly how do you plan on teaching us *witches* spells anyway? Correct me if I'm wrong, but don't warlocks perform their magic differently."

"And you must be Astrid, your reputation precedes you," said the professor as he turned to address his student.

"As does yours," quipped Astrid, her arms folded as she waited for his answer.

The professor snorted, he quite liked Astrid's cheek. "Well, to answer your question, Miss Harper, you're correct. Warlocks wave their hands and witches click their fingers, as someone decided for us years ago. However, anyone who's familiar with the sisterhood's text would know that magic is just an energy and any magic user can perform it any way they so wish. I happen to be well practised with both methods. Perhaps, it would be prudent for you to have a read of that text after all."

The classroom broke out into quiet sniggers led by Sapphire, and Astrid momentarily retreated, her cheeks heated. The professor cleared his throat and the sniggers stopped.

"Now that we've got all questions out of the way we can get on with learning, as it's your first duelling lesson I would like to see what levels you're all at and the spells you already know. There are enough practice dummies for one between two so if you pair up and just try any spells, and I'll come around to observe your current level. Don't worry, every great witch has had to start somewhere," explained Professor Phelonius. With a flick of his wrists, the dummies awoke from their slumber ready to duel with the witches.

Astrid looked around. Everyone had already paired up and they paid no attention to Astrid on her own. She caught a frank smile from Hesper across the classroom before Sapphire roped her back in to help her with a spell. *You don't need her pity.* Astrid turned around and spotted a dummy that wasn't being used, but Professor Phelonius stepped in her way, his shadow towering over her. Astrid's back straightened, and her eyebrows lifted.

"The thought of using a training dummy must be a bit insulting for you. Perhaps you'd prefer something a little more challenging?" probed the professor, walking Astrid slowly over to the orb.

"I'm not one to shy away from a challenge, what did you have in mind?"

"A duel with a live opponent?" The professor studied her expression carefully; the corner of her mouth lifted, and her eyes glowed with excitement.

"Sure." Astrid shrugged her shoulders and placed her palm on the orb.

"Have you duelled with anyone before?" queried Professor Phelonius, keeping his hand off of the orb for now, he didn't want to overstep. He'd been warned of that before with some of his more gifted students.

"Just a handful of times," she replied coolly unconcerned, her expression equable.

"Good. Let's see what you can really do."

Professor Phelonius placed his palm on the orb opposite Astrid's. A steel-based platform rose from beneath their feet, expanding across the classroom. The orb dissolved, its energy spanning over and around the platform keeping the duel and all spells thrown confined. Stray spells flying across classrooms was a sure way for an accident to happen. Astrid ran her hand along the translucent barrier and then took her place opposite the professor, just a few strides between them.

"We can stop at any time," informed Professor Phelonius, shirking off his robe.

"We can stop when I win," muttered Astrid, her hands ready.

A smile flicked across the professor's face, he waved his hands and the dummies returned to their dormant position. "This will be a good opportunity for you all to observe a duel first-hand." Mutters echoed through the room as the rest of the class crowded round the platform, craning their necks to get a better look.

Astrid clicked her fingers and caught the professor off guard, with a thrust of her hands she threw a flare of blinding light from her palm. The professor quickly guarded his eyes. Astrid flicked her other wrist launching the professor across the platform. The witches winced as his back hit the ground but cooed in awe as he quickly regained his balance.

Professor Phelonius swivelled as he stood back to his feet and with a fluid wave of his hands encircled himself in a roaring ring of flames. The flames grew taller and the professor moved covertly as a shadow, hidden amongst the hissing blaze as he controlled their every flick. The flames recoiled with every spell Astrid tried to throw through them and then flickered back, she yelped as they whipped at her hands. One flame mirrored Astrid's every move and then snapped at her like a snake striking out. She leapt out of the way, diving to the floor. She cast a shield of water above her as the flame struck again, its jowls sizzled as they came down on her.

The platform beneath them was slowly getting hotter and hotter. The metal seared on Astrid's palms and she snatched them back. Astrid glowered at the professor. His self-assured smirk was pretty clear through the flames he still hid himself within. Frustration festered through her very being and her temper sparked. She clicked her fingers and threw her hands out and a great wave of water surged across the platform. The water flooded the platform, crashing against the barrier and extinguishing the professor's flames in one fell swoop.

The professor was bent over on his hands and knees in the corner of the platform, soaked to the bone and spewing water. He went to stand up, but he felt the arms of his robe wrap around his ankles pulling them together. He tugged at the material as Astrid wandered towards him, her eyes burning with focus. She pulled the robe tighter and tighter with her magic. Casting her hands towards her, she tugged at the robe and dragged the professor along the floor. He clambered for something to grab and then waved his hand tearing a sheet of steel from the platform and throwing it at Astrid. The steel grazed her head as she ducked out of the way and lost her hold on the robe. Professor Phelonius ripped the robe from round his ankles and stood to his feet just in time to wrestle the panther Astrid had transformed into. She lunged at her teacher, her jaws wide, and he threw her across the platform sending her back into a witch.

Astrid lay crumpled on the platform. Her arms trembled as she tried to get up and then collapsed beneath her. Shapeshifting wasn't meant to be easy for witches and warlocks, it put great strain on any magic user.

The professor held out his hand to Astrid. "Truce?" Astrid glared at the hand and sighed. She reached out to take it and then clicked her fingers hurling the professor across the room. The barrier rumbled as he crashed against it. The class ran to his corner, their faces animate with worry. Astrid lay at the other end, a satisfied grin stretching from ear to ear. *Totally worth it.* She stood herself back up and dusted herself off.

"I think we'll just call it a day," croaked the professor. He winced as he limply flicked his wrist and the barrier fell, blurring into the orb that once again hovered in the centre of the room. The platform slowly deflated, and the witches swarmed around their professor.

"Professor Alexander, are you all right?" chorused the worried witches. They all fussed around him. Sapphire made sure she was first to help him back to his feet, gently wrapping her arm around his waist as she did so.

"I'm fine girls, just a couple of bruises and perhaps a broken wrist which I'm sure Professor Peverel wouldn't mind taking a look at," muttered Professor Phelonius, shrugging their wandering hands away. He rubbed his back and rolled his shoulder, his chest heaved with a sigh of relief as it clicked, and he returned his attention to Astrid. "Some schoolyard duelling rules in play there, but a good duel nonetheless." It was mainly his pride that had taken a beating.

"Some students would get expelled for using those sorts of spells," said Sapphire sternly, her glare cutting at Astrid. Astrid raised a brow and scoffed.

"Now. Now. There's no place for bitterness in duelling," warned Professor Phelonius. "Duelling is worth nothing if it doesn't prepare you with a dose of reality." Sapphire rolled her eyes and stepped away. "Now I think that will do for today, go take an early lunch. I think you've all earnt it."

The witches smiled in thanks and quickly gathered their belongings before leaving for lunch in the Grand Hall. Astrid grabbed her satchel and noticed the professor's tatty robe on her way out. She picked it up and turned back to hand it to him.

"I hope this wasn't a favourite of yours," remarked Astrid uneasily.

Professor Phelonius sighed as he gently took it from her grasp. "I've got a whole wardrobe full of them, thank you." An apologetic smile flickered on Astrid's face and he quickly placed a soft hand on her arm as she turned to leave. "You really don't disappoint, Miss Harper. Those were some advanced charms you used back there that I wouldn't expect from a witch of your age. I look forward to seeing what else you've got."

Astrid looked almost surprised at the professor's complimentary words as though it was rare for her to receive such kind praise. The professor expected some pert remark, but instead she thanked him with a small smile and then proceeded to leave for lunch. Alexander hoped he'd find another opportunity to speak with her properly. Something about Astrid Harper troubled him, but he just couldn't quite put his finger on it. He wondered if she might confide in her head of house, perhaps his trip to Professor Peverel could prove helpful in more than one way.

Alexander checked the time. He'd dismissed his students a little premature for lunch however, Professor Peverel taught less and less classes these days since she became head of Armungus, so he was sure she'd still be free. Professor Peverel had many responsibilities that she had to juggle since becoming one of the youngest heads of house. She was a considerate ear for students to confide in and was frequently visited for her medical advice and skills. Prior to learning of her magical gifts, she'd trained as a doctor of human medicine and then came to Vistaldors to teach history of human/magical integration classes.

Alexander had a hunch she'd be studying in her office in the Armungus tower. She did that a lot, always wanting to better herself for her students. He'd stumbled across her door many times recently, finding himself watching her through her open door. She would usually be too engrossed in her books to even notice he was there.

There she was this time with her book open on a stand, so she could read and practise what she learnt at the same time. Her precious pink, china teacup hovered next to her as she used one hand to stir her two lumps of sugar. Always two lumps, Alexander remarked. Alexander went to knock but before he could, Professor Peverel had already noticed him standing in the doorway and smiled as she removed her half-moon glasses.

"To what do I owe this pleasure, Professor?" she smiled, taking hold of her teacup and tucking a stray strand of golden hair behind her ear. She felt her eyes wander to stare at the sun-kissed chest beneath his damp shirt and noticed the tufts of dark hair springing from the few buttons he left open. Professor Peverel scolded herself and quickly adjusted her inappropriate gaze.

"Sorry to interrupt," he stumbled, trying to not get distracted by her striking teal eyes, they'd been harder to notice behind the frames she often wore. "I'm afraid I had a little accident in one of my classes."

"Of course, have a seat, Professor." She summoned her first aid kit and noticed his limp left hand.

"Just Alexander please." He winced as she examined his hand though her touch was as gentle as he'd imagined.

"Well, you may call me Skylar then," she remarked as she held his broken hand sandwiched between hers and whispered a spell under her breath with her eyes closed. White light radiated from her hands. Alexander barely noticed the pain as he watched the professor at work. Skylar caught a glimpse of his curious expression as she opened her eyes. She quickly released his hand and turned back to the seat at her desk. "How does that feel?"

"Much better," he softly replied, finding some motion had returned to his hand already.

"Your bones should only take about a day to fully heal, so just wear this wrist brace for a couple of days to be safe. May I ask how you managed to break all of your carpal bones quite so impressively?"

"That would be thanks to one of my students, Astrid Harper. She's actually the other reason why I wanted to come and see you."

"Here I was thinking you just enjoyed the pleasure of my company," laughed Professor Peverel, her attention tweaked at the mention of Astrid. "She's got quite the reputation these days. You wouldn't be the first teacher to talk to me about her. If you're going to ask me about why she wasn't in school for two years, I'm afraid I can't help you."

"I know you have a certain confidentiality with your students but surely that's something her teachers should know. There's something about her that worries me and there's definitely something she needs to talk about, it's pretty plain to see," he ranted, standing from his chair. "Surely, the duty of care we have to our students takes precedence here, can't you understand that."

"I can't help you because I don't know myself so don't take that tone with me, Professor," she retorted. Her thin lips twisted, and she placed her glasses firmly on her nose and summoned the book she was reading to her desk, ignoring the rueful look transforming Alexander's face.

Alexander calmed himself and sat back down. "I'm sorry, I just assumed."

"You assumed wrong. Look, your concern for your students is touching but I can't force anyone to confide in me. My students know my door's always open for them and as for Astrid, don't assume that I don't have any concerns myself. She's not the sweet girl that I once taught and don't think I haven't noticed, so if that's everything I'd quite like to get back to my reading now."

Alexander could tell he'd offended her, he hadn't meant to, he knew she cared for her students and had their best interests at heart, but he also knew that there was something more to Astrid's absence. He apologised and graciously left Professor Peverel in peace before he annoyed her any more.

Once Alexander had gone, Professor Peverel rubbed her temples and snapped her book closed, she couldn't concentrate now. She found Astrid's file from her cabinet and began to flick through wondering if there was something obvious she'd missed. Perhaps this was just a belated adjustment phase; growing up in care in the human world couldn't be easy for someone with powers. But then perhaps there was something more to it. The ringing of the lunch bell snatched her thoughts from her, and she proceeded to the Grand Hall. Astrid Harper's incomplete history would just have to wait.

The corridors were packed once again with students, shoulder to shoulder, rushing towards the Grand Hall. Many students feared that all the best food would be gone, but what they didn't realise was that there was no such thing as running out of food in the school of Vistaldors. Every student sat at their house table ready to begin, anticipating what delectable food would be on offer today. The five popular witches pardoned themselves from the formal meal time rules and fashioned their own small table with their magic. The teachers eyed them carefully, but none of them dared to argue. Their daddies donated too much to the school, especially Sapphire's. Sapphire, Hesper, Crystal, Blaze and Delilah all sat gracefully and waited for the food to be served.

The food would only be served once everyone was seated and, of course, there were always the last few stragglers that the masses of ravenous students would glare at as they took their seats. Once the last student had sat down, the mahogany doors swung open and a parade of golden trolleys charged into the Grand Hall all full to the brim with an endless selection of delectable dishes. There was fine roast beef with all the trimmings, honey glazed gammon still oozing with honey, divine duck breast and even a vegetarian option of courgette flower risotto with a bottomless basket of freshly baked bread.

Several trolleys arrived at each table and the enchanted dishes distributed themselves evenly amongst the students and once all the main courses were served, the trolleys refilled with dessert. The students tucked into the succulent meal plated before them, washing it down with a gulp of fruit punch trying not to spill any on the fine silk cloth hand woven by the elves in the outlawed forest of Eldor.

Astrid was sat with her fellow peers belonging to the Armungus house but there was a single empty space either side of her. She'd become a social pariah of sorts. There were already enough rumours circulating concerning her long absence, it seemed her performance in duelling class had only added fuel to that fire. Not that she particularly cared. She sat alone prodding the food on her plate. She could hear the other students whispering about her. *Let them talk.* Astrid straightened her back and tried to ignore the gossip. The gossip quickly changed when Xander took the seat next to her.

"Don't you have anything better to talk about," snapped Xander. His truffle brown eyes darkened as he glared at the gawping students sat at the table. The whispers ceased, and the students stopped staring, quickly returning to their own conversations.

Xander was in the year above Astrid and he was not a warlock to be trifled with. He was the star player of the Solonious Shacklebolt team and his popularity made him practically untouchable, though his athletic physique certainly helped warn off challengers. Xander had had his fair number of fights in his time, mostly protecting Astrid. They'd known each other for years, having grown up together in care. He'd been her protector and big brother when Astrid was at her most vulnerable. He understood her like no one else ever could.

"I'm assuming this seat isn't taken," he smiled, stealing the leg of duck from Astrid's plate.

“I’d be careful sitting next to me, haven’t you heard? I’m the witch who broke Professor Phelonius’ wrist and god knows what other rumours people are spreading about me,” Astrid sighed, returning to pushing the food on her plate around and around.

“Ha, since when are you one to care about what people think of you?”

“Oh, I don’t. I’m just fairly certain the Xander fan club will have something to say about it.”

“Ah so it’s my credibility that you’re worried about, nice to know how little you think of me,” he scowled, passing a hand crossly through his dark, ruffled hair.

“No, wait, I’m sorry.” Astrid looked up at his crestfallen expression. “I’m sorry for thinking that, a lot can change in two years. Would you just sit down, please?”

Xander reluctantly sat back down, his face unchanged even with Astrid’s forced apology. “You’re right, a lot can change in two years, not that you’d know anything about how my life’s been going.” He could see he was starting to make her feel guilty but continued nonetheless, “We’ve been friends, actually family, for years and then you up and disappear. No goodbye. No word. Nothing. Do you get how that made me feel?”

“I do and I’m sorry,” replied Astrid flatly.

“I don’t think you do. Anything could have happened to you. I had so many different scenarios going through my mind. I… look at you… you’re sitting there looking at me like I’m the unreasonable one.”

The corner of Astrid’s mouth quirked, “I’m really not.”

“What happened to you?” he asked more calmly, swallowing down his frustration. The other students had started staring at them both again.

Astrid grasped his hand tenderly in hers and stared ruefully at his sombre face. “I’m here now, Xander. I’m sorry, I really am. I’m sorry I disappeared like that, it wasn’t by choice, believe me. I can’t say any more than that, but I just need you to know that I didn’t want to.”

Xander’s face softened and his jaw relaxed. “Maybe you can tell me how you broke Professor Pretty Boy’s wrist then?”

Astrid laughed and eagerly shared the spell-by-spell account of her duel with Professor Phelonius. Xander hung on her every word, his face alive again with his impish grin. Astrid liked seeing him like this, anger didn’t suit him so well.

Before long, Xander’s friends from the Solonious house had finished their food and were calling him over. “Look, I told the others that we’d go and get some Shacklebolt practise in during our free afternoon, but I’ll catch up with you a bit later. Not a request, okay,” said Xander, jogging over to his friends before Astrid had a chance to argue, not that she had many plans herself.

Astrid returned her attention to her plate, her appetite suddenly much improved. Most of the other students had already finished their food and moved onto their desserts, even the teachers had left the Grand Hall.

One blissfully innocent, young witch had moved with her plate of rhubarb custard to another house table to sit with the rest of her friends. The teachers usually left by dessert and by that time the standard rules didn’t seem to apply. Not according to everyone.

Sapphire immediately noticed the witch and took the rest of the popular witches at her back to confront the girl. Sapphire found any excuse to pick on a younger student far too inviting. She tapped the young witch on the shoulder glaring down her pointy nose. The witch swivelled round in her chair, her face scrunched in confusion as the rest of her friends quickly made themselves scarce.

"Well, well, well, what do we have here? Pretty sure, you don't belong at this table," Sapphire bitterly remarked. Delilah, Blaze and Crystal crowded the little girl, stopping her from leaving. "You're supposed to eat with your house. It's the rules. Do you know what we do with people that disregard those rules?"

"But… but… you all eat together on your own table," stuttered the young witch, trying to keep a brave face.

"Excuse me. Do you know who we are? Perhaps I should remind you," sneered Sapphire.

Sapphire clicked her fingers and summoned a jug of cold custard from one of the trolleys into her hand. The other popular witches giggled as Sapphire trickled the entire jug of custard onto the young witch's head. The young witch bowed her head in shame. The custard soaked her thick raven hair and dripped down her face with her quiet tears. Her cheeks flushed red with embarrassment as the rest of the students around the table began to snigger.

"What was that?" Sapphire laughed, leaning her ear towards the whimpering witch. "Oh, you're absolutely right, no one eats custard without jelly, how thoughtless of me." She beckoned the serving plate of strawberry jelly to her hands, but her laugh was cut short as the plate of jelly struck her in the face. Sapphire shrieked, furiously wiping the jelly from her face. The Grand Hall fell silent as the other witches looked around for the culprit, Sapphire never misjudged a levitation spell.

"Who did that?" bellowed Sapphire, her eyes now roaring with anger. No one made her look like a fool and got away with it. She looked around frantically at the other students, but no one said a word.

Astrid stood up from her seat and waved, smiling from ear to ear. "Did I get the wrong flavour?" Astrid questioned sweetly, stepping back from the table as Delilah, Blaze and Crystal all flocked to their leader's side waiting for her next move. Astrid scoffed looking goadingly at the witches.

"You're going to wish you hadn't done that," warned Sapphire, removing the last bit of jelly from her hair. She nodded at the other witches and the other students quickly scuttled out of the way.

Delilah, Crystal and Blaze all clicked their fingers levitating the chalices from each of the house tables and then charged them at Astrid firing one or two at a time. Astrid ducked and dived using one hand to form a small shield of sorts and the other to fire more spells. She dropped for cover behind one of the enchanted trolleys still trying to fight the others off as they simultaneously walked closer towards her.

Crystal had run out of chalices and moved onto the plates, which hurt even more when they hit Astrid. One chalice knocked Astrid square in the head and soaked her with sticky fruit punch. Astrid's eyes narrowed, her temper simmering. She tucked her hair behind her ears and jumped up from behind the trolley, taking out two of the witches with a couple of the enchanted trolleys and evading the flying plates at the same time. Astrid then clicked her fingers pulling the silk cloth from the Armungus table and trapping Crystal within it. Crystal shrieked as the cloth wrapped itself tightly around her and held her down on the floor.

Astrid pointed her hands towards the paper lanterns and then whipped them downwards with her magic. The whites of Sapphire's eyes flickered with fear as the lanterns swarmed towards her. Sapphire grabbed her chalice, still filled to the rim with water, clicked her fingers and threw it up into the air and blew the water. The water expanded, flooding the lanterns and putting out their fire.

"You want to play with fire, you got it," grinned Sapphire maliciously. Sapphire grabbed the last lit lantern and furiously threw it to the floor. She clicked her fingers at the embers that still softly burned, and the flames ignited taking the shape of a ferocious snake. The flames slithered towards Astrid, striking so fast that not even Astrid's quick reflexes could stop it. Embers spat from the snake's mouth, exploding with a great thunder as it hit Astrid's trembling hand. Not exactly what either of the witches were expecting. Astrid's face was caped in soot. She coughed and held her fingers on the ends of her cindered hair.

Sapphire cupped her mouth and then burst out laughing in hysterics. "Well, what an improvement," sniggered Sapphire, looking rather pleased with herself.

Astrid wiped the soot from her eyes that now seared with irrepressible rage, Sapphire hadn't quite realised the anger she'd unleashed. Astrid exhaled heavily, her hands trembling with fury.

"Nothing clever to say, Astrid, or are we all out of puff?" Sapphire continued to laugh as she turned her back and went to uncover Crystal from the enchanted cloth.

Sapphire pulled the cloth from Crystal's head. Crystal's eyes widened and she frantically tapped Sapphire, urging her to turn around. Astrid stood a few feet behind them, her eyes closed and her hands in a tight fist either side of her. Astrid held her fists in front of her and the floor beneath Sapphire's feet began to rumble.

Sapphire looked down as a great force of water burst through the floor beneath her and she was hurled into the air landing on a couple of spectator students. She quickly got back up, soaked to the bone, and screamed. The sonic pitched screech shattered the stain glass window as her mascara dribbled down her face. A flock of ravens darted through the broken window and headed straight for Astrid.

"Stop!" bellowed Hesper, holding Sapphire still with her magic. The birds were immobilised with Sapphire's silence, their beaks practically inches away from Astrid's eyes. Sapphire struggled, flapping her hands from side to side in an attempt to click Hesper away. Astrid clicked her fingers and broke Hesper's spell, sending the birds out of the window and releasing Sapphire.

"Where the hell have you been, Hesper?" roared Sapphire as she stormed towards Hesper.

"I've been gone for ten minutes and you two are destroying the Grand Hall," replied Hesper. She kept herself in between the two witches who were both eyeing each other up across the gap. "Stop acting like children, both of you."

"How dare you talk to me like that, I'm the leader of the popular witches and if you value your spot in *my* group you better get out of my way, now," exclaimed Sapphire, facing off with Hesper who didn't even move an inch.

"You know what, stuff your group and stuff you for that matter. You're a bunch of bullies with money and I'd rather be kept out of it," retorted Hesper, getting right back up in Sapphire's face. Sapphire cowered slightly, taken aback by Hesper's tone. She'd never known Hesper to have a backbone and she didn't like it.

"I suppose family money can't buy you everything," perked Astrid, looking proudly upon the destruction she'd brought.

Sapphire diverted her attention once again to Astrid and barged Hesper out of the way. "At least I have one of those, a family that is."

Astrid's eyes reddened, she pushed Hesper out of their way with her magic before they both took aim again and clicked their fingers. Nothing happened. They both looked down in confusion, their magic wasn't working. The students were baffled, no one's magic was working.

"I can take this witch down without any fancy spells," exclaimed Sapphire, removing her earrings as she did so.

"Oh, bring it on," Astrid barked, tying up her scrappy hair.

Professor Towinni barged through the mahogany doors holding a crystal mirror and the room fell silent again, every set of eyes was on the professor. She held the crystal mirror of Neron, one of four in existence. The mirror repressed the magical abilities of every creature in one room leaving the one holding it in control.

The professor was not at all happy. Her eyes seemed darker than ever as she glared viciously at the two girls and stared speechless at the mess they had managed to create. She looked around at the broken chalices scattered along the floor and the cracks in the marble floor through which the burst water pipe still leaked. She tutted. She clicked her fingers restoring the Grand Hall back to its former glory; the marble pieces fell into place, the tables were no longer singed, and they were laid once again for the dinner service with repaired crockery and stainless cloths.

"You two, with me, now," ordered the professor, grabbing the two witches. These were times where she wished that using some of her private supply of concoctions on the students was still allowed at Vistaldors. She had various thoughts of the perfectly detestable potions she could brew to serve as punishment for these two.

"Actually, this really isn't a good time for me, professor. I have a non-refundable deluxe serenity package booked with the

Elvish spa in Alsek and I really need it. You have to slip those elves a lot of extra silver pieces to let a witch get a spot like that," replied Sapphire, attempting to walk away.

Professor Towinni grabbed her by the collar and pulled her back. "Oh dear, I think you've mistaken me for someone who cares. The rest of you, back to your dormitories. Now," shrieked the professor. She then continued to drag Astrid and Sapphire out of the Grand Hall and flashed them back to her classroom.

The professor shoved the quarrelling witches into two crocodile skinned seats and sat behind her desk. She clicked her fingers and the arms of the chairs wrapped themselves around the witches' hands keeping them firmly still. Their bickering stopped, and the room fell silent. If one of them went to open their mouth, the restraints only became tighter. They sat in silence listening to the spine-chilling patter and tapping of the leftover beetlebugs shut in a chestnut case whilst the professor locked away her crystal mirror and crossed her legs.

"Well, well, well. It looks like little Miss I'm-so-good-at-everything, and little Miss look-at-me-look-at-me decided to have themselves a fight in the Grand Hall," stated the professor smugly. She dared either of them to say anything, but both the witches were smart enough to not trifle with the professor today. "You're lucky I'm not allowed to use my old methods of punishment, if anyone had broken the window in the Grand Hall ten years ago, they wouldn't be sitting here right now. Fighting is not tolerated at Vistaldors, you two will be on community service for the rest of the week. You can invite that little blonde friend of yours as well, don't think I didn't see she was involved and if I catch so much as you two kicking each other under the table then there will be a two-week suspension on your powers to match. Now leave."

The restraints released, and Sapphire rubbed her tender wrists. "I'm sorry for our disgraceful behaviour, professor, it was just a small misunderstanding over pudding really. Maybe you could have my spot at the Elvish spa and we can forget all about this, what do you say?" smiled Sapphire, heading towards the door.

"How thoughtful, Sapphire. I say *two* weeks of community service should get the message across then. Would you like to go for three? You two and your friend will report to me every morning before class," screeched the professor, slamming the door once the witches had left.

Astrid and Sapphire glared at each other in mutual disdain before heading their separate ways. They'd try to keep out of each other's way for now as bickering would quickly turn to another fight and neither of them wanted to have their magic suspended. Sapphire was unlikely to let the humiliation slide and would surely find a way to repay Astrid at some point. *She could try.*

Astrid took her books and flashed to a small green space on the edges of the school grounds that was hidden behind the apple orchard and cornucopia of plants grown for potion ingredients. She didn't have to listen to the wittering gossip of the other students when she was there. It was her and Xander's spot to talk and play all those years ago, before things got complicated. She laid on her back beneath the sun and closed her eyes content with what she'd accomplished today. It felt good standing up for that witch, she thought to herself, and splitting up the witless witches was an added bonus.

CHAPTER 2

A fresh blanket of snow lay across the hilly slopes of Curo; it had settled neatly upon the leaves of the trees with just a light dusting on the roof of Vistaldors. The harsh winter cold thrashed across the students' sore red faces as they firmly wrapped themselves in layers and layers of their winter uniform and made their way across the grounds. Classes had been dismissed for the day as a reward for the recent improvement in academic performance, so the students could actually enjoy a day of the snow that had come early to Vistaldors, before the winter storm truly arrived.

Astrid sat in the Armungus dormitory for the majority of the morning. Whilst the others were outside hurling snowballs at each other and building snowmen, Astrid sat in front of the spitting fire studying her favourite book, Larissa Lawson's Book of Advanced Spells. She hadn't had much time for reading during her community service stint, scrubbing cauldron pots and tending to the ground's horticulture weren't going to aid her spellmanship. She had wanted to get some extra practise before her next duelling lesson, and they'd be quite useful should Sapphire decide to try her luck with Astrid again.

It had been a quiet couple of weeks without any altercations with Sapphire. They'd both taken Professor Towinni's warning pretty seriously. Apart from the odd encounter here and there, the two witches had managed to keep their distance from one another. Neither of them had fancied testing Professor Towinni's threat and risking a temporary suspension of their powers, the community service had been punishment enough.

Besides, Sapphire was too preoccupied trying to recruit a new popular witch for her to even notice Astrid. She was too concerned with her group's image, she'd realised her group was fast losing its standing amongst the other students. Without Hesper, Sapphire had been left with three nitwits who had more money than real power. She knew it wouldn't be easy to replace Hesper, especially considering her rare mind-reading abilities, but no one had even expressed interest in the position. Sapphire had a lot to be angry with Astrid about.

Astrid first made sure she was alone in the dormitory, she thought most of her house would be outside helping to build the giant snowman that was slowly creeping up to the height of the dormitory window, but it didn't hurt to check. She started with some of the easier spells before trying anything too flashy. With the click of her fingers and a read of the incantation, she managed to shrink the armchair she'd just been sitting at to a handheld size. Astrid leant in closer to examine the chair. She stumbled backwards as the chair burst back to its original size and she lost her balance knocking her book over as she fell.

Astrid glanced around as she sat on the floor, luckily no one had been around to see it. She went to pick up her book but paused as another hand grabbed it first. Hesper beamed from ear to ear as she stood over Astrid and waved with the book she held in her hand.

"Yeah, I saw that," laughed Hesper, walking away as she flicked through Astrid's book. "You know, you should really read the warnings underneath these spells."

"And maybe you should find someone else to creep up on," remarked Astrid, snatching her book back and sitting in the armchair. Her cheeks had flushed red with embarrassment.

"Just try and imagine your day without me, it's not nearly as fun," joked Hesper, perching on the arm of Astrid's chair.

"No but it's a hell of a lot quieter, imagine all the work I could get done."

"Okay, I'm bored of grumpy Astrid now. Daily playful banter aside, can we go do something fun or do I need to give you an Oxford dictionary definition of fun first?"

"Surprisingly, I'm actually familiar with that one," quipped Astrid, looking up from her book.

The laughing was something Astrid had missed about having friends. Hesper had always been the funny one in their friendship. Working so closely, over the hundreds of cauldron pots they had to scrub, had been the perfect time for Hesper and Astrid to reconcile. Astrid had been reluctant at first. She'd tried hard to not speak more than a couple of words to Hesper, but that was easier said than done. It wasn't easy not being drawn into conversation with someone as amiable as Hesper, she was just going to keep talking until Astrid responded anyway. She was as stubborn as Astrid remembered. Besides, they had to pass the time somehow and apologising was a good place for Astrid to start. From there, the witches were quickly reminded why they'd been such good friends before.

"Reading a spell book doesn't count," responded Hesper. She rolled her eyes at how stoic her friend could be.

Astrid's forehead creased. "I like reading, maybe if you picked up a book every once in a while…"

Hesper snatched the book from Astrid's hands before she could finish her sentence and threw it down the spiralling stairs.

"You basically just threw my bible down the stairs." Astrid breathed heavily staring at where her book should have been as she clenched her fists.

"Consider yourself liberated," beamed Hesper, grabbing Astrid's coat and gloves from the table.

Astrid glared at Hesper, but her temper simmered as she turned her attention to the stranger knocking lightly on the door frame. He stood in the doorway holding Astrid's tattered book in one hand and using his other hand to rub his honey haired head. He had quickly drawn the two witches' attention, and for a very good reason.

"Someone's got a very good aim," he smiled, beaming with ivory white teeth. His copper brown eyes locked with Astrid's glare for a second and then they returned to Hesper.

"That would be me," perked Hesper, raising her hand and smiling innocently.

"Sorry about her," apologised Astrid, taking her book back from his loose grip. The stranger's mouth dropped slightly, but he said nothing. Astrid's brows knitted, she wondered what he was staring at. "Is there something else we can do for you?"

"Huh?" the stranger questioned, still mesmerized by the modest beauty before him.

"You know, are you looking for someone, casually strolling round the grounds or just understandably stalking us. I'm going to go with the third choice, it's more plausible," joked Hesper, slowly flicking her golden locks.

"Oh sorry, I'm new… I'm… my name's Caius, Caius Haye," he stumbled, regaining himself as he looked away from Astrid's enticing violet eyes. "I was supposed to be finding my room, but I get the feeling I'm in the wrong place."

"You're a perceptive warlock," Astrid rudely remarked, returning to her seat with her book.

"Ha, I'm not a warlock. I'm a shapeshifter, top of my class," he corrected, watching Astrid's indifferent expression closely.

"That's really interesting," she blandly replied, not lifting her eyes from the open pages of her book.

"Maybe one of you could direct me to the right place?"

Astrid said nothing and continued to study her book waiting for the stranger to leave.

Hesper rolled her eyes and quickly stepped in. "Sure, we were literally just trying to figure out something fun to do with our day off, weren't we Astrid?" Hesper hinted, nudging her friend.

"Nope, that was just you," muttered Astrid.

"Well, I'm Hesper and my wholesome friend here is Astrid." Hesper coughed and raised her eyebrows at her rude friend contemplating how far she needed to throw the book this time to get Astrid's attention.

As if Astrid could sense what Hesper was about to do, she quickly slammed the book closed and gave in, another trip down the stairs would surely break the binding of her treasured book. "Fine, fine, at least if we give you a tour this shouldn't happen again," said Astrid, whisking her coat from Hesper's hands.

"Actually, I just remembered I left one of my potions on the flame but you two go ahead, I'll catch up with you later," winked Hesper, flashing out of the dormitory before Astrid could argue.

Astrid scowled at where her friend had stood and then turned to face Caius with her best attempt of a smile. She would try to be polite. *At least he's handsome.* Her mouth had gone dry at the sensual thoughts that had crept into her head. *That kind of thinking will get you into trouble.* She buried her desires and began marching down the endless staircase with Caius right behind her.

They firstly took a tour of the grounds surrounding the school. In the first breeze of the biting cold wind Astrid clicked her fingers wrapping herself in her warming cashmere scarf and gloves. Caius liked the way she clicked her fingers. He made sure he was always only two steps behind her and Astrid made a point of turning around to check. She wondered what he kept staring at. Maybe she had something on her face or maybe there weren't many witches wherever he was from; the rest of the magical regions were known for their segregated communities.

Caius kept trying to make conversation, but Astrid found small talk tiresome and wanted to get the tour over with, so she could just return to reading her book in peace. He had nice eyes and Astrid couldn't deny he was attractive, but she'd always been taught that shapeshifters didn't make good company for a witch.

"As interesting as the grounds are, I'd much rather you told me a bit about yourself?" probed Caius, walking beside Astrid as they traipsed over the bridge to cross the frozen pond. "Or we can talk about something else. Teachers, your friends, sports, the weather. Anything really."

"Do I look like I want to talk to you about the weather?" quipped Astrid flatly.

"You look like you want to bite my head off," smirked Caius.

"Why don't we just focus on getting back into the warmth," she replied, quickening her pace.

"I'm guessing you're from somewhere warm then?" he continued, lengthening his strides to keep beside her.

Astrid stopped to glare at him and then continued marching. "Nowhere you'd know," she muttered.

Caius perked his lips, delighted by the challenge. "I'm sure I could hazard a guess." Astrid sighed, but said nothing. "You don't like to give much away. Why don't I start? I'm from a little town on the outskirts of Alsek, funny you should ask, we're pretty used to the cold up there and being shapeshifters we of course can…"

"Alsek, where the elves are from?" Astrid interrupted, stopping outside the entrance to the Grand Hall. The Elvish weren't keen on associations with witches and warlocks following a disagreement amongst their ancestors a long time ago.

"That got your attention," Caius laughed. "The Elvish are good friends of the shapeshifters, some of my best friends are Elvish. They're good people. Not many witches in Alsek though, I suppose that's the way they like it."

"Why did you come here then?" she asked bluntly. He wouldn't find any Elvish at Vistaldors — a ruling by the elves rather than Vistaldors.

"There's a lot of out of date thinking back at home, I wanted to experience the rest of the world for my own, good and bad," he replied.

"Well, you've come to the right place," said Astrid, her lips lifting with a small smile. She admired his honesty and the small talk wasn't all that bad.

The doors of the Grand Hall swung open allowing the two of them entry, the sudden warmth thawing them both. Astrid welcomed the warmth gladly and removed her coat. Caius on the other hand found it less than pleasurable. Shapeshifters, being the warm-blooded creatures that they are, aren't accustomated to hot environments, especially athletically built shapeshifters like Caius. His cheeks flushed ruby red, and he quickly had to remove several layers before he felt comfortable again. Astrid chuckled, she was well acclimatised to heat by now.

Caius and Astrid quickly passed through the Grand Hall and into the corridors passing a small group of Year 7s on the way that had to say 'hi' to Astrid. Astrid coyly waved back and continued walking.

"What was that all about?" questioned Caius, intrigued by what he could uncover.

"I'm kind of a big deal to some of the younger years since I stood up for this witch who was being bullied," she bragged, finding his expression of approval pleasing. "May have also wrecked the Grand Hall in the process."

"Note to self, stay on your good side," remarked Caius.

Astrid smiled, she could see herself getting along well with this shapeshifter, perhaps a little too well. The smile disappeared from Astrid's face and she immediately retreated into herself as her walk quickened. "You'll find most of your classes will be down this corridor," she said blankly.

Caius shivered with Astrid's sudden frostiness, he feared that he may have said something wrong. "Won't we be in the same classes?"

"I'm a witch. We won't be having lessons together." Astrid saw Caius flinch. It had come out harsher than she'd intended, but she bit her lip and continued walking.

Caius opened his mouth to say something but stopped himself. Astrid was the first witch he'd ever met, and she wasn't what he'd expected. The elves had a lot to say about magic users, not much of which was complimentary. The elves always spoke of them as self-serving, untrustworthy creatures who thought of themselves as superior; so far, Astrid wasn't doing much to disprove that. Caius couldn't quite recall what really started the conflict between the two species. All he remembered from history class was that it ended with the death of the Elvish leader and a lot of witches and warlocks were exiled from Alsek as punishment. There was a lot of bad blood between them, and shapeshifters had been allied with the elves for as long as Caius could remember. Caius' family wouldn't be keen on Astrid.

Caius continued to follow Astrid and took a quick look into one of the classrooms Astrid had said she presumed was for the shapeshifters. The room was significantly smaller than the ones he'd already seen. The posters were falling off the walls and the furniture was falling apart; wood mites had clearly left their marks on the half-eaten desk legs. Pathetically thin cushions had been propped over areas of the rock-hard benches that had started to splinter, their stuffing sprawling from the rips in the material. Some of the desks had words scribbled into them, none of them were worth repeating; for a school that boasts equality, Caius didn't feel all that welcomed so far.

"I wouldn't worry yourself with that tripe, Caius," said Hesper, scaring Caius half to death, he wasn't used to witches flashing into rooms and creeping up behind him. "Sorry. Sorry. I didn't mean to startle you, although Astrid will probably tell you a different story."

"It's all right, Hesper, something I'll just have to get used to," replied Caius, wandering back out to the corridor.

"What, the flashing or the slander?"

"Both I suppose."

"Some of the students aren't as accepting but there aren't many of them." Hesper didn't even need to read Caius' mind to know what he was thinking about the school. "You do realise that's not actually one of your classrooms, it's a detention room."

"But Astrid said..."

"She doesn't know everything, but don't tell her I said that," laughed Hesper, happy that Caius had managed to crack a smile though his attention was quickly drawn, and his body stiffened. He was watching Astrid attentively. She was talking to a tall boy in the corridor. He saw the boy put his hand on her arm and his jaw clenched. Astrid laughed, he liked the sound of her laugh.

Hesper watched eagerly as Caius wandered over to Astrid, his muscles suddenly tensed. Caius coughed as he stood with his arms crossed behind Astrid and the boy took his eyes from Astrid to look at him. Caius didn't like the way he'd been looking at Astrid.

"You all right there, buddy?" questioned the boy with a friendly expression, it was making it harder for Caius to dislike him. The boy extended his hand. "I'm Xander, I hope Astrid's been looking after you all right."

"Caius." He shook Xander's hand, their grip equally firm. Astrid's brows raised when she noticed Caius flex a bicep. "She's a good guide."

"That she is," said Xander wryly. He looked around uneasily, irritated at how quickly the shapeshifter had sucked the life from his and Astrid's conversation. "So, are you an Armungus man too?"

"No. My house was called something like Solicious?" Caius quickly pulled out the key that had turned green on his arrival.

"Solonious? I'd expect a shapeshifter to remember that," muttered Astrid candidly.

"Shapeshifter huh? We could do with one of those on our Shacklebolt team, big guy like you would be perfect. Do you play?" questioned Xander.

"We have our own version of the game where I'm from but I'm sure it can't be that different," replied Caius.

"A new guardian isn't going to make much difference, Xander. We're still going to beat your ass like we used to," insisted Astrid, her expression oozing with confidence.

"We?" Xander queried surprised, his brows knitted. "Do you think that's such a good idea after two years off?" Shacklebolt wasn't exactly the safest game, Xander was right to be concerned.

"Why didn't you play for two years?" queried Caius innocently.

"I don't really see how that's relevant to be honest," Astrid snapped, throwing a glare at Xander; Caius asked too many questions anyway without Xander baiting him. She didn't understand why her personal life had become everyone's business all of a sudden.

Astrid stormed off before they could probe her about more things that didn't concern them. She glanced behind her to check that she was still within Caius' sight. She still needed to get him to the Solonious common room, but she preferred to do it without the inquest. All Xander's comment had done, was give Caius something else for him to ask more questions about.

"Astrid, slow down," called Caius, breathing heavy as he reached the top of the Solonious steps. He quickly regained his breath and leant against the emerald green armchair. He stripped his coat off as he fidgeted uncomfortably with his collar beneath the stifling heat. The fire was still burning even though the common room was empty.

"And this is where we say goodbye, maybe I'll see you on the Shacklebolt course some time," said Astrid, accidentally walking into the armchair as she tried to make a quick exit.

"Smooth," chuckled Caius. "Are you trying to brush me off with the old 'see you around'? I'm still waiting for you to tell me a bit about yourself." Caius calmly stepped closer behind her, close enough that Astrid could feel his breath on her neck.

"I'm an open book," she murmured sarcastically. She could feel her heart racing through her chest. He leaned in closer and traced his fingers on her bare arm, his touch was so light, she could barely feel it. She sucked in a breath. It was taking every ounce of Astrid's self-control to not turn around. Her mind raced with lustful thoughts, how good it would feel with his lips on hers as he ran his hands along her body. *Stop. Lust is for the foolish, and love is for the weak.* Astrid stepped away and turned around with her hands out in front of her, keeping Caius, and all his temptations, at arm's length. "Let's just park that, right now," she said strongly.

"Sorry. I overstepped, I just thought… clearly I was reading the wrong book," trailed Caius. He shook his head and scratched his light stubble, taking a few strides back and away from Astrid.

"Oh hun, it's not you, Astrid's just emotionally constipated," mocked Sapphire as she waltzed into the common room and sat herself provocatively on the arm of the chair next to Caius. She winked at Caius and admired his arms. "How have we never met before?"

"You two will get along well. Just be careful, you'll find the photos on the walls aren't the only snakes around here," advised Astrid, this time executing a much smoother exit.

Caius shirked Sapphire's overfamiliar hands from his arms.

"You're getting good at running away, Astrid, your parents must be so proud," taunted Sapphire, trying to get a response from Astrid, but she kept walking towards the steps. It had been far too long since Sapphire had had such a prime opportunity to wind Astrid up and she did enjoy it so, after all Astrid was the reason why the popular witches were no longer the respected group they once were. "Oh wait, I forget, your parents never wanted you in the first place."

"All right, that's enough now," demanded Caius, stepping in before Sapphire could spew any more of her vindictive words. She was clearly upsetting Astrid and he didn't like it. He felt protective of her whether Astrid liked it or not.

Sapphire looked up at Caius curiously, observing the stern expression on his face, but she wasn't going to let a shapeshifter tell her what to do, no matter how handsome he was. "I bet your father was just looking for someone to waste a bit of time with," she continued, "And your mother was some junked-up witch he found in a gutter somewhere."

The entire tower trembled as Sapphire finished her sentence. Frames fell from the walls and sculptures clattered off the mantel as Caius tried to catch them, tripping over as he did so. Sapphire stumbled off the arm of the chair and steadied herself as the floor continued to shake, before she could even scream, Astrid threw her against the wall with her magic. Sapphire struggled but it only tightened the grip of the spell Astrid had around her throat. Tighter and tighter she squeezed, watching Sapphire claw helplessly at her throat.

Astrid slowly walked towards her, her hands trembled with rage. Caius tried to get up to calm her down, but he was too uneasy on his feet as the quaking continued.

"Just say one more word about my mother," warned Astrid.

Sapphire tried to speak, but the spell was too tight around her throat. Astrid leant in closer and loosened her grip to allow Sapphire the chance to beg for mercy. "What mother?" rasped Sapphire, grinning from ear to ear.

"Astrid, don't," bellowed Caius as he clambered to his feet and rugby tackled Astrid.

Sapphire fell down the wall coughing as she rubbed at her stinging throat. Caius struggled to hold Astrid to the floor, her arms and legs were flailing as she screamed at Caius to get off of her.

"Or was it that your daddy had anger management issues too and your mummy didn't think you were worth sticking around for," goaded Sapphire, she enjoyed watching Astrid struggle.

Caius would have loved to give Sapphire a piece of his mind, but he was too preoccupied trying to hold Astrid down. She was a lot stronger than she looked. And as Astrid got angrier, the trembling of the tower got stronger and some of the rocks began to crumble from the walls. Sapphire quickly flashed out of the tower whilst she still had the upper hand and left Caius to it. He tried to soothe her as he held her down, but it didn't seem to work. She screamed, propelling Caius across the room and the trembling stopped.

The students who had been watching the tower shake from the ground below, all clambered up the stairs to see what the commotion was about. The Solonious common room was a wreck. There was shattered glass spread along the floor from the broken frames that had fallen off the walls, the furniture had been overturned and Caius was straining to stand back up, rubbing his back after he'd been hurled across the room. He winced and saw Astrid hunched in the corner surrounded by a flurry of broken glass. She clutched her knees tightly to her chest, her knuckles white. Her chest heaved as she sobbed into her knees.

The other students huddled round her to point and stare. They whispered frenetically amongst themselves, but none of them knew what to do with her. Caius just wanted to take her in his arms and tell her everything was okay. He wanted to yell at the other creatures to stop staring at her and he wanted to find that spiteful witch and make her regret every word she'd said, and yet he couldn't move. His feet had suddenly gone as heavy as two cinder blocks.

"Oi, get out of my way!" Hesper barged her way through the crowd and leant down next to Astrid trying to find her friend's gaze, which was firmly fixed to the floor. She threw her arms around her friend and flashed the both of them away from the gossiping crowd before a professor arrived. Who knew what they'd do if they found Astrid in this state.

Hesper had chosen an office that used to belong to Professor Peverel before she became Head of House, now it was abandoned and an excellent place to keep away from other people. The room was still decorated with the professor's old things though it had collected a lot of dust in her absence and the posters and frames on the walls were now blank and empty. She sat Astrid down in the burgundy velvet armchair and grabbed a chair for herself, so she could face her friend. Astrid was silent, her gaze empty and still fixed on the floor. Her bottom lip quivered, and her shoulders sagged as she dropped her head in the palms of her hands.

Hesper threw her arms around her again. Astrid's feelings of pain and loss pulsed through Hesper, her head throbbed with the heart-breaking memories Astrid allowed her to see. Memories that Astrid had never shared with her before. She watched the slow death of Astrid's mum and the effects of her father's absence for years afterwards. She glanced at the years Astrid had spent being pulled from one foster family to another in the human world, rejected by so many. All alone in the world. Hesper swiped at the tear that trickled down her cheek as she cleared her throat.

"Astrid, I'm so sorry. I didn't know," apologised Hesper, releasing Astrid from her hugging clasp. She rubbed her head, it still throbbed from Astrid's overwhelming feelings.

“You wouldn’t, no one does,” sniffed Astrid, wiping her swollen eyes. “It’s not really something I talk about.”

“You don’t have to if you don’t want to,” replied Hesper.

“How much did you see? Of her?”

“Enough to know why you don’t talk about it.”

Astrid’s cheeks stiffened with a pitiful smile. “I was only four when she died. I remember we’d go out into the garden and try to catch fairies, she’d be watching and laughing. I can still hear her laugh.” Astrid started chewing on her lower lip. “She laughed a lot before, you two would have got along well. The illness took its time, it was slow, it… it was… painful…” She swallowed back the lump choking her throat. “But she wouldn’t let it show when she was with me. She’d play with my hair, she’d sit and read to me for hours, and after every nightmare she’d hold me until I fell asleep.” Astrid took a deep composing breath.

“She sounded like a wonderful woman.” Hesper gently rubbed Astrid’s arm, her lips tweaking with a sympathetic smile.

“She was. She certainly doesn’t deserve Sapphire talking about her like that. That bitch can think what she wants of me, but not my mum,” said Astrid through gritted teeth, she could feel fresh anger thrumming through her veins. It pleased her to think of how good it felt grasping Sapphire’s pretty little throat and squeezing.

“Astrid, stop,” cautioned Hesper, her whole body shivered with the wicked thoughts suddenly filling Astrid’s head.

“I think you should just stay out of my head,” murmured Astrid as she quickly rebuilt the walls around her thoughts.

“Look, Astrid, I get it, I really do, but losing your temper like that isn’t going to achieve anything. Do you think your mum would want you to get yourself expelled or worse if Caius hadn’t have stopped you?”

"He shouldn't have stopped me, it would have been worth it," uttered Astrid, her expression cold.

"No, Sapphire's not worth it," insisted Hesper sternly. "You can't honestly think like that."

Astrid stared back at Hesper and her corrupt thoughts cleared. She needed someone like Hesper to make her stop and think, to help her see the difference between right and wrong. "You're right, Sapphire said those things for a reaction and I gave her exactly what she wanted."

"I'm not saying she didn't deserve some of it," smiled Hesper, one eyebrow raised.

Astrid smiled back releasing a heavy sigh and wiping away what was left of her tears. "I need to find Caius and apologise," she blurted. She suddenly leapt from the chair as she realised how crazy she probably looked to him now, she wasn't sure he'd even want to talk to her after that.

"Now that's a good idea, he looked a bit bruised after you threw him across the room. Don't think he's having the best first day of school," joked Hesper, holding out some makeup she'd pulled from her bag. "You might want to put a bit of this on, that boy clearly likes you."

"I don't have time for any of that," Astrid replied, shrugging the romantic thought from her mind.

"But you like him too."

"It's irrelevant really, I like him as a friend."

"And that's all?"

"Nothing more, there can't be any more Hesper so let's just drop it, okay? I need to go find him." She went to flash out but then turned back to Hesper with a grateful expression. "Thank you."

Astrid flashed in and out all across the school searching for Caius, she wasn't sure where he'd be, but she didn't think it would be this hard to find him. After all, he hardly knew many places. A lot of the other students she encountered almost seemed scared of her; it was likely that they'd already heard about what happened in the common room, rumours spread like wildfire at Vistaldors.

One of the professors would surely be looking for her by now and Astrid doubted Sapphire's own account of events would be in her favour. She had to find Caius first before she got herself expelled. She suddenly stopped as she saw him across the glassy pond sitting alone on a bench beneath one of the towering trees frosted with snow. She quickly trudged through the snow, trying to think of how she could explain herself as she wandered over to him.

"Hey." That's all she could come up with.

Caius shot up and smiled, he was just happy to see her. "Are you okay? I didn't hurt you earlier, did I? I swear I've never touched a woman like that before, but I just didn't want you doing something that you'd then regret," Caius explained as if asking Astrid for forgiveness. Astrid was confused, she thought she was the one that was supposed to be apologising. "What? Of course not, Caius," she replied, joining him on the bench and pulling at his hand for him to sit back down.

"Oh, thank god, I was so worried that I'd hurt you." His shoulders dropped with relief and he removed his gloves, placing his other hand on top of hers.

Astrid trembled at Caius' warm touch. She went to withdraw her hand, but she found it all too comforting and so left her hand where it was. "You were right to stop me, thank you," she smiled.

"And I'm sorry for throwing you across the room, I'm not very good at controlling my temper."

"Is that because of your dad or…"

"No, no, look Sapphire doesn't know anything about my parents, me and her don't get along and she just knows how to push my buttons," Astrid replied. She wasn't ready to tell Caius any more about her family, she'd only just met him, and she'd done enough crying for one day.

"I can't say I blame you. If someone was talking rubbish about my family, I'd probably punch them in the face, not as dignified as using magic of course but got to work with what you've got," laughed Caius.

The corner of Astrid's mouth lifted. "I would say magic's a bit cleaner, but everyone saw what I did to the common room. Half the school's afraid of me and the professors are probably looking for me as we speak. I just wanted to apologise whilst I still had the chance."

"Well, I'm not afraid of you," said Caius, gently squeezing Astrid's hand.

"Should we be?" questioned Professor Peverel. She stood cautiously in her winter cloak behind Caius and Astrid with Professor Phelonius and Professor Munroe either side of her.

Caius and Astrid stood up immediately and shot around looking equally as worried as each other. Astrid had accepted this would happen sooner or later, but she didn't want Caius to be involved, he had nothing to do with her outburst. She released Caius' hand and smiled at him as she went quietly with the professors. Before Caius could jump to Astrid's defence, they'd flashed to Professor Peverel's office, leaving him behind once again.

Astrid sat of her own free will in the chair opposite Professor Peverel's desk. She recognised the seriousness of what she'd done and had expected there would be some equally serious consequences. Professor Munroe stood to her left and Professor Phelonius stood to her right. They both looked concerned and on guard, it was almost as if they were afraid of her, she wondered what they thought she was going to do.

Professor Phelonius looked down at Astrid with a half-smile and placed his hand on her shoulder in an attempt to reassure her. Usually Astrid would shrug it off, but she found it oddly comforting. She noticed him glare at Professor Peverel almost as if he was angrier with her than Astrid.

Professor Peverel sat at her desk placing her glasses on the top of her head, she cleared her throat and then gestured for the other professors to leave. "I think it would be best if I spoke with Miss Harper alone," explained Professor Peverel.

Professor Munroe raised her eyebrows with an expression of concern, she didn't seem to trust Astrid as much as the other professors did, not that Astrid was surprised.

"With respect Professor, I think I'd prefer to stay," replied Professor Phelonius sharply.

"Well, with respect, I'm Astrid's Head of House and so what you think on the matter isn't really relevant, Professor," Professor Peverel retorted. "I don't think Miss Harper intends on getting herself into any more trouble."

Astrid shook her head, she had respect for Professor Peverel and she'd much prefer to speak with her alone.

"Fine." Professor Phelonius sighed and reluctantly gave in, leaving with Professor Munroe.

Professor Peverel clicked her fingers to close the door behind them and turned to smile at Astrid. She offered Astrid a cup of tea, but Astrid declined. The professor sat with her pink china teacup stirring the spoon with her magic without saying a word.

Professor Peverel closed her eyes as she pressed the edge of the cup to her lips and she took a long sip. "There's nothing quite as calming as a good cup of tea, something the humans very well know," remarked the professor, placing the teacup carefully on her desk. "Perhaps that's something you could try, Astrid, because taking your anger out on other students is absolutely unacceptable."

"I'm sorry, Professor, there's no excusing what I did," Astrid accepted, bowing her head in shame, she wasn't proud of her temper.

"Saying that, I understand it wasn't exactly unprovoked and I know you've got plenty to be angry about Astrid," the professor said compassionately, she cared about her students.

"Professor, I'm not sure what you've been told."

"I've been told enough, and the rest is your business. I'd love for you to confide in me, but I also understand that trust is earnt, and we don't know each other all that well any more. You should know that if you ever need to just talk to someone about any of it, my door is always open," explained Professor Peverel with a sincere smile.

"I appreciate that Professor," Astrid replied. She had always liked Professor Peverel before she'd left the school and she could think of no one that deserved the position of Head of House more than her, but there were some things that she couldn't bring herself to talk about, even with her.

"Under the circumstances, I'm giving you a second chance here, Astrid. Nevertheless, you need to understand that I don't condone your behaviour and there won't be any third chances should this happen again, do I make myself clear?" Her tone was much sterner than before. "I'm suggesting you find yourself a healthier outlet for your anger."

"Thank you, Professor. I'm considering taking up Shacklebolt again."

"I'd say that's an excellent idea, I'm sure I speak for all of Armungus when I say that I look forward to seeing you out on the course again. Now try not to get yourself into any more trouble," said the professor, dismissing Astrid from her office.

Astrid smiled appreciatively and left, breathing a heavy sigh of relief as she closed the professor's door behind her. If Astrid had been expelled, she wasn't sure where she'd go next. Astrid turned around. Hesper, Caius and Xander had all been waiting nervously for her outside the professor's office, none of them wanted to see their friend expelled especially over something like this.

"You won't be getting rid of me that easy," said Astrid.

The others beamed from ear to ear and Xander was first to run up and give Astrid a hug, whisking her off her feet and spinning her around as he did so. Her cheeks flushed red with embarrassment as he put her back down and she locked eyes with Caius. He forced a smile, but his eyes said something else. *Not your concern.* Hesper grabbed Astrid for a hug, despite Astrid's best efforts to avoid another one. She wasn't quite used to all the public displays of affection.

"I'd really like to see if there are any leftovers in the Grand Hall, we missed dinner and I'm absolutely famished," complained Hesper, thinking about her rumbling belly now that she didn't have to be concerned with Astrid's future. "I know the rest of you are thinking it too."

They all looked at each other and agreed, some food would be appreciated right now and with the formal meal time being over, they could all sit together. Astrid needed the support of her friends; the other students would be gossiping even more than usual, and Astrid wasn't quite her hardened self.

The doors of the Grand Hall opened as they approached, and they found there was still a trolley full of leftovers. Hesper's eyes widened when she spotted the glistening honey roasted ham. Other students were still finishing up their dinner, but their knives and forks remained still for a moment as they saw Astrid wander into the Grand Hall.

Sapphire abruptly halted her conversation with the rest of the students she'd sat with. They'd all been hanging on her every word, she'd likely been spreading some more vicious lies about Astrid. She glared in disgust at Astrid and stood up from her seat taking her entourage of gullible students with her.

"More lives than a damn cat," spat Sapphire, passing Astrid and leaving the Grand Hall.

Astrid shrugged off Sapphire's snide remark, refusing to waste another thought on the spiteful witch. She proceeded to sit down next to Hesper with a modest plate of food she'd taken from one of the trolleys. Students at the same table quickly scurried away with their half-eaten plates, whispering as they got up from their seats. Astrid rolled her eyes. They were definitely scared of her. Hesper gave her friend a reassuring rub on her shoulder and then resumed stuffing her face with the food she'd managed to find, she really was ravenous.

If it hadn't been for the others, Astrid probably would have taken her food back to her room to eat alone. She fidgeted under the glare of the other students in the Grand Hall, they were probably all waiting for her to do something else crazy. When, to

Astrid's surprise, the young Year 7 witch Astrid had defended just a few weeks ago came and sat at their table and then a few of her friends followed. Astrid hadn't spoken to her since Sapphire had poured custard over her head, but she seemed sweet enough.

"I'm Molina, not sure if you remember me, is it all right if we sit with you?" Molina smiled sweetly at Astrid.

"I remember you," Astrid replied as she nodded and returned the smile.

"I realised that I never actually thanked you for what you did."

"Don't mention it, Molina."

"Well, I just wanted you to know that me and my friends don't believe anything that Sapphire says about you and we're not afraid of you."

"Thank you, I appreciate that." Astrid acknowledged how mature the witch was for her age and respected her nerve, not all witches her age would be quite so brave to go against someone like Sapphire. It gave Astrid some comfort that not everyone was gullible enough to fall for Sapphire's lies, not that she concerned herself with the opinions of people like that, but it was comforting all the same.

They quickly finished up their food and then retired to bed before anything else could happen, there had been enough drama for one day. Hesper noticed how Astrid had smiled when she said goodnight to Caius and Xander as they left for the Solonious dormitories.

With an enthralled look on Hesper's face, she went to say something to Astrid, but Astrid stopped her before she could. She was tired and didn't want to talk about it any more, Astrid knew Hesper wasn't going to let it go, but she didn't want to argue about it again. They'd both planned to go ice skating with Caius tomorrow on their free afternoon, so Hesper was likely to bring it up again then. Astrid wasn't sure what had possessed her to agree to ice skating, she knew she was going to make a fool of herself as she'd never actually done it before, it wasn't really her idea of fun. She didn't even like the cold.

After their lessons had finished in the morning, Astrid, Caius and Hesper sauntered on down to the frozen pond. Astrid had tried to get out of it but had been unsuccessful, the others had even threatened to physically carry her there, which would just be far too undignified. She thought she'd save her humiliation for the ice.

The pond was a popular place for the students to ice skate in the winter and had been charmed by one of the professors to ensure it could withstand the weight of all the students. They knew the students would use it whether it was allowed or not so better to use it safely. Astrid felt more at ease when she saw some of the other students struggling to get around the ice, there was no side for them to hold onto, but most had found themselves a more balanced student to lean on for support.

Caius leant himself to Astrid whilst she gained her balance. Meanwhile, Hesper showed off her skills, she'd had a pond at home that her and her sister would skate on every winter when it froze over. She was by far the best on the ice, gracefully skating round the pond countless times, she'd even slip in a neat spin every time she'd skate past Astrid. Astrid on the other hand, was as unbalanced as a one-legged fawn on ice. She may have been beautiful, powerful and clever, but she was terrible at ice skating. For some, ice skating just came naturally, for Astrid it did not.

"This must be hard for you," chuckled Hesper, joyfully skating around an unsteady Astrid.

“What?” snapped Astrid, tempted to use a charm to trip Hesper up.

“Well, we’ve found something I can do, and you can’t.”

“Very funny, Hesper. Don’t get too used to it,” replied Astrid bitterly.

Hesper continued to laugh and tried to throw Astrid even more off balance. She made sure to whizz closely past her, cackling every time Astrid flinched. Hesper was enjoying it far too much, but Astrid let her have her fun. She owed Hesper.

Astrid gripped Caius’ coat tightly refusing to let go; Caius wouldn’t have minded if she hadn’t been gripping some of his skin as well. Whenever he tried to loosen her grip she merely held on tighter believing it was one of his attempts to get her skating on her own without anything to hold onto which she didn’t enjoy, they never went very well. He even tried to skate behind her and gently push her along, which she didn’t mind initially but then he’d get carried away and push her a little too fast for Astrid’s liking.

“You just go on ahead. Don’t let me hold you back,” exclaimed Astrid, nudging Caius onwards.

He swivelled round, an irritating grin plastered on his face. “I don’t think that’s a good idea. I’ll stop pushing you fast, we can go at whatever speed you want.”

“I’m fine. I’m fine,” Astrid muttered stubbornly. She continued to shuffle herself awkwardly on the ice, refusing to take Caius’ arm.

“You’re so stubborn, did you know that?” grumbled Caius with an exuberant sigh. “It’s okay to accept help sometimes, you don’t have to be the best at everything.”

"You say stubborn, I say determined," retorted Astrid, scuffing one skate in front of the other as she watched her feet closely.

Another skater passed Astrid too closely and she quickly lost her balance. Her legs flew forward and she fell onto her back, pulling Caius down with her. She slid across the ice squealing as she went and taking down a lot of other unsteady students in the process. She slid head first into the thick snowy bank at the side of the pond.

Caius and Hesper quickly skated over to Astrid and laughed as she emerged from the snow bank with a frosty dusting of snow in her hair. She didn't find it quite so amusing. She was cold, she was wet, and she was embarrassed. Astrid quickly stood herself up and removed her skates. She grumbled all the way back to the common room, much to Caius and Hesper's amusement.

After a few days, the other students had stopped gossiping about what had happened between Astrid and Sapphire and had moved onto the next big thing to talk about. Astrid soon resumed her position amongst the other students out of the spotlight with her select few friends. She'd accepted that she preferred not to be completely alone, and they began to spend a lot more time together enjoying the snow whilst the wind was still gentle and not too cold. Although, Astrid knew what was on the horizon and she knew that the days ahead were set to become much colder.

CHAPTER 3

Not too far from the school grounds, in the steep slopes of the mountains of Gorgon, there stood a cave carved into the mountain face on the edge of the steepest mountain drop where not even the most thrill-seeking creature dared to climb. The painful cries echoing from within the cave could be heard for miles, but no one knew who they belonged to and no one dared to find out.

The entrance to the cave was enough to make any creature run in fear of what may live inside. Many rumours surrounded the cave known as Trepidor, but no one could be certain whether there was any truth behind them since anyone who entered was rarely seen again.

It was a small, dark and murky cave. Puddles of grimy water filled the craters in the gravel ground, some stained brown with stale blood of rotting victims. Blood-curdling cries echoed off the deadly walls in symphony with the drops of caps of ice leeching from the ceiling. The putrid stench of blood and sweat descended from what seemed to be an endless cavern. A blast of stifling heat, carried from within the cavern, fought fiercely against the piercing cold of the icy slopes surrounding Trepidor, taking hold the further someone ventured through the soul-sucking cavern.

A mysterious cloaked figure flashed inside the cave without making a sound. The figure wore a long black cloak that hid all features including the creature's identity. Impervious to the eerie surroundings, the figure continued, dragging the bottom of their cloak through the murky puddles. The figure passed a skeleton, draped with shreds of what used to be clothing, slumped up against the icy wall. Maggots wormed from the empty eye sockets of the skeleton's skull and carnivorous raptors picked at the rotting flecks of flesh. The figure watched the birds strip the bones bare, with their sizeable beaks, barely batting an eyelid.

The figure arrived in the heart of the cave where the smooth icy glaze of the walls thinned as the stone continued upwards and domed high over the bottomless pit in the very centre. Mists of dust crumbled from the stone above as the cobble stone floor quaked with each surge of searing steam that came from the pit.

The figure peered over the brick wall edge surrounding the pit, studying the sheer drop to the bottom. Hundreds of cramped cells filled the pit encircling around its drop, stacked on several floors. Creatures whimpered from within their cells, screaming at the piercing strike of each cruel whipping. Some sat clinging to the bars and yelling through their grimy hair and soiled tattered clothing as the clink and clank of their shackles rang through the figure's ears. Others sat with their knees firmly clenched to their chest, rocking back and forth muttering senseless drivel to their cell mate.

A handful of creatures looked up and saw the figure staring down at them. They cried out to the figure, begging for mercy, but the figure remained impassive, their expression blank as they turned away. The figure shuddered slightly, showing only a thimble of emotion.

A long wooden table came into view just beyond the pit. The table had been carved using the bark of the last wilmore tree and then painted with a coat of pure liquid gold and silver. Draped across the table lay a puce linen cloth and upon that, three golden chalices containing an exquisite red wine that was only drunk when celebrating. Stood behind the table there were three more cloaked figures and a fearsome troll looming on either side, a hefty club in hand.

One figure was dressed in a maroon cloak and stood to the right tapping her fingers in haste of the news the mysterious figure would bring. Another was dressed in an olive-green cloak and stood to the left waiting patiently. The last figure stood in the centre, a step in front of the others, dressed in a dark red cloak gently leaning on a spiralled mahogany staff. At the very top of the staff a small amethyst stone sat within an intricately carved swirling pattern, its violet, crystal surface glistened in the flamelight.

The amethyst stone was known as the Acroyo gem, one of a handful of objects made from the birth of magic. Its power was limitless, but only to those who knew how to wield it. The gem's magic allowed it to channel a person's full potential power and could even be used to drain the power of another and harness it however they saw fit.

The middle figure stepped closer, the trolls emulating his steps. He studied the person before him and his face softened as he immediately recognised her. He removed his hood and the other two did the same, following their master's lead.

"I didn't expect to see you back so soon, daughter." Vincentrio quickly adjusted the piece of chestnut brown hair that his hood had brushed from his neat back comb and opened his arms to embrace his daughter. He held her close against his broad chest. She felt different, like there was something wrong. He pulled away and gently lifted her chin with his finger studying her closely with his piercing, emerald green eyes. "What's wrong? Has something happened?"

Vincentrio's fatherly values were his only redeeming quality. He hadn't always been the malevolent, power-hungry warlock he was today, though nothing about his life had ever been ordinary. Vincentrio was born a true magical creature, unlike the rest of the magical population. His mother had been a shapeshifter and his father a warlock, and with that blend of magical blood he'd been born with powers far superior to any other warlock, powers that had been declared by magical law as too much for one creature to possess.

The breeding of magical creatures of different species had been outlawed for years, but Vincentrio's parents had disregarded the law in the name of true love and they paid the price. The magical authorities, known as the Guard, soon discovered their criminal act and secretly murdered Vincentrio's parents when he was just a child. He was none the wiser for years, believing they were just the unfortunate victims of a demon attack, wrong place, wrong time.

The Guard's mistake was leaving Vincentrio alive, they thought that when he came of age they could manipulate his power to their own advantage, to control him. After all, most of the great creatures of old had been of blended magical blood. They had been the ones to use their power to cleanse the magical world of dark demons after the birth of magic awoke all manner of creature, but demons were the least of the Guard's worries. When Vincentrio discovered what the Guard had done to his parents, he allowed his anger to consume him and using his true power, he hunted down each person responsible, exacting his revenge in the cruellest of ways.

Once he'd finished, he'd found himself a portal to the human world and hid there amongst the humans until he became sloppy and publicly slaughtered several humans. He was detained by the few surviving members of the Guard and brought back to the magical world to pay for his crimes. Though they couldn't contain him for long. He escaped before they could execute him and fled to Trepidor where he'd been ever since, gathering a band of loyal followers and plotting his ascension to power. His supporters were fast growing, witches and warlocks remained in the higher rankings, though most creatures were accepted if they shared in his core beliefs. Every creature had a role to play. Especially his daughter, he understood that the blood that ran through her veins gave her a strong power that would help with the part she had to play in what was to come.

"Nothing's happened, Father," she replied, keeping her face poised beneath the shadow of her hood.

Vincentrio pressed a finger to his taut, clean-shaven jaw and his forehead creased with his furrowed brow. He lifted his chin and resumed his position, a hand firmly wrapped around the stem of his staff.

The witch in the maroon cloak eyed Vincentrio's daughter closely. "So why are you here then?" the witch asked tersely. She arched her thin brows. "Well, it must be something good to take the risk of someone following you." Vincentrio's daughter remained silent, barely acknowledging that the witch had even spoken to her. The witch's ruby red lips flicked with a snarl. She disapproved of the blind faith Vincentrio placed in a child. She was a firm believer that trust had to be earnt with blood and sweat, and, in her eyes, his daughter had not done that.

"Enough Crista," snapped Vincentrio, throwing the witch an icy glare.

Crista was Vincentrio's second in command, his General of War and so much more. She knew what she wanted, and she was ruthless enough to take it, something that Vincentrio found disturbingly attractive. He'd snap at her and remind her of her place, but with a bat of her luscious eyelashes and a flick of her long, golden locks, he'd forget her insolence and she'd be back by his side doing what she did best.

Crista revelled in the deeds Vincentrio had her do. She'd insisted on taking the lead with most of the tortures of traitors they captured, their screams gave her joy, she'd lick her lips at the very thought of the pain she could inflict. Vincentrio rarely said no; her power and skill made her so very good at it and her lust for blood made it even more enjoyable.

In Crista's case, the evil was born rather than made. Unlike Vincentrio, she'd been wicked from an early age; she used her magic to taunt other creatures, including her own sister. One day, a prank went exceedingly wrong and ended with her younger sister drowning. She'd insisted it was an accident, but the unsettling smile on her face when she was taken away to a special school for disturbed magical children said otherwise.

At the school, Crista met more creatures as equally unhinged as her and the violent tendencies only worsened. By the time she was sixteen, Crista was leading a group of like-minded magic users, reaping havoc on communities and creatures across the magical world. They littered the fields of small villages with the mutilated bodies of elves and shapeshifters, any non-magic user they could pick on. They'd hunt them like wild animals, stalk their prey and then strike, killing slowly and painfully. It was sport to Crista and her group.

The Guard eventually caught up to Crista and her comrades. She'd killed many and she'd been careless with it, her bloodlust controlling her. Crista was sentenced to be executed when she reached eighteen and would remain imprisoned till that day. It was in this prison that she heard rumours of a powerful warlock who'd escaped no less than a few weeks previous and was plotting to cleanse the worlds of those he deemed undeserving.

She was enthralled by his stories and it was those rumours that impelled her escape. After multiple attempts, Crista finally escaped just days before her scheduled execution. She found her way to Trepidor and met the warlock she'd idolised during her imprisonment, and the rest was ancient history.

"Forgive me, master," said Crista sincerely as she bowed apologetically.

"Forgiven," he muttered, ushering her back.

Crista lifted her head; her icy blue eyes glaring mercilessly at his daughter. She pursed her lips and quickly took her place next to Vincentrio.

"We may as well do something useful whilst you're here, daughter. Bedelia, anything to share?" Vincentrio turned to the witch in the olive-green cloak.

"I'm still waiting to hear back from our scouts in Hirtshelm and Pelion, but I visited some of our colleagues in Lagen. Whilst I was there, there was an unfortunate accident involving the Headmaster at the Academy," reported Bedelia, her dark pained eyes surveyed the room carefully as she spoke. "But our dear friend, Professor Fletcher Quinn, was more than happy to step in during their difficult time."

Crista scoffed. "I'm sure he was."

"That's good. Fletcher has always been sympathetic to our cause. Tell me, Bedelia, what *accident* has befallen the old fart?" questioned Vincentrio, his lips twitched with excitement.

"Something in the cherry pie I brought didn't seem to agree with him," she replied flatly.

"Poison?" Crista smiled, mildly impressed by Bedelia's actions.

Vincentrio fiddled with a strand of Bedelia's brown black hair. She watched him carefully, her breaths fast and shallow. He smiled. “It never ceases to amaze me how far you’ve come.” Bedelia’s shoulders relaxed and she lowered her head, relieved that she’d pleased her master.

Bedelia was much younger than the rest of them, she sought the approval of her master like a child craving a parent’s attention. It felt good when he praised her, and she liked it. She’d been given a sense of purpose by Vincentrio, acting as his council and advisor and, when a situation required someone a little more tactful than Crista, Bedelia was the first person he’d entrust. Vincentrio saw both her potential and her innate need for a purpose, and he exploited them both.

Many of the professors from the Academy had similarly noticed Bedelia’s potential. She’d always been a relatively gifted witch, but it was her cunning and perceptive abilities that they had tried to nurture. Bedelia had been gifted with a sixth sense that allowed her to sense a creature’s true nature. It was rarely wrong, but sometimes it could be misleading, blurred by conflicts of personality raging within a person.

The Academy helped Bedelia to refine her senses, cultivating an ability that gained her a highly sought position in the Guard. In celebration of their achievement, Bedelia and a couple of her close friends ventured on a trip exploring the mountains, but one night they ventured a little too far. The mountain range surrounding Trepidor was an unforgiving temptress plagued with unpredictable conditions, unscalable cliff edges and packs of wild chimeras.

Bedelia took shelter with her friends inside Trepidor. Not realising where they were, they allowed their curiosity to get the better of them and continued to explore the cave. Intruders were not well-treated in Trepidor. The cave immediately alerted Crista of their presence and she dealt with them swiftly. She lured

Bedelia and her friends into the maze-like passageways, split them up and then brutally attacked each of them, one by one, leaving them to die alone in the depths of Trepidor. She left Bedelia till last and dragged her before Vincentrio for questioning.

Fearing for her life, Bedelia revealed what secrets she knew of the Guard; locations of the different units, details of operations underway and names of members she knew were involved. When she had no more information to give, she told them of her perceptive sense and, though Crista was reluctant, Vincentrio gave her a chance to prove herself. Something she'd done many times for her master, earning herself a place by Vincentrio's side.

Vincentrio had followers and officers scattered across the regions, all in positions of high standing, which they could use for their master's benefit, but Crista and Bedelia were his most trusted of them all. They both had a place by his side, but Bedelia knew Crista didn't particularly like her. She wasn't sure if she felt threatened or was jealous that Vincentrio listened to her as well. Either way, Crista made Bedelia feel uncomfortable, so she tended to stay out of Crista's way. It was obvious which one of them Vincentrio would choose if it came to it, and Bedelia would prefer that choice never need be made. She knew that Crista was waiting for the day she could finally finish what she'd started.

Crista watched as Vincentrio summoned Bedelia to walk back with him to the table to discuss the next phase of his plans, plans he'd already shared with her whilst tangled in his bedsheets. She wasn't interested in swapping cherry pie recipes with Bedelia either, poison wasn't her thing. The knife was always so much more satisfying.

Crista shrugged her shoulders, finding herself bored by Bedelia's drivel. She slowly wandered over to the cloaked figure whose hooded head hung down as if she was trying to avoid Crista's spiteful glare.

The figure listened closely to Crista's hollow footsteps and the tapping of her boots on the cobble stone floor, and she slowly looked up to see Crista grossly studying her. Crista was trying hard to look through the concealment enchantment the figure had used to disguise herself, the enchantment that blurred her face with a shadow.

Crista's ruby red lips curled. She'd spent a lot of time in the past couple of years with Vincentrio's daughter. They'd been enjoyable for Crista, but perhaps not so much for his daughter. In that time, Crista had observed the extent of his daughter's power, helped teach her to use it, and yet, she'd never gotten any better at concealment charms.

"You've lost your touch," uttered Crista as her thin brows lifted.

"Excuse me?" replied Vincentrio's daughter.

"Your concealment charm still hasn't improved. I can still see the colour of your eyes, so very unique and *recognisable.*" Crista leaned in closer as she spoke, towering over the cloaked figure. She expected her to cower, but she didn't. She wasn't intimidated in the slightest.

"You know what they say, a bad teacher blames their student," quipped the figure calmly.

"You disrespectful, stupid…" Crista stopped. Her hand was held frozen above her as she'd raised it to slap the figure for her impertinence.

"She's absolutely right, Crista," remarked Vincentrio. He walked down the steps holding Crista's hand still with his magic. His eyes narrowed at Crista's raised hand, his protective fatherly instincts thundered within him. "You know full well that violence is meant as a punishment, my daughter has done nothing to be punished for."

"Master, I was only…" Crista cried out as her wrist snapped backwards and she dropped to the floor.

"Like that. Now apologise," demanded Vincentrio without raising his voice by so much as one decibel.

"I'm sorry," said Crista through gritted teeth. She bit her bottom lip and whimpered as she snapped her wrist back into place.

"Forgiven." The figure smiled smugly and made sure to traipse the bottom of her cloak over Crista as she followed her father towards the main table.

Crista trembled with rage. She slowly hauled herself back to her feet whilst the figure's back was turned and clicked her fingers pulling one of the troll's club from his hands. The figure smoothly swerved out of the way and burst the club into splinters with a click of her fingers. The figure removed her hood and the weak concealment charm, and swivelled back around, her eyebrows raised.

"You taught me better than that," sneered Astrid.

An arrogant smile flicked across Vincentrio's face as he stood proudly behind his daughter and gently squeezed her shoulders. "Now let's talk about what I need you to do next."

"Anything you need, Father, I won't let you down."

CHAPTER 4

The first term at Vistaldors was not a favourite for most; the hours of daylight grew shorter with every day, the air turned colder, the snow fell heavier, and mid-term exams were fast approaching. All year groups were subject to them, though some students took them more seriously than others. Some students spent hours in the library squeezing in study time whilst others left their textbooks to gather dust.

Astrid, on the other hand, had much larger matters to be concerned about. Her father had entrusted her with her duties and she knew Crista was keeping a very close eye on her, waiting for Astrid to slip up and make a mistake. Her father had defended her and placed his trust solely in her, she couldn't let him down. She wouldn't. Astrid knew all too well what her father would do to her if she failed or, even worse, what he'd let Crista do. Failure was not an option. Exams were the least of Astrid's worries.

For the students frantically stressing about their mid-term exams, the fortnightly day trip to the neighbouring village, Tarrin, was a grateful distraction. For a single day, the students didn't have to think about studying, they could simply enjoy a restful day exploring the village that was just on the other side of the Perimere Lake.

Astrid wasn't so keen on the idea. Not only did she have more important things to be doing, but she also knew how closely she was being watched and she'd been trying her best to shield Caius and Hesper from both her father's and Crista's sight. Hiding them from Vincentrio's watchful gaze wasn't easy, the charm was draining on Astrid's energy and the more time she spent with them, the more she had to hide them.

"What do you mean you're not coming?" questioned Hesper, barging into Astrid's room, it wasn't like Astrid to still be in bed at this time.

"Give me a break, Hesper, I just don't fancy it, I've got too much reading to catch up on," replied Astrid, rolling back over.

"Nope, not a good enough answer," retaliated Hesper. She clicked her fingers unrolling Astrid from her duvet burrito. "Having a day without reading is not going to kill you. Hurry up and get dressed or I'll drag you out of bed myself."

You could try. Hesper raised her eyebrows at the challenge and Astrid sighed as she realised Hesper must have heard that thought. Blurring her father's vision and blocking her thoughts from Hesper were not easy things to do simultaneously, even for Astrid. Some thoughts were bound to slip through. Astrid considered summoning her duvet back and then decided it wasn't worth the effort. Hesper was a stubborn old boot when she wanted to be. Hesper smiled and left Astrid to get ready. Astrid could put aside the thoughts of her father and responsibilities for the one day.

All the students eagerly gathered by the main gates of Vistaldors where they awaited the arrival of the shuttle bus to take them across the lake. Caius beamed as he saw Hesper flash from the Armungus dormitory with Astrid alongside her. He wasn't sure if she'd come, she'd been somewhat distracted recently and more distant than usual.

"Hey stranger, long time no see," smiled Caius, though he noted her face looked thinner than usual.

"Sorry, I've had a lot of things to do," replied Astrid, quickly turning away from his concerning expression, all she wanted to do was hug him.

"This will be your first visit to Tarrin, something to commemorate, Caius," said Hesper, trying to change the subject. "I wonder where we should go first, any thoughts you two?"

"People have stopped talking about you, if that's what you've been worrying about," explained Caius, completely ignoring Hesper's attempt at diverting the conversation.

"I don't know what you mean," replied Astrid.

"I'll just talk to myself then," muttered Hesper. She stepped forward, so Caius no longer had to talk over her head to Astrid.

"I thought maybe that's why you've been missing meal times," Caius responded.

"I've just been busy, okay," she bluntly replied. She didn't want to turn this into an argument and ruin the whole day.

"Let's go to the bakery first," interrupted Hesper, noting the tension brewing between the two of them and resuming her position in the middle. Neither of them replied and they all stood awkwardly in silence waiting for the next shuttle bus.

The bus's horn sounded as it sharply pulled up outside the gates of Vistaldors. Relieved at its opportune arrival, Hesper was the first to climb the steps onto the bus. Professor Phelonius stood in his casual winter clothes with his hand held out waiting for the permission slips to be placed in his palm. Without a signed permission slip, students weren't allowed on the bus and he was well accustomed to what fake signatures looked like. Astrid was next to hand over her slip and the professor paused as he took a moment to check its authenticity. Astrid was well used to lying about her father. Her father had forged practically all of her school documents himself and he'd made sure Astrid had practised the signature till she got it right. The professor looked doubtful but allowed Astrid past nonetheless and she took the seat next to Hesper.

"Why are you looking at me like that?" questioned Astrid as Hesper gave Astrid her best meaningful stare.

"No reason, just wondering who's signature you used," Hesper replied.

"I don't know what you're talking about," smirked Astrid, the two of them laughed and Astrid quickly changed the conversation, happy that they could talk properly again. She hoped her father wouldn't bother to watch her so closely outside of school.

Caius sat on the seats opposite them and questioned what they were laughing about, but rather than answering they both continued to laugh and found with his confused expression it was even harder to stop.

The bus was soon full of students all eager to get going and explore the village, only a few had been turned away by the professor and left behind. The bus sounded a different horn this time and then abruptly pulled away, racing towards the Perimere Lake. They travelled quickly through the forest line of Vistaldors allowing the students only a brief time to admire the scenic views in its frozen state.

The Perimere Lake was completely frozen with a solid sheet of ice. In the summer the bus would usually skim across the surface of the lake barely leaving a ripple behind, but the ice, however solid, would not be strong enough to hold the bus's weight. The driver continued to accelerate towards the snowy bank of the lake and then sharply pulled the giant lever to his left and the bus lifted swiftly into the sky gliding through the air across the lake. The younger students all ran to the windows either side of the bus gawping at the sight beneath them. The older students weren't so surprised, the driver always left the take off to the last minute. The village soon came into view and the bus began its descent as it reached the other side of the lake. The bus smoothly landed in the central square of Tarrin and the students briskly clambered off the bus.

It was a rather quaint little village home to countless creatures that had all been settled in the peaceful village for years. The students walked along the cobble stone path of Main Street to the centre where the dancing fountains of Pateesh lived as they sang their blissful tune that rang throughout the village. A towering stone warrior stood either side within the fountains ready to protect the church of Tarrin from those not pure of heart and their dark intentions.

The church of Tarrin was a magnificent height made from crumbling stone that had stood at the centre of the village for over five centuries, it was the oldest building in the village. The intricate clock face at the very top of the church was what the village was most famous for, other than the delicious cakes. Its face had an elaborate design; gold plate with an intricate black design of dancing flowers and curves with the sapphire-like Perrero gem in the very centre of the face.

The Perrero gem was one of the most powerful magical stones in the magical world. Like the Acroyo gem, it was made from the birth of magic and there were very few creatures in the magical world strong enough to wield it. The Perrero gem was known for its portal-opening power; in the right hands, the gem could be used to open a portal and allow the user to travel in between any region in the magical world.

There were many stories of the power the Perrero gem held if it was used with its sister gem, the Acroyo gem, though no one had been brave enough, to attempt it. It was rumoured that the Acroyo gem could amplify the power of the Perrero gem more than ten-fold and the wielder would be able to create portals between worlds, something that was near impossible for most. On the odd occasion a portal would randomly open somewhere in the magical world, but it wasn't a common occurrence.

Astrid instantly recognised the gem, she knew exactly what sort of power it held. Unfortunately, she could also recognise a fake gem and the so-called Perrero gem that sat in the clock face was exactly that. She recalled her father telling her about how he uncovered a fake in its place when he'd been searching for the gem for himself. The mayor was the only other person to know of the stone's disappearance and had deceived his people with the fake to keep their faith alive.

Once the clock struck twelve, the crystal bell chimed throughout the town. Everyone stopped and watched as the clock face opened, and a small blue bird was released. It flew over the heads of each student twirling and spinning within the air. When it landed on the floor, the bird smoothly shifted into the mayor of the town. Everyone gasped in wonderment at the mayor's extraordinary trick as the man emerged from the crowd to greet his new arrivals.

His name was Sir Robert Perigee. No one knew exactly how old he was, they only judged upon his appearance. He had long silk silver hair tied in a black velvet ribbon with a short piece of curled hair hanging down the side of his face. He hid his deep mauve eyes behind crescent shaped glasses. He had a few wrinkles and stress lines beneath his bushy eyebrows and a thin moustache that was hardly noticeable. The mayor was dressed in a deep blue robe that he wore over a white shirt, and black trousers. Supposedly, the mayor was a warlock with a remarkable ability of clairvoyance; with one touch he could see a person's past, present and future. A gift that came with its very own price.

"Welcome to our village, please enjoy," he smiled as he readied himself to leave back to the clock face where he watched over the village. Before he left, Sir Robert tripped on an out of place cobble stone and fell onto Astrid who caught him before he could fall. When their hands met, he unintentionally looked into the deepest part of her soul taking Astrid with him as he delved into her past.

For a moment they both travelled to Astrid's mother's bedside where her younger self sat weeping. Before they could watch any more, Astrid resisted and threw them both back into his own past. A young Sir Robert sat happily with his wife and children, and around his neck he wore a patterned golden pocket watch with the Perrero gem set in the clock face. Then they were back in present day Tarrin, amongst the crowd of people blissfully unaware of what had just transpired.

"Intriguing," muttered Sir Robert in a daze. He'd never experienced anything quite like that before.

Astrid helped Sir Robert to his feet, but before she could say a word he flew back to the clock and left Astrid stunned and confused. She touched her hand to her face and found a single tear that she briskly wiped away. Turning to Hesper and Caius, she could see they were none the wiser and Hesper's hankering for this bakery was written plainly across her face. Hesper grabbed Astrid's arm and barged her way urgently through the dispersing crowd of creatures to the bakery. Astrid had never seen Hesper move so fast, she pitied the person that came between her and her tasty treats.

They soon came to Fluffy Buns bakery on the corner of Main Street, it was jam packed with magical creatures all scrambling for the award-winning cakes. Fluffy Buns bakery was renowned throughout Curo for its delectable treats. Creatures travelled far and wide just to taste the confectionary Fluffy Buns bakery had to offer. Astrid was dreading trying to squeeze into the shop, but she thought it would be a bad idea to hold Hesper back.

Before Astrid followed the others, she placed her hands on the glass and peered through the window to take a look at their collection of cakes and biscuits, even she was impressed with their vast selection. Spotlighted in the centre sat the three most sought after desserts: a delectable triple chocolate cheesecake drowning in fresh double cream, a delicate strawberry pavlova and a scrumptious chocolate soufflé oozing with steaming fudge sauce.

Hesper found her favourite treat amongst the extensive cookie selection in the middle of the shop where most of the creatures flocked to first. She fought viciously through the crowd of innocent creatures clawing her way to get to the last cookie, the crazed look in her eyes scared most of the other students off. After all, it wasn't just any cookie, it was a double decker white chocolate and raspberry cookie sandwiched with a sweet layer of strawberry sauce and half-dipped in creamy white chocolate.

Astrid decided to wait outside for Hesper, it was a little too early for something that sweet and she couldn't face having that many people in her personal space at once. She thought it would be more fun to watch from the outside. She could see Hesper using Caius as her personal battering ram as Hesper bulldozed her way towards the last cookie.

A commotion erupted from within the shop and Astrid rushed to the window, watching as someone snatched the last cookie from the rack just as it was inches from Hesper's wanting hands. Sapphire smiled as she held up the cookie and threw her money at the shop person before Hesper could say anything about it. Luckily for Sapphire, there were a few people between herself and Hesper, so she had time to quickly dive out of the shop before Hesper went to snatch the cookie bag from her hand. Astrid jumped out of the way stunned as Hesper missed the cookie bag and tackled Sapphire to the floor, she really wanted that cookie.

"Don't you think you've had enough already, packing on the pounds Sapphire!" yelled Hesper, trying to prise the cookie bag from Sapphire's unyielding fingers.

"Coming from you," squealed Sapphire, pushing Hesper off her stomach. "I'm not the one who ate practically half of *my* birthday cake last year."

"As if, that cake tasted like dirt."

Astrid frantically snatched the brown paper bag from Sapphire whilst Caius hauled Hesper off Sapphire, another one who was stronger than she looked.

"Can't you just stay out of something for once, Astrid," said Sapphire, scrambling to her feet.

"Go find something else to stuff your face with, this cookie's mine," sneered Hesper. Her smile quickly disappeared as she watched Astrid hand the bag to Sapphire and a hard line formed between her brows.

"Ha. Catch you later," beamed Sapphire as she teetered off with her cookie bag in hand. Hesper turned to Astrid with her arms crossed and a livid expression to match, Caius stood behind her wondering if he'd have to drag Hesper off Astrid next. "You know how much I wanted that cookie, was that payback for me dragging you out of bed this morning. Low, real low," groaned Hesper.

“You might want to take a look in here before you say anything else,” Astrid advised, waving a brown paper bag in her hand.

Hesper gingerly took the bag and looked inside to find her double decker white chocolate and raspberry cookie, she looked up with a smile on her face and threw her arms around her friend.

“I didn’t want you doing something you’d regret later on,” smiled Astrid. She’d been doing duplication charms for years so Sapphire wouldn’t even notice the difference until she went to eat it, Astrid had made just a small tweak to the flavour.

“Can I try a bit?” questioned Caius. He went to break off a piece of Hesper’s cookie and then quickly rethought his decision as he remembered how much he liked to keep his fingers and could have sworn he heard Hesper growl.

“I’ve earnt this cookie,” mumbled Hesper, her mouth full of the crumbling cookie, she wasn’t bothered about looking lady-like in front of her friends. Hesper was enjoying her cookie and that was all that mattered to her, she also didn’t care that she looked like she’d been dragged through a hedge backwards. The cookie was worth it.

“So now the beast has been fed,” said Caius, glancing at Hesper as she stuffed her face. “What’s next on the grand tour?”

“Well, I wouldn’t mind checking out this book shop that if I remember correctly should be just around this corner,” replied Astrid keen to get into a shop out of the cold wind.

Astrid continued around the corner and then abruptly stopped finding herself unable to move her feet. Caius suddenly walked into her as he wasn’t paying attention and noticed it was the pet shop on the other side of the road she was staring at. *It couldn’t be the same one surely*, Astrid thought to herself as she edged closer, curiously examining the shop’s exterior. Its wooden frame had seen better days but sure enough the same sign stretched across the doorway reading Fisher's Furry Friends. She continued to the shop undisturbed by Caius crashing into her.

The display through the frosted glass still looked exactly the same and as Astrid opened the doorway and wiped her snow-dusted boots on the mat, she heard the same bell ring. A petite, curious older dwarf emerged from beneath the counter picking up his spectacles as he came to greet his customers. Astrid was very good at remembering faces and Eli Fisher was a particularly friendly face she couldn't forget. The years had been kind to Eli; his honey-coloured hair had barely greyed at all and he only had the odd wrinkle beneath his light green eyes. He fixed his tweed bow tie and plaid waistcoat before welcoming them to his shop, as he got closer his expression turned into one of realisation.

"Could it be, is that Astrid Harper?" questioned Eli, he stopped and studied Astrid dubiously through his spectacles.

"How you doing Eli?" Astrid simpered, greeting him like an old friend. The last time she'd stepped foot in Eli's shop was probably one of the last few happy memories she had from her childhood. She was a lot younger and a lot smaller back then, Eli did well to recognise her.

Back when her mother was alive, Astrid and her mother would come and visit Eli and his menagerie of creatures every Saturday morning. Eli taught her everything she knew about caring for magical creatures. He took her to see her first herd of minavous that he'd rescued on one of his many travels and showed her how to coax the red-furred ringbat from its hidden burrows. Eli and Astrid's mother had been friends for years after meeting on their respective travels in Hirtshelm, sharing in their interest in the wild creatures that roamed the hills there. Astrid's mother found joy watching her daughter share her passion and respect for those creatures.

Astrid remembered on their last visit to Eli's shop, her mum had finally given in to letting her take a creature home with her. She'd chosen her favourite from the nest of orphaned red-furred ringbats she and Eli had been hand rearing. Ringbats were not the easiest pets for anyone to keep; probably the smallest distant descendants of the wildcat family, just about reaching the size of the average cat but their flexible hand like paws and retractable furred wings made them difficult to keep in one place.

Astrid's ringbat was a sweet little thing she'd called Peewee. Peewee was more concerned with curling around the back of Astrid's neck with his bushy brown tail swishing across her back rather than flying off with his brothers and sisters. It had been difficult to separate them even before Astrid formally owned him, so Astrid was delighted when her mum said she could finally take Peewee home. It wasn't long after that Astrid's whole world was turned upside down; she found out her mother was dying and they all relocated to the human world, the place where everything went wrong. It was the human world where her mother died, it was the human world where her father descended down his dark path and it was the human world where she'd been left completely alone.

Astrid hadn't returned to the shop since, even now she could see her mother's face in every corner of the shop and she wondered how Eli did it. She assumed Eli would have moved on after hearing about her mother's death and gone to start his minavous conservation project that he and her mum had always dreamed about.

"It's been a while, my dear. I was so sorry to hear about your poor mum, she was a special witch," said Eli sympathetically as he cupped Astrid's hands in his. His frail voice almost broke as he said it, but he quickly wiped at his eyes and sniffed before either of them started crying. Astrid smiled and lightly squeezed his hand, she knew this couldn't be easy for him.

"Why don't we have a look around, whilst you two catch up." Hesper nudged Caius and dragged him to the other side of the shop, she got the gist of the history from Eli's thoughts.

"I'm just sorry it's been so long, I never even..." paused Astrid, now feeling guilty for never having thought of the effect of their disappearance on Eli, they'd practically been his family.

Eli shook his head. "You don't need to apologise for anything, it's brought me so much joy just to see you here alive and well, and look at you now," he said, admiring how grownup she'd become. "I bet the boys can't keep their hands off you."

"I wouldn't say that Eli," she blushed, glancing over at Caius at the other end of the shop playing with a group of hornbill hamsters.

"Well, I'm not one to pry," he smiled, raising an eyebrow as he noted her subtle smile.

"I didn't think you'd still be here after all this time," remarked Astrid, quickly changing the subject.

"Neither did I, I considered going back to Hirtshelm for some more travelling, but I just couldn't bring myself to get rid of this place. I still go here and there rescuing creatures," he explained. "Speaking of which, I think there's someone else that will be happy to see you."

Astrid waited at the counter intrigued as Eli disappeared through the curtain that hung over the doorway behind his desk. Whilst she waited patiently, Caius slowly made his way over to where she was standing.

"Are you sure you're all right?" questioned Caius, placing a warm hand on her arm.

"I'm fine, it was just a bit of a shock at first, I only ever came here with my mum and… she… well… you know." Astrid half-smiled back at him. Caius understood, he didn't need her to say it if she didn't want to. It still amazed Astrid how deeply Caius seemed to care for her despite how many times she pushed him away. She wanted him to hold her close again and she looked hungrily at his lips, but then she reminded herself that her desires weren't important. Caius was far too good to get himself mixed up with someone like her.

"I'm sure it never gets any easier," Caius responded compassionately before removing his hand from her arm and taking a step back. He quickly looked around to avoid her broken eyes and stopped as he stared intently at the picture hung on the wall by the front counter. Eli was crouching on the forest floor with a woman, a family of wild ringbats at their feet. The woman had short brown hair swooped back behind her ears and intense violet eyes that he'd only seen once before. The woman was smiling, almost laughing. He quickly took a double take looking at Astrid as she turned to glance at the photo Caius had clearly been staring at.

"Yep, that was her, my mum," she smiled longingly, looking at the photo she could hear her mum's laughter. She often found herself imagining how different everything would be if her mum were still alive, not that it made any difference to her now.

Before Caius could say anything else, Eli returned from behind the curtain with a bushy tailed, red haired creature cradled over his shoulder. Astrid beamed from ear to ear as soon as she saw him. The creature squealed and released his wings swooping into Astrid's open arms. She was overjoyed, it was Peewee, her

Peewee, a little bit older and bigger but she could recognise those golden and blue eyes anywhere. She'd lost him in the human world when her father was imprisoned by the Guard and she'd assumed the worst, she thought she'd never see him again.

"Where in the world?" exclaimed Astrid overcome with joy.

Hesper quickly rushed over to give the little guy a tummy scratch, the fluffy tummy was difficult to resist.

"They have amazing memories, don't they? So, a couple of years ago some of our wildlife had managed to get themselves stuck in the human world, no idea how, and whilst I was over there, I stumbled across our old friend here," explained Eli, pleased to see Astrid laugh as Peewee tickled her ear with his nose. "Some humans had found him and clearly thought they could make some money from him."

"What do you mean?" questioned Astrid, knowing what she was about to hear was going to make her angry.

"I found him in a cage at one of their cruel circus events, he was in such a state, but he looks incredible now and let's just say he hasn't wanted to get himself fostered. I think he's always been waiting for you to come back," replied Eli, trying to keep Astrid focused on the positives.

Caius and Hesper had already gathered round to fuss over Peewee as Astrid held him cradled in her arms, he'd always loved the attention ever since he was a young cub.

"This is my oldest friend, Peewee," Astrid explained, introducing him to the others. He was a rare find for them since getting close to a wild ringbat was near impossible, especially with their impressive camouflaging abilities.

"He's just got a face you want to squish," said Hesper. "But not sure what the professors are going to say about him." Astrid raised one eyebrow and smiled slyly. "But rules are there for breaking, right?" grinned Hesper, she knew Astrid wasn't going to leave him behind, so she may as well help.

"If that's all right with you, Eli?" queried Astrid as she turned to look at Eli.

"I think he's already made his decision, don't you?" smirked Eli, looking at Peewee curled contently round the back of Astrid's neck like a fashionable scarf. Eli reached for Peewee's basket and gave it to Astrid. "If you get tired of him round there, he loves his snug basket."

"Thank you, Eli, I'll try and bring him for visits when I can."

"You're all welcome here any time, maybe don't leave it quite so long next time. Take care of yourself."

Astrid leant down to the open basket. Peewee happily obliged, strolling down Astrid's arm towards the cosy blankets in his basket. He brushed himself around Eli's legs before he hopped in. He'd be warmer in the basket anyway. Ringbats were usually well adapted to the cold, but Peewee was no normal ringbat. Astrid closed the basket and held her hand on the lid as she muttered a charm to disguise it as a shopping bag, best to try not attracting too much attention with the domesticated ringbat.

"Pub time?" suggested Hesper, looking at her watch. Hesper didn't want to leave without her Mermaid Inn pub lunch, best seafood this side of the Vestour sea.

Astrid hugged Eli goodbye and then wrapped herself back up in her coat and scarf before they left for the Inn, the snow was falling much heavier now.

The students and professors at Vistaldors often frequented the Mermaid Inn. It was a historic-looking pub that had been around since the village's inception with its black and white timber beam build and straw thatched roof that often leaked, not that the patrons seemed to care. A hanging wooden sign swung above the front door with the mermaid of the inn perched on the frame, her shimmering tail fin dangled daintily as she sung her sweet siren's call to invite the customers in. The mermaid's melody was usually drowned out by the chorus of drunken singing and general chatter, which echoed from the pub every time the door swung open.

Astrid and her friends were welcomed by an ensemble of noises as they scrambled to the last few seats Caius spotted in the corner of the crowded pub. They sat close to the spitting fire, so Astrid was content.

Everyone else was squeezed around the centre stage where the house band of fawns were playing another toe tapping jig, the customers could barely keep still as they played their fiddles and banjos dancing across the stage as they did so. The drunken creatures sang along to the classic tunes, swaying with their drinks in hand and clinking with the creature next to them spilling most of their drink on the table beneath them. Astrid noticed a group of some of the professors sat on the table closest to the stage all singing and swaying to the music, they'd clearly had one too many drinks. Astrid noted how a couple of the professors were sitting just a little too close.

Caius quickly returned with their drinks balanced between his hands placing them carefully on the table before he squeezed himself next to Astrid in the booth. "So, I managed to convince the guy behind the bar that I'm 19," smiled Caius, taking a long sip from his frothy beer.

"How much bribing did that take?" questioned Hesper, her brows arched with surprise. The barman was usually a stickler for the rules, even more so when the professors were around.

"Being a shapeshifter can come in handy," he winked. "But kitchen's closed I'm afraid, Hesp, so you'll just have to drink up."

"Great, bottoms up," said Hesper, rolling her eyes as she began to gulp down her beer hoping to keep her grumbling stomach at bay momentarily.

"You can help yourself to mine as well." Astrid pushed the drink over to Hesper who was more than happy to accept. Caius turned to Astrid with a confused expression and Astrid's forehead puckered. "I just don't really drink, no real reason."

Astrid's father never approved of drinking alcohol, she'd learnt that the hard way when her father once found her after having one too many. She wouldn't make that mistake twice. She still bore the scars of his punishment. Astrid had learnt very quickly how to hide her scars with enchantments. Vincentrio told her that alcohol dulled the senses and weakened a person's power, and he'd never have a daughter of his appearing weak.

"You don't need to explain, not everyone can handle their alcohol," Caius remarked, waiting for a reaction.

"That was an awful attempt to get me to drink," Astrid laughed.

"It's fine, not like you've got anything to prove." He was a persistent one, Astrid would give him that much.

Astrid snatched her drink back from Hesper and began to take a sip just to wipe the smug smile off Caius' face. He laughed as she continued to gulp half her pint down. Before Astrid could drink any more, she suddenly dropped her glass, and it smashed into pieces as it crashed onto the floor. No one else in the pub even seemed to notice, broken glassware was hardly a new thing to them, but Caius and Hesper looked worryingly at their friend. Her eyes were closed, and she was vigorously massaging her head in her hands as a numbing pain pierced through her skull. Astrid tried not to squeal with the pain, but the pain was all too much, and her eyesight began to blur.

"Astrid, what's wro—"

Astrid quickly clambered over Caius and ran out of the pub before he could stop her. She stammered past some people loitering outside the pub who laughed, they clearly thought she'd just had one too many. She came across a quiet back alley and hid quickly out of sight from the others. Caius had got up and followed her, and Astrid had a good idea as to what was causing the pain, she didn't want him to be around.

The pain crippled Astrid and she shrunk down against the wall, her vision completely gone now. Heat seared through her bones and before she opened her eyes, she knew where she was. Her father stood boldly over her and she instantly recognised she'd been transported to Trepidor, yet the pain didn't stop even as she begged at her father's feet. He was angry with her, she hated it when he was angry.

"Please. Father. Stop," Astrid begged desperately, clawing at his trouser legs.

Vincentrio leant down to his daughter's level and looked coldly into her eyes. "And why should I do that?" he queried, calmly pinching her chin when she tried to look away from his eyes. "You've been hiding from me."

"No, I haven't, I…" She writhed in even more pain.

"Don't lie to me." He stopped the pain momentarily to let her talk.

"I don't know what you're talk—" Astrid yelped with the sharp slap her father delivered.

Vincentrio took a step back. He hated hurting his daughter, but he hated her lying to him even more so.

Astrid took a deep breath and spat a drop of blood on the floor, she rubbed her cheek and then composed herself. Finding her confidence once again, she stood to her feet and stared right back at her father's cold, unforgiving eyes, she could see a flicker of shame in them.

"Let's try this again, why have you been hiding from me?" He was calmer now, but Astrid knew she still had to tread carefully.

"I told you, I haven't," she replied confidently now that she'd recovered from the pain.

"Don't test me, I haven't been able to find you all day."

"That's no doing of mine, I think it may have something to do with the Perrero gem in the village." Mentioning the gem had instantly drawn his attention.

"The gem's been missing for years, why should I believe that it's returned now."

"I just have a feeling." Vincentrio narrowed his eyes on his daughter and Astrid lifted a brow. "Surely it's worth investigating?"

"Fine. Don't disappoint me again," Vincentrio replied. He knew if someone else had the gem it could cause problems for him later on. "One more thing."

"Yes, Father?"

"I shouldn't have to tell you what I'll do if I find you drinking again."

Astrid nodded and then found herself standing in the back alley behind the pub. The pain had gone, and she'd been reminded just how powerful her father was, she couldn't keep him out indefinitely. She'd allowed herself to lose focus recently and she couldn't bear to disappoint her father, for all his faults he was still her family. Despite the things he'd put her through, he gave her a sense of belonging that she'd only ever had when her mother had been alive, and Astrid only ever wanted to make him proud. Although she'd felt his rage before and seen him do unpleasant things, she'd also seen a side to him that no one else had. Vincentrio moved heaven and earth to reunite with his daughter, and she understood his pain and loss. Astrid often found herself pondering how different things would have been if she hadn't lost her mother, they'd been such a happy family. Nevertheless, she just had to deal with what she had.

If Astrid was going to help her father, then she'd have to see what she could find out about the whereabouts of the gem, and she could think of only one person that would know that. Sir Robert. Astrid could hear Caius and Hesper calling her name, but she couldn't let her friends distract her now. She flashed to the entrance to the church of Tarrin where she suspected Sir Robert would be, whether he'd want to talk to her was another matter, but she'd learnt a few extraction techniques from Crista that she wasn't afraid to use.

It was beginning to get dark, the square was eerily quiet with no one to be seen. Beneath the dim lamplight Astrid could see the fountains of Pateesh lay dormant either side of the church walkway, their singing had stopped. Astrid buttoned up her coat and then confidently began to walk past the fountains trying not to think about her dark intentions, but as she stepped across the threshold the statue to the right violently swung his stone sword just millimetres from Astrid's head. She managed to duck just in time. She could see the doorway. The other statue took her by surprise, knocking Astrid off her feet. She lay winded on her back as both statues crouched with their swords armed and ready at Astrid's chest.

"Enough," bellowed Sir Robert. He stood in the church doorway and waved his hands. The statues immediately obeyed releasing Astrid and returning to their resting position in the fountains.

"Thank you." *What a warm welcome.*

Sir Robert had already returned to the church leaving the door open ajar. Astrid clambered to her feet and quickly followed wondering what other protective charms he may have used indoors. She gingerly opened the door and stepped through.

The church was lit by candlelight alone in the evening, but Astrid could still appreciate its grandeur. She looked up to see a beautiful painted piece of creatures stretched across the ceiling all centred around a cloaked figure holding the Perrero gem in one hand and her father's gem in the other.

Astrid continued to walk down the centre aisle between the wooden pews looking to the end of each row as she passed them. In front of each stained-glass window along the wall stood a stone statue of a creature and at the base of each statue was a plaque describing the great figure above it. She recognised most of them as famous figures of their world, most children had grown up on the tales of their triumphs.

Another candle came alight on the balcony at the other end of the church. Astrid watched Sir Robert's shadow disappear through another door and then up more steps that ascended to the clock tower. She clicked her fingers, flashing herself into the clock tower.

The room was packed with stacks of papers and books scattered across the floor, and just a simple desk sat in front of the clock face, which was similarly full of open books and a single photo frame face down. Astrid noticed an empty whisky bottle next to the frame and shards of glass on the floor. She picked up the cracked frame. She recognised the people in the picture from her vision earlier on.

"Simpler times," muttered Sir Robert, emerging from the darkness of the corner and gently taking the frame from Astrid's hands. He caressed his thumb over the woman's smiling face and wiped the dust from the children playing on the grass beneath her and then stood it upright on his desk. "Sorry, I didn't mean to startle you. I was wondering when you'd come and find me, you've come to ask me about the gem for your father no doubt." Astrid held her fingers ready, rubbing electric sparks between them, she didn't trust him. "There'll be no need for any of that, Astrid." She relaxed slightly, but still kept her fingers poised. "Do you think I would have just let you in here if I thought you were anything like your father?"

"You presume to know a lot about me," Astrid replied, standing tall and confident.

"I don't need to presume anything, I'd recognise the daughter of Vincentrio anywhere, but there's more of your mother in you than you realise."

Her eyes flickered at the mention of her mother, she wasn't sure what game he was playing, but she wouldn't let him draw her focus. "All I need is some answers, there doesn't have to be any trouble."

"I don't have the answers you want I'm afraid." He wasn't intimidated in the slightest, it was almost like his mind was elsewhere.

"Just tell me where it is." Astrid stepped closer to Sir Robert, she could hear the voice of her father in her head encouraging her to push him further as she held her hands at the ready, she couldn't go back to her father with nothing.

"The gem could be anywhere. I lost the pocket watch along with the rest of my treasures." He glanced solemnly at the cracked photo. "Even if I did know, I wouldn't be sharing that information with that evil man."

The snake-like voices raged now in Astrid's head, she pushed him against the wall with her magic, surprised when he didn't bother to retaliate. "Everyone's always so concerned with labelling people as good or evil. Life isn't that simple. No one knows him like I do."

"But you know his anger, you've seen the things he's done, I don't believe you want to hurt people," reasoned Sir Robert. He could feel Astrid second guess herself as she loosened her hold on him and began to back off. Before Astrid could change her mind, Sir Robert reached out grasping Astrid by the arm taking them both into a memory she'd kept locked away.

Astrid frantically looked around confused at what he'd done, then she realised exactly where he'd brought them both. They were in a crowded carriage on the London Underground in the human world some many years ago. Astrid remembered they'd only been in the human world for a short time whilst her mother was ill, and they often took the tube into the city to pick up her mother's favourite flowers.

Her four-year-old self was sat on a seat opposite where Astrid had landed, her feet dangling off the edge of the chair. She was wearing her red polka dot dress and her hair was neatly tied up in pigtails with two pale pink ribbons, just the way her mum liked it. The young Astrid nursed a bouquet of bluebells within her arms as she wiped away her tear-stained eyes and nestled her head into her father's side. He was sitting next to her in his deep blue suit with his tie loosened and top button undone. *Mum loved that suit.* He stroked his unshaven chin and rubbed at his red raw eyes trying to comfort his daughter. Astrid recalled he hadn't slept for days; her mother had only just passed away and she had nightmares every day following it, but her father cradled her every night trying to help her sleep.

The tannoy sounded indicating the next stop, Oxford Circus, and Astrid knew what was about to happen. As the tube approached the next station, the carriage sharply halted rattling side to side as it came to a stop. A young man stumbled, accidentally falling on to the young Astrid and knocking her off her seat. She began to cry and wail as most four-year olds would when they'd fallen over and the man profusely apologised, anyone could see it had been an accident, but not Vincentrio, already mad with grief. Astrid tried to get her young self to stop crying, but she was just a ghost in her own memory and she couldn't change what was about to happen.

"Please Sir Robert stop. I don't want to see it... I... I'd chosen to forget it, please," pleaded Astrid in desperation, but Sir Robert stood unmoved. She tried to resist him and take them back before anything else happened, but her emotions were stifling her power, she couldn't concentrate enough to do anything. She looked on helpless, watching her father's eyes burn red with rage. She remembered it all so clearly. It was the first time she'd witnessed his fury and it wouldn't be the last.

Vincentrio waved his hands, throwing the young man up against the ceiling as he clutched the human's throat with his magic. Vincentrio slowly squeezed, tighter and tighter. A malicious smirk spread across his face as he watched the man's eyes bulge. The man's hands dropped, and he took his last breath. One of the other humans ran at Vincentrio in an attempt to tackle him, but Vincentrio saw him coming and with the flick of his other hand he snapped his neck.

The young Astrid squealed in horror as she looked at the body that lay next to her, his cold eyes staring at hers whilst his body twisted the other way. She frantically shuffled against the wall almost being trampled by the other humans who fled as fast as they could once the doors had opened. The other man dropped from the ceiling falling to the other side of the young Astrid. She tried not to look and covered her eyes. She cried and cried thinking her father might stop, but he was overwhelmed with his anger and how powerful he felt when he took life away from the humans. He laughed as the others fled. The young Astrid tugged at her father's trousers begging him to stop. He brushed her to the side consumed by power and continued to wreak havoc.

Astrid was huddled in the corner in defeat, every emotion she had felt that day surged through her and then some. She felt helpless as she watched her young self, crumble into pieces before her. She looked up at her father. The man she'd idolised, the man who cared for his heartbroken daughter rather than mourn his own loss, disappeared in front of her own eyes as Vincentrio took his place.

Human policemen arrived fully armoured with their guns aimed at Vincentrio and had surrounded the carriage. They gave him one warning with their megaphone before opening fire. Vincentrio dealt with them quickly before the bullets could reach him; cupping his hands he released roaring flames from his palms burning everything in his path. The young Astrid cowered beneath the seats with her hands over her ears desperately trying to drown out their screams as their bodies charred right in front of her. Then they stopped.

Astrid looked around, she was huddled in the corner of the clock tower and Sir Robert had crouched next to her, his face full of regret. The memory had stopped, but she could still hear their screams, the screams that had haunted her nightmares for years.

"I think you've made your point," Astrid callously said, keeping her eyes fixed on her feet. "I know he's done some horrible things, but he's also had horrible things happen to him."

"You can't make excuses for murdering innocents, a lot of people have horrible things happen to them," Sir Robert replied.

"More to some than others," she mumbled as she thought about the events that followed, the things the memory didn't show.

Before Vincentrio could butcher any more humans, the Guard arrived to take control and although he put up a good fight, he was outnumbered and weary. They overpowered him and imprisoned him back in the magical world, but not one member of the Guard realised his daughter was there still cowering under a seat. Astrid had been left amongst the dead, she was so scared, she had no one.

Eventually, a policeman found her whimpering amongst the rubble like a wounded animal, and he took her to a care home where she stayed for several years being pulled from pillar to post in and out of foster homes. Her powers had started manifesting after the trauma she'd been through and without someone to guide her, she didn't know how to use them. There were accidents that she couldn't explain and behaviour that foster parents soon tired of. The other children thought she was a freak, they called her names, they bullied her, she was made to feel like nothing, alone in the world. Things got better when she met Xander, he took her under his wing and protected her, being a magical being himself he understood. But even Xander couldn't be there for Astrid all the time. He was adopted, and she was all alone again. When Vincentrio finally escaped a few years later, Astrid was his priority. He found her, he rescued her, he protected her, and he loved her. They'd both been damaged, but they were family.

"He's still my father." Astrid looked up at Sir Robert. "He just lost his way."

“Some souls can’t be saved, Astrid, but that doesn’t mean you have to follow the same path.” Sir Robert lifted her chin with one finger and winced at the mark Vincentrio had left on her cheek from earlier. “A good father would never lay a hand on his daughter, you don’t owe him anything.”

Astrid’s brows knitted, and she drew her bottom lip between her teeth. “No, I don’t think you really understand. He made me into someone, he made me who I am, I owe him everything,” said Astrid. She truly believed that the things he did to her were out of his love for her, all he asked for was her help and some respect, which she knew she neglected to show sometimes. Astrid stood up confidently and wiped away the tears that stung her eyes.

“You really don’t understand, Sir Robert,” smirked Vincentrio as he appeared with his hands on his daughter’s shoulders. He looked down approvingly at his daughter.

Astrid turned around startled by her father’s presence. For a moment she’d forgotten to hide herself from her father. Astrid looked apologetically at Sir Robert as he shot up from where he was crouched and turned around to see Crista stood behind him. Vincentrio continued to wander round the room, he frowned as he noted the empty whisky bottle.

“I’ve been ready to die for quite some time now so just be done with it,” said Sir Robert, preparing himself for a deadly blow from Crista. He could see she was practically salivating at the thought.

“There’ll be a time for that, old man, but today isn’t that day. You have something I want,” hissed Vincentrio, staring at the pocket watch Sir Robert wore in his portrait on the wall. Vincentrio turned to his daughter and gently kissed her on the forehead. “Well, done, Astrid.” He smiled and then the three of them had vanished, leaving Astrid alone with the tang of her guilt.

Astrid felt awful, she hadn't meant for Sir Robert to be taken. All she'd wanted was some information from him that she could have used to satisfy her father, but he had to be stubborn.

People would surely notice Sir Robert's absence and it wouldn't take long for them to become suspicious that something unsavoury had happened to him. Thinking fast on her feet, Astrid clicked her fingers and returned the room to its original state before Sir Robert had finished his whisky bottle. The books ordered themselves neatly on the bookcase, the photo frame stood back up uncracked and the crystal glass and full bottle returned to the drawer in his desk. She then quickly wrote a note using Sir Robert's stationery and imitating his handwriting with the help of some letters she'd found in his drawer. She kept the note short and attributed his departure to a long overdue trip round the regions, that should hopefully buy a bit of time before people started asking questions.

Astrid turned off the lights and briskly left the church with the hood of her coat up. She ran around to one of the side streets and hoped no one had seen her though it was dark now, so they shouldn't have been able to recognise her even if they did. She stopped for a moment and took a deep breath; the guilt was overwhelming, and she could feel her knees almost buckle. So much had happened in one day, she hadn't had a minute to process any of it. Pieces of memories that she'd buried had now resurfaced to circle round in her head and so many emotions were pulsing through her. If she had any hope of regaining some control and protecting her friends from her father's gaze, she needed to get herself together, but she was finding it difficult.

Suddenly, Caius appeared around the corner and Astrid couldn't have been happier to see his friendly face. He practically ran towards her and she almost collapsed in his arms as she threw her arms around him and nestled her head against his chest. Tears flooded her eyes as all her emotions burst from her at once.

Caius had no idea what had happened, but he just stood and held her. He felt a disturbing ache rumble through his chest as she cried against him. "What happened, are you okay? You've been gone for hours, we were all so worried," asked Caius. He softly stroked her hair and looking down at her sad eyes he almost cried himself. He wanted to know what had upset her so much, but more than that, he wanted to make it stop.

Caius brushed the hair out of Astrid's face and stroked the mark on her cheek. An unnerving anger coiled in his stomach as he thought of someone laying a hand on Astrid and what he'd do to that person when he found them. His jaw clenched, and he shook the furious thoughts from his head.

Caius brushed his thumb over Astrid's lips and then went to take his hand back, but Astrid held his hand closer, his touch was so soothing for her. He leant in, placing his forehead on hers and then brushed his lips gently on hers. She kissed him back tenderly as Caius caressed her face with his hands. Her knees almost buckled again as she wanted more. She wanted to stay in his arms and she wanted him, the kind, caring Caius she was starting to fall in love with, but she knew she wasn't good for him, so she abruptly pulled away.

"I'm sorry," she said quietly, she rushed back to the bus that was waiting to take the students back to Vistaldors, leaving Caius alone in the snow, confused and dumbfounded.

CHAPTER 5

Astrid and Caius hadn't spoken since they shared a kiss. It had been over a week now and they still avoided each other wherever they could. Neither of them had the courage to talk to the other about what had happened, and Astrid hadn't even spoken to Hesper about it.

The law was clear when it came to inter-species relationships. No one would approve, and Astrid's father certainly wouldn't approve. She feared what he would do if he found out she even had feelings for someone, regardless of their species, let alone if she started a relationship like that. Nevertheless, Astrid often found herself day dreaming about how good it felt when he held her and how the feel of his lips against hers made her hunger for more. She craved his touch and his love, but it was just a silly fantasy for a life that she knew she could never have.

Astrid's thoughts were no longer safe from her father, so she had to be more careful, she had to at least try to stop thinking about Caius with whatever distraction she could muster. Preparing for the first Shacklebolt game of the season was exactly the distraction she needed. Though she'd certainly noticed the effect her two-year absence had had on her game and she wasn't the only one, she'd barely made the Armungus team at try outs. Luckily for Astrid, her teammates remembered how she used to play. She'd once been the best Runner in the school and no one could forget how she'd won her school team a place at regionals. Though her father had removed her from school before she could lead her team to victory.

Astrid knew her father would respect her decision to take up the sport again; he understood that before, it had had its place disciplining Astrid's mind, but now it would particularly benefit her in combat. Witches and warlocks could be vicious on the field. They were ruthless players and the rules of the game were flimsy at best, practically anything was allowed much to the disadvantage of players not gifted with magical powers.

The objective of the game was simple: each team has a selection of five house banners scattered in their area of the course and the aim for each team is to not only find and protect their own banners, but to steal all five of the other team's. It's essentially a game of capture the flag with just a few alterations. For one, the game is not played on a simple field of hills and banks, instead the stadium contains a perilous course of towering rocks and tunnels with traps set in unpredictable areas. Secondly, the game is not played on foot; each player wears a pair of winged boots, so they can swiftly manoeuvre through the course, though players gifted with wings usually opted to use those instead. And thirdly, players are allowed to use any means necessary of stealing their banners back from the other team. If anything, physical contact was encouraged, and it made for a more interesting game. Once a banner was stolen, it was a matter of how quickly that player could fly away from the other team and how long they could keep hold of that banner.

There are six players in each team and each member has an essential role in securing a win for their house. The team is made up of three Guardians to find and protect their own team's banners, two Scouts to find the other team's banners and help steal those banners. But keeping those stolen banners relied solely on the Runner whose responsibility was to hold onto the stolen banners and evade the other team's Scouts and Guardians. A good Runner required speed, agility and stamina, without those qualities the game would soon be over.

The first game of the season was between Armungus and Solonious, an anticipated game for most of the school since the team representing Vistalus was never really much of a contender. Astrid had even more to prove with both Xander and Caius having positions on the Solonious team. She still thought it was ridiculous how quickly they'd made Caius one of their new Guardians. He'd said he'd played the game before, but she imagined the game in an Elvish region to be a lot gentler than one with witches and warlocks, not to mention that Vistaldors was known for its treacherous course, Caius was sure to get hurt. *And it will be his own stupid fault.*

The stakes were high for all the team members thanks to the rumours circulating around the school concerning the presence of talent scouts, they often watched games at schools across the regions to handpick fresh talent for the professional teams. Astrid had once dreamed of becoming the next star player of the Hawcranes, though that was the dream of a young foolish child who hadn't quite realised the fate her father had planned out for her.

Everyone was invested in the games of the Shacklebolt season, even the professors had their teams that they supported. The Headmistress of Vistaldors allowed a day off for the entire school whenever there was a game taking place. It was an opportunity for students to come together in support of their team however, the headmistress was rarely seen attending the games herself. She wasn't a fan of the violence but allowed it at her school only if the students still showed good sportsmanship.

By the time the greatly anticipated first game of the season came around, the ice and snow from the recent flurries had disappeared and the students were grateful for the temporary rise in temperature. It would have been no fun watching the game in the freezing cold, as some games could go on for an unprecedented amount of time.

"Doesn't look like you'll be needing your winter uniform out there today," remarked Hesper as she pulled back the curtains and flung the window open.

Astrid shot awake and glared at her friend for interrupting her sleep, something she didn't get much of since her nightmares had returned. Hesper was dressed head to toe in the Armungus colours, her deep red knit jumper was embroidered with the eagle emblem of their house and she'd even sprayed red streaks throughout her golden locks.

Hesper lifted a brow. "You can glare at me all you like, I'm not letting you make your return to Shacklebolt on an empty stomach," said Hesper. She perched at the end of Astrid's bed and raised her hand before Astrid could interrupt. "I've given you your space whilst you've been training. I haven't mentioned anything about whatever happened between you and Caius. I haven't even pushed you to talk about the nightmares that I know you'll deny you've been having. But I'll be damned if you lose this game for us today."

"No concern for my safety at all then," said Astrid wryly. She hadn't realised quite how invested Hesper would be in the game.

"Of course, I don't want you to get hurt," replied Hesper with a more caring tone to her voice. "Plus, I've got ten silver pieces riding on us winning, so don't get caught with those banners."

"Hesper you know it's against the rules to bet on games."

"Like how it's against the rules to have pets hiding underneath your bed."

Astrid perked her lips. "Point taken. We won't be losing on my account, don't you worry about that," Astrid smiled. She knew she had a lot to prove to the others and although she didn't particularly care what others thought of her, she had wondered if her father would be watching. If he was, she wanted to make sure he was watching a daughter he could be proud of.

"Glad to hear it, now get dressed and then we can go get some food in you," instructed Hesper, leaving her friend to it.

Astrid lifted the sheet hiding the underneath of her bed and waited for Peewee to emerge from his snug and calmly climb up her open arms; she hoped a quick snuggle with Peewee would help calm her nerves. She quickly got dressed into her uniform, fastening the Velcro tightly on her shoulder-pads. She then tied her boot laces and grabbed the fingerless gloves from her drawer, trying to ignore her trembling hands as she did so.

"Breathe in, breathe out, in and out," Astrid muttered to herself before opening the door. Her pride wouldn't let her show anyone how nervous she was, not even Hesper, though she could see from the sympathetic look on her friend's face that she probably heard those thoughts through the door. Hesper was beginning to understand when it was appropriate to press Astrid to talk about things and she knew now was not the time. Without even attempting to probe, Hesper clicked her fingers and flashed them both to the Grand Hall.

The Grand Hall was echoing with the chatter of students excited for the game ahead. It never was usually quite so busy at that time in the morning or at least not as noisy. A grand buffet had been laid out for the students on their day off, but Astrid didn't think she could stomach more than a bowl of cereal. The noise seemed to resonate more than usual for Astrid, she could hear every scrape of the metal spoons along the bottom of the cereal bowls and every slurp of coffee. She felt her hands tremble even more.

Ignoring the obvious tremor of her hands, Astrid went to grab some cereal for them both, whilst Hesper found some empty seats. A warm hand brushed over her knuckles and her tremors all of a sudden settled. She sucked in a breath as Caius lightly traced his finger down the palm of her hand and tentatively interlocked his fingers with hers, his touch was reassuring, and she found herself focussing on the sound of his breathing, deep and slow. She knew it was Caius and she was grateful for his discretion. Astrid never wanted to let go, she wanted to turn around and explain herself, he deserved that much, but she couldn't face him, not yet.

Astrid sharply took back her hand, poured the cereal into the bowls and hastily rushed back to Hesper before she could convince herself to turn around and look at the poor boy. She let out a deep breath as she took her seat next to Hesper. "Just don't," she warned, noting the expression on Hesper's face.

"Was only going to say thank you," Hesper replied sheepishly. She looked back and saw Caius at the breakfast buffet. He weakly smiled back at her and then returned to the Solonious house table where the other team players were laughing with their avid supporters.

Astrid looked up momentarily from the bowl of cereal she'd been shovelling into her mouth and saw Sapphire, dressed in her emerald green uniform, laughing as she fondled Caius' arm whilst he ate. The girl was all over him, flicking her auburn hair every time he said something. Not that Astrid cared, she couldn't have him anyway, so he was free to do as he pleased. Yet she couldn't help but feel a tang of jealousy as she watched on.

"Are you going to sit and scowl at them all day?" questioned Hesper. Astrid hadn't even realised the sour expression she'd been wearing on her face.

"I didn't even know *she* played Shacklebolt," she remarked, finishing her bowl of cereal.

"None of us did, I would say she bought her way onto the team but according to Caius she's the fastest flier he's seen out on the field."

Astrid scoffed and rolled her eyes, clearly the pair had become fast friends in her absence. "I'm sure he's got plenty of nice things to say about her," she murmured under her breath.

"Oh, don't get your knickers in a twist, they're just teammates and nothing more, Caius is just too polite to tell her to shove off."

"I don't care, he can do wha—"

"Yeah, yeah, yeah. I don't see you being so bothered about Sapphire working closely with Xander," jibed Hesper. Astrid couldn't think of anything clever to say, so Hesper continued, "You don't want to talk about it, I get it and if this is what you need to help you win the game then by all means rage on sister."

Astrid exhaled, she hated that Hesper was so right about everything. The boys had both been lumped together with Sapphire unwillingly and as Hesper said, they were too polite to say anything to her until they'd at least won a game. Nevertheless, she still loathed Sapphire and she didn't like her behaving like that around Caius whether he reciprocated or not. She looked down at her hands that had stopped trembling now, and she could feel her confidence returning.

“We’ve got a game to win,” Astrid smiled, getting up from her seat and clicking her fingers to tidy their bowls away.

“That’s more like it,” beamed Hesper, joining Astrid as they went to leave for the stadium.

The game would be starting soon and most of the other spectators had already began making their way to the stadium to get some good seats. Astrid turned around stumbling into the wall of muscle that was Xander’s chest. The rest of his team stood shoulder to shoulder behind him.

“We just wanted to wish you luck on your return to the course,” said Xander, placing his hand reassuringly on Astrid’s arm.

“You’re going to need it,” snickered Sapphire just loud enough for Astrid to hear her.

Xander threw her a dirty look and then went to embrace his friend before she could object. “Be careful out there,” he whispered gently in her ear as he released her.

“May the best team win,” she smiled graciously, ignoring Sapphire’s presence altogether.

Astrid didn’t recognise the other three members of their team, so she had no idea what kind of players they were. She’d see it for herself soon enough. Her eyes then met with Caius’ and they both nodded with a silent exchange of good luck, the last thing she wanted was to see Caius get himself hurt. She pushed the thought of that aside for now and left with Hesper to the Armungus team room.

The rest of the team were already in the team room, sitting at benches making sure their bootlaces were double tied, if not triple, and tightening their fingerless gloves round their wrists. Astrid looked around the room, she recognised most of the team from before when she’d been captain. She was hoping things hadn't changed too much, they'd been a tight group of friends prior to her leave of absence.

Katy Nickelson scraped back her raven hair into a French plait away from her deep brown eyes. Astrid noticed she now wore the captain's mark on her sleeve. She wasn't in the least bit surprised. Katy had been the youngest witch to play on a house team having tried out immediately once she'd turned thirteen, the headmistress didn't allow any students younger than thirteen to play simply due to the dangerous nature of the game. Katy quickly progressed from the reserves team to be their number one Scout in just her first season and was happy to help Astrid when she first joined the team, a Runner was only as good as their Scouts.

Astrid recognised their other Scout as Grayson Smith, a warlock with a flair for playing practical jokes on other students. She recalled how he used to drive Katy crazy when they used to train, she was usually the target of his practical jokes and very rarely did she see the funny side of them. Although it seemed he'd done some growing up in Astrid's absence and, from what she'd heard, Katy certainly approved of how he'd changed. She didn't blame Katy; his charcoal hair and darkened stubble were appealing to the eye and it was difficult not to get caught in the piercing gaze of his icy blue eyes. He was tall and handsome, but still lean enough to be a fast Scout. Astrid was sure the two of them had plenty of fun training together.

Astrid looked to where the three other players were sat discussing tactics as the Guardians of the team. She didn't recognise two of the boys who were both similar looking and certainly close in age, neither of them had been at the group training sessions she'd attended. The other girl she remembered had been on the reserves team whilst Astrid had been playing.

She looked athletic and at least a year younger than Astrid herself, but she couldn't quite recall the girl's name. The girl turned and smiled sincerely at Astrid as if she could feel Astrid trying to work out who she was.

"You won't have met our Guardians yet, Astrid," said Katy, walking Astrid over to where they were all talking.

All three of them immediately stood up for their captain smiling. The boys were clearly built to be Guardians, they towered over the rest of the girls and Astrid was frankly surprised they'd managed to find shoulder-pads wide enough to cover their broad shoulders.

"These two are Zack and Reuben," explained Katy as she gestured towards the brown-haired lads who nodded simultaneously.

"Brothers?" questioned Astrid, the resemblance was uncanny though one brother donned more facial hair than the other.

"Would you believe this lump is actually my *younger* brother," remarked Reuben, the smaller brother of the two.

"And I'm Erin," smiled the girl, shaking Astrid's hand.

"Our little sister," finished Zack. "Mum's not too happy about us all playing, but at least we can watch each other's backs, that's what families for right?"

"Right," Astrid muttered. Her mind began to trail off as she imagined what it would be like to be in a family like that, but then she focused herself again and went to check her laces for the third time.

"You all right there?" questioned Katy, the two of them hadn't really talked much since she'd come back to school.

"It's just been a while." Astrid half smiled trying to shake off the conversation, though she appreciated Katy's concern.

"I'd say there's a bit more to it than some pre-game jitters," Katy implied, sitting on the bench next to Astrid. "We were pretty good friends before whatever happened to you, I hope we could become good friends again?"

Great, another person to protect from Father. There'd been a reason why she'd tried to separate herself from other students. She sighed. "I'd like that, Katy."

"For now, let's go win this game," exclaimed Katy, quickly standing up from the bench to be met by a chorused cheer from the rest of the team as they made their way up the steps and out onto the course.

The team could hear the rumbling of applause and chanting of students as they strolled out in formation. Astrid looked back to see an encouraging smile from Hesper as she mouthed good luck before flashing to her seat. Astrid lifted her head high and joined her team to walk out onto the course, her hands were steady, and her breathing had calmed. She saw the Solonious team emerge from the underground tunnel across the course with Sapphire leading them out. She noticed how Caius' eyes widened when he first saw the course, it could be quite intimidating at first sight.

Contained within the stadium, the rocky course towered high with fragile tunnels already crumbling from the tremors of the roaring crowds. Astrid smiled reassuringly at Caius, swallowed hard and then allowed a stern expression to spread across her face. *Time to focus.*

The two teams met in a small dusty patch in the centre of the course where Professor Munroe was waiting for them. Each team took their place either side of her, standing in their formation facing each other. Caius stretched a great pair of eagle wings from his back whilst the rest of the players summoned the ankle wings from their boots. Reuben, Zack and Erin had all taken their griffin form, wearing just their team t-shirt across their auburn feathered chest. The professor raised her hands and the chanting silenced as the teams awaited their starting signal.

"Your banners have been hidden in your side of the course, but tread carefully, this course is not forgiving, and neither is your opposition," bellowed the professor, her voice echoing throughout the stadium. "Let the game… begin."

The stadium echoed with thunderous applause and the professor swiftly flashed to where the other teachers sat to observe the game. The Guardians of each team had quickly taken flight to protect their banners whilst the Scouts and Runners gingerly followed awaiting a signal from their Guardians that all of their own banners had been found. Katy pretended to stick close to their own Guardians, but then signalled to Grayson and diverted course to stalk the Solonious Guardians. Caius and Xander weren't difficult to keep track of, it was their third, much smaller, Guardian that managed to slip through unbeknownst to the others. The course remained quiet and stable whilst they located their own banners. Once the stealing starts, that's when the true fun begins.

Astrid caught a glimpse of the other Solonious Guardian as he snuck through a small tunnel in one of the rocks. The rest of her team had separated, so she chose to follow. She'd flown halfway through the tunnel when the first piece of rubble fell and then the walls began to crumble as it collapsed around her. Someone must have already stolen a banner. She had to get out before the walls fell in on her. She picked up speed to the end of the tunnel dodging the rocks as they began to fall quicker. She saw the light and raced towards it emerging from the tunnel seconds before it collapsed entirely.

The Armungus crowd cheered as Katy darted towards Astrid holding a Solonious banner firmly in her hand. Sapphire was close behind her, her face red with anger. She was throwing spells and Katy dodged each one. Astrid flew towards Katy to retrieve the banner when Sapphire raised a wall of rock separating them. Katy quickly flew upwards to avoid flying into it and Astrid followed the rock upwards on the opposing side.

All of a sudden, the Guardian Astrid had been following burst from the rock in the shape of a dragon. He stretched his wings outwards and widened his jaws. Fear crossed Astrid's face as she saw the fireball release from his mouth and she dived out of the way. She rolled onto the ground and formed a protective wall of water above her when the dragon spat more. She clicked her fingers, splashing the water at the dragon giving her just enough time to dash into the air and back to help Katy.

Sapphire was relentless in her pursuit of Katy and she'd recruited their other Scout in the process. The two were throwing spells at Katy that she was only just about quick enough to dodge. Katy dived through a narrow shaft she'd spotted in the rocks and the others followed her, as she knew they would. Once she'd reached the end of the tunnel, Katy turned around and clicked her fingers at the rocks pulling the rocks down on the exit, they'd have no other option than to turn back. Katy smiled and took flight again. She swivelled around defensively as she felt someone tap her on the shoulder, but she quickly lowered her hands as she saw Astrid standing behind her.

"Jesus Astrid, I almost took you out there," barked Katy. She hooked the stolen banner quickly onto Astrid's belt. "You better not lose that." Astrid smirked and the two took off ready to find their next banner.

They both flew round the course when Astrid spotted Xander brooding over a banner he was protecting as he hovered in the centre of a crater, it almost looked too easy. Astrid signalled to Katy and they both descended whilst his back was turned. Katy reached for the banner but yelped as Xander threw her to the side with a wave of his hands. She quickly regained her balance before he'd thrown her from the crater. She formed a shield of rocks in front of her and flew straight towards Xander before he could react, tackling him with the rocks and then herself. Whilst Katy kept him busy, Astrid swooped in stealing their second Solonious banner causing the entire course to rumble again. This time the floor began to crack and fearsome steam and fire spat from beneath. The stadium echoed with thunderous applause.

Astrid tagged the second banner onto her belt right before a rope wrapped around her ankle. Sapphire stood on the ground grasping the other end of the rope in her hands. Astrid resisted its pull as she tried to fly against it. She screamed as a burning pain pulsed through her ankle, the rope had begun to sear like a red-hot poker. Sapphire smiled and yanked at the rope whilst Astrid cried out in pain, bringing her crashing down to the ground in a flurry of dust. Astrid bit back the pain from the shoulder she fell on and quickly removed the rope from her scalded ankle.

"You've got something that doesn't belong to you," sang Sapphire.

Astrid could see Sapphire's shadow emerging through the flurry of dust. Thinking on her feet, Astrid clicked her fingers and stirred the small puff of dust into a storm surrounding the two of them. She could see Sapphire clearly now, but Sapphire couldn't see her. She was disorientated, flailing her hands around in front of her.

"Astrid, where are you?" shrieked Sapphire.

Astrid sniggered as she flew off with her two stolen banners and left Sapphire behind within the small storm of dust.

Sapphire screamed expelling the storm she was encased in. She could see Astrid flying off in the distance and went to follow, but then heard the Solonious Runner calling for help. The course rumbled once again and this time great rock creatures broke off from the course swinging gravel batons. Sapphire saw the Armungus banner flapping against her Runner's belt and then saw the two hefty griffins not far behind.

"I can't believe you let him sneak up on you like that," squawked Reuben, barging into his brother as they both chased the Solonious Runner.

Zack rolled his eyes and flapped his wings harder pushing himself ahead of his brother in their pursuit. He screeched with his talons poised to take out the Runner when a rock creature burst from the wall beside them, knocking Zack to the side. Zack regained his balance and flew into the rock creature's body in an attempt to cripple the beast. Reuben quickly joined his brother snatching the steaming baton from the beast's grasp as he'd tried to swing it at his brother. Sapphire flew behind the rock monster controlling it like a master puppeteer. The Solonious Runner got away in the opposite direction returning to steal the other banner the brothers had left unguarded in their haste.

With another shudder of the course and a roar from the Solonious crowd, the rock creature shed its rocky shell revealing its molten form underneath as lava oozed from every crack in its skin. Reuben yelped and dropped the baton that was now too hot to touch, and the two brothers raced away narrowly missing the creature's searing grasp. Sapphire summoned another creature on the other side of them and then left to steal the rest of their banners.

Reuben and Zack were trapped with a molten monster either side, their eyes widened as the monsters moved inwards.

"Any great ideas, Reuben?" quivered Zack as he backed up to his brother.

"I'm thinking, I'm thinking," he muttered, frantically scanning the crowd. His gaze focused on a student in a back-row chugging down a bottle of water. "I've got it."

Zack turned and saw what his brother was looking at, instantly clicking onto his plan. They swiftly flew either side, diving beneath the monsters' arms and swiping through their molten armour with their razor-sharp talons as they did so. The beasts roared as lava poured from their wounds. Zack and Reuben swooped over the crowd snatching a few bottles of water, they then smoothly turned and ripped open the bottles splashing the water over the molten monsters. The monsters howled as their molten skin hissed with the water, but it only made them angrier.

"Got any better ideas?" laughed Zack, narrowly missing a swing from one of the beasts.

"I'm all out," Reuben replied, clawing at one of the beast's eyes.

A surge of water suddenly burst from a crack in the ground beneath them and the boys dived out of the way. The beasts howled and crumbled to pieces as Grayson emerged behind the two brothers. "Think you just needed a bit more water, boys," smirked Grayson.

Reuben and Zack laughed with relief when another shudder echoed through the course much stronger than before and more molten creatures burst from beneath. Solonious had managed to find another two of their banners Reuben had hidden away, leaving only one banner before they won the game.

"What do they do now?" whined Zack, rolling his eyes as two molten monsters charged towards them spitting fire as they ran.

"You two go help the others, I'll deal with these jokers," ordered Grayson, fashioning himself a shield of water. He flew towards the molten monsters, allowing the brothers time to get away and help the rest of their team.

The Solonious Runner sped past Zack, the four banners on his belt slapped Zack's beak as he flew past at such a speed. Katy threw spells from behind as she flew after him, but the Runner was good, he was fast, and he was nimble. He disappeared into another tunnel and Zack pursued them both to help, he knew his wings could carry him faster than Katy's boots. Reuben heard his sister's call and went to help her instead.

Erin had only one of their banners in her possession, but she'd managed to keep it safe for the majority of the game, playing it smart and not staying in one place. Unfortunately, the other Solonious Scout had caught on to what she was doing and was now in pursuit. Erin was fast, and she was smaller than her brothers, so she could fit through much smaller gaps. She'd been leading the Scout through some tight scrapes, trying to wear him out as she flew deeper and deeper into the core swerving to avoid the molten beasts as she flew. As Erin flew into the open, the Scout yelled a charm expelling chains from his hands. The chains wrapped around her wings tightening into her body as she plunged to the ground. She squawked as she plummeted, struggling to break her wings free of the chains.

Reuben appeared over the top of one of the rocks grabbing his sister before she hit the ground. He let her go gently close to the ground and then raced towards the Scout with his talons poised. Before the Scout could use another charm, Reuben shrieked in his face and dug his talon into the Scout's shoulder pad spinning him round and throwing him across the course like a shotput. The chains holding Erin vanished and she flew away with the remaining Armungus banner and Reuben at her side.

With Katy in pursuit of the Solonious Runner and Grayson being preoccupied with a couple of molten monsters, Astrid was solely left with the duty of stealing the three remaining Solonious banners and she needed to do it quick. She couldn't rely on her team keeping their last banner out of the other team's grasp for long. She searched frantically looking from above the course, when she caught a shine off Caius' armoured wings from a small area atop a steep rock. She quietly flew round the back and noted he'd attached the two banners to his belt and stood calmly on guard waiting for a challenger. She knew she'd be a fool to try and tackle him, he was far stronger than she was, and his shapeshifting skills were untested. She'd be better off to knock him out with her magic and then swipe the banners from him whilst he was unconscious. She hesitated. She didn't want to hurt him, but then she didn't want to lose either. She could use her magic some other way.

Astrid hid behind a rock out of his sight. The crowd were making enough noise watching the other team members fight to distract Caius from what was happening behind him. She clicked her fingers and quietly muttered a charm summoning the banners towards her hands. They gingerly unhooked themselves from his belt without him even noticing, the banners were inches from her grasp. Then she froze. She couldn't move.

"Nice try, Astrid," beamed Xander as he landed next to Caius. "You've got to watch your back with this one, she used to do this to our old Guardian."

Caius swivelled and snatched the banners back. Astrid noted how annoyed he looked with himself, she hoped he wouldn't hate her for what she was about to do next. Xander, in his arrogance, hadn't bothered to freeze her other hand that was hidden behind the rock. She smiled and Xander immediately realised his mistake. She clicked her fingers blasting the rock she'd been poised behind.

Xander dived out of the way and Caius ducked as a shard narrowly missed his head. Astrid took flight, deflecting spells Xander threw at her. She crashed to the floor with her palm flat, splitting the rock the pair stood on and forcing Xander into the air before she ran towards Caius. She clicked her fingers, rocking the ground beneath his feet and dived to his side to snatch the banners whilst he was off balance. Caius jumped out of the way and span his armoured wings around him throwing metal feathers at her as he took flight. She leapt into the air and grabbed hold of the banners on his belt, veering him downwards. He shifted into a snake and from her grasp, taking the banners with him.

Before she could chase him, Xander trapped Astrid in a ring of fire allowing Caius time to get away. Astrid was overwhelmed by the heat, a stifling heat that she'd felt before. She coughed and spluttered as the smoke swarmed overhead, it was enough to keep her contained without totally hurting her. She stood screaming with her hands out to the side summoning a surge of water from the sky and blasting Xander off the rock he stood on.

Astrid emerged from the water, dripping wet, when she saw Reuben swoop down and snatch Caius from between two rocks when he'd tried to make his escape. Caius quickly shifted back mid-air but was winded as Reuben dropped him in surprise. Astrid flew upwards to help Caius gain some balance before he fell. He released his wings and sorted the rest out himself looking grateful for her help. The course shuddered intensely, and he looked at Astrid. The smile had left his face as he saw her holding the other two banners. She'd snatched them from his belt whilst helping him. She smirked and raced off to find the last banner.

Caius and Xander quickly raced after Astrid as she desperately searched for the final Solonious banner. Astrid swerved and darted round the course in an attempt to lose them, when she saw the flicker of emerald green from Sapphire's belt. She chased after her, clicking her fingers to summon the molten monsters behind her, they'd keep Caius and Xander out of the way.

Sapphire saw Astrid charging towards her and grinned. She stopped mid-air and fired a bolt of lightning from her palms, hitting Astrid square in the chest. Astrid landed in one of the craters writhing in pain, gasping as Sapphire landed next to her and reached for the banners Astrid had stolen. Astrid screamed, forcing Sapphire away with her magic before she could grab any. Astrid stumbled to her feet, her fingers poised and ready.

Sapphire flew into the air and Astrid followed. Sapphire summoned spikes of glass from the crater below as Astrid narrowly avoided each one. One rose and sliced her on the leg. She squealed and threw one of the spikes with her magic. The spike speared through one of Sapphire's shoulder-pads pinning her to a wall of rock.

Sapphire wriggled tirelessly, trying to free herself, but Astrid used the rest of her power to hold Sapphire in place as she sauntered towards her. Sapphire viciously spat at Astrid, as she snatched the last banner from her belt and held it up to the crowd to be met with roaring cheers from the Armungus crowd. Armungus had won.

Astrid beamed from ear to ear. It was a win that not even her father could take away from her. She could be happy even if it wasn't for very long, she could feel proud of herself. But before Astrid could turn and return to her team, Sapphire clicked her fingers and screamed, shattering the spikes of glass and throwing Astrid across the course and taking her off guard.

Astrid stumbled to her knees, winded by the force of Sapphire's piercing screech. As she stood up, pain seared through her stomach and she looked down to see her hands warm with blood. Her vision began to blur, and she wavered fumbling back to her knees. Caius had rushed to her side and caught the rest of her body before she fell. She saw his dusty face looking down on her, he seemed to be saying something to her, but all she could hear was a constant ringing as she fell into the black.

CHAPTER 6

The cottage where Astrid had spent her mother's last days in the human world wasn't particularly memorable; it was secluded and away from prying eyes, somewhere no one would think to look for them. The cottage was surrounded by green fields as far as the eye could see with not a person in sight for miles and behind the cottage was a beautiful garden of bluebells Vincentrio had grown just for Astrid's mother. In the days where she felt strong enough to walk, he'd help her outside, so they could sit together on the bench and watch the sun set whilst Astrid would chase the flittering birds. They'd laugh as Astrid would leap in the air and call for the birds to come back.

Those days were few and far between, especially towards the end. The image of one room inside the cottage was so clear now. Astrid could feel the cold, wooden floor against her bare feet. She could hear the soothing chirp of crickets sounding through the open window and the warmth of the log burning fire that blazed even whilst her mother slept. Her mother slept peacefully on the canopy bed tucked up with plenty of blankets, she felt the cold more towards the end.

Astrid looked down and watched her mother sleep; her cheeks were sunken, and the colour had almost faded from her olive skin. Astrid knelt down next to the bed and dropped her head as she sobbed into the sheets, her mother had suffered for so long like this, too long. Her hand tingled and she looked up as she felt her mother reach out with her frail hand. Her eyes were open, those violet eyes were once so full of life and now they were almost empty. She smiled and gently stroked her daughter's hair.

"Save your tears, my love." Her voice was almost musical, it had been so long since Astrid had heard her mother's voice.

Astrid tried to speak through her tears, but she couldn't find the words. She jumped into the bed and dropped her head on the pillow. Lying next to her mother, she looked upon her ghost pale face.

"Look at the young woman you've become, so brave, so strong," admired her mother, caressing her grown daughter's face. Astrid leant into her mother's hand and sighed. "But you can't stay here."

"I don't want to leave you, not like this, let me stay, just a little longer." Astrid held her mother's hand tighter, it felt as real as anything and she never wanted to let it go again.

"Oh, I wish you could, my love, I wish you could."

"I love you, Mum," Astrid cried as the outside began to fade. She reached out for her mother, but she evaporated in front of her as the dust fell through her fingers and the room vanished. Then she opened her eyes.

Astrid looked around and found herself lying on a hospital bed in the ward at Vistaldors. She could see it was dark outside, but she had no idea how long she'd been unconscious for. Her hands tingled from her mother's touch and she could feel the fresh tears staining her cheeks, the dream had felt so real. She heard a low murmur and deep breathing as she saw Caius slumped in the chair next to her bed; he was fast asleep with his hand resting on her bed by her side. His face looked almost angel-like in the glow of the moonlight.

Shaking off the temptation to reach out to Caius, Astrid went to lift herself up from the bed, but her stomach twinged, and she threw her head back against the pillow as the pain stabbed at her core. Her jaw tightened and her face pinched as she clutched at the tender wound sprawled across her stomach. *One scar Crista won't be able to take credit for.*

Caius jolted awake and stood up at Astrid's side in one fluid motion. "Careful there, if you move too much, you'll pull your stitches out," Caius whispered, gently laying his hand on top of Astrid's.

Astrid felt the tremor of her hand settle with Caius' gentle touch and the pain waned. "How long have you been sitting there?" she questioned, noting the heavy bags beneath his eyes and the mucky Solonious uniform he still wore.

"Not long, I'm just glad you're okay," he said, his lips lifting with a heartrending smile. The corners of his eyes creased, and his face softened. "You had me worried for a second."

"Can't get rid of me that easy," muttered Astrid as she watched Caius tenderly trace his finger along her knuckles.

"Good, I'd prefer it if you stuck around a bit longer," he murmured.

Caius slowly leant over her. Astrid could hear his shallow breaths as he closed the space between them. Her knees would have buckled if she hadn't already been lying down. Her chest quivered, and she gently shook her head. "Caius," Astrid whispered, stopping them both whilst she still had some control. "We can't."

Caius pulled back, quickly snatching his hand away and he cleared his throat. Astrid flinched at the blatant hurt that clouded his soft features; her heart ached for him, but she had to ignore it for both their sakes. If she chose to pursue her feelings for Caius, it would only end in pain and misery for them both.

Astrid's brows knitted with a stern expression. "You know the law, Caius, I didn't write it," she said, trying to keep her voice quiet for the other patients still sleeping.

"Screw the rules and since when do you care about abiding by them?" he replied moodily, standing away from her bed.

"We're not talking about some silly little school rules; do you know what they'd do to us?" Astrid thought of how her grandparents had suffered and the vengeance her father had taken in their name, all for following their hearts. She wouldn't do that to Caius and she certainly wouldn't involve him in the mess that was her life, he deserved much better than that.

"I don't care, no one would have to know." Caius dropped to his knees by her bed and cupped her hand between his.

"They'd find out and when they do they'd…" Astrid paused, "I don't want to see you get hurt, we're not worth it, we have to stop." This time she pulled her hand away and turned onto her side, she couldn't bear to look at his sad eyes any longer. She held back her tears until she heard him slam the door behind him. He was gone. So, she allowed herself a single moment to fall apart.

The moment had passed. Astrid took a deep breath, wiped away her tears and collected herself, she needed to get out of the ward and concentrate on the task her father had set her. No distractions. Astrid swivelled her legs to the edge of the bed, she paused to curse at her throbbing stomach and then staggered to her feet. She reached out for the bed rail to keep her steady. As soon as she began walking, a pinching pain pulsed up her leg and she stumbled, falling to the stone floor. The burn on her ankle had completely slipped her mind.

"You're supposed to be on bed rest," exclaimed Hesper, rushing to Astrid's side.

"What are you doing here, Hesper?" questioned Astrid, leaning on Hesper as she helped her to her feet and back into bed.

"I was on my way over to see how you were doing and I bumped into Caius on the way," she paused, waiting to read Astrid's reaction, but Astrid said nothing. "He looked pretty upset." Still no reaction from Astrid, Hesper rolled her eyes. "You do know he downright refused to move from that chair for the past two days until you woke up."

"Well, I'm awake now," Astrid replied coldly.

"Jesus Astrid, you don't make this easy, do you?"

"What?"

Hesper raised one eyebrow. "His thoughts were pretty loud, I'm just waiting for you to tell me what in the world you were thinking."

"Don't worry, I shut it down before it went any further, he…"

"No, no, I meant what you were thinking rejecting him like that, you two are clearly in love with each other so why deny you both the happiness," said Hesper.

Astrid darted a glare at her friend and tried to hush her voice. "It's against the law, Hesper, there's no place for us together so just drop it," snapped Astrid, looking around uneasily at who could overhear them.

"How would anyone find out? I'm not going to say anything and he's not going to say anything. This is true love. Don't just throw it away."

"Hesper, please. Drop it," begged Astrid. She looked tired and she felt defeated, it had been hard enough pushing Caius away when she wanted him so badly, she didn't want to ruminate on it any longer and she certainly didn't want to discuss it.

"Drop what?" questioned Professor Peverel, surprising both the girls as she wandered into the ward.

"Nothing, Professor. Astrid just doesn't like being told to get back into bed," said Hesper, quickly improvising.

"Yes, I'd heard you'd woken up, how are you feeling?" queried the professor, perching on the foot of Astrid's bed.

"I'll feel much better when I get out of this bed," Astrid replied, wincing as she went to get up again. She clicked her fingers to summon the crutch that leant against the end of her bed, but it didn't move. She clicked again and still nothing. "What's happened to my powers?"

"Astrid, you need to give yourself time to heal," advised the professor caringly. "You hit your head pretty hard out there, that needs to heal before your powers return."

"But they will come back?" she asked frantically, her face stricken with worry. Without her powers she wouldn't be able to serve her father. She was weak without them, and she knew what her father thought of weakness.

"They should do, we just don't know how long it might take. In the meantime, you need to rest," instructed Professor Peverel, giving Astrid a reassuring smile as she left. "Everyone takes their own time to heal."

Once the professor was gone, Astrid whipped off the covers and attempted to get up again, this time grabbing the crutch before trying to stand. Hesper rolled her eyes and gave in holding her arm out for Astrid to lean on whilst she flashed them both back to their dormitory. She was going to try and leave anyway, may as well save her the walk, Hesper thought to herself. Astrid smiled and took her friend's arm.

They appeared in the Armungus common room. Astrid fell into the armchair as they arrived, it had been a while since she flashed somewhere as a passenger. She sighed, she didn't see how she could be so tired when she'd just been unconscious for two days and yet she was struggling to keep her eyes open. She was so much weaker without her magic. If her father could see her now, he would find her state most distasteful.

"I think you'll sleep a whole lot better in your bed," remarked Hesper as she held out her arm again to help Astrid hobble into her room.

"I'm just going to rest my eyes for a couple of minutes here," yawned Astrid, falling back into the armchair.

"Sure." Hesper rolled her eyes and grabbed the blanket from the sofa, gently laying it over Astrid. "I'm out this evening, but I'll be back a bit later."

Astrid murmured softly, acknowledging Hesper leave and then she let her eyes close, it couldn't hurt to have just a quick rest. Her mind slowly drifted, and she fell into the darkness once again, unsure what memory would resurface this time.

The city streets of Aberdeen were still overflowing with life in the early hours of the morning; music blared from the clubs along the road as people began to clumsily leave and make their way home, clutching the hand of a person they'd just met. Astrid stumbled in her heels on the cobble stones. She steadied herself against a shop window and glanced at her reflection. A shadow of her former self peered back at Astrid with the tired eyes of a person who was just trying to forget.

A warm arm wrapped around Astrid's waist and she swiftly turned around and away from her pitiful reflection. A laugh burst from her mouth as she snatched the bottle of vodka from the boy's other hand and took a long swig. Astrid raised her eyebrow as she saw the hungry look in his dark brown eyes and he pulled her close, devouring her lips with his. She tugged at his lip and pulled away. Her cheeks were red raw from his dark stubble and they dimpled with an impish grin.

The boy draped his arm around Astrid's shoulder as he led her to a spot he knew along the harbour. Astrid recalled his name as Damon, some rugged older boy she'd met when she was sixteen and had escaped to Aberdeen. Her father had recently taken her out of school and explained all of his plans to Astrid, including her role in it all. She'd wanted to escape her father, her destiny, herself and alcohol seemed to help with that, it numbed her.

Astrid hadn't been around normal people in a while and, at the time, Damon seemed to be exactly what she needed to take her mind off everything. It was a fast and heavy romance. They had fun together and she didn't have to think about the person she was supposed to be, in fact, she didn't have to think at all. He was tall and handsome and had his own motorbike and she fell hard in those two days, taken up by the thrill of it all. She knew now that what she felt for him wasn't love. Looking back at it now, Astrid was ashamed of her younger self, but she couldn't change it. She was trapped in the drunken memory until she awoke from what was about to become a hellish nightmare.

They'd found a private spot along the docks looking over the River Dee. Damon had gently placed his leather jacket around her shoulders. He must have said something funny as Astrid felt a smitten laugh escape her throat. She licked her lips and he leant in, swiftly devouring her lips again with his. He pulled her closer against him and grasped the back of her neck, running his fingers through her thick brown hair. She fell back as his kisses got hungrier and moaned as he left his mark on her neck. Her thighs tingled as she felt his hands slowly sweep under her skirt and she eased them away trying to slow things down. Damon backed off, leaving a gentle kiss on her lips as he pulled away and smiled down at her.

Damon's smile suddenly disappeared as his eyes reddened and begun to bulge. Blood spluttered on Astrid's face as he fell to the side of her, coughing and clawing at his throat. Astrid didn't know what to do. She ripped his shirt off and watched his chest begin to collapse. She heard his ribs crack and screamed as Damon choked on his own blood. She tried to think of a spell or maybe she could run and get help, but then his broken ribs burst from his chest, erupting in a spurt of blood and he stopped struggling. His body lay still, his face stained with his own blood and his eyes wide.

All Astrid could see was Damon's lifeless eyes and all she could feel was his blood staining her hands. She crawled backwards as the realisation set in. She held her hand over her mouth in an attempt to muffle her own screams through the tears that surged from her eyes.

"Such a pity." The witch's voice sent a cold chill down Astrid's spine.

Astrid looked up and saw the blonde witch standing over Damon's lifeless body. A wicked grin flicked across Crista's face and she slowly uncurled her fist releasing Damon from her spell. She casually stepped over him, lifting her cloak so not to stain the edge with his blood.

"St-stay back," stuttered Astrid, holding her shaking hands in front of her.

Crista's thin brows quirked. "I don't think I'm the one to be afraid of right now," she said as her gaze flicked to the figure that towered behind Astrid.

Astrid's eyes widened, and she swivelled around. "Father," she gasped, looking up at her father's stern face. She quickly looked away from his icy glare.

Vincentrio's eyes narrowed as he looked at the boy and then the ruffled state his daughter was in. He pinched her chin with his fingers and lifted her off the floor, so his eyes met hers, she couldn't move. "Someone's been busy," he spat, disgusted with his own daughter.

The red raw mark on his daughter's neck and the wretched stench of alcohol on her breath drew Vincentrio's attention. A muscle in his jaw twitched and he struck Astrid across the cheek. She yelped, crumbling to the floor next to Damon, cowering like a wounded animal. He slapped her again as she tried to say something, this time making sure he used the hand he wore his rings on.

Crista kicked Astrid down as she tried to get up and then struck her face again. Astrid whimpered on the ground, clutching at her eye as she tried to crawl away from them. Vincentrio held her ankles with his magic and dragged her along the flint rocks, she screamed as the shards scraped at her skin. Vincentrio leant next to his daughter and pried her eyes open as she tried to escape his glare. A pitiful mewl escaped her mouth.

Vincentrio's lips twisted in disgust. "You think that you can just walk away from me and everything that I am doing, everything that I am doing for you, to drink and whore yourself," he hissed, not even needing to raise his voice. "You would be *nothing* without me." Vincentrio's grip eased and his face softened, "Don't you understand how worried I was about you."

"I'm sorry, Daddy," trembled Astrid, shielding her face as she braced herself for the next blow. "Pl-please forgive me, please."

Vincentrio sighed and released her from his hold. He took a step back and tamped down his temper. "We're going home. It's time for you to find your true power."

"Th-thank you." Astrid's shoulders sagged with relief and she stood to her feet, grateful for her father's kind mercy.

A hard line formed between Vincentrio's dark brows and he paused. "But first, let Crista remind you exactly how I feel about alcohol." He nodded to Crista and turned his back.

Astrid stepped back in fear as Crista marched towards her, a furious ball of flames flickered in her palm and her icy blue eyes gleamed with an undeniable satisfaction. Crista struck Astrid in the stomach and Astrid jolted awake, feeling the sting like it was all too real. She rolled up her shirt and saw the old burn mark beneath her stitches.

"I remember giving that to you," smirked Crista, leaning to look at the marks on Astrid's stomach.

Astrid leapt out of the chair and frantically scanned the room for any other unwanted guests, but the common room was deserted. She rubbed her eyes. *Am I still dreaming?*

"It's not your imagination, my dear," said Crista with a gleeful cackle. She revelled in the panic flickering in Astrid's face, the panic she knew she was responsible for.

Astrid certainly wasn't dreaming any more. She took a deep breath and straightened her shoulders as she tried not to lean too much against the armchair. "What a pleasant surprise."

Crista arched her brows. "Hm, I'm sure." She circled Astrid like a vulture round its food. She noted the bags beneath Astrid's eyes and the lack of colour in her face, she looked positively awful. "You don't look too good."

"Been having trouble sleeping," Astrid replied, glaring coolly back at Crista. "I'm sure you didn't come all this way to give me beauty tips. Why are you here, Crista?"

"I suppose that nasty cut along your tummy doesn't help. Who gave you that one?"

"You want to swap tips with them?"

Crista cackled. "Something like that, I should hope the other person is worse off." She licked her lips at the lustful thought. "Or am I right in thinking you've gone soft?"

Astrid's cheeks stiffened. "I'll only ask once more. Why are you here, Crista?" barked Astrid sternly.

Crista perked her lips and backed off. She walked over to the mantelpiece where she could fiddle with the trinkets on display, Astrid's gaze followed her every move. "You've been unreachable for the past couple of days, your father was sick with worry and I, his dutiful servant, volunteered to make sure you were okay," she explained all too sweetly.

Astrid raised her eyebrows, she was not convinced. "Making sure I haven't run off is more like it," scoffed Astrid.

"Well, it wouldn't be the first time," Crista muttered.

"Well, you can tell my *anxious* father that I was injured by a sore loser at the end of my Shacklebolt game, but I'm healing now, and I haven't forgotten what he tasked me with. I won't let him down."

"Oh, I can tell him more than that," said Crista, her lips curled with a devilish grin.

"And what's that supposed to mean?"

"Let's just say I met a lovely fella earlier today, someone I think you've made quite the impression on," said Crista, taking a small vial from her cloak pocket. Astrid's eyes widened as she saw the wisps of Caius' memories trapped inside. Crista could see how agitated Astrid was becoming, provoking her was far too easy and far too enjoyable. Crista wiggled the vial playfully and continued, “I’m sure your father can’t wait to see these.”

“Give those back or I’ll—”

“You’ll what?” probed Crista, her brow creased with curiosity.

Astrid lunged for the vial, but Crista flashed out of the way. She pretended to drop the vial and a wicked cackle erupted from her lips as she saw the fear flicker in Astrid’s eyes. She bit her bottom lip playfully and slipped the vial back into her pocket where she’d keep it safe and sound. Before Astrid could do anything else, Crista clicked her fingers, thrusting Astrid up against the wall. Astrid squirmed and wriggled but Crista’s hold was strong and without her magic, Astrid was powerless.

Crista tilted her head as she studied Astrid curiously. It had been a while since Crista had bested Astrid, she almost forgot how good it felt. “I’d heard you’d lost your powers, wanted to see it for myself,” teased Crista, delighting in Astrid’s helplessness. She held Astrid’s lips together with her magic, she didn’t care for what clever thing Astrid had to say. “I’m sure your father won’t make it quick for him, you’d be amazed how much pain the body can withstand, well—” she paused, gesturing at Astrid’s body. “You’d know all about that. I want to know if he’ll be quite so masculine when he starts screaming.”

Astrid could feel a surge of power pulse through her body as the thoughts of Caius in pain crossed her mind. She couldn’t let anyone hurt him, she wouldn’t. Astrid clicked her fingers throwing Crista across the room. Crista fell into the wall, cracking the mirror that hung there. Astrid was released from Crista’s grasp and landed on her feet. She quickly limped to

Crista's motionless body and snatched the vial of memories from her cloak pocket whilst she was still unconscious.

Crista's eyes opened, and she grabbed Astrid's injured ankle. Astrid squealed as Crista's blade-like fingernails drew blood beneath her bandage. Astrid clicked her fingers, repelling Crista's grip with a sharp shock and then flicked her wrist, holding a shard of the glass mirror poised at Crista's neck with her magic. Crista stopped and eyed the glass warily. Astrid's eyes reddened as she pressed the glass slowly into Crista's neck, drawing just a few drops of blood. She'd happily end the witch's life with just a click of her fingers and then Caius would certainly be safe, for now.

Crista licked her lips. "Go on then," she spurred, relishing in the look she saw in Astrid's eyes. "I know you've got it in you."

Astrid breathed deeply, swallowing down the anger that so quickly consumed her. She eased the glass away, this wasn't the person she wanted to be. "No." She dropped the glass and relaxed her hands.

A wave of disappointment transformed Crista's face. "Shame, that's the only chance you'll get," she said, smoothly standing to her feet. She pressed her finger to her neck and pursed her lips as she stared at the drop of blood. "I hope the boy doesn't mean too much to you."

As Crista waved her hand to vanish, Astrid clicked her fingers, plucking the memories of Caius from Crista's head and into an empty vial. Crista sucked in a breath as the wisps were snatched from her skull and then her face went blank. She turned around, her face scrunched as she stared at the mess around them.

"I hope you're going to clean this up," remarked Crista, throwing her hood over her head. "We'll be watching you closely."

Crista swiftly made her exit and swung the door open just as Hesper went to push it from the other side. Without saying a word, Crista looked Hesper and her guest up and down, and then swatted them from her path as she continued down the stairs.

"Well, she seemed nice," said Hesper dryly.

Hesper stepped gingerly through the doorway, unsure what state she'd find the common room in considering the hurry the stranger was in to leave. Hesper's guest followed warily behind her, observing the mess the stranger had left behind. She instantly looked down as her foot cracked on shards of broken glass on the floor and she noticed the drops of blood stained into the carpet. She pressed her finger to the spot, noting the freshness and stood back up immediately with her hands poised when Astrid emerged from her room.

"I thought you were supposed to be napping," grumbled Hesper, gesturing to her guest to lower her hands as she approached Astrid.

Astrid eyed Hesper's guest nervously and then clicked her fingers, repairing the shattered mirror and returning the common room to its former condition.

Hesper lifted a brow. "And I see you got your magic back, you've been busy."

"Who's this then?" questioned Astrid, choosing to ignore Hesper's remarks whilst she thought of a lie to tell her.

"This is Paige, my older sister," she explained.

Now that Hesper stood next to her sister, Astrid could see that the resemblance was uncanny. Paige had a few more worry lines and was perhaps an inch taller than her sister, thanks to the thick sole of her boots, but that was where the differences ended.

Paige tucked a piece of her dark blonde hair behind her ear and then held her hand out confidently to Astrid. "Nice to finally meet you."

Astrid shook Paige's hand warily and they both smiled politely at one another, though Astrid could see how uncomfortable Paige felt. "I don't usually break things," said Astrid, trying to put Paige at ease. "Me and my aunt don't always see eye to eye."

"I'm guessing there's a good story there," probed Paige, draping her red leather jacket over the arm of the sofa as she took a seat.

"Sorry, Astrid, nosiness seems to run in the family," said Hesper, glaring at her sister. "My sister finds it hard to switch off from her job."

"I didn't even ask a question," retorted Paige, rolling her eyes.

"What is it that you do?" questioned Astrid.

"Nice. Diversion tactic," remarked Paige. "I'm an investigative field agent for the Guard and I'm also very protective of my family."

"Paige," scolded Hesper.

"It's all right, Hesper, the situation doesn't exactly look great and no doubt you've probably heard some other stories," suggested Astrid, no doubt word had spread outside the school of her destructive behaviour.

Paige pressed her lips together and shrugged her shoulders. "One or two, but I like to give people a chance before jumping to conclusions," she replied, urging Astrid to explain herself. Paige had a gut feeling about Astrid Harper and it wasn't a good one.

"She's my father's sister, my father who I haven't seen since he left me after my mother died," said Astrid. She could feel

Paige examining her closely as she spoke, as though she was studying her face for any subtle tells she was lying. Luckily, Astrid had had plenty of practice by now, the lies became so natural.

"Astrid, you don't have to," comforted Hesper, giving Astrid's arm a gentle squeeze.

The corner of Astrid's mouth tweaked, and she continued, "Let's just say my father isn't the nicest man, he's left his marks and my aunt managed to track me down in an attempt to reconnect us. I don't have a lot of nice things to say about him and she didn't react well, I guess violence runs in his side of the family." *Not a total lie.* Astrid could see her story was good enough to throw Paige's suspicions for now. Not too much detail, but enough to satisfy Paige's curiosity.

Paige's apprehension eased. "I'm sorry, our father left his marks too." Paige smiled ruefully at her sister. Astrid recognised that pained expression. Paige's expression hardened, and she looked back to Astrid. "I told you, I'm protective of my family."

"Hesper, you never said anything," said Astrid, realising she'd never even thought to ask about Hesper's family, she'd assumed that with her wealth came happiness. Now that she thought of it, Hesper had never really spoken much about her family, not even before Astrid disappeared.

"It's hardly a thing that comes up in conversation," laughed Hesper half-heartedly. "Besides, Paige took the brunt of it and as soon as my mum realised, he was out on his ass with not a penny of her money."

"Well, that conversation was cheery," joked Paige, leaning back into the sofa. "How about we talk about the important stuff now like are there any boys my sister hasn't told me about?"

"Don't answer that, Astrid." Hesper punched her sister's arm as she joined her on the sofa. Astrid laughed and then realised she'd almost forgotten she still had Caius' stolen memories.

"Actually, I've just realised I need to return something to someone, but it was nice meeting you," explained Astrid, excusing herself before Hesper could probe her about who she was going to see.

Paige still watched Astrid carefully. "I'll be staying around for the next few days," she said, a tone of warning to her words. Hesper turned to her sister confused. "On Guard business, sis. Maybe we can continue this conversation some other time, I've got plenty of stories to share about my baby sister and something tells me you've got a few stories of your own."

Astrid's cheeks stiffened. It was pretty obvious Paige didn't trust her in the slightest, despite the believable sob story she'd fed her. "I look forward to it," said Astrid, forcing a sincere smile.

Astrid grabbed the vials she'd stashed away in her room and then made her way down the spiralling steps. She'd have to worry about Paige and her scepticism later. With a little time and work, Astrid was sure she could quell Paige's suspicions and, if she couldn't, her father had taught her well enough, she'd deal with her swiftly. Astrid shook the troublesome thought from her head. *Let's hope it doesn't come to that.*

As Astrid stepped out into the cold, she shivered, feeling suddenly far too underdressed for the sub-zero temperature. It had been a few days since Astrid had stepped outside, it was easy to forget how cold it was. She clicked her fingers, wrapping herself in her winter coat and scarf and rubbed her hands together. She could see her breath, as she hobbled over to the figure she saw crossing the bridge in the distance. The pain in her ankle seemed to have dwindled since she'd got her magic back.

The figure had reached the other side of the bridge and Astrid could tell now that it was Caius. She kept her distance and took the two vials from her pocket, emptying the one that contained Caius' memories into her hand and dropping the other one back in her pocket. The wisps steadied themselves on Astrid's open palm. She softly blew them in his direction and watched them drift towards him, memory wisps always knew where they'd come from.

Caius stopped still as the wisps reached him and vanished into his hat-covered head. He turned on his heel, a great smile stretching from ear to ear. He called out to Astrid and then briskly jogged over to her before she could flash herself away. Astrid didn't want to talk to him, but she also didn't want to walk away from him. Watching him coming towards her, she could feel her desire take over and it took every ounce of restraint to stop herself from running towards him and into his arms.

As soon as Caius reached Astrid, he threw his arms around her almost lifting her as he did so. Astrid fell into him wrapping her arms around his waist and leaning her head against his chest, she could hear his heart with every beat and she felt his warmth radiate across her own body. Her grip tightened around him.

Caius glanced down at Astrid. "I've been thinking about what you said." His hushed husky tone made her legs tremble. "And I care about you too much to just let you go."

"Maybe I care about you too much to let you in," she whispered, sighing as he softly caressed her face with his hand.

Leaning in closer, Caius locked his eyes with hers. "We *are* worth the risk." He closed the last bit of space between them and gently brushed her lips with his, taking her with a tender kiss. This time Astrid couldn't pull herself away, she leant in to him as his kiss became more passionate and she took his lips with all the emotion she'd repressed for so long. She wanted him, she needed him, and she couldn't push him away any longer.

Caius released her lips leaning his forehead against hers, breathing heavily as he held her.

"We have to be careful, Caius," muttered Astrid, feeling so at ease in his arms.

"I know," he replied, gently kissing her forehead.

"I'm serious. No one can find out. I don't want anything to happen to you," she said, looking up at him.

"And nothing will."

Caius took her hand with his and then led her quietly along the bridge over the pond. The grounds were always so tranquil in the evening and there wasn't a student or professor in sight, they wouldn't have to hide anything for now, they could just enjoy being with one another. Astrid smiled as they walked hand in hand around the pond. She allowed herself to forget her worries and just enjoy the moment she was having with Caius.

CHAPTER 7

Astrid had always considered herself good at keeping secrets, she'd had enough experience with it. No one knew who her father was, no one knew what plans he had in store for the magical world and they certainly had no idea of Astrid's role in it all, and yet hiding her relationship with Caius from everyone else was proving to be her biggest challenge yet.

Astrid had spent so long trying to ignore her feelings for Caius. She couldn't afford the distraction and she knew it would only end in heartbreak for them both, but now she'd given in to her selfish needs, she couldn't let it go again. She didn't dare to consider what would happen to the both of them if someone found out. No one could know. Not the professors, not the students and certainly not Paige. She may have been Hesper's sister, but she was also a direct link to the Guard and Astrid was well aware of their view on the matter.

With all the lies Astrid had told, she thought it would get easier, but it didn't. During the day, Astrid and Caius had to act like friends and nothing more, which was proving difficult for both of them. For now, their moonlight walks were the only time they could spend together as what they really were. Every evening, once everyone else had gone to bed and Professor Munroe finished her evening rounds, the two would sneak out of their dormitories and meet each other on the bridge crossing the pond. There they could just talk and be together.

"As much as I love all of this," said Caius, locking his fingers with Astrid's. "I think it's about time I got to take you on a real date."

Astrid paused, placing the palms of her numb hands on his rock-hard chest. "Caius, I thought we talked about this, if anyone even suspected—"

"I know. I know. A fate worse than death and all that," he sighed, rolling his eyes.

A hard line formed between Astrid's brows. "It's not a joke, I thought you realised what you signed up for." Caius had gone quiet and Astrid noticed he was avoiding eye contact, she scowled, pulling away from his warmth, and continued to walk ahead.

"Astrid, wait," Caius called after her, but she'd already clicked her fingers and vanished. He blew out his cheeks with an exasperated sigh, sometimes he forgot how temperamental she could be.

Caius shook his head and took off towards the Armungus dormitory at a brisk jog. He took the stairs two at a time just, so he could catch up to Astrid before she went to bed. He'd have no chance of talking to her otherwise. Knowing Astrid, she'd probably take a good few days to simmer, if he didn't apologise now, though he wasn't entirely sure what he was apologising for.

Once Caius reached the top of the steps, he wiped a bead of sweat from his brow and caught his breath. He gingerly poked his head around the door and his lips curled as he spotted Astrid warming her hands by the fire. She looked annoyed. Caius checked the room was otherwise empty and then crept up behind her without making a sound.

Astrid sucked in a breath, as she felt his broad body behind hers, so close she could feel his warm breath against the back of her neck. He brushed his fingers along her bare neck as he gently removed her coat and draped it across the top of the armchair. He swept her hair to one side and began to leave a trail of gentle kisses down her neck. A soft moan left her throat as he wrapped his arms around her small waist and drew her in closer to the heat of his body.

"All I want is you," Caius whispered tenderly into Astrid's ear. He could feel her tremble at his touch.

"I just hope I'm enough," she murmured, staring down at the fire.

Caius' brow furrowed and he stepped in front of her. He lifted her chin, forcing her to look into his eyes. "How could you not be?" He took her lips with a gentle kiss and pulled her close as she nuzzled her head against his chest.

"And where's my goodnight kiss?" questioned Hesper. She stood leaning on the doorframe to their bedroom with her arms folded across her silk pyjamas.

Astrid swivelled around, throwing a fireball and narrowly missing Hesper's head as she ducked out of the way. "What the hell, Astrid?" shouted Hesper. Her eyebrows knitted as she stared at the singed doorframe that could have easily been her face.

"Shit, Hesper, I'm sorry. I didn't realise it was you. You startled me," Astrid apologised, her face stricken with guilt.

Hesper shrugged her friend's gentle hand from her shoulder, apology not accepted. "Jesus Christ, who deserves a fireball thrown at their face?"

"Come on, Hesp, Astrid said she was sorry," interjected Caius, trying to settle the situation.

Hesper threw Caius a sharp glare and her eyes narrowed as she jabbed his chest with her bony finger. "You don't get to talk."

"Woah, what did I do?"

"You lied to me, I expect that from Astrid but you—" She paused, her face saddened. "Well, I just expected more. I've been in your corner from day one. I just don't appreciate the sneaking around."

"Have you finished huffing now?" questioned Astrid, she no longer felt guilty. Caius eyed Astrid, warning her to be careful, but she ignored his cautionary glare. "You're pissed we didn't tell you, but we did it to protect you and I'm not sorry about that."

"Says the girl that just threw a fireball at my head," quipped Hesper. "You were thinking about yourselves, let's not dress it up as something else." Hesper really didn't like being kept out of the loop.

"You know that's not true." Astrid turned back to Caius. "I think you should go."

"Don't leave on my account," said Hesper bitterly.

Caius nodded and tried to catch Hesper's eye with an apologetic smile, but no luck. He looked back at Astrid who urged him to leave.

Astrid watched the door close and clicked her fingers, putting the fire out before she returned to their room to smooth things over. She never wanted to deceive Hesper, but the more she knew, the more danger she'd be in. *If she wasn't in enough already thanks to me*.

Astrid softly knocked on the door as she gingerly pushed it open. "Can I come in?"

"It's your room too," remarked Hesper, sitting cross legged on her bed as she twiddled her thumbs.

"I wanted to tell you, Hesper, but you know what would happen if anyone found out," Astrid said, perching on the end of Hesper's bed.

"So, you didn't trust me to keep your secret."

Astrid flinched, trust was hard for her, but Hesper was one of very few people she'd found she could trust. "That's not fair. You know that you'd be punished too if they found out you knew and with your sister in the Guard as well."

"You thought I'd go and blab to my sister then, do you really think I'd do that?" asked Hesper, hurt flickered in her eyes.

"Of course not. I didn't want you to even be put in that situation in the first place, you shouldn't have to lie to your sister. Not for me," said Astrid. Hesper's eyes still looked down at her thumbs. "I am sorry, Hesper, please try to understand."

Hesper sighed and gave her friend a half-smile. "I do."

Astrid threw her arms around her friend, glad she'd sorted that out. The secrets had begun to weigh heavy on Astrid's shoulders and it was a relief to at least be able to share some of them with her best friend, the rest she'd have to bear alone.

Hesper's face brightened, and she leaned forward eagerly. "Right tell me everything, where did he take you on your first date? Have you kissed, of course you have, is he a good kisser? What changed your mind?" The questions spilled from Hesper like verbal vomit.

Astrid laughed waiting for Hesper to finish. "We haven't been on one, yes and *yes*." Astrid smiled fondly. "I guess someone made me realise what's really important."

"Why haven't you been on a date yet?"

"Oh, don't you start too, Hesper, it's too risky, if someone saw us—" Astrid was beginning to get tired of having to repeat herself every time.

"So, go somewhere no one will see you," Hesper suggested.

Astrid went to shut down the ridiculous idea and then paused for a second as she considered it, it was possible. "But we're not allowed to just leave the grounds, we'd have to ask one of the professors for permission and then what if they became suspicious?"

A sly smile stretched across Hesper's face. "I believe that's where I can help." Intrigued, Astrid waited for Hesper to continue, but instead Hesper tucked herself into bed and clicked her fingers, switching the lights off. "Goodnight, Astrid."

Astrid rolled her eyes, she could tell her friend was smirking in the darkness. She quietly changed into her pyjamas and climbed into her bed, trying not to disturb Peewee who was quite content curled up atop her other pillow. She closed her eyes hoping the dreams of her past would leave her alone for just one night.

Sunlight filled their room as Hesper threw the curtains wide and Astrid squinted as she woke. She'd slept through the night and she could hear Hesper's cloying humming, things were finally getting back to normal. Astrid rubbed her eyes and reluctantly stepped out of bed, summoning her school uniform from her wardrobe as she did so.

"You won't be needing those today." Hesper clicked her fingers and opened the wardrobe doors, smiling as she watched Astrid's uniform hang itself back up. "Lovely day for a date, don't you think?"

"What are you talking about, Hesper?" yawned Astrid, her eyes half closed.

"I had an idea about how you two can leave the grounds together without rousing any suspicion. It's brilliant really, not sure why you didn't let me in on your little secret sooner," rambled Hesper, studying the clothes hanging in Astrid's wardrobe.

"And are you going to tell me about this brilliant idea or just brag some more." Astrid wasn't the most patient person, especially in the morning.

"Hm not sure, feel like I've got more bragging I can do." Hesper's smirk eased as she felt Astrid's cutting glare. "Fine, I can save the rest for later. I spoke to Professor Peverel this morning and told her my sister needs some help with the missing mayor case in Tarrin—"

Astrid's ears pricked. "She's investigating his disappearance?"

"Yeah, well it is her job. Anyway, the professor is allowing both you and me to go down there to help Paige with the case," continued Hesper, dismissing Astrid's sudden interest in the case.

"Why, what have I got to do with it?" Astrid kept herself calm, she saw Hesper's expression change slightly as she noticed the unease in Astrid's voice. "I mean why would the professor let both of us miss lessons, she's *your* sister after all."

"I just told her you knew the village better than me. Me and Paige are hardly locals."

"Right," Astrid smiled convincingly, and her mind eased. "I fail to see how that helps get Caius off the grounds though."

"Get yourself dressed and then you will," said Hesper, shutting the door behind her as she left Astrid to change into the outfit she'd picked out.

Astrid didn't see the point in arguing. She trusted Hesper knew what she was doing and quickly got changed.

When Astrid emerged from their bedroom, Hesper was stood waiting outside the door wrapped in her winter coat. She held out her hand for Astrid to take and smiled. "You ready for our date?" Astrid snatched her hand away, the person looked like Hesper but the voice that left her lips was that of a man. The Hesper lookalike laughed as he grew taller and Caius appeared before her in his normal form.

"That wasn't weird at all." Astrid laughed nervously, still a little confused.

"Did you just forget your boyfriend's a shapeshifter?" sneered Hesper, appearing from the corner of the room. "How have neither of you thought about using that?"

Caius shrugged. "I guess neither of us are as brilliant as you."

Hesper smiled slightly, she could see Caius was trying to get back into her good books and the flattery was helping.

Astrid rolled her eyes. "And what happens when someone realises Caius isn't in any of his classes?" She held up her hand before either of them could respond. "You'll get in trouble. That's what will happen."

"Astrid, give me some credit," snorted Hesper.

Caius yelped as, without warning, Hesper snatched a single hair from his head and wrapped it round the arm of a small patchwork doll she pulled out from underneath her cloak. "Voodoo?" Caius questioned, a hint of fear in his voice.

"You've got such a mortal opinion of witches," scoffed Hesper, carefully sitting the doll on the armchair. Slowly she raised her hands and muttered an incantation. The other two stepped back as they observed the doll grow in size. Caius went quiet. He crouched down to study the face of his newly formed lookalike whose copper brown eyes stared right back. He stretched a finger out to touch his mirror image's shoulder, but the lookalike grunted as he lurched back.

"Problem solved," smiled Hesper, looking particularly proud of herself.

"How did you get your hands on a Genevieve doll?" Astrid was genuinely intrigued; the use of the dolls amongst the witch community was frankly frowned upon, no respectable witch owned one or at least wouldn't admit to owning one.

"Sometimes Paige brings things home from work," shrugged Hesper. "And sometimes one of those things might go missing."

"Hesper!" Astrid liked this side of her friend.

Hesper smiled innocently. "I have an interest in curious objects. Anyway, we'll send the doll to sit in Caius' lessons, you guys can skip off into the sunset and I'll get a day out on a case with my sis. Everyone's a winner."

"I don't know, Hesp. Something feels off about this," stirred Caius, folding his arms sternly across his chest.

"You were all up for breaking rules before," remarked Astrid.

"But he can't even talk."

"He'll just sit at the back of the class and stare into the distance, it'll be fine," Hesper replied confidently.

"Not like anyone will notice the difference," smiled Astrid playfully.

"Ha, I guess I set myself up for that one," he sighed and gave in. "He'll have to get going if he wants a seat at the back."

Hesper whispered a few words into the lookalike's ears and then clicked her fingers sending him on his way with a book under his arm. Astrid pressed the palm of her hand reassuringly onto Caius' tight-muscled back and gently rested her head against his arm, he was tense. He knew enough about witch law, to know where the use of Genevieve dolls fell. *Imagine if he knew who you really were*, the little voice niggled inside her, but she dismissed it and felt him relax at her touch.

"Don't worry, I'm sure a few shapeshifting classes won't be too taxing for him," she teased, gently smiling when she heard him chuckle.

"Are you quite finished?" he questioned, looking down at Astrid. His brows arched as a playful smirk stretched across his face.

Astrid sighed with relief. She'd put him at ease, "Just about."

Caius took her hand in his and shifted back into Hesper in one fluid movement. Astrid couldn't help but laugh as he winked at her, it would take a little while to get used to that.

"You two get going and make sure you're seen leaving the grounds like that." Hesper paused before flashing out. "Although, maybe keep the handholding to a minimum, I'm sure you're a catch Astrid but don't want the other boys thinking I'm already taken."

Astrid pursed her lips and blew a kiss.

"Don't do anything I wouldn't do," exclaimed Hesper, leaving for the village in a single flash.

"Best not waste any more time." Caius tugged at Astrid's hand grabbing her coat from the sofa as they left. "You'll be needing that." Of course, he knew how much Astrid loved the cold. Astrid rolled her eyes and quickly followed the Hesper lookalike who was practically jumping down the steps.

The grounds were covered in a thick layer of snow. It lay almost untouched, a perfect white glaze, barely a footprint to be seen or even a morsel of green in sight. Caius had gone ahead, leading Astrid through the orchard where the trees gracefully arched over the walkway, the snow perfectly balanced on the leaves that remained. Caius continued through a rusted steel gate hidden at the very end of the orchard, the gate could easily have been mistaken for just an entanglement of vines. Astrid didn't even realise this part of the grounds existed. She hesitated for a moment. She couldn't see Caius on the other side, just the back of a tall, frosted hedge. She tried to look through it but could only see its broken tips and thorns.

"Caius?" she called.

"Aren't you coming?" he replied, his voice was clear, but she still couldn't see him. "Time for you to trust me."

A hand appeared through the hedge, waiting for Astrid to take it. She gingerly took it and closed her eyes waiting for the scratch of the hedge as Caius abruptly pulled her through. The hedge parted immediately, and she fell into Caius' rock-hard chest. For a minute, she kept her eyes closed and leant into his warmth as he held her. She pulled herself away and opened her eyes.

"I never even knew this was here," she murmured, looking around at the tranquil woodland dip they'd stepped in to. She could see the edge of Perimere Lake in the distance through a gap in the trees. The area was completely undisturbed by the school, she wondered how many people actually knew that gate existed.

"I found the gate on one of my walks and wondered what was on the other side." He stood behind her and wrapped his arms gently round her waist leaning down to her neck. "No one can see us out here."

Astrid trembled at his whisper. She melted into him as she clutched his arms tighter and looked up at his handsome face, his expression so tender and it was all for her. "Is this what you brought me all the way out here for?"

Astrid gently ran her hands over his, entwining their fingers. Caius spun her around and tenderly pressed his lips to hers, caressing her cheek. She licked his lips and he took her mouth with his, this time with need. Astrid threw her arms around the back of his neck, pulling herself closer to his body, wishing she was just that bit taller as she stood on her tip toes. This was what she wanted. He groaned, with his arms on her waist he lifted her around him pushing her against the trunk of one of the trees. A dusting of snow fell from the branches above them and they both pulled away, their breathing heavy. He gently pressed his forehead to hers and they kept each other's gaze as he carefully dropped her to the floor.

"I've been wanting to do that for a while," he said gruffly. He cleared his throat and then took her hand, leading her through the trees. "This is what I actually brought you out here for."

In the middle of the trees a wild minavous stood on his slender, charred hind legs, leaning against the trunk of one of the trees. His thick neck stretched, and he lapped with his lengthy tongue wrapping it around the branch and pulling the snow-stricken leaves from their stem in one swoop. He dropped onto all four hooves and swiftly turned his horse-like head when he heard the leaves crunch beneath Astrid's boots. She stopped. The creature's ice blue eyes widened, and he flicked his wings out to the side snuffling as he followed his nose to where Astrid calmly kept still.

Astrid held her hand up to stop Caius interfering and allowed the minavous to approach. She slowed her breathing and held her hand out for the creature to sniff, being almost completely blind she knew the creature relied heavily on his sense of smell and sound. His velvet muzzle twitched as he cautiously approached her hand, he exhaled heavily and relaxed into her hand, nudging his soot-stricken face into her chest and urging her to stroke him. She stroked his velvet tipped long ears and laughed as the creature ruffled his muzzle through her hair. She knew her mother would be proud if she could see her now.

"He's here every time I come this way on my walks," explained Caius, pulling a couple of apples from his pocket. He patted the creature's neck fondly as the minavous continued to munch. "I don't think he's got anyone else, he's always walking around on his own."

"No doubt some locals ran his herd out of the area, people don't like creatures that are different. They call them names, fear them," she muttered bitterly, noticing the lash marks across the creature's back.

Caius squeezed her shoulder trying to find her gaze. "Not everyone's like that."

"I know," she smiled, looking into his caring brown eyes.

"I've been trying to track where his herd might have gone, but I'm no expert. We don't have many in Alsek," he trailed off. Astrid could see how disheartened he was at his lack of success and it only made her want him more. *Mum really would have loved him.*

"This time of year, they've probably already migrated to the Hirtshelm forests." She empathised with the poor creature, no one deserved to live alone.

"Hm, I thought as much," he sighed. "Guess you'll be stuck with me through the winter, Cormac." The creature flapped his wings and snorted.

"Cormac?"

"He needed a name and it just kinda stuck." His compassion for monsters would never cease to impress Astrid. *I wonder if he'll think the same of the demons inside of you,* the sarcastic niggling voice was back. She shook the thought and turned her attention back to their date.

Caius scratched Cormac behind his ears and then ran his hand down the creature's neck to his withers. Cormac gracefully fell onto his front legs and pulled his wings into his body gesturing for the pair to climb on.

"After you, me lady," said Caius, giving Astrid the front seat.

"You're mad, Caius, totally mad," she laughed, climbing onto the creature's back.

Caius jumped on behind her and Cormac rose to his feet, stretching his wings out to the side and arching his neck with a high-pitched whinny. Astrid slid back into Caius' body. He wrapped his arms around her, taking hold of the short tufts of grey hair on the creature's neck as some form of steering. She felt safe with his warmth around her. Her bare skin tingled with the feel of his breath on her neck and her lips had gone dry. She could tell he was smiling behind her.

"Think I get some points for originality." Caius loosened his grip on Cormac's hair and urged him on. The creature responded almost instantly galloping towards a fallen tree. Astrid couldn't help the shrill that escaped her throat as the creature used the broken tree trunk to leap into the air, flapping his wings and pushing himself off from the fallen tree as he took flight to the open skies.

The cold winds whipped against Astrid's cheeks leaving them red raw, her lips began to crack, and her eyes began to water with the cold, but she didn't care. She felt free. She watched the school disappear beneath them and her worries faded with it. The school grounds and surrounding village appeared so small from where they flew, and the people that filled it were like ants now. She'd flown before with her boots or on the back of Ender, but never like this before. Never this high. Never of her own volition. And never with someone, someone like Caius. She stretched her arms out to the side, she knew he wouldn't let her fall. Laughing she reached for the clouds as they swooped past, swerving round the mountain peaks.

"Where exactly are we going?" she exclaimed, battling against the gushes of wind.

"You'll see," he replied. Astrid narrowed her eyes and turned around to see the grin Caius smugly wore.

"Well, can I at least have a go at steering," she queried, trying to take hold of the hair Caius only gripped tighter. She huffed and gave up.

"You really hate not being in control." Caius laughed when Astrid sighed even heavier. He playfully leant forward, so he was close behind her ear. "Good thing I have a thing for control freaks."

Caius kept hold of the handful of Cormac's hair and threw his hands forward along Cormac's neck. Cormac threw his head back with a whinny and then pulled his wings close, diving beneath the cloud line. Astrid gripped Caius' arm as they swooped through the valley and Cormac spread his wings open, swerving round the mountain face.

The sky cracked with thunder and the heavens opened. The rain began to pour, the drops were almost warming on Astrid's bare skin. As the rain got harder, they could barely see past the mountains and Caius urged Cormac to land. He spotted a small clearing atop one of the smaller mountains, they'd be sure to find some cover there whilst the storm passed.

They gracefully landed amongst the thick, wet grass on the clearing and Caius leapt off. He grabbed Astrid by the waist and lifted her off with one fluid motion. Once they were both off, Cormac took his leave and flew back above the cloud line and out of the rain. Caius noted a small cave at the edge of the clearing and took Astrid's hand in his, running to escape the pouring rain. Astrid stopped for a minute. She threw her head back and laughed, soaking up every drop of rain as it soaked her to the bone. She liked the feel of a downpour and its cleansing power. Caius smiled and shook his head, she looked so happy. He took her hand again and gently dragged her into the cave where they could at least try to dry off.

As Astrid entered the cave, she felt a sharp pulse in her gut and faltered.

Caius caught her as she stumbled. "Are you okay?" he asked, sweeping her dampened hair away from her face.

"It's nothing, I'm fine honest," Astrid replied, trying not to grind her teeth at the twinging pain in her stomach, she'd almost forgotten she still had stitches in.

"You're going to freeze in all these wet clothes," he remarked.

Astrid was soaked through and through. Caius gently removed her coat and then went to remove her sodden jumper. She trembled as his warm hands brushed her bare skin and he pulled the jumper over her head. She leant into his hand as he gently caressed her cheek, tracing beneath her hypnotizing eyes and brushing his thumb across her ruby red lips.

"I had the ideal spot picked out for us you know," he murmured, leaning in closer. "It had flowers, a waterfall, the works. I wanted it to be perfect."

"This is," whispered Astrid, closing the space between them. She took his mouth with hers, pulling him in closer as she threw her arms around his neck and tussled his dripping hair with her hands. Their heavy breathing matched the rhythm of the rain falling on the cave. He licked her lips with his tongue and she reciprocated with her own and playfully bit his bottom lip. He groaned and gently dropped her to the floor leaving a trail of kisses down her neck as he continued downwards about to lift the thin tank top she had left on. She cried out and clutched her stomach. Caius immediately stopped and saw the red begin to soak through. He lifted her top and saw the blood seeping from her still fresh wound. It didn't seem to have opened but it was still bleeding.

"Shit. Astrid, why didn't you say anything?" Caius yelled, frantically ripping at his shirt to use to put pressure on the bleeding.

"It's fine, it's not even open, it's just—" She screamed writhing in pain.

"This is not fine, Astrid. Hold that on there and I'll go call Cormac. He can't be far. I'm taking you back. Now," he instructed. Caius ran out into the rain calling for Cormac in the clearing.

"Caius, wait," she called after him. The pain had stopped. Astrid looked down at her stomach and the blood was gone. Her hands were clean.

"Come back, Caius," whaled Crista mockingly as she appeared kneeling beside Astrid.

Astrid almost jumped out of her skin. She leapt to her feet with her hands held defensively in front of her.

Crista cackled and clicked her fingers, whisking the two of them away to the entrance of Trepidor. Astrid looked down, she was fully clothed, and they were bone dry as if she'd never even been out in the rain.

"We don't want your daddy knowing what you've been getting up to with that shapeshifter boy," Crista teased, fixing Astrid's hair into a sleek plait with one click of her fingers.

“I don’t understand, I took your memories, I—” Astrid stuttered confused, she was sure the vial of Crista’s memory wisps was still hidden in her room.

Crista’s face pinched and she wiggled a thin brow. “Did you really think I wouldn’t notice a few memories missing, foolish girl. You’ve always thought you’re smarter than you are.” Crista continued walking through the murky tunnel, Astrid could have sworn she almost had a spring in her step.

“But if you remembered everything, why haven’t you told my father?” Astrid questioned, cautiously following.

“I thought it would be more fun to let things play out a bit longer.” Crista smiled sinisterly.

Astrid grabbed her by the shoulder making her face her. “If you so much as go near him—”

“Now, now, now. Don’t start something you won’t be able to finish,” warned Crista, her brows arched. Astrid released her, and they continued walking. “Your daddy wanted me to fetch you so here we are.”

The pungent odour of sweat and blood immediately hit Astrid; she wrinkled her nose and quickly swallowed down the bile that had surfaced, it had been a while since she’d endured the conditions at Trepidor. She wriggled in the stifling heat and adjusted the collar on her thick, winter jumper, never breaking her confident façade.

Vincentrio stood watching over the rancid pit in the centre of the room. He swiftly turned when he heard the sound of two sets of footsteps echo through the main chamber. A genuine smile stretched across his face when he saw his daughter and he held his arms out to hold his child in a warming embrace. He gave her a gentle squeeze and she rested her head on his soft shoulder. Astrid could see Crista snarling out of the corner of her eye, but she ignored her and concentrated on the warm embrace she was having with her father. She exhaled softly, she'd been worried for nothing.

"I'm glad to see you, Astrid." He smiled, rubbing his hands on her arms. "In one piece as well, I'm still struggling to understand how you let a player take you out like that."

"She just took me by surprise is all, Father," dismissed Astrid.

"And then let her get away with it?" His smile had disappeared now, she could see he was questioning her resolve.

Astrid straightened her shoulders. "She'll get what's coming to her," said Astrid, sternly glaring at Crista when she scoffed.

"And a scar to match I hope?" queried Vincentrio.

"If she's lucky," remarked Astrid.

"Hm." Astrid could tell her father wasn't completely convinced.

"Why did you call me here, Father?" She'd realised by now that her summoning wasn't entirely related to his concern for her wellbeing, there was something else he was holding back.

Vincentrio clicked his tongue. "Weaknesses come in all forms, Astrid, and some of us seem to have more than others." *He's digressing, this can't be good.* "I don't think I raised you to be weak, did I?" She could tell it was a rhetorical question and remained quiet for him to continue. "If anything, I did the opposite. I snuffed out your weaknesses. I made you strong. I made you powerful. A power to be respected, to be feared and yet do you know what I see in you before me now?" He kept his voice low and took one step towards his daughter, he tipped her chin up and stared sharply into her eyes. "I see weakness." He practically spat the words at her, but she didn't cower. He let her go and summoned his staff, turning his back to look over the edge of the pit again.

Astrid wondered what he had planned as a *reminder* this time, he'd always been so creative in the past, but that was as far as she'd let her mind wander. She wasn't weak. She was ready to face what test he had planned, she would not fail.

Astrid peered over the edge and saw the tortured souls shackled in their prisons, screaming through the bars. Those were the lucky ones. She stood up straight, maintaining her emotionless face. "I will do anything to prove myself to you, Father."

"We'll see," he murmured, she could hear the doubt in his voice. He tapped his staff, whisking the three of them to one of the small chambers at the very bottom of the pit. Astrid knew the room just by its smell; a distinct tang of stale blood and other bodily fluids stung her nose much worse than that upstairs. She hadn't stepped foot in her father's torture chamber for a while and yet it was still oh so familiar to her. She'd counted the number of stones in the walls dozens of times and noted every crack in the concrete floor, it was not a place a person could easily forget.

Crista clicked her fingers and lit the flame torches that stood against each corner of the room before making her way towards her table of tools all neatly laid out. She chose her favourite curved blade knife and caressed its tip, keeping her eyes fixed wickedly on Astrid's as she did so. Astrid twitched as she remembered how Crista had chosen that blade the first time Astrid needed punishing, even now she could feel it slice against her skin.

Crista's thin lips quirked. "I'll admit one thing about the mortals, their torture techniques can be quite… invigorating," said Crista, turning her attention to the battered body slumped on the wooden chair in the centre of the room. "Something about the feel of a knife as it cuts into flesh, the satisfaction you sometimes don't get with magic." She grabbed the man by his silver, sodden hair and pressed the end of her blade slowly into his swollen cheek. The man woke with a stifled scream and she stopped.

"You remember our old friend Sir Robert, don't you Astrid?" questioned Vincentrio, leaning in closer to the old man.

Astrid's eyes widened. She had barely recognised him; his cheeks were swollen and bruised, his eyes were vacant, and he wore an expression of such despair now.

"He's been Crista's plaything for some time now, but he hasn't been particularly forthcoming with information," Vincentrio continued turning back to his daughter. Astrid noticed the blood that stained Sir Robert's once white clothing. "This is how I'd like you to prove your strength."

She knew exactly what he was asking her to do. "Why haven't you extracted what you want yourself?"

"I've tried, he's somehow able to resist my mind manipulation. Something the two of you have in common," he muttered. "We all know your powers of Concilium are far stronger than ours, a talent from your mother no doubt."

Astrid winced, she knew her mother had it and chose not to use it on others. Concilium magic was too dark for her mother to develop her talents any further than simple suggestive thought placement. Astrid, on the other hand, had used it to twist so many minds in the past, some had been accidents, and some had not.

"It's been a little while since I practised," admitted Astrid as she removed her cloak and crouched next to Sir Robert.

"I think it's time we changed that," Vincentrio responded sternly. Crista had joined him by his side eager to watch what was left of Sir Robert's mind be broken. "I want to know all his secrets; the deals he's made with the Guard, the plans he has in place for his town, where he's hidden what's left of his family and most importantly, where he hid the gem. And you know what to do with him once you're finished, Astrid." Astrid gulped and nodded solemnly. "Because you know what happens to things that don't bend." He lightly squeezed his daughter's shoulders. "They break."

Vincentrio and Crista took a seat in an observation area just next-door to the torture chamber, he'd had it built to keep a close eye on how loyal his followers were to his cause. Sometimes, he just enjoyed seeing them at work, particularly Crista, she had such a creative flare. She was like an artist, an artist who only painted with blood. He found nothing more attractive than watching her carve into a traitor, his mouth had gone dry at just the thought. He quickly turned his attention back to his daughter, he needed to watch her more carefully.

Astrid was still crouched next to the man who once was Sir Robert. Vincentrio twitched when she gently squeezed what was left of the warlock's hand, she did it so quickly she probably thought he wouldn't notice. He did. She'd moved her hands to either side of his head and had closed her eyes. She was having to dig deep from her power, she was more out of practice than he'd realised. He scowled and, as if she'd felt his disapproving glare, Astrid scraped harder through Sir Robert's mind.

The warlock's eyes rolled into the back of his head and his knuckles were pale where he was gripping the arms of the chair so tight. He threw his head against the back of the chair and screamed as he began to shake uncontrollably. Vincentrio watched as his daughter continued to torment his mind. Her face was cold and emotionless, but he saw a flicker of determination in her eyes that he hadn't seen in a while.

Astrid fell backwards to the floor and her connection was lost. Sir Robert had stopped shaking, his body slumped in a heap on the chair. He was still alive, but Astrid had hollowed him out, removing everything that made him who he once was. Only an empty shell of the once great warlock remained.

Astrid looked up to see her father's hand stretched towards her, he looked pleased with her. She focussed on her father's face rather than the horrors she'd just inflicted on Sir Robert. She couldn't even look at the man she'd just broken; she'd used his every regret against him, made him relive his darkest moments in unimaginable ways. His screams would remain with her forever. Her blood ran cold as the regret sank in. She cleared her dry throat and took her father's hand rising to his side.

"I think we've got a few things to discuss," grinned Vincentrio. "Crista, I can trust you to find our *friend* somewhere suitable to stay, once you're finished of course."

"With pleasure, Sir, there's still plenty more fun to have here," cackled Crista, returning to her tray of tools.

Astrid closed her eyes and turned away disgusted, trying to maintain her stern expression. She swallowed hard and gestured towards the door. "After you, Father."

CHAPTER 8

Astrid gently closed the door to her father's chamber and made her way back down the spiralling steps, away from where her father could see her. She stumbled on a step and found her balance again leaning against the cold, stone wall. She pressed her back against it and then felt herself slowly slide down it. She dropped her heavy head into her palms and took a few deep breaths as an overwhelming guilt consumed her.

Astrid was bound by her loyalty to her father to obey him and tell him everything, yet she still felt a burning feeling of compunction. It made her sick to her very stomach. Her father had been so pleased with what she'd done as well. He'd hugged her, he was proud of her, he'd even trusted her with another vital task, but still she felt dreadful. All Astrid could see was the desolate face of Sir Robert.

Even in Sir Robert's weak state, his mind had tried to safeguard his secrets, though it couldn't maintain it for long. His life had been so normal once; he'd been a loving father to three talented children and a doting husband to his beautiful wife. He was devoted to them until he found the Perrero gem, its power had corrupted him and all those around him that sought it for themselves, a tale Astrid knew all too well.

Once Sir Robert had found the strength to destroy the gem himself, it was too late. A power-hungry warlock stole the gem in the middle of the night and set their house ablaze assuming Sir Robert would be taken with it. Instead, he'd been out that night, looking for his courage at the bottom of a whisky bottle in his local tavern. When he returned, all he found was the rubble of what remained of his home. The gem had gone, and his entire family had perished with it.

In his shame, Sir Robert tried to hide what really happened that night. He told a very different story claiming how he'd fought off the thief, but at a grave cost. He mourned the loss of his family and the entire village rallied behind him, appointing him as their mayor to use the power of the gem to watch over them like he'd tried to do for his family that night. Sir Robert forged the fake gem and placed it in pride of place for all to see, a warning for others who thought they could take the power for themselves. Consumed by his guilt, he'd continued to reach for his whisky for comfort, yearning for the day when he could finally join his family and hold them in his arms once again.

Sir Robert had blamed himself for everything and Astrid had used that self-loathing as part of her attack against his mind. She'd twisted each beloved memory he'd had of his family, turning the people he loved against him. They'd turned on him so quickly; his wife spat blame at him for the loss of their children as they watched them burn in front of them. His daughter who'd idolised him so, stared at her father in disgust and contempt as the skin melted from her face. Astrid replayed their piercing screams over and over again in his head until he'd crumbled in his own mind surrounded by echoes of his deepest and darkest fears. Astrid had watched as his guilt ate away at him, picking at his mind like vultures with a dried-up carcass.

By this point, Astrid had already extracted the plans Sir Robert had in place to protect his village people from the likes of her father. She'd discovered how he'd been working with the Guard investigating creatures he suspected Vincentrio had already influenced, a final attempt at his own redemption. She'd been impressed with how right he was. Her father had pawns in many places, she knew how far his reach spanned. Still, she continued to twist his mind, she found herself revelling in watching his demons torture him, like she'd convinced herself he deserved it. After all, the warlock's legacy had been built on a lie, a terrible lie. His ambition had cost him his family, a family he should have been there to protect. She'd continued, adamant that it was divine justice she was dealing.

Then she'd stopped. Astrid looked at him through her own eyes, not her father's. She saw a man who'd experienced a massive loss, a feeling she knew too well, and a man who'd tried to repent by dedicating his life to protecting others, penance for failing his own family.

Just as Astrid was about to release Sir Robert from his pain, his mind revealed one last secret, a secret he'd protected his entire life in his own shame. His eldest son, Aramis, a teenage warlock at the time, had survived the fire. When he discovered why his father hadn't been there to protect them, he'd confronted him, he'd found his father deep in the web of lies he'd spun about that night and disowned him. The boy swore one day he'd take his revenge on the man who'd murdered their family, but he'd do it without his father's help. Sir Robert never saw his son after that.

Astrid only wished that she could end Sir Robert's suffering altogether, to give him what he's wanted for so many years and reunite him with his loved ones in the land of the dead, but her father wouldn't allow it. Only Vincentrio would be allowed to decide when his time was up, and she had an unsettling feeling that that wouldn't be any time soon.

Astrid had told her father everything. His eyes glistened when she mentioned a survivor of the fire. The boy would be a similar age to Vincentrio by now and he was hopeful that he'd done what he'd vowed and tracked down the warlock who'd stolen the gem. At the very least, he'd be able to tell them who the warlock was, leading Vincentrio one step closer to its power.

Vincentrio sent Bedelia to uncover Aramis' true identity, no doubt he'd changed his name to keep hidden from his father for so long. In the meantime, he'd tasked Astrid with finding Sir Robert's list of names he'd formulated from his suspicions of who Vincentrio had corrupted. Sir Robert had been right about many of his most important allies, he didn't want to risk them becoming compromised by the Guard.

Astrid wiped her bloodshot eyes that stung with her tears and took a deep breath, pulling herself to her feet. She had a job to do and she couldn't allow herself to dwell on mistakes she continued to make. Her regrets would continue to stack against her and she'd learn to deal with them at some point when this was all over, but, for now, she hid them away. Her compassion was her weakness and she could not let her father see that, or anyone for that matter.

Crista stood waiting at the bottom of the stairs, she looked revitalised as if torturing Sir Robert's body had given her energy. Astrid held her head high keeping eye contact with Crista as she came down the stairs.

"I hope you gave him some good news, Astrid. Your father always has so much more energy when he's in a good mood," remarked Crista, licking her lips.

Astrid felt her skin crawl at the very thought of Crista with her father, touching him with her blood-stained hands. "I'm sure I've left him happier than you will," smirked Astrid. She knew her father had only ever loved one woman and Crista was no more than a scratch for his itch.

Crista laughed. "I've never left your father unsatisfied, it seems your mother wasn't much of an act to follow." She could hear Astrid gritting her teeth. "But then I suppose he's used to disappointment with you as a daughter."

"And you as his hussy," retorted Astrid. She knew Crista was trying to get a rise out of her and she refused to give her the satisfaction.

Crista perked her mouth mockingly. "I will try not to blurt anything out, I wouldn't want to ruin the mood by mentioning what his precious little girl has been getting up to." Crista continued up the steps. "But I can't promise anything, your father can be so insatiable."

Astrid's eyes narrowed, but, before she could respond, Crista had whisked her back to the cave where she'd been waiting for Caius to return. The rain still pounded outside, and her tank top was once again damp and bloodied, her hair was a sodden mess and she was on the floor still clutching at her stomach as if she'd never left. She cried with the pain and noticed a couple of her stitches had snapped. She rolled her eyes and bit back the pain, Crista had wanted it to be believable.

Hooves splashed across the muddy clearing and a pair of boots moved even faster through the puddles. Astrid shivered, she needed to adjust from the scorching heat in Trepidor. She reached for her jumper, cursing Crista as her whole side twinged. Caius rushed in from the rain, running a hand through his wet hair. He grabbed her jumper before she stretched herself even more.

"Astrid, I told you to keep pressure on that," Caius scolded. He grabbed the blood-soaked piece of his shirt and pressed it back on Astrid's stomach, he winced as she flinched.

Astrid couldn't help but study his handsome face as he knelt over her; the worry lines stretched across his furrowed brow and the concern in his darkened eyes was so striking she felt her aching heart still. No one had ever looked at her like that. *And how will he look at you when he finds out what you just did*, the niggling voice was back.

"It's okay, it's barely bleeding now," she replied softly. She placed her hand over his and gently pulled the rag off her stomach.

"Sorry, I guess I panicked a bit." His lips tweaked with a small smile.

"What are you apologising for? I'm the one who ruined our first proper date." Astrid clicked her fingers placing two new stitches in her wound, she bit her lip as her magic pulled them together.

"Don't be stupid, I'm just glad you're okay, I thought I'd—" Caius looked away and dropped his eyes.

"You could never hurt me, Caius." Astrid pressed her hand to his cheek and pulled herself up to leave a gentle kiss on his lips. "I'm sadder that we didn't get to finish what we started."

Caius arched his eyebrows and chuckled. "How about we continue that when you're not so… fragile."

She sighed. "Fine. I suppose that would be the sensible thing to do."

"Waiting makes the heart grow fonder, Astrid."

"I think the phrase is actually absence makes the heart grow fonder," corrected Astrid, wrapping her arms round the back of Caius' neck.

Caius rolled his eyes playfully and lifted her up, swooping her into his arms. She giggled and rested her head against his warm chest. She closed her eyes and just listened to his heart beat, with her hand she played with the few golden hairs that were peeking through the top of his shirt.

"All right, Miss Know-it-all, I think we should get you back to school so the professor can take a proper look at those stitches," said Caius, carrying Astrid with ease in his arms out to the clearing.

It had stopped raining now and the sun was beginning to shine through the cracks in the clouds, and the clearing looked all of a sudden so beautiful. "Can't we stay here, just a little longer," suggested Astrid, clinging to his warmth. She just wanted him to hold her and not let go.

"I suppose we could stay for a little bit," he sighed, walking closer to the edge where they could sit and admire the scenery. He carefully dropped Astrid onto her feet. "As long as you're not bleeding to death."

"Cross my heart," she smiled.

Astrid clicked her fingers, drying off a patch of grass for them both to sit on and then took her jumper that still hung over Caius' arm; the wind was still icy cold when it blew past them and her jumper was dry now. They both took a seat and Caius wrapped his brawny arm around Astrid, pulling her close into his warmth again. She nuzzled her head into his neck and he pressed a gentle kiss to her forehead. They both rested on their backs and Caius pulled Astrid in tighter. She rested her eyes for a moment and just listened to his rhythmic breathing.

The sky had cleared, and the blood orange sun had started to drop lower as the daylight was beginning to wane. Cormac had returned from his venture chasing woodland creatures across the clearing, he was getting restless. He whinnied and bent down to nudge Caius' chest and then snuffled Astrid's hair. They both stirred, and Astrid turned around to tickle Cormac's chin. She could see he'd been running around the clearing, his legs were caped with mud.

“I think someone wants to take us home,” remarked Astrid, gently nudging Caius awake. He groaned and went to roll over, but Astrid grabbed him more firmly. “Caius. If we get back too late someone’s bound to notice.”

Caius rubbed his eyes and sat up slowly. “What time is it?”

“Well, the sun’s beginning to set so I’d say it’s time to go.” Astrid pulled at Caius’ arm, but he was far too heavy for her to get him to his feet.

“All right, all right, a little nap never hurt anyone,” he joked, lifting Astrid onto Cormac’s back and then jumping on himself behind her.

Caius wrapped his arms around Astrid again and grabbed the tufts of hair before kicking him on. Cormac eagerly obliged, taking flight to the skies. Astrid could have sworn he knew they were in more of a rush this time as he flapped his wings faster, soaring between the mountain peaks. He swung back around and Vistaldors slowly crept back into view.

Cormac swooped down towards the piece of undisturbed woodland just next to the rest of the school grounds and landed softly, squawking as he did so. Astrid patted the creature’s neck and waited for Caius to lift her off; Cormac’s back was quite a way from the ground when he was standing, and Astrid was tired. Concilium magic was draining for anyone.

Astrid stroked Cormac’s head and then clicked her fingers, pulling a crisp red apple from behind her back. He took the apple from her palm and pushed it round the floor as if he wanted to play with it before he ate it, Astrid had almost forgot he was only a youngster.

Caius took her hand in his and then led them back through the steel gate, leaving Cormac to amuse himself. He quickly shifted into Hesper once they’d reached the orchard; classes had finished for the day and students were still wandering around the grounds. Astrid only hoped that Hesper hadn't returned already, two Hespers wandering around could raise a few questions.

The two of them briskly climbed the stairs to the Armungus common room and, to Astrid's relief, it seemed Hesper still hadn't returned. A couple of students were studying in the common room, but most were still in the Grand Hall eating their dinner. They glanced at them for a second and then returned to reading their books, one of them glanced up again looking somewhat perplexed. Astrid smiled politely and then quickly pulled Caius into her room, shutting the door behind them.

"Let's not forget this is my room too," exclaimed Hesper quickly. She sat cross legged on her bed playing chess with the Caius lookalike who welcomed his original with a nod and a grunt.

Caius had shifted back into himself and perched on the edge of Astrid's bed, trying to keep his distance from the lookalike.

"When did you get back?" questioned Astrid, taking a seat next to Caius. She noticed the unsettled look on his face and gently placed her hand on his thigh.

"About ten minutes ago," Hesper replied. Hesper scrunched her face when the lookalike made his next move. "Caius 2.0 may not be able to speak, but he certainly knows his way around a chessboard."

"Can we not call it that," snapped Caius.

"What would you prefer I called *him*?" queried Hesper, surprised by Caius' sharp tone.

"I'd prefer it if *it* wasn't here at all."

"Caius," cautioned Astrid, giving him a warning look, there was no need to be rude.

"If you're going to use dark magic, I'd just prefer it not to have my face plastered on it," explained Caius.

"How is he any different to you pretending to be me?" defended Hesper.

"I'm a shapeshifter," he retorted.

Hesper laughed sarcastically, "So that's all right then."

"Oh, stop squabbling," interjected Astrid. She snatched her hand away from Caius and turned to him. "Both of you. Hesper did something nice for us, what's your problem?"

"I'm just not comfortable with you two using dark magic, I've got a lot of friends at home who've been on the receiving end of it too many times," Caius admitted sharply. "And lost some of them because of it."

Astrid opened her mouth to say something but couldn't find the words. He looked so angry. She was hardly the best example of a *good* witch, just look at what she'd done in one day. She'd dabbled so much with dark magic, she couldn't be sure how much light was left within her. *If only he knew*. If he had only seen her today, let alone all those times before. Seeing him now, Astrid realised there was no way she could tell him the truth. He surely wouldn't be able to forgive her if he knew everything she'd done, and he certainly wouldn't be able to love her. Not that she would blame him, she knew she wasn't deserving of it and she'd accepted that, but that was all before. Having someone to love meant she now had more to lose.

Hesper scoffed and rolled her eyes. "This is hardly the same."

"Dark magic is dark magic, Hesper," replied Caius adamantly, he was not about to change his mind.

"Jesus, everything's so black and white with you," Hesper sighed. She clicked her fingers and the lookalike shrank to the Genevieve doll it was before. "Happy now?"

"Much," he responded bluntly as Hesper folded her arms across her chest. "There's no need to be a witch about it."

"I think it's probably best you leave now," advised Astrid, swinging the door open with a click of her fingers.

Caius leaned in to drop a gentle goodnight kiss to her lips, but she flinched and turned away. "Astrid, you know I didn't mean anything against you, I just—"

Astrid pressed her finger to his lips. "Goodnight, Caius." She softly pecked his cheek and forced a smile before she gestured politely towards the door.

Caius opened his mouth but then thought it better not to say anything else, he'd said enough for one day. He left, and Astrid quickly closed the door behind him pressing her forehead to the door and closing her eyes. *Keep it together*.

"You, okay?" questioned Hesper. Astrid still pressed her head to the door. "Why don't you come and sit down?"

With a heavy sigh Astrid turned and sat next to her friend, she dropped her head onto Hesper's shoulder and remained silent. She was afraid if she spoke, her voice would break, and she'd surely cry.

"I'm sorry if I crossed a line with the doll, he didn't seem that bothered this morning and I just wanted to help you guys out. I didn't mean to make more trouble for you two, the situation's hard enough without me riling him up like that," said Hesper, trying to comfort Astrid.

Astrid pulled her head back up and stared at her friend. "Don't be stupid, Hesper, you did something incredibly nice for us and he's got no right to be so ungrateful."

Hesper dropped her shoulders with relief and smiled. "Oh, thank god, I thought you were annoyed at me for a second there."

"Of course not," laughed Astrid, forcing herself to ignore the ache she was feeling in her chest.

"I really didn't expect him to react like that, he's got a pretty insulting opinion of witches that boy. Using a Genevieve doll is hardly a crime," scoffed Hesper.

"Certainly not compared to some of the things I've done," murmured Astrid. She desperately wanted to tell Hesper everything, but she couldn't.

Hesper looked seriously at Astrid. "Astrid, we've all done something we're not proud of."

"You've seen my darkness and so has Caius."

Hesper rolled her eyes. "We've all got a bit of darkness, even narrow-minded shapeshifters like Caius," teased Hesper, pleased when she saw Astrid crack a smile. "The boy's an idiot, but then he's a shapeshifter so we just have to forgive his ignorance."

"He's very thoughtful at arranging a date at least," praised Astrid, trying to lighten the mood and enjoy some normality with her friend.

"Well, he's got that going for him then," smirked Hesper.

Astrid raised her eyebrows playfully. "He's got a few things going for him."

"Astrid, you didn't?"

"To be continued," she replied elusively.

"Well, you're going to have to try and keep your hands to yourself at the dance tomorrow night, no point spoiling all this sneaking around," cautioned Hesper. Astrid stared at her blankly. Hesper could practically hear the cogs turning. "You forgot, didn't you?"

Yes. "No, of course not," she replied quickly, wracking her brain as to what dance Hesper was referring to.

Then it came to her, Astrid had forgotten about the invitation she'd received earlier in the week. It must have slipped behind the books that were gradually piling up on her bedside table. The school were throwing their annual winter dance, but this year there was even more reason to celebrate; a select few Shacklebolt players had been shortlisted for the next provisional Hawcranes squad. The team were the reigning inter-regional champions and had been for the past three years, most students could only dream of being considered to join them. Of course, Astrid had had more pressing things to be thinking about, forgetting about a dance that she hadn't intended to go to was hardly surprising.

"You can't not go," declared Hesper, listening to snippets of Astrid's thoughts.

"Hesper, I just don't think I should go," replied Astrid.

"Who's being stupid now? You know Xander is one of those players that might be shortlisted. I'm sure he'd appreciate your support." Hesper knew Xander was like a brother to Astrid, she knew she wouldn't want to let him down. "Like he's supported you, been there for you when you needed him, shall I go on?"

"All right, all right," agreed Astrid, she didn't have the energy to argue. "You really don't play fair."

"I'm not going to a dance full of eligible bachelors without my wing-woman. Plus, you're taken now so you'll be far more impartial," smiled Hesper. "Right, I think we both need to get a bit of beauty sleep, some of us need it more than others."

"And which one of us would you be referring to?" laughed Astrid, getting up from her friend's bed.

"I don't think you need me to answer that one." Hesper rolled over to her side and quickly shut her eyes yawning. "You can tell me more about what other things Caius has got going for him, in the morning. Night, night."

Astrid rolled her eyes, she envied how quickly Hesper could fall asleep, she clearly had significantly fewer problems to be keeping her awake at night. Astrid clicked her fingers changing into her cosy pyjamas and then climbed into bed. She let her head fall onto the pillow and pulled her blankets close, wrapping herself in them. She reached over and blew out their bedside lamp. "Goodnight, Hesper."

Astrid yawned and rubbed her eyes; keeping so many secrets was exhausting and the conflict of the two sides within her was slowly taking its toll. She sighed, she was so tired and yet she found herself lying awake staring blankly at the ceiling, a hundred thoughts all running through her head. She winced when she imagined what Crista did with Sir Robert after she'd finished psychologically torturing him, she thought about how she'd broken him and all the minds she'd broken before his.

The voice of her father quickly smothered the remorse she felt. He reminded her exactly how good it felt to use that power, and she had to agree, it was almost addictive. If she was being honest, she'd revelled in it, she'd hungered for more of it and then there was her father, he'd been so proud of her. But every thought she had, came back to Caius. The beautiful, compassionate shapeshifter that was Caius. She loved him more than she could admit, and she knew, eventually, she'd have to make a choice. Unfortunately, she also knew she'd make the wrong choice and there was very little she could do about it. She stirred at the thought of the path that had been set out for her, it had been set in stone for years, she knew she had no say.

Peewee emerged from underneath Astrid's bed and she smiled when he jumped up. He sauntered towards her head and snuggled himself against her as if sensing her unease. She pressed her head against his fur and closed her eyes allowing her mind to rest at last.

Astrid stirred when she heard movement in their room. She couldn't hear the calming breathing of Peewee next to her and when she opened her eyes, all she saw was darkness. She went to get out of bed, but her body didn't respond. She was frozen, fixed where she lay. When she managed to force her body to move, metal shackles appeared on her wrists and ankles, pulling tighter every time she struggled. She tried to cry out, to scream for help, but nothing came out. She tried to calm herself, to focus, but her magic wasn't working. Panic gripped hold of her as she thrashed even more violently until the shackles were pulled so tight that she couldn't move at all.

The door opened and from the light, a line of hazy, hooded figures appeared. One by one, they drifted through the doorway surrounding Astrid's bed. The door slammed shut as the last one entered. The figure stood at the foot of her bed and removed his hood. It was Caius. He stared blankly at Astrid and pulled a curved knife from beneath his cloak.

The others had removed their hoods. She looked upon their faces and saw ghosts of her past, faces she'd tried to forget and some she'd succeeded in doing so. Amongst the figures were students she barely knew, students she'd simply passed in the hallway. Their hate-filled eyes were all fixed on Astrid as they each cradled a knife in their hands.

Astrid opened her mouth to protest her innocence, but nothing came out. One by one, the figures plunged their knife into Astrid's body. She threw her head back with every stab, screaming as she felt the cold blades slice her flesh. She could feel their rage with every vengeful stab and she sobbed knowing she deserved each one. She lay in a pool of her own blood, her face pale and her breath weak. Caius proceeded to her face, looking down upon her he smiled wickedly and plunged his knife into her heart. She wailed as he twisted the blade.

"Please. Caius. You're. Not. A killer," she spluttered. Her Caius wasn't capable of this, she closed her eyes, shaking her head as she faintly chanted to herself, "This is just a nightmare."

He leant in close and cruelly pressed on the blade forcing her to look at him. A wicked grin stretched across his face and his eyes glistened an icy blue colour. The voice of Crista slithered from his lips, "Someone has to finish what you're too weak to do."

Astrid jolted awake, throwing a spell at where Crista had stood over her. The curtains caught on fire and she clicked her fingers, extinguishing the flames. She could feel her heart pounding through her chest and her breath was fast and heavy. Her pyjama top was soaked in sweat. She quickly lifted it and checked for the slashes the figures had made, but all she felt were the scars of old wounds, nothing new. She couldn't be sure if it was a nightmare of her own creation or if Crista had wormed her way in, but either way the message was clear.

Hesper stood in the doorway holding her toothbrush still in her mouth. She looked at the singed curtains and then back at her wide-eyed friend sitting upright in bed. "What did I miss?"

"Just had a bad dream is all," replied Astrid, stepping out of bed. She wandered to her wardrobe and pulled out her uniform, she still had lessons and she knew how important it was to keep up appearances, for now. Astrid could feel Hesper reach into her mind and she immediately threw her out. "Leave it alone, Hesper."

"Ouch," exclaimed Hesper, rubbing her head. "I was only trying to help you."

"I don't like you crawling through my head like that," barked Astrid. She winced at her own short temper and then turned back to her friend ruefully. "I'm sorry, I can be a bitch when I'm tired."

"Yeah, you can," retorted Hesper, clicking her toothbrush away. "I suppose I could try asking instead, did Caius have anything to do with your bad dream?"

"Maybe." Astrid clicked her fingers and changed into her uniform. She proceeded to make her bed, making sure to avoid eye contact with Hesper.

"Want to tell me any details?" probed Hesper, grabbing the other side of the duvet.

"Not particularly." Astrid didn't know where she'd even begin; being stabbed by Caius, being chained up by other students or her *Aunt* Crista's crude warning. *I wonder which one Hesper would choose to psychoanalyse first.*

"Look, I don't know what he did in your bad dream, but it wasn't real."

"I know how a dream works, Hesper."

"So, you know it's your subconscious' way of messing with you then, if you try just talking to Caius, I'm sure—"

"It's okay, I know what I have to do now," said Astrid, grabbing her books from the bedside table.

Hesper didn't look convinced. "I hope that involves actually *talking* to Caius."

"Yes, yes, Hesper, I will," she muttered, and she would, once she'd found out where the list of names was. She was almost certain it wasn't in the Guard's possession yet; they'd have started tracking people on the list by now and her father would surely have made her failure known to her. The list must have been hidden somewhere in Sir Robert's office, but with the Guard combing that area for evidence, it would be difficult for Astrid to get in there to have a proper look herself. She'd have to think of some other way. For now, they had classes to get to.

"Hurry up, Hesper, maybe we'd actually be on time for once if you focused less on my dreams and more on getting yourself ready," urged Astrid. She hated being late and Hesper had a habit for dawdling.

"You really are cranky this morning," Hesper remarked, changing into her uniform with a click of her fingers. She swooped her thick hair back into a high ponytail and fixed her robes before checking herself in the mirror and grabbing her books. She threw Astrid an exaggerated smile. "Ready."

"Let's not give Professor Towinni another reason to shout at us."

"Like she needs one," laughed Hesper as the two of them flashed to their Advanced Potions class.

Professor Towinni was being particularly difficult today; the whole class had to line up outside the classroom along the stone wall until she returned from a meeting with the other professors. She'd been brewing an extraordinarily intricate potion in her classroom for the past couple of days and was close to finishing, she wasn't running the risk of having one of her students spoil it by leaving them unattended.

The witches were clucking outside like a brood of hens, describing every intricate detail of the dresses they'd be wearing tonight and how they'd be styling their hair. Astrid left them to cluck away, she wasn't even sure if she had a dress to wear. She was too busy thinking about where Sir Robert would have hidden his list and, more importantly, how she was going to get her hands on it, the rest was like white noise.

Astrid turned around when she heard Professor Peverel's door open down the end of the corridor and a handful of professors emerged still talking amongst themselves. A slender, dark haired woman stood with them with her arms folded across her smart, black dress. She pressed her olive-skinned hands to either side of her head pulling her worry lines taut. She smiled sincerely at her colleagues and then walked the other way donning a long, deep red robe embroidered with subtle patterns of green, red and blue.

"Was that Professor Ryback?" questioned Hesper, interrupting Astrid's chain of thought.

"As in our headmistress? Surely not," replied Astrid. She wondered what could be so important.

"Well, she looks a lot like the portrait in the Grand Hall," noted Hesper. Neither of them had actually seen their headmistress in person before; the headmistress had been kept busy the past few years working on inter-species relations across the regions. She was a spokeswoman for the witch community especially with the select few humans in government that know of the magical world's existence. Astrid wondered what had grabbed her attention so suddenly at the school, it had to be something important.

Astrid wandered to the back of the line edging herself closer to where the professors were coming from. She saw Professor Phelonius standing with Paige, she didn't realise Hesper's sister was still around the school. They were talking in hushed tones, just out of Astrid's earshot, but she could see by the sober look on their faces that it was something serious. Professor Phelonius had stopped talking, she could have sworn a hint of sadness glistened in his eyes. Paige rested her hand reassuringly on his shoulder, but he quickly shrugged it off and their conversation became more heated.

Astrid began to walk closer to investigate when she heard Professor Phelonius speak her father's name, surely if they were talking about her father, they must have also been discussing his list. Paige would know, she must have known about Sir Robert's deal with the Guard, she would know where the list is, thought Astrid striding towards Paige.

"And where do you think you're going, Miss Harper?" Professor Towinni stood firmly in Astrid's way with her eyebrows arched and lips pursed, she turned Astrid around without a word from her and shooed her back down the corridor. "My classroom is this way, as you well know."

Astrid thought best not to bring any unwanted attention to herself and continued back into the potions classroom. They had a duelling lesson later on before lunch and she'd make sure she had a private chat with Professor Phelonius afterwards. It seemed he knew more than he was letting on. She knew better than to go straight to her best friend's sister. She knew Paige didn't fully trust her, despite what Hesper had told her. She was probably right not to, her instincts served her well. For now, she'd have to wait till then to get some answers.

CHAPTER 9

Professor Phelonius hadn't been himself all lesson, Astrid could tell he was somewhat subdued since his heated discussion with Paige earlier that morning. He barely batted an eye to any of Astrid's playful jabs or Sapphire's outlandish advances, much to Sapphire's disdain. In fact, Astrid was sure the professor had been purposely avoiding her throughout the lesson, it was almost like he couldn't bring himself to even look at her. *Maybe he's figured out who you really are.* Astrid shook the paranoid thought, she was surely reading too much into it, she was just a bit on edge herself with everything that had happened recently.

"I think that's enough for today, girls," announced Professor Phelonius. With a wave of his hands, the practice dummies packed themselves away and the room returned to normal. They'd been practising offensive spells using the elements so there'd been quite the mess.

"But Sir, we haven't even done any duelling yet," whined Sapphire, looking sharply at Astrid. Astrid's brow creased, she welcomed the challenge.

"How about you all save that enthusiasm for our next lesson?" he suggested, gently shooing the girls out of his classroom. He could hear them all complaining. "I promise we'll do more next time, since when do you girls moan about a longer lunch?"

"We do when it means less time with you, Sir," remarked Sapphire softly as she grabbed her bag from the corner of the room. She made sure to brush past him as she left, pausing for a moment. “I hope to see you at the dance later, Sir, my dress will be quite something.”

The professor rolled his eyes and shook his head as he closed the classroom door behind him. He sighed and turned to see Astrid still standing in the middle of his classroom. He looked away and then continued briskly towards his office as if she wasn’t even there. She wasn’t imagining it, Professor Phelonius was certainly avoiding her and she was about to find out why. She called after him and followed him up the steps. He’d slammed the door to his office firmly behind him and Astrid could feel herself beginning to lose her temper, not that it took much these days. She took a deep breath and knocked on the door before entering.

“Sir, I was just wondering if I could have a quick word with you,” questioned Astrid politely.

“How about five, I’m not in the mood,” he replied coarsely, sat at his desk with a mess of papers. He didn’t even look up from the piece of paper he was reading.

“Please, Sir,” she said through gritted teeth, trying to keep her temper in check. “I was just looking for someone to talk to, someone who might be able to help me.”

“I’m sorry, I’m being rude,” sighed the professor, placing the piece of paper down and finally lifting his head to look at her. Astrid could have sworn she saw him flinch. “Why don’t you sit down, and I’ll make us some tea.”

“Let me,” insisted Astrid, making sure he stayed sitting down.

His lips curved with a small smile and he nodded gratefully gesturing to the brass teapot on top of his cabinet of curious objects.

Astrid held her hands around the pot and continued to heat it until it sang. The professor was tidying away the many documents and books he had open on his desk, he was too busy to even notice the sands of morpheus Astrid had sprinkled into his teacup. She put the two cups down and then sat in the chair across from the professor.

"Thank you, Astrid." He took a long sip from his teacup and then put it back down.

Astrid smirked and continued to drink hers waiting for the sands to take effect. She noted he looked about as tired as she felt, perhaps the sands would do him some good.

"You must forgive me, I had some rather unsettling news earlier about someone I never thought I'd have to hear of again," explained Professor Phelonius. Astrid remained silent as he took another sip. "Of course, that doesn't give me an excuse to shirk my responsibilities to my students. What was it you wanted to… erm… to talk abo—"

The professor yawned. Astrid pulled his cup out of the way before his head crashed to the desk. She took one last sip of her tea and then pocketed the rest of the morpheus sands. She needed the professor to be fast asleep for her to interrogate him properly and if she'd simply used her Concilium magic then he'd remember everything, and it would be another disappearance for her to stage. Quite frankly, Astrid wasn't in the mood for that extra work, although she had expected him to be a tad more resistant to the sands' effects.

Astrid propped him sitting up against the back of his chair and took her place in the seat opposite him. She then clicked her fingers and summoned his subconscious from his slumber to speak with her, she was ready to get some answers.

"What was the meeting about this morning?" she questioned, looking across at the professor, he didn't look nearly as handsome whilst he slept.

"So many meetings, so many problems, blah, blah, blah, blah," muttered the professor in a daze with his eyes still closed.

Astrid rolled her eyes, the subconscious could be a fickle thing. "What did Paige talk to you and the other professors about? Why was the headmistress there?"

"Such a nosey student, aren't you, what a big nose you have," he sniggered. "And you strut that big nose around like you own the place, I know I strut like a peacock but you—"

Astrid's patience was running thin, his subconscious was trying to make this difficult. "I don't have time for this."

"Tick tock goes your clock," sang the professor's subconscious as he reeled his head and Astrid began to search the papers on his desk, perhaps they'd be more helpful.

"Your father didn't have much of a sense of humour either," remarked his subconscious, that caught Astrid's attention.

"What did you just say?"

"The spawn of Vincentrio," he said in a mockingly deep voice.

"And who else knows?" she asked sharply, her hands poised ready to grasp his neck.

"Just me." He was serious now. "The others only know he's up to something, no one else knows he even had a child."

Astrid pursed her lips. She was intrigued why he'd kept this to himself all this time and what was stopping him from telling anyone else. No matter. He was distracting her from the information she really wanted. "So, you know about the list as well?"

"Shopping list?" he joked.

She huffed. "Where's the list?"

"None of you ladies can find your shopping list, whatever will you do," he continued hysterically.

Astrid had had enough of this, his subconscious was irritating and the sands wouldn't last much longer. She clicked her fingers sending back his subconscious and his head crashed to the desk once again. She'd have more luck searching his office. He clearly knew what list she was talking about and if he had it with him, she was going to find it.

Astrid rustled through the papers Professor Phelonius had moved from the desk, examining them for any names she might recognise, but all she found was notes he'd written, scribbles. She pulled open the drawers in his desk and shook them out onto the floor, but still nothing. She needed to find that list, she needed something. Astrid went to open the bottom drawer, but it didn't move. As she passed her fingers over it, she could sense the magic he'd used to seal it shut. Something important was in that drawer.

Astrid closed her eyes and placed her hands on the drawer, muttering the incantation she drew the magic from the drawer and heard it unlock. She gingerly opened it and found a bounded leather folder inside. The folder was full of old looking pieces of parchment, some had more scribbles, she wasn't sure of the language, but she noticed a faint coloured drawing of a gem on the corner of some of the pages. On some it was the Perrero gem and on others it was her father's, it seemed the professor had been investigating him for some time. Still there was no sign of the list.

Astrid's ears pricked when she heard the door to his classroom shut and then the sound of someone's footsteps fast approaching, someone had come to see the professor. She shoved the papers back and then went to put it back in the drawer. A photo had dropped out of the folder, she turned it over and stopped still. Her mother's bold, violet eyes sparkled as she smiled back at Astrid. What was the professor doing with a photo of her mother, she thought turning over the back of the photo where the message read 'My Mia.' He knew her.

The footsteps got louder, and Astrid reluctantly tucked the photo back in. She didn't have time to question him again, his visitor was almost at the door. Astrid sealed the drawer with the same enchantment that had originally been protecting it and, with a click of her fingers, she returned the room to exactly how it had been. The professor woke up just as Professor Peverel walked in and Astrid slipped into his wardrobe, concealing herself amongst the professor's many cloaks. She held her breath and tried desperately not to think about the photo in his drawer. *It's just a distraction.*

"Have I caught you at a bad time?" asked Professor Peverel, noting the slither of drool on the side of Alexander's cheek.

"Not at all, Skylar, I must have dosed off," he replied, quickly wiping it with his sleeve.

"I just thought I'd come and check up on you," she explained softly.

"On me?" He'd leant forwards in his chair, Astrid could tell there was something between the two of them.

"You looked upset earlier after the meeting, I was concerned," said Professor Peverel, her mouth lifted with a sweet smile. "I hope you don't mind me asking, but what was Paige talking to you about?"

Astrid leaned her ear closer to the crack in the door, perhaps Professor Peverel would have more luck getting some answers from him.

Professor Phelonius' lips formed a hard line. "She gave me some bad news concerning an estranged family member, it was a bit of a shock." Professor Peverel looked almost as disappointed as Astrid by the ambiguity of his answer. "Skylar, I really can't say any more about it, it would only put you in danger."

Professor Peverel's gaze dropped to her hand as he took hold and held it intently in his grasp, she smiled and gently squeezed his hand. "Okay. I'd be lying if I said all this Vincentrio stuff didn't scare me, I just can't believe he's still alive."

Astrid was glad Professor Phelonius hadn't shared his discovery with any of the other teachers although she still didn't quite understand why. *He must have a hidden agenda*. Both of the professors had gone quiet, she peeped through the crack in the wardrobe to check if they were still there. Alexander held Skylar in his arms, both leaning on one another for support. A sense of shame crept over Astrid, like she was spying on an intimate moment between the two of them. She pulled herself away from the crack and waited for them to leave.

"I don't suppose I could ask you a favour," queried Alexander.

"Of course, whatever you need," she replied in a heartbeat.

"I have something important to do this afternoon, something I need to finish." Astrid wondered if he was talking about the list. "Would you mind covering my lesson this afternoon? I need to help Paige and I'm not sure how long I'll be."

"Say no more."

"You star." He dropped a gentle kiss to her forehead and grabbed his coat. "I should be back in time for the ball, perhaps you could save a dance for me?"

"Perhaps." She smiled fondly and opened the door for him.

The office door closed, and Astrid was certain they'd both left. She cautiously stepped out of the wardrobe and brushed herself off, he really needed to clear out that old wardrobe. Alexander must have left to help Paige find the list, which meant Astrid had no chance of going there herself without arousing some suspicion, especially now Alexander knew exactly who she was. She'd have to be patient and wait for one of them to return with it. Paige wouldn't go back to the Guard headquarters without first saying goodbye to her sister and she was sure Hesper had mentioned she was coming to the ball later on. If Paige came back with the list, Astrid would get her hands on it, one way or another.

Astrid walked towards the door but paused for a second. She wanted to go back in that drawer, to look if he had any other photos of her mother or just to steal a look at that photo once more. Her father had locked away the few photos he had of her, he didn't like to dwell on the past. Astrid was only permitted to look at them on the rare occasion, he didn't want her love to weaken her. Most of the time, Astrid only had the few memories of her to think of what she looked like. *Never mind, it would do no good.*

She pulled herself away and rushed out of his classroom before anyone saw her, though if anyone did, she could easily lie about wanting to get some more practice in. Luckily, no one was in the corridor, so she could save that lie for another time. The underground corridors were relatively quiet at this time with everyone probably eating in the Grand Hall. Astrid continued towards the flame lit spiralled steps that led back up to the Grand Hall. She was hungry, and she'd be no good at finding anything on an empty stomach.

Halfway up the steps, she crashed into a broad chested body where she was in such a rush and dropped her books. She clicked her fingers catching them before they travelled too far.

"You should really watch where you're going," she cautioned sternly, summoning her books back to her before looking at who the clumsy student was.

"Because you were really looking yourself," Caius remarked, picking up one of the books she'd dropped.

"I didn't realise it was you, sorry." She smiled and took the book from his grasp. He couldn't help but caress her fingers as she did so, she quickly snapped it back. She knew it hadn't been him, but every time she looked at him all she saw was him with that knife. "What are you doing down here?"

"I came to find you. Hesper said you were still down here," continued Caius, a little bit hurt by her sudden withdrawal.

"And I'm trying to get back upstairs, would you please move?" insisted Astrid, trying to find a way around him without actually looking at his face.

"Can we just talk about it?" Caius lifted her chin gently, forcing her to look in his eyes. His brown eyes, not icy blue, this was her Caius. "I realise now that I may have come off a bit harsh last night, that dark magic stuff just made me feel uncomfortable."

"Uncomfortable?" she snorted and pulled away, ducking her way past him to continue up the steps.

"Astrid, I'm trying to apologise here," he sighed wearily.

"And you're doing a piss poor job too," she sneered. She'd realised she was channelling a lot of the resentment of his dream self, not to mention she was tired and hungry, but it didn't make her feel any less right.

Caius leapt in front of her on the steps again and this time stopped her passing with his whole body. "Just stop." She really didn't want to, she wanted to go get some lunch from the Grand Hall, but she couldn't keep avoiding him.

"I'm sorry for what I said last night, I don't think witches are bad at all. If anything, I think your magic is beautiful," he smiled edging himself closer. "I wish I could do half the things you can. I just want it to stay beautiful. Call me old-fashioned, but I just have this need to protect you all the time, even if that is from your own magic."

"Caius." Astrid had learnt to protect herself from such an early age, sharing that with someone else just felt odd to her.

"Or from yourself," he murmured, pulling her close to his chest.

Astrid dropped her books and rested her head. *A bit too late for that now*. She closed her eyes and just breathed as he stroked her hair, his touch was so gentle, she could fall asleep there and then.

"Hesper told me you had a bad dream," said Caius softly.

"What else did that big mouth say?"

"Just that you wouldn't talk to her about it."

She lifted her head and sighed. "Caius, I'm not one of those girls who just can't stop talking about their feelings. That's not me and if you want one of those then—"

"How many times do I have to say this, Astrid? I want you. I just wish you'd start sharing some of that weight you carry round with me."

Astrid really wished she could. She wished she could tell him everything. She wished she didn't have to do the things she had to do, but Astrid had learnt many years ago that she would never get her happy ending. *This would just have to be close enough.*

Astrid wrapped her arms around the back of Caius' neck and pulled him in close leaving a tender kiss on his lips. He took her lips with his, but so tentatively this time, with care rather than need. She teased his lips with her tongue and he pinned her up against the stone wall with his body. She inhaled suddenly as he pushed against her and he stifled her soft moan with his mouth, she could feel his rock-hard affection. He continued to press himself against her slowly, with such restraint. Astrid quivered as he ran his hand along the side of her face, stroking her cheek so softly with his thumb, she wanted him, she craved him, all of him. Then he smoothly pulled away taking control.

"You're such a tease, Caius," laughed Astrid, quickly sorting out her ruffled hair and picking up her books.

"We're just lucky no one else uses these steps," he smiled, bending down to help Astrid. He then whispered in her ear, "Kind of exciting though, isn't it?"

She chuffed and hit his chest playfully. "Don't get any ideas." They were very lucky no one had been around to see them, for a minute she hadn't been thinking clearly and she'd let herself get carried away. She wouldn't let it happen again. "I swear if they've ran out of food in the Grand Hall, I'm blaming you," she warned Caius, continuing back up the steps and towards the Grand Hall. She'd be lucky if lunch was still being served; it was almost time for lessons to start again.

"I will accept the consequences," laughed Caius, grinning from ear to ear as he followed closely behind her.

By the time they'd got to the main floor, students were flooding out through the towering wooden doors on their way to their next lesson. Astrid turned and frowned at Caius who couldn't help but laugh when he realised where everyone was going.

In the crowd of students, Caius gave Astrid's hand a gentle squeeze and leant in close against her. "I'll make it up to you later," he murmured and then started walking to his lessons as he shouted across the heads of students, "I might see you later at this dance thing." He winked, and Astrid couldn't help but smile, even if she was still ravenous and about to shout at the next student who barged past her.

One student walked right into the back of her and Astrid felt her tolerance snap. "Would it kill you to say excuse m—" She turned around sharply to see Hesper smiling sweetly and sighed.

Hesper held out a small pot of the beef stew they'd been serving for lunch and Astrid's eyes instantly lit up. "Sorry, who's the most amazing witch in all of Curo?" jibed Hesper.

"Most definitely you," exclaimed Astrid, grabbing the pot and tucking in exuberantly as they walked to their next class.

"You might want this as well," remarked Hesper, holding out her hairbrush, she'd noted how out of place her friend's hair was. "I take it Caius found you."

"Enough of that," dismissed Astrid through a mouthful of stew. "And enough of this," she exclaimed as yet another student pushed past her.

Astrid flashed the two of them to Professor Peverel's classroom before anyone else had the chance to barge past her. No one else had arrived yet, so Astrid took her usual seat at the back. They had an hour of human/magical integration and then they were free for the rest of the afternoon, plenty of time for Astrid to find herself a dress to wear for the dance. Although, Astrid could think of a number of things she'd rather be doing in that hour than listening to Professor Peverel witter on about human history, it wasn't anything exciting.

Astrid couldn't help but daydream throughout the lesson; she wondered how well Professor Phelonius knew her mother and, by association, her father. Surely, if the professor realised how serious the threat her father was, he'd soon share her true identity with the other professors, and if that happened, she wouldn't be able to stay in Vistaldors for much longer. She needed to know why the professor hadn't said anything, otherwise she'd be living the rest of her time at Vistaldors constantly on edge. As if she didn't have enough to worry about already.

Before she knew it, she'd daydreamed the entire lesson away and Hesper was prodding her, pulling her away from her thoughts. "Did you listen to a word I just said?" complained Hesper, collecting up her belongings.

"Huh?" Astrid quickly snapped out of her daydream, practically the entire class had already left.

Professor Peverel was rubbing something off the chalkboard at the front of the class, she turned around and looked over her half-moon glasses. She'd realised Astrid hadn't really been present throughout her class and she couldn't help but feel concerned. She'd noticed the bags beneath her eyes and a somewhat nervous energy that was altogether very out of character for Astrid.

Hesper rolled her eyes at her friend and continued to leave the classroom, nodding to the professor as she left. Professor Peverel reached out a hand stopping Astrid as she made her way towards the door. "Is there something troubling you, Astrid?" Astrid hesitated. "I can't help you if you don't talk to me," said the professor soothingly, searching for the student she used to know.

"I'm fine, Miss." Astrid forced a smile and politely proceeded through the door and joined Hesper outside.

"What was that all about?" questioned Hesper.

"No idea," shrugged Astrid as they both flashed back to the common room.

Hesper had realised there was more to it but decided now was not the time to push her for any more. She'd be at risk of putting Astrid in a bad mood and that would just spoil everyone's evening.

"So, can I show you the dress I'm planning to wear later, I'd really like someone else's opinion," questioned Hesper hopefully, she left her books on the table and ran into their room before Astrid could respond.

"I'm not sure if I'm the best person to ask, Hesper," she sighed, rubbing her head as she took a seat in one of the armchairs. She had a pulsing headache. "Why don't you ask your sister. isn't that why people have sisters?"

"Paige had to go back out to work, sounds like there's been some sort of development in the case. She's not sure if she'll be back in time," called Hesper from the other room. "You'll just have to do."

Hesper emerged from their room in a stunning, powder blue evening gown; its perfectly fitting shape, trimmed nicely inwards to her delicate waist with a gorgeous plunge neckline decorated tastefully with several diamantes. Astrid's mouth dropped, and she was rendered speechless, which was the effect Hesper was going for. Hesper gleamed, and span round pleased with her choice of dress.

"Wow, you look amazing," exclaimed Astrid, standing up from the chair to get a better look, she took her friend's hands and smiled. "I don't think you're going to need my help looking like that."

"Thanks, Astrid, gird your loins boys," Hesper laughed. "Let me see what dress you're planning to wear."

"Maybe later," dismissed Astrid, returning to their room and perching on her bed.

"We have a couple of hours before getting ready, later is now," remarked Hesper. She threw open Astrid's wardrobe to look at the dress she was planning to wear, but there wasn't a dress in sight. She frowned. "Astrid, you do have a dress, don't you?"

"Yes, of course I do," yawned Astrid, finding her duck feather pillow extraordinarily tempting.

"Of course," groaned Hesper, rolling her eyes. "How about you go for a little nap and then we'll see what we can rustle up."

"And this is why we're friends."

Astrid heaved a heavy sigh and threw herself back onto her bed pulling her duvet close, resting her eyes for just a little while. She could hear Hesper pottering about their room, but the noise was rather comforting. Her mind had gone quiet and she drifted off, the thoughts that had been troubling her all hushed for now.

A rattling chirping noise finally woke Astrid and she opened her eyes to see a clockwork bluebird sounding on her bedside table. *Hesper must have left it there*. She groaned and pulled her covers over her head in an attempt to drown out its vexing shrill. She'd felt so rested after that sleep, but now all she could think about was how hard she was going to throw the damn thing at Hesper.

"Hesper," called Astrid through her covers. No response. She threw her covers off and sat up glaring at the mechanical bird. She picked it up to look for an off switch, but its alarm only rang louder drilling right through Astrid's head, she had no idea how to turn the bloody thing off. With a huff, Astrid clicked her fingers and the clockwork toy burst into flames in the palm of her hand, that shut it up. She poured away the ashes and jumped out of bed feeling practically rejuvenated as if all her worries had worked themselves out of her head as she'd slept.

Astrid walked to her wardrobe and opened the doors to see for herself the lack of ball attire she really had. Hanging from a hanger on the inside of one of the doors was an elegant, strapless, ruby-red evening gown. Astrid ran her hands through its delicate material and smiled, she had some idea how the dress had got there. She found some diamante strapped heels that would go perfectly and slipped into the dress before sorting her hair and makeup. Sitting at the mirror, she carefully styled her hair up, curling it into an elegant low bun. Astrid reminisced how her mother loved to play with her long hair as she slid another pin to keep the simple do in place. She placed a fine gold necklace around her neck and then thought of the last thing she needed.

Astrid lifted her dress as she went onto her hands and knees reaching blindly underneath her bed; her arm flailed about as she felt a few random objects that Peewee had clearly collected whilst she hadn't been looking and then she found it. She pulled out the small wooden box she'd kept under there for safe keeping and scanned the room to check no one was around before she opened it. The box held some of her most valued possessions, to anyone else it was just bits of tat and some old photographs, but to Astrid they were memories. She found a small hair grip shaped like a comet tail and delicately encrusted with amethyst gems, the piece had belonged to her mother. It was the one thing her father had salvaged from the wreck of their house after the Guard began hunting him down.

"Astrid are you in here?" called Hesper, teetering into their room on her nude high heels. Astrid quickly slipped the box back under her bed and placed the grip just above her low bun. "What are you doing down there?" she questioned, helping Astrid back up onto her feet.

"I just dropped something," replied Astrid quickly as she brushed herself off and adjusted her dress.

Hesper frowned as she tucked her golden, curled hair behind her ear. "There is nothing worse than lending someone a dress and them looking better in it than you."

"Thank you, Hesper, you're like my very own fairy godmother," smiled Astrid, throwing her arms round her friend almost knocking them both off balance.

"We better get going now if we don't want to be late, it's going to take me long enough in these shoes," remarked Hesper, getting a head start out of the common room.

"Oh, we're not walking," said Astrid. She clicked her fingers and flashed the two of them to the corridor just outside the Grand Hall where students were already flocking in to take their seats.

"Of course, when do we ever walk," laughed Hesper, linking arms with Astrid to make their way in together.

The Grand Hall looked grander than it ever had before; thousands of lanterns lit the ceiling above them like stars in the night sky, their flicker reflecting off the dazzling, crystal chandeliers. Satin banners and streamers ran between each chandelier, their hem littered with gold dust. The house tables had been moved and in their place were a series of smaller round tables all set with silver cutlery and crystal glassware upon a satin table cloth laced with gold dust. In the centre of each table stood a beautiful arrangement of deep red roses entangled round an ice sculpture of a stag, the sigil of their school.

Students and professors alike had dusted off their suits and evening gowns for this formal occasion, and the Grand Hall's walls echoed with the chorus of their conversations whilst a string quartet played softly in the background. Wooden waiters made their way around the room carrying silver trays of crystal chalices and a selection of hors d'oeuvres.

Astrid felt like she couldn't let go of Hesper's arm, she was mesmerised. It had been such a long time since she'd been able to attend one of these dances, she'd almost forgotten what they were like.

"Hey stranger." Astrid immediately turned around and threw her arms around Xander's neck, laughing as he picked her up and span her round. Everyone turned to look, and he quickly put her back down narrowing his eyes as he urged the nosey students to return to their conversations. "Don't you scrub up well, give us a spin," he marvelled, holding his hand out, he couldn't remember the last time he'd seen Astrid wearing a dress.

"And look at you, you've actually combed your hair," teased Astrid. She leant up to his chest and quickly adjusted his black bow tie. "But you were always hopeless with these." She stroked the black lapels of his suit jacket and smiled. "There, much better."

"I'm going to go and get myself a drink, it was nice to see you again Xander. I hope you get that spot on the Hawcranes squad," said Hesper feeling rather awkward as she excused herself and hurried off towards the refreshments.

"You too," stuttered Xander forcing the words out, his mouth had gone dry and he found himself staring as she walked away.

"You too? Smooth, Hesper doesn't even play Shacklebolt," remarked Astrid. "Is there something going on there I should know about?"

"Absolutely nothing," he replied, running a hand adversely through his thick combed hair as his eyes wandered round the room. The headmistress had begun wading through the crowds to her seat at the professors' table, a seat anyone rarely sat in.

"I think it's time for us to go find our seats," said Xander, quickly changing the subject. Astrid propped her hands on her hips, there was definitely more to it. "I'll come find you for a dance later, think it's definitely overdue."

"Sure," agreed Astrid, gently squeezing his hand before he walked away, she understood how much this place on the Hawcranes squad meant to him.

Xander had been right; Professor Ryback stood by her chair, the red chiffon trail of her dress formed a pond around her feet. She gently clicked her fingers quietening the strings of the quartet. The conversations concluded, and the groups of students dispersed to their respective tables. Astrid scanned the room for Hesper, hoping she'd found a good table for them to sit on. Then she spotted her, her curls bounced as she laughed with Erin who sat next to her. Astrid briskly walked to join them realising she was one of the few people still standing. She greeted everyone with a small smile and quickly took her seat next to Hesper.

"I thought you'd like to sit with your team," whispered Hesper who had positioned herself opposite Reuben and Zack.

Astrid had noticed how the boys were looking at Hesper. She didn't know either of them well enough to judge them completely, but she threw them a friendly, warning stare, which seemed to work pretty well. Their eyes quickly diverted rather sheepishly towards their headmistress instead. Astrid heard

Katy's laugh that she'd tried to stifle, she'd quite clearly noticed herself. Though Astrid was surprised she'd noticed at all, her chair was positioned rather close to Grayson's and she could see their hands firmly entangled out of the corner of her eye. She felt a pang of jealousy in her chest, those two didn't have to sneak around deserted corridors or find hidden spots to meet up. They could just be. She dismissed her envy and returned her attention to their headmistress.

Professor Ryback was smiling with a chalice in her hand, waiting for everyone's full attention. She'd done well covering the bags beneath her eyes with her makeup, but Astrid still noticed them. It seemed the headmistress was also struggling to sleep, but she's a strong woman who wasn't going to let the uncertainty of the dangers ahead ruin the evening. She was there to bolster her students and that's what she'd do.

"I'd like to start off with saying how lovely everyone looks this evening and how proud I am of you all," announced the professor. "I think you've all faced your own challenges this year, but what amazes me is the way you all face them, with the grace and decorum that our founder would be proud of. So, first off here's to all of you." Everyone raised their chalices to her toast and took a sip of their fizzle juice. "And on to our talented Shacklebolt players, I won't keep you waiting any longer. I hope you'll all join me in congratulating the four students who have been handpicked for the Hawcranes trial: Finn Clarke, Katy Nickelson, Erin Cosgrave and Xander Black."

The room roared with thunderous applause as the students and professors cheered for their players. Katy squealed with excitement, throwing her arms around Grayson and hugging him tightly, he whispered something in her ear and then nudged her to stand up, keeping hold of her hand as she did so. Astrid smiled and leant across the table to congratulate both Katy and Erin. Erin looked so surprised when she heard her name, her face had stopped still until her brothers were on her and pulling her up from her chair.

Astrid scanned the room to see if Xander was standing. It wasn't difficult to find him, she could hear the gruff cheers of his friends who all sat at the same table hammering their fists in triumph for their friend. She found his dark eyes and mouthed her congratulations as she held her hands up and continued to clap enthusiastically. She couldn't be happier for him, he was so deserving of this chance. He'd talked about playing for them for as long as she could remember, every year he'd save up his chore money and scrape together just enough to go to their last game of the season. Astrid had even managed to procure a signed photo of his favourite Runner, Torin Knight, for his birthday four years ago. She knew for a fact that he still kept it above his bed.

"Now let's enjoy the rest of the evening," chimed Professor Ryback.

The wooden waiters flooded through the open doors, balancing plates of delectable food on their timber. Everyone returned to their seats and the Grand Hall was once again humming with conversation as they dug into their dinner. Their golden plates were teeming with a gourmet meal of poached lobster sitting delicately on a bed of crunchy garden peas and succulent white peach pieces. The wooden waiters promptly returned with hand crafted china bowls of freshly baked bread and crisp green lettuce, scattering them amongst the tables. The conversation was flowing, and everyone was enjoying themselves, drinking their fizzle juice between bites, their chalices refilling every time they were low.

Astrid was enjoying herself, all thoughts of her father or the things she'd done, or the uncertainty of the future had vanished from her mind. She could have normal conversations with the others, she even found herself laughing with the boys, Reuben and Zack were quite the charismatic pair. Plus, they'd stopped staring at Hesper like a piece of meat, which certainly helped.

"It's a real shame you weren't considered for one of the spots on the team, Astrid," said Katy, dabbing her lipstick with her napkin. "I think you'd have given us all a run for our money."

"I definitely shouldn't have got a place, so I must confess I was relieved," admitted Erin as her cheeks flushed.

"Don't be silly, you earnt your spot, both of you," declared Astrid, she hadn't been eligible thanks to the time off she'd had from the game.

A coy smile stretched across Erin's face and she pushed her half-eaten plate aside. "If I eat another thing, someone's going to have to roll me to training tomorrow." They all laughed and polished off what they could from their plates, some of the girls started to regret the tight-fitting dresses.

They rested back in their seats as the wooden waiters returned to remove the empty plates and the string quartet had begun to play again, this time accompanied by an acoustic guitar and bass giving the students a more upbeat tune to dance to. Students and professors began to take to the dancefloor as the tables slid to the side. Grayson waved his hands and a red rose corsage appeared in his palm, which he tenderly wrapped around Katy's wrist. He held out his hand inviting Katy for a dance and spun her around as she stood up. Reuben and Zack had already descended on a pair of girls they'd seen across the room.

"I suppose that just leaves us three," sighed Hesper, leaning against the back of the chair to watch the other couples dance.

Finn Clarke appeared by their table sweeping his red hair back nervously as he congratulated Erin and proceeded to ask for a dance. She looked back apprehensively at the other two as if asking what she should do. They both glared and nodded her on, she'd be silly not to dance with Finn, he was a strapping young griffin who plenty of girls fawned over.

Astrid watched on as the boys placed one hand on their partner's waists and stepped in time with the beat, gliding across the dancefloor like skaters on ice, even the younger students were giving it a go. Though she couldn't see Caius dancing, in fact she hadn't seen him all evening. She couldn't help feel a little disappointed by his absence.

"And then there were two," remarked Hesper, taking a long sip from her chalice.

"Why don't you go and dance with Xander, he likes to waltz," said Astrid, studying Hesper's face for a response.

"I'm sure he's got girls lining up to dance with him," she said rather bitterly.

"Did something happen with you two?" Hesper's reddened cheeks had prompted Astrid's curiosity. Hesper threw Astrid a stern glare and then finished off the rest of her chalice, she covered her mouth quickly as a burp burst from her lips. "I'm beginning to think there's more than just fizzle juice in that cup," said Astrid, snatching the cup from Hesper as it refilled, she put it to her nose and pursed her lips. "Definitely not fizzle juice, I think that's enough of that."

"It was just a small tipple," huffed Hesper, taking her chalice back that was now full of water. "And yes. Something might have happened."

Astrid perked up and pulled her chair closer. "Well, you're going to have to elaborate on that."

“We may have had a moment the other day when I was in the village.”

“A moment? Is that all you’re going to tell me, what even is a moment?” smirked Astrid. Considering how invested Hesper had been in her love life, she wasn’t very forthcoming with details of her own.

Before Hesper could answer, the doors to the Grand Hall swung open and Professor Phelonius sauntered in adjusting his black bow tie as he found Professor Peverel for a dance. Astrid’s attention wandered, and she noticed Paige standing just outside the Grand Hall fiddling with her bag. She was sure she saw her fold a piece of parchment and tuck it away in her clutch. She sealed it with an enchantment and then continued to enter with a smile painted on her face. Astrid could think of only one thing that would have been important enough to seal in her bag.

“Paige, you made it,” squealed Hesper as she quickly ran to greet her sister with a hug and invited her to sit down with them.

Paige greeted Astrid and sat herself down taking care with the trail of her black dress and placing her clutch on the table. “So, what did I miss?” questioned Paige, she sounded almost out of breath.

“Oh, not much, Hesper was just about to tell us about a moment she had with Xander,” replied Astrid, trying not to stare at the clutch on the table.

Paige grinned. “Oh really, tell us more, dear sister, about this moment.”

Hesper laughed and grabbed her sister’s hand pulling her to her feet. “How about we have a dance first?”

“I daren’t say no,” said Paige before Hesper dragged her away. “Astrid, would you look after my bag for me? Thank you.”

"No problem," replied Astrid, watching the two make their way to the centre of the dance floor.

When Astrid saw the two were far enough away, her attention was pulled back to the bag and before she could even think to stop herself, Astrid had picked it up and started to make her way briskly out of the Grand Hall. She purposely left her own bag behind on the chair; their bags were so similar it would have been easy to mix the two up, at least that's what she'd tell them if anyone asked. She turned around to check they were still dancing but stumbled into Sapphire in her haste towards the door. Sapphire shrieked angrily and glared at Astrid with her jaw clenched. Sapphire had spilt her fizzle juice all down her forest green gown.

"What the hell," whined Sapphire, quickly dabbing at the stain.

Astrid cursed her clumsiness, she really didn't want to make a scene. "Oh crap, I'm so sorry, Sapphire. I really didn't mean to," apologised Astrid as she quickly brushed past her.

"Next time I'll make sure one of those rocks cut you a bit deeper," muttered Sapphire under her breath.

Astrid bit her lip and continued walking, ignoring Sapphire's provoking jibes.

"I hope that dress isn't too tight on that scar of yours," sneered Sapphire. She smirked when she saw Astrid walk back towards her.

"You're just lucky I didn't get the chance to return the favour," whispered Astrid, she narrowed her eyes. "We'll see how confident you are when other people aren't around."

"Is that a threat?" questioned Sapphire confidently.

Astrid's mouth lifted, she could see a flicker of fear in Sapphire's eyes. "You decide," she replied, walking out of the

Grand Hall with a smile on her face. She'd been waiting for her chance to get back at Sapphire and it seemed she'd certainly ruffled a few feathers.

Astrid continued walking calmly down the corridor, there were too many people hanging around outside the Grand Hall and she didn't want to attract any unwanted attention. She came across one of the smaller classrooms and checked no one else was in there before pulling the door ajar. She placed the clutch on the table and then tried first to open the bag, perhaps she'd just imagined Paige placing an enchantment on it. Astrid pulled her hand back sharply and bit her lip as a shock ran up her arm. She hadn't imagined it. A simple protection charm wouldn't be difficult for Astrid.

With the clutch on the table, Astrid hovered her hands either side and closed her eyes muttering a reverse incantation. The magic from the bag slowly seeped towards her palms and she stopped. Bedelia had taught her reverse incantations years ago, they were a bit more civilised than just breaking things. Astrid cautiously went to open the bag again, she didn't fancy another magic shock. This time the bag opened, and Astrid quickly dug through. It was impressive how many products Paige had managed to fit in such a small clutch. She emptied the bag's contents onto the desk and snatched the piece of folded parchment as it fell from the bottom of her bag. She frantically unfolded it and saw the names.

Astrid took a second to read the list and then sighed with relief. She'd found it. She'd done what her father had asked of her. It was clear why it had been such an urgent task; there were about thirty names of Vincentrio's followers on there, half of them in highly influential positions. She just hoped that Paige hadn't had a chance to properly read the list, otherwise that would leave another loose end for her to deal with. Astrid dismissed the sinister thoughts that were creeping into her head, she'd cross that bridge when she came to it. For now, she needed to finish the task and destroy the list. Astrid clicked her fingers, setting the list alight and dropped it into a metal bin, she watched as the flames burnt away the names.

"What are you doing in here?" Astrid almost jumped out of her skin as she turned and saw Xander standing in the doorway.

Astrid waved her hands and extinguished the flames, stepping quickly in front of the mess she'd left on the desk. "I just wanted a bit of space," she replied as she turned to tidy the products back into Paige's bag. "Why aren't you in the Grand Hall celebrating?"

"I was looking for you, I said I'd come find you for a dance, remember?" Xander explained, dubiously eyeing the products scattered on the desk. "Astrid, that's not your bag."

"I know, I'm such an idiot. I picked Paige's up by mistake, not sure how I didn't notice the difference by the weight with all this rubbish in there," she said, casually closing the bag. She took his hand and went to lead him out of the room. "Now, how about that dance?"

"Astrid." Xander stopped and closed the door. He'd noticed the ashes in the bin and could tell when Astrid was lying, she wasn't as good at it as she thought. "Why don't you tell me what's really going on here?"

"I don't know what you mean." Astrid held her ground, there was no way she was involving Xander in this mess.

"I'm not stupid and I'm not blind like lover boy." Astrid's eyes widened, and he continued, "Oh yeah I've noticed that too, but we can discuss that idiocy another time. Let's try again, what are you really doing with Paige's bag?"

"I told you, I picked it up by—"

"Astrid, just tell me the truth," he shouted. Astrid stood back, she hadn't heard Xander yell before or at least not at her. He gritted his teeth and brushed a hand through his hair, his expression softened. "I want to help you, so just… let me help you."

"I can't," she admitted faintly, avoiding eye contact. "Let's just drop it and you forget you ever saw anything, I picked the bag up by mistake."

Xander clenched his jaw and sternly stood in Astrid's away. "Enough with this cock and bull, Astrid, I know you well enough to know when something's wrong. I could make you tell me." Astrid stiffened, he'd never threatened her with magic before. Xander could feel himself losing it; he cared too much for Astrid to let it carry on, he'd seen her through too much, they were practically family. "You've been sneaking around classrooms, keeping to yourself and now sneaking around with *him*, a shapeshifter. I mean come on Astrid, you're smarter than that, well at least you used to be! And now this. You've been different ever since you came back. I know you and this isn't you," he said, his face had gone red, but his eyes looked defeated.

"Maybe that's just it, Xander," remarked Astrid. "You don't know me any more."

Astrid closed her eyes and started to walk, trying to keep her expression cold even though she felt like she was going to lose it any second and start crying. Xander grabbed her arm firmly before she could leave and then loosened his grip still holding her there, allowing the silence to fill the room. Astrid tried so hard not to look at him, her eyes were watering and she bit back a sniffle.

“Astrid, just talk to me.” His voice was soft now, compassionate.

Astrid really wanted to turn around. Her secret was on the tip of her tongue, she had to tighten her lips to keep it from bursting out of her.

“What happened to you?” pushed Xander.

Astrid couldn’t hold it any longer, she looked up at Xander and the tears began to fall streaming down her heated cheeks. “Please, Xander, you wouldn’t understand. I can’t talk about it, I just can’t.” She crumbled on the floor and he caught her, she looked up at his eyes and pleaded, “Don’t make me tell you.”

He softly stroked her hair as she sobbed into his chest. He hadn’t held her like this since he told her he was leaving the orphanage all those years ago, he almost gave up his chance of adoption to stay and protect her. She’d had no one else to do it.

“Astrid I will understand, me and you are like family.” Xander’s cheeks stiffened and he corrected himself, “We *are* family.”

Astrid pulled herself away from him and wiped her eyes trying not to ruin her makeup even more, she muttered, “If I tell you, you’ll be in danger and I can’t do that to you. I owe you too much.”

“You owe me nothing,” Xander said assertively. “But if you don’t tell me, I might just lose my mind imagining what could be so bad and I will find out what it is. I won’t let it go.”

Astrid breathed a heavy sigh and lifted herself back up to her feet. She pulled herself together and helped Xander to his feet. It was time. “I don’t think I can tell you.” She held a finger to his lips as he opened his mouth to protest. “But I can show you. Before I do, will you promise me one thing?”

"Anything," he replied caringly, he was just relieved she was going to share the truth with him.

"Just promise me that you won't think any less of me." Astrid trembled as she held out her hand.

"I promise." He took her hand and Astrid closed her eyes taking them both back through her memories, memories she'd fought to forget, memories that only haunted her nightmares. Then she stopped and they both opened their eyes.

The heat was unbearable and the stench detestable, even in a memory walk the essence of Trepidor was enough to turn Astrid's stomach. Xander's eyes were drawn to the rotting corpses propped up on the floor against the wall. A bird was picking at the stringy flesh left on their bones and Astrid could see Xander swallow the bile that had surfaced.

An all too familiar scream echoed off the walls and Astrid followed it, she knew exactly where it led. Xander paused, he too had heard the screams and was clearly apprehensive about discovering their source. She could see he was rethinking whether he really wanted to find out what she'd been hiding, but she'd brought him here now and she needed to follow through. If not for Xander, then for herself.

Astrid squeezed Xander's hand, drawing his attention away from the decaying corpses. "Whatever you do, don't let go of my hand or you'll be thrown out of my memory," said Astrid calmly. She could feel the sickening feeling of dread twist in the very pit of her stomach, but she refused to let it get the better of her. "And don't forget what you promised me."

"I know, I know," he nodded. He swallowed dryly and followed her down the spiralled staircase. If Astrid could be brave enough to show him what she clearly feared, then he would be strong enough to hold her hand throughout.

The steps seemed to go on forever and the screams were getting louder. As Xander heard them more clearly, an unsettling feeling stirred, and he dreaded what he was about to see next. He lifted his chin and gripped Astrid's hand a little tighter, reminding her he was there with her.

They'd come to a room at the very bottom of the pit. The screams had gone quiet for a second and Astrid could hear the flicker of two torches, she remembered they'd been the only light in the room. She froze at the doorway. The door was so distinct. She instantly recognised the beautiful carvings etched into its woodwork and it had been open. They'd always left the door open. Her heart was practically bounding through her chest and she felt herself tremble, she couldn't stop it. She could hear the voice inside her, it was warning her to turn back, to run away, but she ignored it and led him through the doorway.

In the flicker of the flamelight, they could make out a distorted figure whimpering against the wall. There were shackles bound tightly around their wrists, the leather was stained with blood where they'd started to grate into the figure's flesh. The figure had their knees clenched tightly to their chest, sobbing into the ripped rags they wore. The figure looked up and through the sodden mess of her hair, Xander saw such sorrow in his friend's eyes. The young Astrid quickly stood to her feet as another face appeared in the flamelight. Crista. A nefarious smile was plastered across Crista's face as she caressed the tip of her blood-soaked blade.

Xander went to stand in her way as a sudden need to protect his friend swelled in his chest but Astrid pulled him back and forced herself to watch with him.

"You could make all of this stop, if you just fought back," hissed Crista, pressing the blade's edge to Astrid's side. The young Astrid squealed as Crista slowly pressed it harder and then flicked its edge.

Astrid clutched the scar on her side as it seared with the pain as if she was experiencing it all over again.

"Why don't you just fight back," yelled Crista, punching the young Astrid in the stomach. "Come on, stop me." She jabbed her with her knife and twisted it before yanking it back out. The young Astrid slumped to the floor, clutching at her wound that seeped with blood, pleading for mercy. "Father, please, make it stop," she cried out.

"Just look at yourself, you're weak," spat Crista, returning the knife to her table. "You need to learn to protect yourself. To fight back."

Astrid needed to look away, just for a second. She knew what came next, what always came next after Crista had had her fun with her knives.

Crista turned on the young Astrid and clicked her fingers, throwing sparks from her palms. Astrid riled in pain as the current surged through her body, throwing her head back as she screamed. Crista continued, pausing for just a few seconds to allow Astrid to regain consciousness, she wanted her to feel each and every shock.

"Please. Stop," breathed the young Astrid, keeled over on her hands and knees.

Crista knelt down next to her, so they were eye to eye, and uttered, "Make me."

The young Astrid steadied herself back on her feet and looked up, her violet eyes sparked. Crista sneered and carried on. Astrid was thrown back against the wall when the sparks hit her square in the chest, but this time, as she screamed, the floors rumbled, and the walls began to shake. Crista faltered as the stones shook beneath her feet and with a high-pitched screech, Astrid rebounded Crista's magic ten-fold. Crista was thrown backwards falling unconscious in a heap on the floor.

Astrid looked at herself standing over Crista's limp body. She could practically hear the thoughts that raced through her younger self's head. The young Astrid snatched a knife from the table and held it to Crista's throat. Her eyes were dark and thirsting for revenge. She thought she was ready to take Crista's life, to rip her heart out if she could, after everything she'd done to her nothing would please her more. She gritted her teeth wanting so badly to slice her throat open, but her hand just trembled.

Vincentrio had appeared in the flamelight. Astrid knew her father always liked to watch, he wanted to be there to see Astrid's power first hand, to take credit for its appearance. He leant down next to his daughter and whispered softly in her ear, goading her demons, "You want to do it. I can feel that hate inside you, use it. End her. Go on. Do it." And with that, Astrid sliced Crista's throat open and took her first life. Crista's eyes opened with fear as she spluttered and clutched at her neck, slowly she choked on her own blood and then her body stopped moving.

Astrid dropped the knife as Crista's face changed and the lifeless eyes of a stranger stared back at her. Astrid fell back to the floor staring at her blood-soaked hands, her breathing heavy. She looked around and Crista appeared in the corner, she clapped her hands together with joy and cackled, looking curiously at the dead body.

"But you… why, why would you make me do that," young Astrid stuttered. "Who is that?"

"I think you mean who *was* that," giggled Crista, standing next to Vincentrio.

"You can't tell me that that didn't feel good, Astrid," remarked Vincentrio, he looked so proud of his daughter. She'd done exactly what he'd wanted, she'd blackened her soul, and, in truth, it had felt good. That was the moment Astrid truly lost herself, the beginning of her end. They'd broken the girl she once was, snapped her in two and, in her place, remained this darkness.

Astrid saw Xander flinch as they watched her young self, realise how good that control was. She took her father's hand and stood tall. With a click of her fingers, her hair was clean and plaited neatly to the side and gone were her tatty rags. An arrogant smile swept across Vincentrio's face as he embraced his daughter.

"You see power isn't born, it's made, and I can't wait to see it used on all the people that have wronged me. That have wronged us," he stated, taking his daughter's hand in his.

"I will not let you down, Father. I will play my role," she vowed.

And with that, the memory was over. Xander and Astrid fell back into the classroom where they'd argued. He let go of her hand and walked away. He leant on one of the desks and dropped his head without saying a word. He hadn't even looked at Astrid. *You've really gone and done it now.* She hesitated and then went to rest her hand on his back. She wasn't sure if he was upset or angry with her or just in shock, he was keeping his face hidden.

"I just need a minute Astrid," Xander warned. His chest heaved, and she could practically hear him grinding his teeth.

"I'm sorry. It's not fair that I've dragged you into my m—" She stopped, Xander had started to laugh hysterically and she didn't quite know what to do, it wasn't the reaction she'd expected. Then he looked up at her and the laughing stopped.

"No." He bit his lip and his muscles stiffened. "Don't you dare apologise. What's not fair is that I never got the chance to smash that bastard's face in." He echoed and smashed a hole in the desk with his fist. Astrid flinched. He shook his fist and simmered his temper, Astrid had experienced enough violence without his input. "Sorry, I didn't even think."

Astrid held up her hand before he could apologise even more and caressed his splintered knuckles, she muttered a mending incantation and the wounds repaired. They both perched on the edge of one of the desks.

"I don't even know what to say," he murmured.

"There's not a lot else to say really," Astrid responded objectively.

Xander gave Astrid's leg a reassuring squeeze and flashed her a small smile. "Did you ever find out who you, you know?" he couldn't quite form the words.

"Who I killed?" she questioned coldly. "No. Crista had been controlling them the entire time though."

"That woman is pure evil," Xander declared distastefully. He imagined what Astrid must have endured at that witch's hand, his stomach churned as his imagination wandered to some dark and twisty places.

Astrid tipped her brows. "That she is. She was good at finding places that wouldn't simply kill me, she knew what she had to avoid, but she just loved to leave her scars. Wouldn't want me to forget," explained Astrid. She held out her arm and let the scars on her forearm show. "I just got very good at hiding them." Then she made the scars vanish again, but she knew they were still there like the rest of the marks Crista had left.

"And your father just let her do these things to you," he said bitterly. "Your father, Vincentrio. And you're still helping him with his revenge." She could see he was trying to process it all, it was a lot to take in at once. "You need to tell one of the professors, we'll go to Professor Ryback, she can help. They're not going to lay a single hand on you again."

"It's more complicated than that." Xander stared at Astrid in disbelief and she glared back. "He's my father, Xander, he just wants what's best for me. He found me. He's all I have left of my family."

"Astrid, *I'm* your family. Simply providing half your DNA does not make him family. He's murdered innocents and he will keep murdering innocents, are you going to really let him drag you down with him?"

"They're not innocents," she spat. "They're the people that ruined *our* lives, Xander. Me, my mum and my dad were a family. We were happy, and he was good. It was *them* that took that away from us, all because of some silly rule."

"That's him talking, Astrid, not you."

"No, *they* are the murderers. They murdered his parents, my grandparents Xander, and then they tried to use him because they were too cowardly to finish what they'd started. They were afraid of what that sort of power could do to a person, but they're the ones that made him a monster," she argued, frustrated that she was the only one that could see that.

Xander sighed, he didn't want to argue with her. He understood why she was making excuses for him and, though he hated the man, he could see it from Astrid's perspective. After all, he only knew him as this warlock who murdered humans and creatures alike in cold blood, he'd never known him as the man before that, the man that Astrid remembered so well. But she was blind if she thought that that man was still in there, he wouldn't have let Astrid go through those horrors and he certainly wouldn't be putting her through all of this.

"I get it, I really do, but you're not a murderer." Xander had calmed himself down now and he could see Astrid settle too.

"I've done a lot of bad things. I don't want to hurt people," she said pitifully. "Things just aren't as black and white as everyone makes them out to be."

"That's the difference, you feel remorse. You can come back from this. I believe you can, I know it," said Xander, his tone changed as he continued, "I just don't understand how making the same mistake your grandparents made is going to help."

"Do we really have to do this now?" Astrid was emotionally exhausted, and she didn't want to row any more.

"We do."

"Look, I tried. I really tried to stay away from him. As you can see I already have enough on my plate, but I fell for him, I fell really hard, and I can't say I regret it, he's the best thing in my life," she admitted, the love she felt for Caius warmed her through. "And I know I don't deserve it, but I think he loves me too."

Xander's frown eased. "You deserve to be happy," he said, his chest heaved as he exhaled slowly. "I want you to be happy. I just don't see this having a happy ending."

"Finally, something we can agree on." She huffed and dropped her head on his shoulder.

"Are you going to tell him or are you just going to suddenly disappear again?" asked Xander.

Astrid could tell he was worried about the possibility of that happening. "I want to tell him, but he's safer not knowing. If something was to happen to him or Hesper or you, I could never forgive myself."

"That doesn't answer my question."

She rolled her eyes. "Where would I even start?"

"Start by telling him you love him and then take it one step at a time from there. He'll understand."

Astrid stood up and fixed her makeup with a click of her fingers. Xander was right, she needed to be honest with Caius and if she didn't go do that now, she probably never would. Before she left, she threw her arms around Xander and hugged him tight.

"Thank you," she whispered. "You won't tell anyone will you? At least until I've figured something out."

"It's not my secret to share." Xander pulled her tighter and dropped a doting kiss on her head. "I know you'll do the right thing."

Astrid pulled herself away and left the classroom to find Caius. She really wished Xander was right about her, but he didn't quite realise how far her father was willing to go and how far she would have to follow him.

CHAPTER 10

Astrid had at least tried to find Caius, but he was nowhere to be found. She'd popped her head back into the Grand Hall and taken a quick stroll around the grounds and still nothing. It just gave her more time to convince herself what a terrible idea telling him really was. She thought to look for him in his dormitory but hesitated at the bottom of the Solonious staircase. She needed to really consider what she was about to do. *Is this really the right thing to do?* Maybe this was the universe's way of saying it wasn't.

Cheerful laughter echoed down the staircase from the common room and Astrid felt herself turn the other way back towards the Armungus dormitories before she could even argue with her own spinelessness. Now was not the right time. She'd try and find him tomorrow, she'd tell him then. *If you've got the guts*. She brushed off her doubts. She would tell him tomorrow and face the consequences.

The Armungus common room was empty, and the fire burned low dimly lighting the room. None of the other students had come back from the dance yet. Astrid draped her coat over the armchair and started removing her jewellery as she made her way into her room. She'd half expected Hesper to be passed out on her bed, but the room was empty. She heard a light creak from on top of the wardrobe, Peewee had found a new spot. Astrid smirked as she saw his puffy paws twitch whilst he slept. She then grabbed the box from underneath her bed again and carefully replaced her mother's hair grip back to where it had been.

"I thought I might find you up here," remarked Caius, his voice smooth like velvet.

Astrid cursed from beside her bed and slowly stood back up, forcing a small smile. He stood in the doorway and Astrid had to take a couple of seconds just to drink him in. His white shirt ruffled around his muscles and a few tufts of golden hair peaked through the open buttons at the top of his shirt where he'd undone his black bow tie. She heard him swallow. His eyes were fixed on her, mesmerised like she was his siren and he'd answered her call. She couldn't tell him anything when he was looking at her like that.

"Do you know how beautiful you look?" he uttered.

Astrid blushed and then quickly walked over to her mirror. "I didn't see you at the dance," she remarked, removing the other pins from her hair as she tried to avoid looking at him, he was so distracting.

"I thought if I went, I wouldn't be able to keep my hands off you."

Astrid trembled as she felt the soft touch of his hands traipse across her bare back and remove the last pin from her hair. Her hair dropped, and he brushed it over her shoulder. She could feel his rhythmic breathing and quivered as he left gentle kisses on her neck and wrapped his arms around her body, pulling her closer against his warm chest. He slowly began to unzip the back of her dress and she closed her eyes. She wanted to tell him everything like she was supposed to, but she couldn't do it. *You coward.* She shut out the voice and stopped thinking, just for now.

A moan escaped her lips as his kisses became more and he sucked at her bare skin. She turned around and took his lips with hers with her hands holding his beautiful face. Her kisses were needy as she licked at his lips with her tongue and pulled him in closer, she wanted more. She needed to feel him, to touch his golden skin, to run her hands through those fine hairs and explore every line of his muscles. Astrid pulled at his shirt and splayed her hands across his chest, his heart was pounding.

Caius dropped his hands around Astrid and lifted her from the floor, nudging the door closed with his foot as he carried her towards the bed never breaking eye contact. Her dress slipped to the floor as he undid the last part of the zip. His lips went dry and he stopped for a minute taking in every curve of her beautiful body. Astrid threw her arms around the back of his neck and tussled his hair with her fingers. She unbuttoned his trousers and heard him suck in a breath as she took him in her hand.

A few strokes and he threw his head back dropping her onto her bed. He took control pushing her hands up and intertwining his fingers with hers. He licked his lips and continued his trail of kisses downwards. Astrid moaned as he spread her legs and worked his way downwards, lapping with his tongue. She cried softly and writhed as he continued to tease her.

"Caius, please," she called quietly, gasping as he continued with his tongue.

He stopped and lightly tracked his fingers up along her belly and traced her bare nipple. He softly kissed her lips and then kept his eyes locked with hers as he dropped himself into her and slowly began to move. She gasped and pulled his face closer, pressing her forehead to his as she felt the impressive size of him fill her. She wrapped her legs around his and moaned as his thrusts quickened. She could feel they were both close. She pulled herself up sitting up right with their legs entangled round each other. He bit her lip and growled as she moved herself slowly around him, tightening as she did so. Then she let go and threw her head back with a cry as the euphoria pulsed through her body and Caius clenched her tighter filling her with a sudden gasp.

Astrid dropped her head on his shoulder as his chest heaved and relaxed against hers. She carefully lifted herself off and they both fell back onto the bed lying next to one another. Astrid rested her head, leaning into him as she kneaded the few golden hairs scattered across his chest. This was what she'd wanted, what she'd craved. She wanted to stay like this, to fall asleep to the soothing sound of his breathing. He stroked her hair and left a gentle kiss on her head. He wiped the dried tears with his thumb and traced the scars across her body. She could see he wanted to ask her where they were from, the question was on the tip of his tongue, but she nuzzled herself against him before he could. One day she'd tell him about them, but not now.

"I wish we were back in that cave," he murmured, softly kissing the scar across her stomach as Astrid played with his beach blonde hair. "I wouldn't have to leave, and we could do *that* all over again."

"You have no idea how much I want you to stay," she smirked.

"I think I have some idea." His mouth quirked as he felt her tremble to his touch, and then he was serious again. "But I really should go, people could come back from the dance any second now."

"You're right," Astrid sighed, pulling the sheets around her as she leant over to grab her pyjamas.

She could feel him watching her. He groaned as he pulled his trousers back on and adjusted his groin. She smiled. That was all for her, and how she wanted to feel him again, but he was right. She'd let herself get carried away and she needed to engage her brain again. Astrid helped Caius button the rest of his shirt and then wrapped her arms around his waist, leaning her head against his chest. He towered over her without her heels on. She drew in his smell and held him close. If only she could tell him now. She could feel the truth like a lump in her throat and she so desperately wanted to say it, it was right there. But she couldn't do it. *You really are a coward.*

"I love you, Caius," Astrid whispered into his chest. She felt him tense, he'd definitely heard her. At least she could be honest about one thing. He didn't say anything. She was scared to look up. Maybe I shouldn't have said anything, she thought to herself, clinging tighter to his body.

"I lo—" Caius stopped and turned his head towards the door. There were voices coming from the common room and the sound of more footsteps up the stairs. He crept towards the door and slowly opened it a crack to take a peek. Other students had come back from the dance and none of them were going back to their rooms in a hurry.

"Your bag did look similar to Astrid's, she probably just picked it up by mistake and hasn't even realised," said Hesper, trying to calm her sister as Astrid heard them enter the common room.

Astrid cursed herself. She'd completely forgotten she still had Paige's bag. She'd let herself get side-tracked looking for Caius and then with other things.

"I really hope you're right, Hesper." Astrid could hear Paige was worried and she had every reason to be.

"Look she's probably only just gotten into bed, why don't we go ask her."

Astrid's eyes widened, this would not look good. Before she could panic, Caius hushed her into bed and then confidently walked to the door. His hair had darkened, and his shoulders grew broader as he snuck through the doorway and carefully closed it behind him. Astrid held her breath and tightly clung to her duvet with her ears pricked, she could just about make out what they were saying on the other side of the door.

"Xander? What were you doing in there?" probed Hesper. Astrid winced at Hesper's accusatory tone, she didn't want to hurt her friend, but the alternative would be far worse for her and Caius.

"I found her stumbling out of the Grand Hall, I think she had a bit too much to drink," Caius explained, his voice deep like Xander's.

Hesper's eyes narrowed on the misbuttoning of Xander's shirt. "Sure," she said bitterly, clearing her throat to stifle a sniffle as she threw open the bedroom door. Astrid could feel her friend's sharp glare, but she dared not move.

"Leave," exclaimed Paige, following her sister. Astrid opened her eyes for a second and saw the regret on his face before Paige slammed the door behind her. Everyone else had gone quiet in the common room.

"What are you lot gawping at?" growled Caius, storming out of the common room. He'd hated hurting Hesper as much as Astrid did.

"Want me to wake her up so I can give her hell?" suggested Paige. She was angry, and Astrid didn't blame her. From her perspective, she was an awful friend, and perhaps she was.

"Just leave it, Paige," barked Hesper.

"You're not going to let her get away with that, are you?"

"There wasn't even anything really going on between me and Xander, I was just kidding myself. Those two have known each other for years, just drop it." Hesper's voice was shaking, Astrid wanted to tell her it was actually Caius, but she couldn't. Not whilst Paige was here. Instead, she had to let her friend think the worst of her and let her heart be broken. *You really are selfish.*

"When someone hurts my little sister, I find it hard to just drop it."

Astrid could hear Paige walk towards her bed and felt her standing over her, she forced her eyes closed and maintained her sleeping position despite how on edge Paige was making her feel. Paige bent down and picked up the bag from beside Astrid's bed, she'd forgotten that's where she'd dropped it.

"See, there's your bag. It was an honest mistake," said Hesper coldly.

"I don't think this girl knows what honest means," spat Paige. She was very protective of her sister, she sighed. "Are you sure you're going to be okay?"

"I'll be fine, you've got work to do," replied Hesper, unfolding her duvet.

"Fine. But if you need anyone to come sort her out, you come find me," instructed Paige, pulling her sister in for a hug before she left.

"You know I can fight my own battles," she replied defiantly.

"I know, Hesp, but you don't have to." Paige squeezed her tighter and then closed the door behind her.

Astrid hoped she'd wait till she got back to headquarters to open the bag, surely, she trusted the seal she'd placed on her bag enough to wait till then. When she'd find the list missing, she might be suspicious of Astrid, but Astrid had been careful not to leave even a trace of her magic. They'd have a hard time connecting it to her. After all, in Paige's mind, Astrid had been too busy fooling around with Xander to do anything with her bag.

Once Astrid was confident Paige had left, she turned over and lit their bedside lamp. She heard a miffed groan from Hesper who had just gotten into bed.

"You've been awake this whole time, haven't you?" sighed Hesper, turning away from the light of their lamp.

"Just let me explain," blurted Astrid, she at least wanted the chance to try.

"It doesn't matter. I don't care, you're free to do what you want. Why not have two guys on the go, I'm sure we can find another one to add into the mix," grumbled Hesper. Then she sat upright in bed, her face scrunched with frustration. "Actually, no, it does matter. Where do you get off stringing Caius along and pretending to love him when you're off getting busy with Xander?"

"Are you quite finished yet?" questioned Astrid bluntly. Of course, Hesper had the right to be angry, but she could at least let Astrid get a word in.

"Am I finished yet? I don't know, did you ask Xander the same question?" she sneered.

"I get that you're angry, but just give me a second to explain what actually happened."

"It was pretty clear, I don't need your account of the sordid details thank you."

"Hesper just shut up," snapped Astrid, that got Hesper's attention. "If you just listen for one second before jumping to conclusions and making snarky remarks." She lowered her voice conscious of the other students that could still be in the common room. "That wasn't actually Xander that you saw leave, it was

Caius. He and I, well you know, he heard your sister outside and thought it would be safer if *he* wasn't seen leaving my room."

Hesper's eyes widened, and the realisation spread across her face as Astrid's vivid thoughts filled Hesper's head. "Oh."

"Oh indeed," smirked Astrid.

"In all fairness, you can't blame me for jumping to conclusions like that, you two have got… history."

Astrid scrunched her face at the thought. "Hesper, he's like my brother."

"I know, I know, but you and Caius, how was that? Actually, your thoughts speak for themselves," Hesper laughed and then her smile disappeared, and a sombre expression took its place. "This just got serious, Astrid, you know I'm always up for bending a few rules but this—"

Astrid sighed and fell back into her bed, she didn't want to have this same conversation again so soon. She was exhausted emotionally and physically. Besides, Hesper was the last person to be lecturing her on being with Caius when she had a hand in it all. Astrid turned off the light and let her head sink into her pillow.

"I'm just going to keep talking at you," snarked Hesper when she was met by an exasperated groan from Astrid's direction. "I know I encouraged this, but you need to be a bit more careful now. It's still the law."

"And maybe that could change." Astrid scolded herself as soon as she'd said it, the remark had just slipped out.

"I don't see the law changing any time soon. Unless you know something, I don't," fished Hesper.

Astrid shook her head. "It's a medieval law, maybe it's just time for change." And change is exactly what her father would bring to the world. Maybe her father would remove that law for her. Maybe her and Caius could be happy in the new world her father would create. And maybe not.

Astrid could feel Hesper attempting to delve into her mind, she was surprised Hesper even still tried that. Astrid was well practiced at protecting her thoughts from those around her. She heard Hesper sigh and then the rustle of her bedsheets, she'd given up for now. Astrid closed her eyes and let herself drift off, dreaming of more nights she could spend with Caius in this new world she so hoped for.

Astrid awoke suddenly to a numbing pulsing through her head. She looked around frantically holding her palms up to the side of her head, the pulsing was getting harder. It was still dark outside, and Hesper was fast asleep, she didn't even stir as Astrid lifted herself out of bed. A pain like this usually only meant one thing, her father was calling a meeting.

Before she could even grab a coat from her dresser, she'd closed her eyes and opened them to the gloomy caves of Trepidor, she squinted as her eyes adjusted to the light of the searing fires. Her father was sat at his chair beyond the pit. Crista and Bedelia stood either side and a few of his other followers stood before him, their faces were familiar, but she wasn't sure who they were. She heard a couple of them snigger with Crista as she approached; she winced and remembered the silk pyjamas she still wore. No doubt Crista was responsible for bringing her before her father in such haste. Astrid lifted her head and glared at the faces as she stood by her father's side, their sniggers ceased.

Vincentrio's jaw stiffened as he spotted his daughter's appearance out of the corner of his eye, Astrid was sure he'd punish her later. He bit back his tongue and then turned his attention back to his followers gathered before him.

“Thank you for joining us at such short notice, my friends, I’m afraid the news I have couldn’t wait till daylight. As you all know, I’ve been searching for the Perrero gem for some time now and we recently discovered that the last person to see the gem as it was stolen from their home was a young Aramis Perigee.” His followers stirred, the name was not one they knew. “A young man that seems to be alive and well. I’d tasked Bedelia with finding who the boy was now and oh did she deliver.” His lips tweaked, and he gestured Bedelia to continue.

“The boy had hidden his life well, he’d created himself a new life, a new identity that wasn’t easy to find. He now goes by the name Alexander Phelonius, a professor at Vistaldors,” revealed Bedelia, the followers clearly knew that name.

“How can you be so sure?” quipped Astrid in disbelief. He’d be the right age and it would explain a lot, but it didn’t explain everything. Vincentrio sensed the doubt in his daughter’s tone, she could practically feel his glare sear right through her.

“I still have friends in the Guard,” replied Bedelia sternly. “Friends who await the day Vincentrio returns to liberate the world.”

“I’m sure you all recognise his name, the name of the warlock who put your master in chains,” spat Vincentrio.

“My lord, allow me the honour of killing the treacherous bastard,” begged one of the followers.

“No, allow me, my lord,” roared another.

“No, me,” joined another.

Vincentrio smiled at his follower’s loyalty, they shared in his hatred for the man, though it ran far deeper for Vincentrio. Astrid could tell there was more, a part of the story that was missing. “Your dedication means a lot to me, but I need him alive. For now. He has information about the gem that deems him useful. Crista, you will retrieve him for me."

Crista licked her lips in glee. "With pleasure."

"We just need information from him, I don't care how you do it just—"

"Do you think sending your rabid dog is really wise?" interrupted Astrid, the remark spilled out before she could stop it.

The followers fell silent and all eyes fell on Astrid. No one interrupted Vincentrio, but Astrid couldn't help herself, perhaps the lack of sleep was clouding her judgement or maybe it was the thought of losing an unknown connection to her mother. Vincentrio's eyes narrowed as he waited for his impertinent daughter to continue.

Astrid drew her bottom lip between her teeth and continued, "If you want to start a mass panic throughout the school and invite the investigative forces of the Guard to our doorstep then be my guest."

"Leave us," ordered Vincentrio, his hand twitched as he dismissed his followers.

His followers bowed and obeyed their master, leaving quickly with Bedelia and Crista, though they were all keen to see how Vincentrio would reprimand his daughter this time. They all knew he loved his daughter, but disrespect was something he had never tolerated, not from anyone.

The footsteps ceased, and Astrid was left alone with just her father and the howling screams of the prisoners in the pit below. She knew she'd spoken out of turn and she'd done it in front of some of her father's higher-ranking followers. It wasn't something she usually did, but the words had just slipped out.

Astrid dropped to her knees in front of her father and pressed her forehead to his hand. "Forgive me, Father, I didn't mean to be rude, I just think we need to be more careful. They may be slow, but they're onto us, onto you, and without that element of surprise all of this could be for noth—" Astrid was knocked back to the ground, winded by the sharp slap. She pressed a hand to her throbbing cheek and felt the drop of blood where her father's ring had caught beneath her eye.

Vincentrio rose from his chair and glared blankly at his daughter. "I'll take your counsel under consideration," he replied coldly as he walked back to his chamber.

Astrid opened her eyes and she was back in her bed, tucked up beneath her bedsheets. She winced as she rested her head on her pillow, her face would be bruised tomorrow, and she had no idea how to explain it away. *Maybe if you hadn't opened your big mouth.* Astrid cursed her own arrogance. She'd handled the situation awfully and her father had been right to strike her, he deserved more respect than what she'd just shown him. If she was going to handle this mess, she needed to do it more delicately, if she could only get to the professor before Crista had her way. Astrid didn't pretend to like the warlock, but he knew more about her than he'd care to let on. It was about time she spoke to the professor, this time without any pretences.

It was still dark outside, but Astrid was certain Crista wouldn't let the time of day slow her down. Astrid quietly grabbed some clothes from her dresser and snuck out of their bedroom, being careful not to disturb Hesper. She wasn't sure how long she had before Crista carried out her father's order, all she knew was that she needed to get to the professor first.

The corridors were deserted and barely lit, the only sound to be heard was Astrid's brisk footsteps along the stone floor. The door to Professor Phelonius' classroom was open ajar, but she couldn't hear anyone inside. The hairs on the back of Astrid's neck rose as she gingerly pushed the door open.

The room was pitch black, but a light was on in his office, she could see the flicker from beneath his office door. Astrid made her way quietly across the classroom, her fingers poised. Crista could have already been and gone. *Or she could be waiting for you*. Astrid flinched as the classroom door slammed shut. The light vanished from the office door and then the room was black. Astrid stopped still in the middle of the classroom. She could hear another person's breathing, there was someone else here.

"Crista?" called Astrid. She knew how much the witch loved playing games. "You know the darkness doesn't scare me any more." She'd been left in the darkness with far worst demons. She continued round the classroom, listening for the other person's faint movements, they were trying to sneak up on her, take her by surprise. "Enough games," murmured Astrid, holding a ball of fire within her palm.

In the flicker of her flamelight Astrid saw a shadow dart across the room. She threw her fire at the shadow, but it passed right through him singing the wall. Another shadow ran up behind her and she threw another spell, but it passed right through him again. Her eyes widened as another shadow creature sprang at her before she could jump out of the way. The creature had no face, only a mouth with fang like teeth oozing tar. She kicked at the creature as it pinned her down, but she couldn't get a hold of it, her fingers passed right through him. Then another was on her. And then another. Astrid struggled as three shadow creatures pinned her to the floor, they'd bound her with their shadows until she could no longer move. She couldn't move her hands to even cast a spell.

"Show yourself," roared Astrid, her breathing heavy. Crista had never used shadow creatures before, Astrid didn't think she even knew the incantation to summon the demons.

Astrid squinted as the lights came on across the classroom. The shadow creatures squealed through their fangs as Professor Phelonius approached them. He still wore the suit from last night, his bow tie hung round his neck and bags hung beneath his bloodshot eyes. He waved his hands and the creatures obliged, dragging Astrid along the floor and then upright against the wall. Astrid knew he'd been keeping quiet about her identity for some reason, he must have been biding his time, luring her so he could catch her off guard. She spat at him through gritted teeth, her eyes raged as she struggled against the shadow creatures.

"You're lucky these shadow creatures are holding me down," she snarled.

The professor still hadn't so much as said a word, there was resentment in his eyes, but also something else. He took a step closer.

"What are you going to do with me now? Kill me? That would really send a message to my father," said Astrid. His silence was only making her angrier. He was studying her like she was some sort of animal, his expression gave nothing away. "Why don't you grow some balls and get on with it then, Aramis," she yelled.

Professor Phelonius waved his hands and the shadow creatures disappeared. Astrid dropped to the floor. She thought about lunging at him, using her magic to kill him now, but he'd turned his back and was walking towards his office.

"I think it's time we had a real conversation," remarked the professor. He held the door open for Astrid and she chose to follow, her hands were poised in case he tried anything funny. She didn't like the warlock and she certainly didn't trust him.

His office was a mess, papers littered everywhere, shards of his shattered mirror were scattered beneath the frame that still hung on his wall. Astrid noted the blood on the shards and the cuts on his knuckles. An empty bottle of whisky lay on his desk. She sighed, like father like son, she thought to herself. Old photos sat next to the empty bottle, some of the photos were singed, but she could still make out the faces. The same faces that Astrid had used to torture Sir Robert. She wasn't angry any more.

Aramis pulled a photo from the pile and placed it in Astrid's hands. She swallowed hard and fell into one of the chairs as her eyes dropped on the picture of her mother. She looked so young, she must have been about Astrid's age in the photo. She was laughing as she sat beneath a tree, the sun shining over her shoulder.

"You look just like her," murmured Aramis, pulling the other chair next to Astrid's. "I'm sorry about that out there, can't be too careful now that your father knows who I really am."

"How did you—" Astrid's voice broke and she cleared her throat, putting the photo down and out of her sight. "How did you know?"

"How did I know you're Vincentrio's daughter? How did I know your father still wanted me dead? Or how did I know your mother?" He glanced over at the photo and then pulled his focus back to Astrid. "I guess I have a lot of explaining to do. Maybe a drink first?"

"It looks like you're all out," remarked Astrid, gesturing to the empty whisky bottle. Aramis smirked and pulled a bottle of vodka from his desk drawer. Astrid's mouth went dry. "My father doesn't approve of me drinking." Astrid grabbed the bottle and took a long swig.

"Daddy knows best," muttered Aramis wryly as he took the bottle back and held it up before taking a long swig himself. "I could never get used to his new name, Vincentrio, struck fear into a lot of people out there, but it's not as scary when you used to know him as Vinnie."

Astrid couldn't help but snort at the nickname, she took another swig of vodka, she'd forgotten how good it tasted.

Aramis looked longingly at the singed photos as he slumped in his chair. "After I lost my family, I'd decided that I'd make it on my own, I was 13 at the time, but my power lacked discipline, so I took myself off. Went to study at the Academy in Lagen for witches and warlocks. That's where I met Vinnie, and your mother." Aramis paused and took another swig. "Me and Vinnie became friends pretty quickly, best friends. We didn't ask each other too much about the past. It wasn't important back then. Somehow, we always managed to get ourselves into trouble though. And then there was Mia. She was beautiful, talented, boy she knocked us both on our asses a good few times in duelling class." Astrid smiled at the thought. "She really loved your father, Astrid, and Vinnie loved her, I know that. Nothing could come between those two, except—"

"Death," muttered Astrid and then she turned to look at Aramis. "Or you?"

"I—" he stuttered and took another swig. "I loved her, but she loved your father more, and then she had you. I knew there wasn't a future for me and Mia after she had you, you were her world."

Astrid rubbed her eyes and went to grab the bottle, but Aramis held it back. Her mouth twisted as she swallowed the lump in her throat. "So, then what? You betrayed my father because you were, what, jealous?"

Aramis' brows knitted. "Vinnie was like a brother to me," he said, taken aback by Astrid's assessment of him.

"You had an affair with his wife," she yelled, her anger resurfacing. "And then gave him up to the Guard, did you think my mum would have you with my father out of the way, was that it?"

"Astrid, I don't know what lies your father has fed you but I—"

"Oh, save it. I know that my father used to be in the Guard. Everyone there knew exactly who he was and what he was, and they thought they could use him, manipulate him, but he found out the truth. He found out what really happened to his parents and that's when he turned. They made him the man he is today, and so did you." Astrid quickly stood up. "When my mum became ill, we fled to the human world, we hid where the Guard couldn't find us and all you had to do was leave us alone, but you couldn't even do that. My father told me that a man he thought was his best friend gave up where we were hiding and that's how the Guard found us, that's when my father killed all those humans and that's when I got left behind. Now I know that man was you." She clicked her fingers and threw Aramis out of his seat. The bottle fell out of his hands and smashed to the floor beneath him as she held him by the throat with her magic against the wall. She could just see the face of the man that ruined her life, he wasn't even fighting her. Her eyes narrowed. She held his throat tighter and tighter as the rage gripped her.

"Stop," he squealed, his eyes bulging as he struggled for air.

"Give me one good reason why I shouldn't snap your neck," hissed Astrid, she loosened her grip and allowed him to beg.

"Your mother didn't just become ill," exclaimed Aramis, gasping for air.

"You're lying," bellowed Astrid, tightening her grip again.

"It was your father."

Astrid stopped and dropped her hold, her hand shaking as she fell back into the chair.

Aramis massaged his neck and continued, "I went to talk to Vinnie after he murdered those Guard members, I thought I could talk some sense into him. I found Mia and I told her that you and she would be safe if Vinnie just handed himself in, there was still a way back for him. But he came back and saw me talking to your mother. He'd had his suspicions about us before, there was no talking sense to him at that point, he'd got a taste for his power, for blood."

"No, no, no—" muttered Astrid, dropping back into the chair.

"We argued and then he turned violent. Mia tried to stop us both, but she got caught in the crossfire and one of his spells must have rebounded. Astrid, I'm so sorry." He fell to his knees in front of Astrid and gently pressed his hands to hers.

"No, you're lying," snapped Astrid, pulling her hands away. "How do you know it wasn't one of your spells?" But she could see he knew, and yet he clearly still felt as guilty as if it had been his own.

"I wouldn't have used a spell like that on my best friend, what that spell did to your mother I—" Aramis stood back on his feet and started looking for more alcohol in his desk.

"If that were true, why doesn't anyone else know about me? I'm the daughter of the mass murdering maniac, there must be a pretty high price on my head," she questioned, wiping away her tears.

"I wanted to protect you, I owed it to your mother. You're an innocent."

Astrid couldn't help but laugh. "No, I *was* an innocent. If you really wanted to protect me then you would have taken me with you when my father got locked up rather than leaving me alone in the human world. *You* are as much to blame for everything that I've endured and everything that I have done. My father may not be a *good* person, but he is still my father and at least he owns what he is. He doesn't cower behind some hero façade like you."

Astrid had nothing more to say. She briskly walked out of his office and into the corridor before Aramis could say anything. She made it all the way to the gardens outside without even looking back and then her feet couldn't move any further. Her knees buckled, and she fell to the snow-covered ground in a heap. She clenched her knees tightly to her chest and sobbed into them, she cried out as the tears streamed down her red-hot cheeks and then she could feel herself struggling to breathe. It was all too much. Aramis. Her mother. Her father. She could feel her mind cracking.

Then she could hear a muffled call of her name and the crunching of snow as a blurred figure ran towards her. His broad arms were around her and she fell into him, sobbing into his chest. He cradled her and stroked her head, pulling her close.

"Sh, shh, sh, just concentrate on my voice, Astrid." It was Xander. "Breathe with me, come on, in and out, in and out." Luckily, no one else was around; it was still quite early in the morning and Xander had only happened to walk by on his way back from the gym.

"Come on, let's get you out of here," said Xander, feeling how cold she was sitting in the snow, she wasn't wearing nearly enough layers and students would be getting up soon for their breakfast. Xander was certain Astrid wouldn't want anyone else seeing her like this.

Xander took her up in his arms and then flashed them both back to her bedroom and away from prying eyes. Hesper would likely be there, but Xander thought he might need the back up. He'd never seen Astrid in this state before.

They arrived in Astrid's bedroom, scaring Hesper half to death as she walked into the room with just a towel wrapped around her. Xander immediately diverted his eyes before his mind wandered to think about the curves that lay beneath the towel, now was not the time for that. Astrid clung to his coat. She was still sobbing, just quieter now, but she still hadn't said a word. He tried to put her down, but her grip was so tight, she wanted to hold onto the comfort. Hesper immediately dressed herself with a click of her fingers, shut the door and ran over to her friend.

"What the hell happened?" questioned Hesper desperately.

"I don't know. I found her like this outside in the snow, she was hyperventilating and crying, I didn't know what else to do," explained a frantic Xander as he finally managed to set her down on the armchair in their room.

Astrid buried her head in her hands and began to calm her own breathing. She closed her eyes; her head was throbbing. Her father's voice began to whisper in her ear. "Just get out of my head, get out," scrambled Astrid, rocking herself.

Hesper knelt down beside her friend and took her hand gently. "I'm not in your head, Astrid, can you tell me what happened?"

"Get out. Get out. Get out," repeated Astrid over and over again. She could just hear his voice and then flashes of him murdering those humans, of all the things Crista did to her, of all the things she'd done to others. She was breaking, but she didn't want to break, she couldn't break. She tried to fight it. To shut up the voices. To forget the memories. She looked up at Hesper in desperation. "They won't get out, they won't shut up."

"Who won't?" Hesper looked back at Xander concerned.

"The voices. They won't stop," cried Astrid, clenching Hesper's hands.

"All right, all right, let me help you, Astrid," pleaded Hesper. She locked eyes with Astrid's and muttered an incantation under her breath, squeezing Astrid's hands tighter. Hesper fell back to the floor and Astrid was back. The voices had stopped, and she let out a sigh of relief.

"Are you okay?" questioned Xander, helping Hesper back to her feet. "What did you do?"

"Sometimes I can stretch my telepathic magic, I haven't done it very often." She gave Xander a small smile and pressed a hand to her tender head. She blinked away the throbbing pain and then returned to her friend's side. "Astrid?"

"Thank you, Hesper," gasped Astrid. They'd gone from her head, the voices and the images had all gone. Her cheeks heated as she realised the state her friends had just seen her in.

Serious concern gleamed in Hesper's brown eyes. "Who were those people, Astrid? The ones in your head, the ones that were doing such *awful* things to you, was that… real?"

Hesper had seen it all, every cruel memory that Astrid had buried deep in her mind. She'd never seen anything quite like it. She just hoped they were nightmares, and that was all they were, but her heart told her otherwise. Hesper wiped her face with her sleeve and looked at the suffering in Astrid's eyes, she didn't want to ask the question again because she didn't really want to know the answer.

“Maybe it’s time to share it with someone else,” urged Xander.

“Share what?” Hesper glared back up at Xander. “Will someone please just tell me what’s going on? You’re scaring me now.”

Astrid closed her eyes and nodded, “Okay.”

“I’ll leave you two to it,” he smiled and quietly left the girls alone. He was sure to close the door behind him.

“How much did you see?” Astrid’s voice was hoarse from all the crying, but she needed to tell Hesper and she needed to tell her everything.

CHAPTER 11

"You haven't said a single word since I started, not like you to be so quiet," probed Astrid, trying to get a smile out of Hesper. Hesper's face had gone blank since she'd started telling her all that had happened, and she told her everything, starting from the beginning and sparing no detail. She couldn't tell if Hesper was in shock, angry or just didn't quite believe her. "I wanted to tell you sooner, but it would only put you in more danger than you're already in." Hesper's expression turned to confusion. "Hesper, please say something."

"It's a lot for me to process, Astrid, I'm just wrapping my head around it all," muttered Hesper, rubbing her head as she walked around their room.

"Vincentrio is dead," murmured Hesper.

"Well, he's not," replied Astrid.

"And he didn't have a daughter. People would have known. My sister would have told me."

"And yet here I am."

"Here you are."

"Why would I lie about this sort of thing, Hesper?"

Hesper stopped pacing round the room. "Well, if you are who you say you are then I imagine you'd be pretty good at lying, how would I know the difference?"

Astrid winced at Hesper's accusatory tone, she couldn't blame her, but it still hurt all the same. "I don't know what you want me to say," said Astrid.

"Just give me a minute. It's a lot to swallow and if it's true, how can I trust you?"

"*If it's true,*" Astrid snapped and began to unbutton her shirt frantically. "How can I make you believe me. Maybe you want to see my scars, is that it?" She unveiled the burn mark across her stomach. "This was when I ran away from my *responsibilities* at 16." She pulled her shirt to expose the scar on her side. "Oh, or maybe this one, when Crista was trying to get my power to evolve. Let's not forget these, courtesy of Crista and my father." She pulled her shirt off and showed the old slashes on her forearms and then the small burn marks on her hand. "Those were from the human kids at the orphanage. Kids can be cruel huh?"

"Astrid," said Hesper, her face had softened.

"How can I forget this one?" barked Astrid, pointing to the fresh bruise beneath her eye. "My father gave me that one just this morning for showing him up."

"You can stop now, I'm sorry," apologised Hesper, grabbing the shirt Astrid had thrown on the floor.

Astrid's mouth twisted as she swallowed the anger burning through her. "Oh. You don't want to look at them any more. Don't worry I'll cover them up with charms so no one else has to see them, but *I* still know they're there, *I* had to live through them, and *I* still have to," squeaked Astrid, clearing her throat as she felt her eyes water again.

Hesper threw her arms around Astrid and held her close. She didn't want to see the scars because she didn't want to think about her friend being hurt like that. She felt her suffering when she'd seen the memories in her mind, she knew she was telling the truth, but she just didn't want to believe it.

"I guess you believe me now," snarked Astrid, pulling away as she took her shirt back from Hesper.

"I always did, I just didn't want to. Does Caius know?" If he had, he was hiding it very well, thought Hesper, she would imagine he'd want to put Vincentrio through a wall if he could, something she'd be more than happy to help with.

"No. I told Xander yesterday and I was going to tell Caius last night, but—"

The realisation sunk in and Hesper's eyes widened. "Ah, *that* happened. I can see how that might have spoilt the mood."

Astrid had to smile. "Wasn't really the right moment for it."

"You're going to have to tell him at some point."

"Perhaps," replied Astrid.

"Perhaps?" Hesper was confused again.

"And perhaps not. I think it won't be long before my father makes his existence, and mine, very well known," said Astrid half-heartedly. "He's tasked Crista with getting Aramis for him and that witch is about as subtle as a brick through a window. His abduction will cause mass panic and what better time to start his attack. Not that I'm complaining, I don't think I could sit in a classroom with Aramis now that I know the truth."

"You don't mean that," said Hesper, taken aback by Astrid's coldness. "It was your father's spell that killed your mum and what's worse is that he's lied to you about it all your life."

"I'm sure he had his reasons, he's always had his reasons," rationalised Astrid.

"Are you trying to convince me or yourself?" asked Hesper, she saw Astrid flinch. She wanted Astrid to really think about it, the girl she knew wouldn't want to see that many people die.

Astrid's cheeks stiffened. "The last thing I want is for people to get hurt." Astrid's eyes were vulnerable. "But my father is merciful and the world he'll build will be better."

Hesper's brow furrowed. "Listen to yourself, Astrid, he's brainwashed you. I know he's the only family you've got, and you want to see the best in him. I get that, believe me I really do, but he is a monster. Just look at what he's done to you and think of what he'll do to others, do you think he'll be so merciful with the Guard, with my sister?"

"If she follows him, he will," replied Astrid sternly.

Hesper pursed her lips and shook her head. "That won't happen, she'll fight him and so will I. Astrid you're my best friend and I love you, but you need to decide what side you're going to be standing on when the fighting starts." Hesper smiled and then walked towards the door. "I'm going to go find my sister and then we're going to talk to Professor Ryback about evacuating the school."

Astrid clicked her fingers and the door locked before Hesper could open it. Hesper pulled her hand back suddenly as a sharp shock ran from the handle and up her arm.

"I can't let you do that, Hesper," said Astrid, her hands ready. She couldn't fail her father now.

"If I have to knock you on your ass Astrid, I will." Hesper raised her hands, but neither of them made any sudden moves.

"I don't want to hurt you."

"Then help us, help us get the kids out of the school."

Astrid's eyes flickered. "I've done too much already, Hesp, terrible things."

Hesper's face softened, and she stepped towards Astrid. "You are not too far gone, you can come back from this," she said, grabbing Astrid's hand. "What would your mum want you to do?"

Astrid exhaled slowly. "She'd want me to do the right thing." With a click of her fingers, Astrid unlocked the door and she released Hesper's hand. "I can't go with you, but I can try and buy you some time."

"Thank you, Astrid." The corners of Hesper's mouth lifted with a grateful smile and then she left to find her sister.

In the meantime, Astrid would try and stop Crista in the hope of delaying her father's plans. Her mum believed in forgiveness, she'd clearly forgiven her father for what he'd done to her and she'd forgiven Aramis for trying to come between them. Astrid was by no means ready to forgive Aramis, but she also wasn't ready to have his blood on her hands. She quickly tidied herself up and masked the scars on her body, the mark on her face was not so easy. She just hoped that no one would really notice it.

Astrid clicked her fingers and flashed into the professor's classroom. The Christmas holidays had just started, and lessons had finished. The room was bare where Aramis had clearly packed most things away for the holidays. It was a lot less sinister looking in the daylight and Astrid had hoped that he'd retired the shadow demons after last night's altercation. She was sure he wouldn't want a student to be carried away by a shadow demon before they went home for the holidays.

Astrid made her way up the steps towards the professor's office, the door swung open as Astrid lifted her knuckles to knock. Professor Peverel emerged and locked the door behind her, stifling a gasp when she turned around to see Astrid standing there.

"You took me by surprise there, Astrid," remarked Professor Peverel with her hand on her chest. "Is everything all right?"

Astrid could see her staring at the mark on her cheek and her matching bloodshot eye. "I was just wondering if you knew where I could find Professor Phelonius?" she queried innocently, following Professor Peverel back down the steps.

“What’s this regarding?” probed the professor.

“I just really need to talk to him, Professor, it’s about something quite urgent,” pressed Astrid.

Professor Peverel stopped and swept her spectacles onto her head before lowering her voice. “Look, I found Professor Phelonius in a pretty sorry state in the early hours of this morning, rambling about responsibilities after he’d had one too many drinks by the smell of it. I’ve just tidied his office and left him to sober up elsewhere, maybe it’s something I can help with?”

“Oh no, dear, you just won’t do,” smirked Crista, clicking the classroom door shut as she emerged from the shadows where she’d been lurking.

A hard line formed between Professor Peverel’s brows. “Sorry but who are you?” she asked, stepping in front of Astrid. She was wary of the witch’s radiating hostility.

Crista studied the professor curiously as she pressed her lips together. “Why don’t you just make this easy and tell me where Aramis is, then you two can crack on with your little girly chat.” Crista slowly moved towards them as she removed her black leather gloves and tucked them into her cape coat.

“I don’t know an Aramis,” replied Professor Peverel, standing her ground. “I suggest you get off the school grounds and take your search elsewhere.”

Crista arched a thin brow and her ruby red lips twitched. “This day just got a lot more interesting.”

Professor Peverel pushed Astrid out of the way as Crista clicked her fingers and threw one of the classroom chairs at the professor. The professor quickly ducked and then fired a spell at the candle chandeliers above Crista. The chain snapped bringing the lights crashing down. Crista jumped out of the way just in time.

"Now this is going to be fun," cackled Crista, looking up from her hands and knees. She tucked the strand of golden hair that had fallen out of her tight bun behind her ear. Crista screamed as she lurched her hands forward and shattered the glass windows behind Astrid and Professor Peverel.

The professor instinctively retreated to the floor, shielding Astrid from the glass shards. Crista clicked her fingers enchanting the shards of glass, she waved her hands and raised them from the floor. Astrid and Professor Peverel stood up cautiously, they were trapped within a bubble of glass shards. Astrid looked over at Crista unsure whether she'd meant to trap her too or if she was just trying to keep up appearances.

Crista licked her lips as her icy blue eyes gleamed. She'd meant for it to go down this way. "One last chance, tell me where Aramis is and I'll make this quick," offered Crista, tapping her foot impatiently.

"Why don't you just go to hell?" spat Professor Peverel defiantly, using her body to shield Astrid.

Crista's cackles echoed off the walls. "I've already been."

Crista whisked her hands and the glass shards began to swivel around the pair of them. Astrid could hear the glass whistle as it shot right past her and then the glass drew closer. Professor Peverel yelped as the first piece caught her cheek and then another caught her arm and then another caught her side. Over and over again they sliced her skin, cutting deeper as the bubble got smaller. Astrid cried out as a shard plunged into her shoulder. She fell to her knees and screamed through her gritted teeth. Her hand shook as she thought about pulling it out.

"Enough," screamed Astrid, throwing her hands out to the side. The shards shattered, and Crista turned away as the dust cloud passed right through her.

Astrid reached down to help Professor Peverel to her feet. "Are you okay, Professor?"

"I'll be fine, thank you, Astrid. Just a few scrapes, nothing I can't—"

Blood spluttered from the professor's mouth and Astrid's eyes widened as she caught her. Astrid shook as she felt the knife buried in the professor's back and pulled it out before falling to the ground with her limp body. The professor trembled, she tried to speak but the blood choked back her words.

"I'm sorry, I'm sorry," murmured Astrid, taking the professor's hand. Professor Peverel looked desperately at Astrid, her eyes wide with fear.

Crista picked up the knife and stabbed her again. The professor's chest stopped, and her hand dropped. Astrid sat, still holding her limp body in her lap. She looked down at the blood as she tried to wipe her bloodied hands on her bloodied clothes, but it just wouldn't go. She tried again. She took the knife from the dead professor's stomach and slowly stood back up. It was like one of her nightmares. *Maybe that's what this is, maybe it's all in your head.*

"Unpleasant business, had to be done," sighed Crista, taking the blade from Astrid's loose grip. She pulled out a silk hankie and carefully wiped it clean. "Guess we'll have to find this traitor the old-fashioned way, where shall we start? Ehem?" coughed Crista, narrowing her glare on Astrid, her patience was wearing thin at this point. Her ears pricked; there were voices coming from the hallway and then the door swung open.

"I can't believe that you knew about her all this time," exclaimed Paige, frantically storming through the doorway after Professor Phelonius who looked particularly exhausted. "You've endangered so many—" Professor Phelonius had stopped still right in front of her and she stumbled into him. She paused and looked at the horrific scene before them; Astrid was standing coldly over a lifeless body and Paige quickly realised there was no way all that blood was her own. "What have you done?"

Astrid looked up, all the blood had drained from the professor's face as he'd realised whose body it was. His lips trembled, and he dropped to his knees cradling Professor Peverel in his arms. Astrid shook her head as her lip quivered. "I... it wasn't. Wait!" exclaimed Astrid.

Without waiting another second, Paige ran towards Astrid and clicked her fingers, throwing a binding charm at Astrid's dominant hand. Astrid pulled at the charm that cut round her wrist, but it only yanked her wrist closer to the ground. Astrid saw Paige lunge for her other wrist, but she quickly ducked out of the way. She held her free hand up in defence. She could break free from the binding charm with one quick swoop, but she didn't want to fight Paige.

"Stop. Just let me explain, Paige," Astrid pleaded, for Paige's sake more than her own. Crista had concealed herself in the shadows waiting for her moment, a moment Astrid didn't want to give her.

Paige clicked her fingers and bound Astrid's other hand. Astrid didn't even flinch. Paige's face twisted with the fury thrumming through her, she knew she should have trusted her instincts when she'd first met Astrid. "I knew there was something off about you when we first met. Maybe if I'd just listened to my gut—"

“Don’t even go there,” perked Aramis as he rested Professor Peverel’s cold body on the floor and gently closed her eyes. “If there’s anyone to blame for this it’s me.” Astrid’s eyebrows twitched with surprise at the professor’s sincerity. “I’m the one who was naïve enough to believe that *she* was like her mother,” he spat, standing face to face with Astrid. “I’m glad she’s not here to see you now.”

Astrid snapped. With one quick swoop, her hands were free from the binding charms and she clicked her fingers taking tight hold of Aramis with her magic. He clawed at his neck, which constricted with every squeeze of her hand. Astrid found herself smiling, it felt good watching the man who destroyed her life squirm. Watching his eyes bulge and redden. Watching him gasp for air. Then before she knew it, Paige lunged at her, tackling her to the ground. Aramis crashed to the floor coughing and spluttering as Paige pinned Astrid down. Astrid kicked, and her arms flailed as Paige tried to steady her arm to wrap the impotens band around Astrid’s wrist and render her powerless.

“Get off,” yelled Astrid, throwing Paige across the room before she could click the band on. Astrid quickly clambered back to her feet and dodged a near miss charm thrown by Aramis. She clicked her fingers and pulled the floorboards apart beneath his feet. Aramis jumped and waved his hands, encircling Astrid in a ring of fire, keeping her at bay as he tended to Paige.

The flames flickered dangerously close to Astrid’s face when she tried to find a gap and she quickly leapt back, catching a searing whip of a flame on her back. She howled in pain. Her eyes watered as the stifling smoke began to fill her nostrils. She could barely see what they were doing through the flames. With a click of her fingers and a wave of her hands, she duelled with the whipping flames just long enough to escape through a small gap she'd spotted.

The flames began to spread, following Astrid across the classroom and engulfing the wooden chairs and desks as it swept towards her. The flames grew higher and the entire room was soon full of thick smoke. She squinted through her watering eyes at two shadows heading towards the door and clicked her fingers, bringing one of the creaking beams overhead crashing down over the doorway.

"You fancy giving me a chance to do some explaining now or do you want to keep throwing stuff at each other?" called Astrid calmly. Taking control of the flames, she simmered the spread of the blaze just enough to clear some of the smoke that was quickly filling the room.

"Why don't you start by telling us about that list you stole from me, then we'll consider stopping throwing things." Astrid could hear Paige's vexed voice, but she still couldn't quite see where she was.

"I don't know what list you're referring to," she replied evenly with a shrug of her shoulders.

"Oh, don't give me that," said Paige. "The list naming your daddy's followers. The list we recovered from Sir Robert's study. The list that you quite clearly stole from my clutch at the ball."

"I haven't seen my father in years," explained Astrid, the lies left her lips as easily as the truth. "I'm not really sure who you think I am or what I've done—"

"You murdered Skylar, you probably murdered my father and who knows how many others you've hurt," interrupted Aramis defiantly.

Astrid recalled the things she'd done, the sins she'd committed. Too many to count, but Professor Peverel's death was one of very few she wouldn't be held accountable for. "I found Professor Peverel like that, why would I kill one of the only teachers that's ever been in my corner?" posed Astrid. Her voice shook ever so slightly as she thought of that exact sad truth and she took another look at the blood that had now dried on her trousers. Professor Peverel had always been her favourite teacher; her interest in Astrid had been so genuine and she'd been the only professor that refused to give up on her. *And look where that got her,* nagged the little voice inside her head.

"I guess that's another question you'll have to answer when we take you back to the Guard," shrugged Aramis, emerging through the smoke with Paige, the impotens band in hand.

"That's if there'll be any of your little society left by then," snickered Crista, waltzing through the small flames Astrid had been keeping at bay.

Crista clicked her fingers, whisking the band from Paige's hand and into her own. She took one look at it and smiled thinly, pocketing the band in her cape coat. Aramis' eyes widened as a wave of recognition struck him. Her sinister smile and shrilling voice weren't things a person quickly forgot. Before Aramis could throw a spell, Crista had taken control of the flames that still burnt and pulling them with her hands, swept the flickering frenzy round both Aramis and Paige, wrapping around them like jungle vines. A cackle escaped her thin lips and she watched on intently at the both of them, both paralysed, too scared to move for fear of the fires burning through their warm skin.

"What the hell, is that witch doing here?" seethed Aramis, he knew all about the things Crista had done.

"I couldn't let Astrid have all the fun," grinned Crista, playing with the blade she'd used on Professor Peverel. "Or all the credit."

Aramis' eyes widened as he realised who the true murderer was and met Astrid's glare apologetically. Astrid had taken a step back accepting it was Crista's show now and she wouldn't show quite so much restraint as Astrid.

Crista playfully pressed the tip of her blade to her lips. "Oh, how I've waited for this, Aramis," gleamed Crista. "Our master has some prolific plans for his revenge on you."

"Let's not forget my father wants him in one piece," reminded Astrid, spying how twitchy Crista was getting with her knife.

Crista sighed in agreement and proceeded to stroke her blade gently across Paige's cheek. Paige tried not to cower, but Astrid could see the flash of fear in her eyes.

"I don't believe we've been formerly introduced." Crista slowly sliced her blade down Paige's cheek, her smile disappeared as Paige refused to react. "I like this one. Why don't you tell me your name?"

"Paige," she said through gritted teeth as the blood trickled down her cheek.

Crista rolled her head. "Ah yes, the older sister. Where is your little sister? I've heard she's got some particularly interesting talents, think I'd quite like to meet her."

Astrid stiffened. She hoped Hesper wasn't anywhere close.

"If you touch her—" Paige recoiled from the flames that wrapped themselves tighter around her body.

Crista perked her lips. "Tut, tut, tut, if you start throwing threats around, me and you are going to fall out," warned Crista, returning her attention to Aramis.

"I'd leave here whilst you have the chance. Both of you," cautioned Aramis.

Crista couldn't help but laugh. "Are you really that stupid or are you just naive? I don't think you're quite grasping the gravity of the situation."

A long rumble shook the school and Astrid steadied herself as the ground beneath them quaked and dust settled around them from the crumbling walls. The remaining dash of confidence faded from Aramis' face, replaced by concern. Astrid took one look at Crista's cavalier grin and then ran to the doorway to see what was going on. Students were frantically running through the corridors, some were crying whilst others were screaming for their friends. There was mass panic. One student crashed into Astrid as she leant out of the doorway.

"He's here," the girl screamed, quickly re-joining the swarming crowd. Astrid had a bad feeling she knew exactly who they were running from. She hurried back into the classroom.

Crista was at the window craning eagerly to see what was going on outside. "And so it begins," smirked Crista.

CHAPTER 12

"What begins?" questioned Paige frantically. "Hey. Answer me you crazy bitch."

Crista glared back at Paige and then turned to Astrid with a nefarious grin. "Daddy's home."

Astrid knew the day would eventually come, but she didn't expect it to happen all so quickly. She at least thought she'd have some time to protect the ones she loves, try to get them to understand, to join her. *Caius.* She only hoped he kept himself safe, put himself first. *Who are you kidding?* She rolled her eyes, Caius wouldn't do that.

Paige's eyes were wide with panic as the screams crept through the crack in the door. She looked desperately at Astrid. "Astrid you can't want this. What about the little kids who can't defend themselves, what about Hesper?" Astrid glanced back at Paige, conflicted by her emotions, Paige could see a flicker of doubt cloud Astrid's hardened features. "You can help us put a stop to it. Just let us go. We can—"

"That's enough from you," snapped Crista, pinching Paige's lips closed with her magic. "I'm afraid you've outstayed your welcome."

"Wait," exclaimed Astrid.

Crista paused, keeping her blade hovering against Paige's neck, she glared at Astrid and her forehead creased. "What?"

"Why should you get all of the fun?"

Crista smirked and summoned the knife back to her. "I don't need to tell you how to use this," she muttered, placing the knife in Astrid's palm.

Astrid smiled and, without Crista noticing, she murmured a charm under her breath and the flames around Paige's body dropped. Paige took her moment. She clicked her fingers, throwing the remnants of the fallen beam at Astrid and Crista. They both ducked, and Crista returned fire with an assortment of counter-charms. Astrid waved her hand. Crista cursed as a stray piece of wood caught her forehead. She was distracted just long enough for Paige to escape through the doorway.

"Dammit," roared Crista, running after her through the doorway, but Paige was long gone, lost in the panicked crowd. She held her hand to the gash on her forehead and snarled. "I swear if you tell your father about this." Crista eyed Aramis warily, he hadn't so much as moved an inch. She snapped the impotens band around his wrist and then took hold of his arm. "This one's got a cell with his name on it. Make sure you save some blood for me." Crista licked her lips at the thought and then with a flash she was gone.

Astrid took a moment to collect herself. It seemed the stampede of students in the corridor had subsided, yet their screams carried through the time-honoured halls. She stopped and looked around at the scorched classroom. The remainders of Professor Peverel's blood still smeared on the floorboards. The remains of her body were barely recognisable. The flames had not been kind. Astrid took one last mournful look and then clicked her fingers, setting the remains alight and giving the professor some final peace. Once the professor had returned to ash, she extinguished the flames.

Caius. Her priority was him and only him. She had to find him before someone else did.

Astrid made her way towards the doorway and checked it was clear before venturing into the hallway. It had suddenly gone eerily quiet. She looked around but there wasn't a soul to be found. *Where would he be*. She continued down the corridor. A shrilling scream echoed from below, it must have been coming from one of the underground corridors. She quickly brushed it off and continued walking. Another scream sounded from below again, this time it sounded painful, enough to chill Astrid to the bone. *Oh dammit.* She swivelled around and made her way to the underground corridor following the scream.

The underground corridor was barely lit. A single torch remained alight. Astrid steadied herself as she adjusted to the darkness. She stumbled on a few rocks that had fallen from overhead with the initial quake. A limp hand was visible beneath a pile of rubble, but she thought it best not to think too much about it. She continued cautiously around the corner, treading carefully as the light dimmed.

"Hello? Anyone down here?" Astrid called, but there was no answer. *Just turn back.* The coward inside her wanted to run back. Back to the light. Back to the open space. Memories of being trapped in darkness flooded back. The kids at the orphanage quickly realised how well she fit into one of the boy's chest of toys. How easily they could squash her in there, leaving her for hours screaming. She'd sit there whimpering, wondering if they'd ever let her out. "You'll keep your mouth shut if you know what's good for you," they'd snarl under their breath.

The tunnels shook again, and another helpless cry brought Astrid back. She swallowed hard and took a deep breath. She clicked her fingers and held a ball of light in her palm. Holding it out in front of her she could just about make out a small body on the ground. The girl looked up desperately through her ragged raven hair as she heard Astrid approach. A wave of relief swept over the girl's face.

"Astrid?" mewled the girl, her voice hoarse from all the screaming. "Thank god it's you."

Astrid stepped closer, it was Katy. Astrid threw the orb of light above them and rushed to help Katy up, it seemed she was caught on something.

"My leg," cried Katy. It was trapped under a pile of rocks. When Astrid looked closer, she could see a wall of rubble was blocking the rest of the corridor.

"The corridor caved in on me when there was that first quake. What the hell even was that? What's going on up there?" questioned Katy feverishly. She gasped as Astrid tugged at her leg.

"Sorry," winced Astrid. She was trying to figure out how she could dig Katy out without collapsing the rest of the corridor, every rumble of the walls put her on edge.

A shadow darted across the crumbling wall past the rubble. Astrid stopped digging. She could have sworn she saw a figure through the rocks. The hairs on the back of her neck had shot up and she shivered as a soft breeze swept past her, the remainders of a whisper carried by its current.

"Did you hear that?" Astrid's eyes darted upwards. She was sure she heard the clatter of stones echo off the walls. "Was there someone else down here?"

"I'd like to think if there was, they would have helped me by now," replied Katy tartly as Astrid peered through a gap in the rocks. "Can you just help me get my leg out please?"

"Sure." Astrid paused, she shone the light through the gap and scanned the rest of the corridor. "I just thought I saw—"

A clawed paw burst through the stones, grabbing hold of Astrid. She screamed as the razor-sharp claws pierced her shoulder and wrenched her through the rubble. Astrid coughed and spluttered clinging to the throbbing puncture wound on her shoulder. She fumbled on the ground, her eyes adjusting to the dark. She could hear the creature's heavy breathing. He smacked his lips and the stones crunched beneath his hefty paws. She could just about make out a hazy outline of the creature. It was well muscled, crouched on all fours, stalking her like prey or maybe the creature was just playing with her. She saw a flash of his teeth and a gleam of his blood red eyes.

"Astrid?" called Katy, her voice trembling. "What the hell was that? Are you okay? Talk to me Astrid."

Astrid clambered to her feet. She looked up and saw the beast lunge towards her. She leapt out of the way just in time and the beast fell against the rubble wall. Katy screamed as more rocks fell on her foot. Light from the other side seeped through the crumbling wall and Astrid saw the creature shake himself off. He turned back to Astrid, his hackles up and his back hunched. She crept backwards, her breathing heavy.

The creature crept closer and Astrid stopped, her back against the wall. The creature had her cornered. It snapped its jaws and pounced forwards. Astrid ducked out of the way, the beast's teeth narrowly missing her arm. She clicked her fingers and thrust her hands forward. The beast howled as the rocks crushed him against the wall. Astrid pulled the walls apart bringing the tunnel crashing down on the beast. She fell in a heap and threw her arm over her head deflecting the rocks as they fell. The rocks fell around her and she closed her eyes.

"Astrid. Astrid." She could hear a deep voice calling her, it was frantic, distraught. *Caius.* He was digging at the rocks in a frenzy. She tried to call for him, let him know where she was, but she could barely move. It was taking all her energy to keep the rocks from crushing her.

Astrid squinted, dazzled by the burst of light. A warm hand grabbed hers and hauled her from the rocks pulling her into his heaving chest. Caius held her close and she wrapped her arms around his waist, dropping her head against him. It took every piece of her strength not to fall apart. She trembled as he gently stroked her hair, his voice soothing to the ear.

"I'm here. I'm here," he repeated, holding her tightly.

"I'm so glad you're okay," said Astrid as she pressed her head firmly against his chest and savoured the moment. She'd thought the worst and she couldn't bear to let him go again.

"I'm okay? I'm not the one who was stuck under a bunch of rocks." He cracked a small smile and lifted Astrid's chin, leaning down he rested his forehead on hers and took her lips tenderly.

"Don't worry about me guys. My leg's been stuck for a while now, what's a couple extra minutes," remarked Katy with a heavy sigh.

Caius quickly pulled away. He dropped to Katy's side and, with all his strength, he lifted the rock trapping Katy's leg just enough for Astrid to drag her out. Katy could feel the bile rise in her throat as she took one look at her mangled leg, but before she could dwell too long on the ramifications of her injury, Caius had wrapped her arm around his neck and hauled her onto her feet. She squealed as her leg dragged along the floor and Astrid quickly took her other arm.

"Don't worry, Katy, we'll get you to Professor Peverel. She'll know what to do. Your leg will be fine," said Caius reassuringly.

"I think the professor might be a bit preoccupied," lied Astrid, helping Katy up the steps and back to the ground floor hallways.

They were halfway up the steps when the frantic screams started again. Caius and Astrid stopped dead in their tracks. Neither of them had any idea what would be waiting for them at the top of the steps.

"You two hold on here and I'll see what's going on," whispered Caius, propping Katy up against the wall.

"No, wait." Astrid grabbed Caius' arm. "I'll go."

"Like hell," exclaimed Caius, shirking free of her grip.

Astrid lunged onto the step above him and splayed her hand across his chest, nudging him against the wall. "Look. I won't be able to carry Katy anywhere on my own. You can. Just wait here," she ordered in hushed tones.

Caius glared back at Astrid but chose not to argue with her. She had a point.

Astrid crept up the last few steps and, keeping close to the wall, took a look around the corner. A young witch ran straight past her, blood was pouring from her nose and tears were streaming down her cheeks. She barely even noticed Astrid. Astrid retreated against the wall as she heard the sound of more footsteps. Two warlocks raced after the witch, throwing spells ahead of them, purposely missing the witch by a hair's width. It was just a game to them. Astrid held her breath hoping they also wouldn't notice her. She heard them snigger and continue after the witch. Astrid carefully glanced around the corner. They'd both gone and all she could hear were distant whimpers.

"It's clear." She kept her eyes fixed on the corridors whilst Caius carried Katy the rest of the way up the steps.

"Can someone please tell me what's going on," pleaded Katy, noting the blood trail stained along the hallway.

"It's Vincentrio," Caius spat angrily.

"The maniac who killed all those humans?" questioned Katy in disbelief. "He's supposed to be dead."

"He's very much alive," exhaled Astrid. She told herself that she'd explain everything to Caius once they got somewhere safe. Then she'd tell him the truth, all of it. Till then she needed to keep him safe and step carefully. Her father's followers were swarming all over the school and it appeared they weren't looking to take many prisoners.

Astrid glanced back to make sure Caius was following her closely. She peered around the corner and jumped back quickly, ushering Caius against the wall. It appeared the warlocks had caught up to the witch. The witch squealed as they pinned her to the floor. Anger flashed in Caius's eyes and before Astrid could stop him, he'd propped Katy against the wall and strode around the corner.

Caius grabbed one of the warlocks and threw him against the wall. The other warlock looked up suddenly from the girl and was met by a swoop of Caius' fist. The witch trembled on the ground, her face was bruised, and her body battered, her eyes were wide with fear. Caius tenderly offered his hand, but the witch ducked out of the way as Caius was struck by a bolt of lightning square in the back. He howled falling onto his face. The witch stumbled to her feet and ran. The warlock continued to shock Caius, the other warlock massaged his jaw and dealt Caius a weighty kick to the stomach. He sniggered watching Caius writhe in pain.

Astrid leapt from around the corner. Clicking her fingers, she pulled one of the banners from the wall and wrapped it round one of the warlocks. She burned with anger. Clenching her fists, she sucked the banner tighter round the warlock. The warlock gasped, blood spluttering from his mouth as his ribs started to snap. Astrid clenched her fists tighter, her eyes firmly fixed on the warlock.

The other warlock quickly sprang into action. He waved his hands and threw Astrid across the hallway, breaking the hold she had on his friend. He ran to his friend and muttered an incantation, pressing his hands to his friend's panting chest. The warlock gasped and took his friend's hand as he sprung back onto his feet.

Astrid looked up from the floor. Her vision was blurred, and the walls seemed to spin around her. The two warlocks sauntered towards her. One whisked his hands and held her flat on the floor. Before he could do anything, Caius came up from behind bounding towards the warlock in the form of a grizzly bear. With one swipe of his claws, he'd ripped the warlock's arm off. The other warlock swivelled around. Caius had shifted back into himself and threw his whole weight at the warlock, tackling him to the ground. He smashed the warlock's head on the stone and pounded his face with his fist again and again and again. Rage pulsing through his veins.

"Caius. Stop. That's enough," cried Astrid, trying to pull him off the warlock. "You'll kill him." *And that wasn't Caius.*

But Caius continued to punch the warlock again and again until his knuckles bled, and the warlock's face was unrecognisable. Caius fell back to the floor. His chest was heaving, and his hands still trembled as he looked at the mess he'd made. Katy leant frozen against the wall speechless.

"It's okay, Caius. Look at me," ordered Astrid on her knees next to him. She took his hands in hers and pulled his gaze back to her. *He's never had to do this before.* "You did what you had to do. You did it to protect us, to protect me." She could see he was coming back round, his rage was simmering, and his breathing was slowing. Astrid looked around frantically, any one of her father's followers could come across them at any moment. "We need to get out of here. Caius. You need to get up. Now."

"You're right," he stammered, pulling himself back together. He picked up Katy being careful to approach her steadily, he saw her flinch as he walked towards her. Caius then continued down the corridor with Katy in his arms as he led the way to the Grand Hall.

"Where are you going?" called Astrid, briskly jogging after him.

"There's a group of students hiding in the room above the Grand Hall. Professor Ryback and Professor Towinni are there too, we'll be safe there," explained Caius, pausing as he saw a group of Vincentrio's followers approaching the Grand Hall doors.

Crista stood at the helm. She pressed her hand to the grand mahogany doors and grinned as she felt the magic pulse beneath her fingertips.

"Child's play," smirked Crista. She clicked her fingers and burst through the doors, blasting them off their hinges and across the Grand Hall. Crista waltzed into the Grand Hall, the other cloaked followers close behind her. An evergreen forest tree towered in the centre, its crown skimmed the floor of the hidden overhead room. Crista palmed one of the silver ornaments that hung from a low branch and removed it from the tree.

"Merry Christmas," she murmured as she clicked her fingers and set the tree ablaze.

The rest of the followers crowed at the burning tree. They pulled the portraits off the wall and tossed them into the blaze. They smashed the crystal glasses all laid out on the tables ready for the annual Christmas feast and burnt the tables too.

Crista's eyes gleamed with the flicker of the great bonfire. "Find that snivelling excuse for a headmistress. She's cowering around here somewhere. Our master wants her, and he *will* have her," barked Crista, striding through the Grand Hall.

"I don't think anyone's safe in there," remarked Astrid, about to turn back the way they came.

"Professor Ryback enchanted the room so they wouldn't know it was there," replied Caius.

"And how do you suggest we get up there?" chimed Katy.

"Astrid can flash us up there, right?"

Astrid scrunched her face. Her father was sure to have put some enchantment on the school that stopped people flashing in and out, otherwise students and teachers would have easily been able to escape. "I don't think that sort of magic will work. If it did, Professor Ryback would have flashed everyone out of here. Instead, we're all stuck. Trapped," explained Astrid with a heavy sigh.

Caius' brows knitted, and he shook his head. "Not true. I saw one of *them* do it earlier. Maybe he's just restricted it, so no one can leave the grounds."

Astrid's face loosened, she couldn't fault his reasoning. "It's worth a try," she said. Taking hold of Caius' hand, she closed her eyes and clicked her fingers.

Astrid opened her eyes to a room full to the brim with students. Groups of students were huddled together. Older students were trying to reassure the younger ones, trying to keep their cries quiet in fear of being discovered. Professor Ryback was crouched next to Reuben and Zack in the corner, she laid a consoling hand against Zack's back as Reuben cradled his dead sister in his arms. The pang of guilt lay heavy in the pit of Astrid's stomach as she gazed at Erin, her body cold and lifeless, her face swollen and bruised. Astrid forced herself to look. Forced herself to feel the loss Erin's brothers felt. She cursed her father. *Why did he have to do it like this?*

Professor Towinni appeared from the back of the room, immediately leaping into action when she saw Katy's mangled leg. With a whisk of her hand, she'd thrown her unruly hair up into a bun out of the way and helped Caius set Katy down on the floor. Katy squealed as the professor examined her leg, taking care not to touch it too much. She popped the cork off a small vial of thick liquid from her pocket and passed it to Katy.

"For the pain," explained the professor, gesturing to Katy to drink it. Katy took one sip and pursed her lips. "That won't do. All of it, Miss Nickelson."

Katy swigged the remainder and threw her hand over her mouth as she tried to keep it all down. "Can you do anything for it?" pleaded Katy, her eyes filling with tears every time she looked at the mess that was once her leg. Caius tried to reassure her, but even he found the sight of her leg difficult to stomach.

"Maybe," the professor replied sharply. She worked frantically and cut away the remainder of material that clung to her leg. As the professor peeled away the last piece of blood soaked trouser, a shard of Katy's shin bone peeped through the broken skin. Katy wailed as she caught sight of it. "We can't have any more of that," snapped the professor, trying to keep her voice quiet.

"What do you expect? I can see my goddamn bone," screamed Katy through the tears.

"And if you carry on, we'll all be seeing a lot more bones," hissed Professor Towinni, anxious that someone would surely hear Katy's screams.

Grayson pushed through the crowd of cowering students and dropped to his knees next to Katy. Tears streamed down her heated cheeks as he took hold of her hand and dropped a gentle kiss on her forehead. She thought she'd never see him again. "You squeeze my hand as hard as you need to, Katy. I'll be here with you," soothed Grayson, nodding to the professor to continue.

"Be better if she just passed out," muttered Professor Towinni, mumbling an incantation under her breath and snapping the bone back into place.

Astrid winced at the sound of Katy's bone snapping into place. She looked around the room for Xander or for Hesper, but all she saw were the mournful faces of students she barely knew. Professor Ryback looked up from the twins and caught Astrid's gaze. The professor studied Astrid's weary appearance; she noted the dried blood staining Astrid's trousers and the wound still gaping in her shoulder from where the beast underground had attacked her. She eyed her suspiciously. *She definitely knows something about you.* Astrid's eyes darted across the room, but the professor gingerly approached her.

"Sit down, let me take a look at those wounds," advised the headmistress.

"I'm fine, just a few scratches," replied Astrid quickly.

"You look like you've been through it, Miss Harper." Her tone sceptical. "I don't suppose you saw Professor Peverel out there? Or Professor Phelonius, maybe?"

Astrid kept herself guarded, the professor was fishing, it was like she knew very well what had happened to her professors. Astrid looked back at the professor innocently. "No, Professor. I haven't seen either of them since the ball. I just hope they're both okay."

"Liar," growled Paige, emerging from the other side of the room.

Paige strutted towards Astrid, her face flashing red with fury. The room fell suddenly silent and all the students looked towards Astrid who firmly stood her ground even as Paige came towards her.

Caius quickly stood between the two of them in an attempt to calm them both. "I don't know what this is about, but I think you need to just take a step back," warned Caius, ready to defend Astrid, there was no way he was letting anyone else hurt her.

Paige laughed uncontrollably in his face and looked past the wall of muscle at Astrid. "He doesn't know, does he? Absolutely clueless."

"Know what?" probed Caius, turning to Astrid.

Astrid glared bitterly at Paige and bit back her anger, this was not how she wanted to do it. Her jaw relaxed as she glanced at Caius. "I'm… my father—" the words choked in her mouth.

"Vincentrio is her father," interrupted Paige, announcing it to the entire room. "That's right. Daddy's little girl here has been spying for him this whole time. Scheming with him."

The room erupted with angry murmurs, but the only person in the room Astrid cared about was Caius. She reached for his hand, but he quickly snatched it away, his eyes full of hurt. "Caius just let me explain," she begged desperately as he stepped out of the way. He couldn't bear to even look at her right now.

Paige stood face to face with Astrid, her jaw taut. "She helped murder Professor Peverel." The room erupted with more gasps and Paige continued, "She helped abduct Professor Phelonius. Abduct Sir Robert and do God knows what to him. Worst of all *she* let these monsters into this school. Into your home. All that blood that's been spilled today, that's on you."

Astrid bit her lip and took a deep breath. "What about Hesp—" Paige slapped her hard across the face. Astrid touched her hand to her cheek as it throbbed, the slap rivalled the ones she received at her father's hand.

"Don't you dare speak my sister's name," snarled Paige. "No one's seen her, not that you'd care." Her eye's reddened and she swallowed her grief retreating to Professor Ryback's side.

"What shall we do with her now?" questioned Professor Towinni, her fingers poised.

Astrid could feel the glares from the other students. *If looks could only kill.* Her fingers twitched, and her eyes darted across the room assessing how many students were about to pounce.

"Why don't we just kill her?" exclaimed Zack coldly. "Send her body to her father, lure him out."

Astrid glared back, trying not to show any fear though her heart was beating so hard she could hear it drum through her ears. She knew better than to show them weakness. She waited for some sort of protest from Caius, but he'd absolved himself, slumped against the wall. *What did you expect really?*

"Would certainly send him a message," quipped Paige.

"I don't think that would be wise," advised Professor Ryback, attempting to take command of the situation. "For all she's done, she's still just a child of *his* making."

"Threatening me really isn't a good idea," Astrid warned confidently. Professor Ryback shot her a look to keep quiet, but she continued, "Unless you want more to die."

"What are we waiting for? Let's just kill her now," snapped Zack, his anger spiked. A few other students stood up in agreement.

"Tut, tut, tut, tut, you should really listen to my daughter," suggested Vincentrio, appearing next to Astrid with a hand reassuringly on her shoulder.

The students screamed and frantically looked for an escape, but his hooded followers had surrounded them. No one was going anywhere. Astrid looked up at her father surprised, she'd never been so pleased to see him. She dropped to her knees before him and pressed her head gently against his hand in respect. He smiled dotingly down at his daughter and lifted her chin gently.

"You didn't think I'd leave you to the wolves, did you?" He helped her to her feet and examined her, worriedly eyeing the gash still gaping on her shoulder. "Who did that to you?"

"I encountered one of your werewolves in the underground corridors. It's nothing, Father," Astrid assured him.

"Primitive beasts," he spat. Vincentrio pulled his daughter close for a hug and she fell into his embrace, she could feel how proud he was of her and that was reward enough. Then she looked back at the faces of those she'd betrayed, she looked at Caius who still slumped against the wall even with Crista's hostile presence right next to him. The pang of guilt stung all too deep again, but she shoved her shame down and held her head high. Her father's love was all she had now, and, to her, that was worth the hate of all the others.

Vincentrio returned his attention to the rest of the creatures, revelling in their fear. He gazed upon the creatures he'd soon shape into his followers. He saw defiance in some of them. Spirit. But spirits were easily broken and so fun to break. He eyed the headmistress who frowned at him with such resentment, and he smiled. Many of these creatures had thought him to be dead, some probably thought he was just a myth. Few of them really knew what he was truly capable of, but they would soon find out.

CHAPTER 13

Each day that had passed since Vincentrio's ascension to power felt like an eternity to a prisoner in a Trepidor cell. Every day started the same; the prisoners were woken by the snarl of the beast that guarded their cells and fed a bowl full of gruel, just enough to keep them alive. That was when the helpless cries of prisoners would start. Each prisoner would first try to plead and reason with the beast, begging for anyone that could hear them to release them, but the begging would only last a few days. Eventually, the begging would turn to anger, but the anger would only worsen their punishment.

Every day, Crista chose a new victim to torment, to break, she liked to describe it as giving them a fresh perspective. Some prisoners chose to join the cause whilst others — the stronger willed — chose to endure her punishments instead and soon entered the final stage of being a prisoner of Trepidor. Acceptance. For those prisoners, the month of solitude within their cell had not been kind.

A new day was dawning, and the desperate cries of prisoners had started echoing throughout the airless pits. Astrid marched down the endless rows of prison cells, ignoring the filthy hands that stretched through the metal bars desperately trying to pinch a corner of her cloak. She was never sure if they were trying to plead with her or trying to hurt her. Not that it mattered, she never let them get close enough.

Astrid wrinkled her nose and swallowed the bile that had surfaced. She'd grown so used to the stench of Trepidor that it usually didn't bother her, but her stomach was feeling particularly sensitive today. She'd woken with an unsettling feeling early this morning and, for the first time, her fear had given her enough courage to face Caius. Something she hadn't been able to do since *that day.* She needed to see him, just to make sure he was okay, maybe talk to him. *To say what?* Astrid had convinced herself that she'd been protecting him by not visiting; she needed time to plead her case to her father, preferably before one of his minions found out and told him first. *Who are you kidding, you've just been thinking of yourself?*

Astrid stopped still. His cell was just down the end. She knew he was down there, she'd checked many times whilst he'd been sleeping, that way she didn't have to see the hurt in his eyes. She urged herself on, but her legs wouldn't move. *You need to do this.* With a burst of courage, she put one foot in front of the other and continued towards his cell.

"Astrid," called Crista, striding down the cell block.

Astrid cursed and turned around. *Tomorrow.* "What can I do for you?" questioned Astrid, plastering a small smile on her face.

"I'm surprised you still have a reason to be down here," spurred Crista.

Astrid's eyes narrowed, but she did her best to hold her tongue. "Is there something you wanted?"

"There are many things that I want, but right now it's our master's needs that I continue to accommodate." She licked her lips devilishly. "He wants to speak with you."

"You can tell my father I'll be there shortly," replied Astrid, she swallowed the bile that had resurfaced.

"He wants to speak with you *right away*," emphasised Crista. "Your shapeshifter can wait."

"Fine," she said through gritted teeth.

Astrid reluctantly followed Crista to her father's torture chamber. She quickly glanced back, and her heart ached when she saw Caius' shadow linger by the bars of his cell like he'd been waiting for her. She yearned for just the touch of his hand, but her emotions were not important at this time. The more Astrid did to please her father, the more likely he was to be sympathetic to their case, so she'd continue to please him.

The doors to her father's torture chamber opened and two men emerged, dragging a prisoner between them. The prisoner's head hung low and what remained of her tatty rags hung loosely on her frail body. Astrid barely recognised Paige now, it was remarkable the difference a month could make. She took a deep breath and watched them drag Paige back to her cell. *They can't all be your problem.* And yet the guilt still weighed heavy on Astrid's soul, something she was surprised she still even had at this point.

Vincentrio stood over the table of tools in the corner of the room, he carefully laid the poker back in its place and adjusted the rest of the instruments before turning to smile at his daughter. He held his arms open and Astrid obliged, shivering against him as she spotted the wear on the instruments she knew all too well.

"Leave us," ordered Vincentrio to Crista, ensuring the door was closed behind her. Vincentrio turned to his daughter and slowly unrolled the sleeves of his crisp blue shirt as he gestured for her to take a seat. Astrid noted the single chair and sat down, she stiffened when she saw the bloodied chains attached to the chair legs, she remembered all too well how they felt around her wrists.

Vincentrio pulled up a chair next to his daughter and then grasped her hand gently, looking upon her with such pride. "We rarely get time alone these days and I just wanted to take a moment to tell you how grateful I am to you," he said with the deepest sincerity.

"Grateful?"

"I'm grateful that you've stuck by me. I know we've not always seen eye to eye and I won't be winning any father of the year awards anytime soon, but everything I do is because I love you. Like any father I want the best for you. I want to give you everything. I want to give you—" His voice broke and he cleared his throat. "I want to give you the world. The world that people *ripped* away from you, from me… from your mother. And you will have those worlds my sweet."

It had been years since Astrid had seen her father so vulnerable, she saw a glimpse of the father she knew before all the madness and it gave her hope. She squeezed his hand and smiled. "You don't have to explain anything to me."

"I just need you to understand. I was born for greatness but you, Astrid, were born for even greater things and I *need* you to remember that, but first I need your help with something." Vincentrio stood tall and summoned his staff, his superior persona returning.

"Anything," replied Astrid quickly.

"It's not just about our world and the human world any more, it's the land of the dead and the world in between. With both my gem and the Perrero gem I can create portals to all of those worlds and we'll be able to rule it all. Together. Masters of life and death. Exactly as it should be."

"But the Perrero gem is still lost," Astrid muttered, trying to wrap her head around the extent of her father's plans. She always knew he wanted to rule, to have power, but for a warlock to even step into the realms of the dead, it was unheard of.

"That's why I need your help," admitted Vincentrio. "Even without his powers, Aramis is adamant to keep his secrets to himself. Your Concilium magic is far superior to anyone else's. We need it."

Astrid hesitated. The thought of going into that warlock's head frightened her; she'd seen the tricks his father could play on the mind first-hand and she knew there was a history there that she wasn't sure she wanted to see. "I know who he was to you, father. He told me what happened." She didn't want to keep more secrets from him, he would find out eventually. Astrid could see the rush of anger flashing in his eyes and his jaw tightened, but she took his hand and continued, "And I don't blame you. It was an accident. What good would it have done for a four-year-old to learn her father, the one person she has left in the world, was responsible for the death of her mother?"

"None," he replied softly as he tenderly wiped the tear beneath her tired eyes.

"I would do anything for you," she asserted.

"Let's get started then."

The doors swung open and Astrid stood up, making way for the new prisoner Crista trailed in. She threw him into the chair and clicked her fingers, shackling the chains to his hands and bare feet. Aramis sniggered and wiped his bloodied nose on his soiled shirt. He rolled his head back with a heavy sigh and eyed Astrid with a perpetual look of regret and then returned his piercing gaze to Vincentrio.

"I would have cleaned myself up a bit if I'd known I was being presented to our Lord and Master," sneered Aramis. His hair was overgrown and unruly, his stubble unkempt and the dirt on his face made it difficult to distinguish muck from bruises, but the warlock hadn't lost his tenacity.

"It's not exactly the reunion I'd hoped for," remarked Vincentrio.

"How about you take this band off my wrist and then we can make this into a real party," urged Aramis, flinching as he received a nick across the face from Crista's knife. "Did I offend the welcoming committee?"

Vincentrio gave Crista's shoulder a gentle squeeze and she graciously took a step back without saying a word. He leisurely approached his prisoner and leant down, so they were face to face. "I've waited a long time for this. Just to look you in the eye, the man who took *everything* away from me."

"I've been here a month and yet this is the first time you've come to see me yourself. Were you worried about those old feelings I'd stir up? Scared I'd—" Aramis' head reeled as Vincentrio swung the end of his staff across his head knocking him over in the chair. "You always did have a temper, Vinnie. Mia used to say it was your biggest weakness." Aramis paused and spat a fleck of blood on the floor next to him. "And yet she still chose you."

Vincentrio tapped his staff to the ground, pulling Aramis upright. "Attempting to use the past we share against me is not only beneath you, but it's also ineffective."

"Here I was under the impression that Astrid had joined us today to hear some stories of her dear old dad back in the glory days or did I get that wrong too?" Aramis questioned mockingly as he stared at Astrid.

This time Astrid met his glare with one of her own. Vincentrio glanced back at his daughter assessing the stern expression she held on her face. She didn't falter. She'd been playing this game long enough.

"Wrong again," smirked Vincentrio, summoning his daughter forward. "Astrid's here to help us get some information from you, Aramis. Right now, that information is the only thing still keeping you alive."

"Then it would be silly of me to just *give* that information away, considering my life depends on it."

"She doesn't need you to be willing. All you have to do is sit still," instructed Vincentrio.

"So, this is what you do with the gift your mother gave to you?"

"Did you want this to hurt?" cautioned Astrid. She dropped to her knees and placed her hands on his temples, closing her eyes she dug deep into the realms of Aramis' memories.

Astrid found herself on the floor of a desolate courtyard. She looked around and saw what remained of a great hall. Pillars towered all around, but only one full wall remained intact, its crystal glass windows untouched. The night sky flickered above her, stars scattered across its black canvas and all she could hear was the sound of crashing waves against the rocks surrounding the small island. *It's amazing what the mind can conjure.* She marvelled at the intricacy of the patterns marked into each stone.

Astrid spied an archway leading to a set of steps whittled into the rock's edge and she followed them down. The ocean spray splashed her cloak as she wandered down the steps, but it never wet it, reminding her that the steps she was walking were all within someone's head. She came across a cave at the bottom of the rock's edge and, with a flamed torch in hand, she continued inside.

Drops of water trickled from the ceiling and a soft breeze swept throughout the cavern, brushing past Astrid as she ventured through. Stone doors were carved into the wall of the cavern all along its length, all waiting to be opened, a different memory calling from beyond each door. Now she just needed to find the right one. She sensed the call of one as she walked right past it. She glanced back having barely noticed the door, it was almost entirely covered with weeds and vines, just a glimmer of the handle to be seen. Astrid took a hold of the handle and gently pushed the door open, squinting as she adjusted to the sudden light.

The door led to an open green field. A single thatched roof cottage stood in the centre, a beautiful array of flowers surrounding it and a single bench sitting amongst the rose garden round the back of the cottage. A little girl in pigtails ran around the back of the house, a net in hand as she jumped to catch fairies. Her laughter echoed through the fields as the fairies danced around her. Astrid quickly turned back to the door.

"Astrid, slow down." Astrid's heart stopped when she heard her soft voice. It ached so much as she turned to see her mother emerge from behind the house, a smile stretched across her face. Mia laughed as she ran after her little girl, scooping her up and throwing her up into the air. *This was before.* Astrid quickly wiped the tear that had dripped down her cheek and sat down on the grass. Her mother looked so healthy and so happy, her luscious hair bounced across her cheeks and her floral long dress flapped in the breeze as she played with her little girl.

Mia laid in the grass watching her little girl play with the fairies. She propped herself up on her elbows and looked up as Aramis came and sat in front of her. Astrid stood back up. *It was a trick.* She watched Aramis tuck a piece of hair behind her mother's ear and he slipped a pin through her hair. She looked closer and spotted the amethyst gems encrusted in the grip. *It was from him.* Mia looked adoringly upon Aramis and leant her cheek against his hand as she closed her eyes. *She was in love with him.* The realisation stabbed at Astrid and she couldn't bear to watch any more.

Astrid hurried back into the cave and firmly shut the door behind her. She sobbed into the door and her chest heaved, her whole body, aching. This was what she'd feared. It was just more illusions, more mind games. She shook her head and pulled herself together as she continued to the next door. The quicker she found the memory she needed, the quicker she could leave his head. Astrid feared that if her mother was behind too many of these doors, she'd never want to leave. One of the dangers of walking through a person's memories too long, is becoming part of that memory. Soon the memory begins to feel real and the urge to leave disappears.

Behind the next door she found the inside of a classroom. It didn't look quite like Vistaldors and the class was mixed with both witches and warlocks. The desks and chairs had been swept to the side of the classroom and a bearded professor stood in the centre surrounded by young students paired up and sparring spells with one another. Astrid took a seat at the back of the classroom, out of sight. She spotted a young, dark headed Aramis scrapping with another teenage warlock who could have only been her father. She could see the other boys staring, faces full of envy as they watched both boys practise magic far beyond their years. Her father laughed as Aramis sent him spinning on his ass across the classroom.

"Those two just love to show off," said a dark-haired girl, startling Astrid half to death. Astrid quickly swivelled around and saw the girl standing at the back of the classroom, she met the girl's violet eyes as they left the pages of her book. No one had ever seen Astrid in a memory before, this was something different.

"Sorry, I didn't mean to startle you," apologised the girl. She closed her book and took the seat next to Astrid.

"Why don't you show them a thing or two?" questioned Astrid, curious how the girl could see her.

"Witches aren't allowed to fight warlocks," mimicked the girl. "So much for progression."

"Says who?" challenged Astrid.

The girl smirked, left her book on the desk and marched up to the group of warlocks that were still bragging about one another's power. She heard them all laugh in the girl's face, but Astrid continued to watch. Her father accepted the challenge the girl had laid, and, within a few minutes, she'd wrapped him in the rug he'd been standing on. The girl wasn't to be underestimated.

Astrid wanted to stay and watch her parents duel some more, but this wasn't the memory she'd come for. She left back through the door and continued to search for the one door she needed. Going through every door was taking too long. Aramis' memories of her parents were like traps set purposely to keep her from the secrets her father wanted, and she wasn't going to let herself get distracted any more.

Astrid closed her eyes and focused on the memory she was trying to find. She followed the sound of a blazing fire and found another door, a heat radiated from its surface and she could see the flicker of flames through the crack under it. Astrid opened the door and stepped into a house engulfed by flames. She covered her mouth with her cloak and spluttered at the smoke that filled her lungs.

The flicks of the flames passed right through Astrid as she wandered through the burning wreckage. Chilling screams came from behind a door at the top of the landing, she could hear a woman's frantic shouts as she hammered the door from the other side. A young boy in his pyjamas pulled at the wood stuck across the doorframe. He cried as he burnt his hands on the red-hot wood and he looked around panicked at the flames that swept closer and closer.

"Hold on Mamma. I'm coming Anabella," shouted the boy.

The boy waved his hands and formed a wall of water around him, keeping the flames at bay whilst he tried to break through the door. He had managed to break a crack in the door and Astrid could see a woman's bloodied hand reach out to hold the boy's.

A hooded figure appeared in the flames behind him. The figure thrust his hands downwards and snapped the floorboards beneath the boy's feet. The boy yelped and held onto the edge of the broken floorboard. His water wall had disappeared, and the flames continued to swarm. The boy tried to haul himself back up whilst the figure stood over him and watched him struggle. The figure took down his hood and leant down to look the boy in the eye. With a nefarious grin stretching from ear to ear, the stranger summoned a piece of wood and struck the boy across the face.

Astrid ran through the flames and saw the young Aramis unconscious in the rubble, his face bloodied from the gash across his eye. She looked up through the hole in the floorboards and saw just a shadow of the man holding a sapphire like gem in the palm of his hand. *Dammit.* The rest of the house blurred, and the memory began to reset. Astrid fled towards the door and went back into the cavern.

Astrid hammered her fist against the wall of the cavern. She'd been so close. The man who'd stolen the gem was in that memory, but his face blurred, unrecognisable. This was the problem with memories, with time they became hazy, distorted. *Try telling Father those excuses.* Astrid sighed and threw her head into her hands as she slumped against one of the doors. She ran her hand feverishly through her hair and then she eyed one last door she hadn't opened.

The door had been hiding in plain sight, padlocked chains stretched across it. Astrid ran her hand along the chains and felt the magic pulsing beneath her fingertips. She smiled. She clicked her fingers and furiously pulled her hands towards her. The whole door shook, and she roared as she tried to break the chains with her magic. She stopped, her chest heaving. *He's laughing at you.* Aramis' mind was strong, she'd give him that. *Let's see how strong you are after this.*

Astrid carried on down the cavern, opening the door to every memory as she went. The sounds of all his memories filled the cavern, flashes of fire, screams of his family perishing and laughter of her mother. The cavern began to crumble and crack, and Astrid could feel the floor shake beneath her feet. She smiled to herself and ran back to the chained door. Clicking her fingers again, she pulled at the chains and with one last pull they snapped. The door flew open and Astrid jumped in.

Astrid looked around and found herself in the town square of a small village amongst a snowy mountain range. A fresh layer of snow dusted the rooftops and smoke puffed from every chimney along the street. The streets were teeming with creatures bustling around the market place. She was surprised none of them lost their footing on the icy cobble stones beneath them. A huddle of elves brushed past her and then she saw a hooded figure slink into what appeared to be a deserted tavern at the very end of the street. Another cloaked figure snuck into the same tavern and Astrid quickly followed.

The hooded figure was crouched in the corner of the room just behind the stairs. He was hiding a small package behind a few stones he'd pulled from the wall. The cloaked figure stood behind him and took down his hood. Astrid recognised the scar across his face and the spark in his eyes, Aramis must have only been about seventeen.

"I knew I'd track you down eventually," hissed Aramis, holding his hands out poised for a fight.

"I don't want to hurt you, boy," croaked the hooded figure still crouched in the corner.

"Why don't you stand up and face me? I've learnt a few things since we last met."

Astrid could see his hands twitch, she was surprised he even gave him a chance to turn around. She recognised the thirst for revenge in Aramis' eyes all too well. The hooded figure slowly stood up and dropped his hood. His face was pale and his eyes hollow and black, his black raven hair was scraped back and tied away from his face. The warlock's face was sunken, yet he towered over Aramis, his chest broad and heavy.

"Just walk away, kid," warned the warlock.

Aramis waved his hands and shot sparks at the warlock before he could say anything else. The warlock ducked out of the way and waved his hands, knocking Aramis off his feet. The warlock turned back to the bag he'd hidden in the wall and grabbed it. In a flash of blue flame, he was gone. Aramis stood back up and walked over to the pile of ash that was left behind. A black, velvet package remained underneath the ash, he dusted it off and picked it up. He pulled the string and the dazzling glimmer of the Perrero gem shone in his eyes. He quickly looked away and tied the package back up. He pocketed the gem and then left the tavern.

Young Aramis moved quickly through the crowd holding the hood of his cloak closely around his face. Astrid followed him all the way to a frozen water spring just on the outskirts of the village. She stood back and carefully watched him. He looked around surreptitiously and then kneeled down on the ice. Aramis muttered an incantation and then with his hand drew a circle in the ice cutting it away. He took out the package from his pocket and Astrid watched as he dropped it into the water before he waved his hands and sealed over the ice.

Astrid made her way back to the door and locked it up behind her. She took the steps calmly back up the rock's edge and opened her eyes. She was lying on the floor of her father's torture chamber, Crista and her father standing over her. She looked up at the chair and saw the fearful look in Aramis' eyes. He knew exactly what doors Astrid had opened.

"Did you find what you were looking for?" quivered Aramis, already knowing the answer to his question.

"I did," she replied bluntly, taking her father's hand. "Looks like we'll be making a journey to Alsek."

CHAPTER 14

Astrid woke early the next morning, new memories of her young mother jerking her awake. Peewee had nuzzled into her, he always knew when she needed that little bit of comfort. He stirred, and she stopped to give him a fond scratch under the chin before getting up. She stepped out of her canopy bed and walked towards her floor length mirror. She studied the bags that still hung heavy beneath her eyes, it had been a while since her last decent night's sleep. Her mind wandered back to *that night* with Caius, how she wanted to just stay in his arms.

Then the unsettling feeling in her stomach stirred again, but this time she couldn't keep it down. She ran to the bathroom and just about made it on time. With her head hung over the toilet bowl she heaved and heaved until her throat burned and there was nothing left. She slumped on the toilet floor and rubbed her head. *Must be all that guilt.* Astrid brushed herself off, washed her face and found some suitable clothing for the day ahead. She'd need something warm for Alsek, the region wasn't known for its sunny climate.

Astrid grabbed her thicker cloak on the way out and then walked the rows of prison cells on her way to meet Crista. Her father had tasked them both with travelling to Alsek and finding the Perrero gem. Astrid only hoped that the gem was in the same place so at least the task would be quick, and she could spend even less time alone with Crista, the witch had a habit of pressing all the wrong buttons.

Astrid walked a lower row of prison cells today, but she stopped when she was right below Caius' cell. Astrid looked up wistfully. *Today is tomorrow.* Astrid mustered her courage again and turned towards the staircase.

"Where do you think you're going?" probed Crista, sauntering down the steps. She glanced back at Astrid. "Well, come on, we have work to do."

With a heavy sigh Astrid followed Crista towards her father's chamber. *Tomorrow.*

Vincentrio's chamber sat at the tallest point of Trepidor, at the top of a spiralling set of stone steps with a great glass window overlooking the entirety of Trepidor all the way down to the prison pits. The floor was lined with various fur rugs and a grand marble fireplace stood opposite the canopy king-sized bed. Astrid picked up the framed photo that stood pride of place on the mantel, she smiled at the photo of the three of them, smiling, happy together. *Apparently not so happy.* She turned to Crista who was sensually eyeing the ruffled sheets on the bed, Crista perked her lips and Astrid could feel a second round of heaving coming very soon.

"Did you just bring me up here to see me heave?" queried Astrid. She knew her father had got up early to see to one of his new prisoners and wouldn't be back to his chambers for some time.

"Not at all, that's just an added bonus," Crista cackled, picking up a golden globe from her father's desk. "Security's a bit tighter than what it used to be round here. One way in. One way out."

Crista span the globe on the floor in front of them and the piece slowly opened up, a purple flame sprouting from within.

She held out her well-manicured hand for Astrid to take and they both stepped into the flame together.

The two witches gracefully stepped out of the purple flame portal, the snow crunching beneath their boots. Crista pocketed the globe in her cape coat and took out a pair of black cashmere gloves. Trepidor had its faults, but at least it was warm, here they could practically see their own breath.

They took a quick look around to gather their bearings; it seemed the portal had spat them out on the outskirts of one of the small villages below the snowy mountain peaks. It was probably for the best. Streets that were once full of markets and bustling crowds of creatures were now deserted, only Elvish guards could be seen patrolling the streets and they weren't too kind to witches even before Vincentrio's ascension. It would do both witches well to stay far out of their way.

"There's a reason I don't usually come out this far," grumbled Crista, rubbing her hands together.

"I could have handled this fine on my own," remarked Astrid. "The spring where Aramis last left the gem is on the other side of the village. There's no easy way around so we'll just have to go through."

"Ingenious," muttered Crista dryly, taking a bag of black powder out of her pocket.

Astrid threw Crista a demeaning glower and said, "Look, we don't want to bump into any elves so you're just going to have to find a way to blend in for once."

Crista took a pinch of the glimmering powder and blew it at Astrid's face. Astrid scrunched her face and coughed, the powder sticking in her throat. She felt her eyes narrow and her cheeks sink, she touched her bare fingers to her ears feeling their pointed tips. Crista took another pinch of the powder and dropped it on her own face.

"Just two elves finding our way through the village," Crista explained, cringing as she listened to the sudden change in her voice's pitch.

They both pulled their cloaks tighter and continued towards the village, trudging through the snow. Astrid spotted the deserted tavern from Aramis' memory at the end of the main street as they approached the village. She noted how many more of the buildings along the streets appeared just as deserted. Houses were boarded up, some had been burnt down, businesses had closed.

Astrid felt the rustle of a newspaper beneath her boot. She bent down and brushed the snow from the paper, the Elvish Times. The front page boasted some ludicrous headline concerning the long-awaited return of Vincentrio, her father's photo smiling in the centre. The editor had been in her father's pocket for some time. She spied the action snapshot of herself in the corner. *You're famous now.* Then she turned the pages to sheets of names of the missing and the dead. Vincentrio's followers had ravaged far and wide, Alsek was no exception. She saw Caius' name in the list of the missing and her heart ached all over again, she wondered if his family were on the list too.

"Are you still pining after that shapeshifter?" teased Crista, snatching the paper from Astrid's hands and tossing it in the bin. "Do you think he still wants anything to do with you, now he knows who you are? Course you don't. That's why you haven't mustered the courage to go talk to him. You're afraid he'll reject you, which he will."

“You don’t know that. I don’t know that,” replied Astrid, walking ahead so that she didn’t have to listen to any more of her cruel comments.

“Okay. Let’s pretend for a minute that we’re in happy fairy land and he does still want you, what do you think old Daddy would have to say about it?” posed Crista, her eyebrows raised when Astrid threw her a fierce glare.

Astrid turned back around and continued ahead, she wouldn’t let Crista get the better of her. That witch lived for getting a reaction out of Astrid. “That’s something that’s always confused me.” Astrid paused in the middle of the street. “You’ve known about me and Caius from the very beginning. That’s something you could have used to your advantage, to get to me or to get between me and my father, yet you’ve been sitting on that secret all this time. Why? It’s no great secret that we hate each other, so why keep my most important secret? I’m curious.”

“Oh, it’s not out of love for you, let’s get that clear now,” laughed Crista. “Power is power, but knowledge is also power. Something that you and your father often forget. Secrets should be savoured for the right time, something you’d do well to remember.’

Astrid stiffened. Crista’s words sent a distinct chill down her spine, she didn’t enjoy knowing that that witch had something to lure over her. She could use that secret against her whenever she wanted, and it seemed she intended to do just that. Astrid looked ahead and saw Crista stopped, fixed to the spot staring irately up at the wall in front of her. *What’s her problem now.* Astrid jogged to catch up with her.

“Ah,” exhaled Astrid, looking at the artwork on the wall.

The stone wall was plastered with A4 pages clustered together to create a sketched portrait of Vincentrio, his hands red with blood and his boots stained from the pool of blood at his feet. Astrid admired the creativity, if anything they'd made her father look dashingly handsome. Then she spotted the words written from the pool of blood: Down with the Titan, join the cause. *Could have been worse.*

"I've seen this sort of slander before," scowled Crista, tracing her fingers over the upside-down V stamped in the corner.

"I wouldn't necessarily call it slander," murmured Astrid.

Crista threw Astrid a cautionary glare and then stormed off down a small alleyway in the opposite direction.

"Where are you going?" called Astrid.

"To find me some agitators," exclaimed Crista, disappearing around the corner. Her fury had worked up quite the thirst and she knew exactly what she needed to quench it, some Elvish blood on her hands.

"I'll go finish our actual job then," sighed Astrid as she continued surreptitiously through the outlying streets and towards the spring.

The spring was exactly as it had looked in Aramis' memories. A thick layer of ice covered the water's surface and the flow of water had ceased, frozen in limbo as it careened down the rock's edge. Astrid cautiously approached, keeping herself hidden in the tree line that encompassed the spring. She'd realised the powder's effects had worn off and she couldn't risk being recognised. She was vulnerable. Anyone could be lurking amongst the trees and Astrid would have no way of seeing them until too late, it was the perfect spot to be ambushed.

Astrid peered from behind one of the bushes and quickly scanned the area. She emerged from the bushes and her ears twitched at the soft crunch of snow beneath another person's boot. Tree roots burst from the ground beneath her, entangling themselves around her ankles. She desperately tugged at the roots as they fastened themselves tighter and tighter. A tree branch swept from behind her wrapping itself around one wrist and then splitting to wrap around the other, holding Astrid still no matter how hard she tried to pull herself away.

"Come and claim your prize then," yelled Astrid, waiting for the responsible creature to emerge from behind the rustling bushes.

"Astrid?" She heard a male voice call.

"I told you I saw her in the village," a frustrated female voice muttered.

"Well, you've been wrong before," remarked Xander, appearing from behind the tree. He waved his hands and the tree released Astrid and returned to its placid state. "Sorry about that. You stumbled across one of our stronger traps."

"Hey stranger," smiled Hesper, removing the hood of her cloak. She ran towards Astrid and threw her arms around her, pulling her tightly. "It's so good to see you."

"You look good. Both of you," remarked Astrid, studying them both. *Much better than your sister,* the niggling of her conscience was back.

"Oh Paige," whimpered Hesper, her eyes filling with tears as she saw what Astrid had seen just yesterday, the picture was so vivid.

Astrid looked regretfully at her friend and gently squeezed Hesper's arm in an attempt to provide some comfort, but Hesper shirked it off and took a step back. She took a deep breath and let a stern expression mask her grief. Astrid saw the walls Hesper was putting back up and she retreated. Hesper looked at her differently now. Before, Hesper had hope for Astrid's humanity, for her soul, but where there once was hope, there was shame. *Are you really surprised?*

"What are you two doing here?" queried Astrid, eyeing the hilt of a dagger Hesper hid beneath her cloak.

"We knew Vincentrio would send someone for the Perrero gem. We've been waiting here, hoping he'd have the guts to come collect it himself," explained Xander, planting himself between Hesper and Astrid.

"But as per usual he's got someone else to do his dirty work," scowled Hesper, her hands twitching.

"How do you know the gem's even here?" Astrid was intrigued considering they'd held Aramis prisoner for the past month and only just found out themselves.

"Don't," cautioned Hesper, glaring at Xander.

"She's still our friend and I still trust her," murmured Xander, holding Hesper's glare with his own. He gently took Hesper's hand in his and gave it a soft squeeze before turning back to Astrid. "It's not been easy for us. For anyone since your fa… Vincentrio took control. People are scared, and they have every reason to be."

"He only wants what—" Astrid retorted irately, she was quick to defend her father, as quick as everyone else was to judge him, but she stopped herself when she heard the snap of a twig. "There's someone else with you." She readied her hands and looked around warily.

Xander raised his hand and spoke softly, "There's a lot of other people with us. Watching out for us, but that's all they're doing. They don't know who you are, and they won't do anything unless we tell them to."

Astrid let her hands drop and gestured for Xander to continue.

"Vincentrio's followers have been making their way through the regions. Taking what they want. Hunting creatures who aren't witches or warlocks. Butchering those that choose not to follow." He could see a glimmer of guilt in Astrid's eyes, no matter how hard she tried to hide it. "We managed to get a few students out of Vistaldors, but we barely escaped his followers a couple of weeks later. We lost some friends." Astrid saw the mournful look on Xander's face. "But then this other group found us, and we joined them, joined the fight against Vincentrio. It's a large group, started by what was left of the Guard. They had information on the gem's whereabouts and knew Vincentrio wanted it, so they took it. We volunteered to protect it, to keep watch, to—"

"To what?" challenged Astrid. She couldn't hear their companions any more, but she could sense them coming closer.

"We didn't know he'd send you," admitted Hesper, her hand slowly reaching for the dagger.

"You really don't want to do that," warned Astrid.

"I know I don't."

Hesper reached for the dagger beneath her cloak, but Astrid clicked her fingers halting Hesper's hand. Astrid snatched the dagger with her magic and held it poised at Xander's throat.

"Astrid," sighed Xander. He tried to make eye contact with her, but she kept her stare fixed solely on Hesper.

"All you need to do is hand over the gem, Hesp," instructed Astrid.

"I can't give you something I don't have," she replied. "I don't even know where it's kept."

"You'd think that someone who can read minds would be better at lying," murmured Astrid. Xander bellowed as Astrid slowly pressed the knife against his neck.

“Stop,” cried Hesper. Astrid eased the knife away and returned her attention to Hesper. “Astrid, can’t you see what your father is turning you into. Just look at what you’re doing.”

Astrid swallowed hard and her face softened. She glanced at the blood that trickled down Xander’s neck. The knife dropped to the ground and, she took a step back. An elf leapt from the tree behind Astrid knocking her to the floor. The elf wrapped an impotens band around Astrid’s wrist and then stood back up, a crossbow aimed closely at her back.

“Get up,” demanded the elf, her voice didn’t falter. Astrid stayed glued to the snow-covered floor and glared at the band glowing around her wrist as it kept her power at bay. “I said get up,” yelled the elf, she jabbed the tip of her crossbow at Astrid’s back.

Astrid sighed and slowly stood back up, her hands raised in surrender. She turned to face their light-footed comrade and studied her closely. The elf held the crossbow firmly in her gloved hands, her deep green eyes fixed on her target. Her pointed ears twitched at Astrid’s every move. Another cloaked figure emerged from the bushes flicking a curved throwing knife between her fingers. She examined Astrid closely and pursed her lips.

“You’re *his* daughter. I expected you to be more impressive,” remarked the stranger, tracing her blade against Astrid’s cheek. Astrid noted the striking scar running down the stranger’s face from the hairline of her short, dark blonde hair and across her prominent cheekbones.

“How about you hand me one of those knives and I’ll show you how impressive I am,” smiled Astrid, eyeing the hunting belt strapped across the stranger’s torso.

The stranger raised her eyebrows.

"Evelyn, I don't need to remind you what we're here for," remarked the elf.

"Fine," sighed Evelyn. "You never let me have any fun, Ani."

"Astrid knocking you on your ass wouldn't be fun for any of us, Evelyn," said Xander, handing Hesper's dagger back to her.

Hesper smiled and pressed her hand tentatively to the wound still bleeding on his neck.

"It's just a scratch," he assured her, taking her hand and pressing it to his lips, he turned back to Evelyn. "Do you think you can do it?"

Evelyn shifted into the shape of Astrid and looked back at Astrid. "Easy enough."

"It will take a lot more than a cheap copy to impersonate me," said Astrid, a little uneasy.

Evelyn perked her lips. "I don't know, with a bit of arrogance and self-loathing no one will even notice the difference," snarked Evelyn.

Astrid's brow furrowed. "Don't you understand. If *I* return without that gem, I'm as good as dead anyway," pleaded Astrid.

"It doesn't matter," Evelyn replied solemnly. "I just need to get close enough to kill him. I don't care if I die, that's not important."

"There's a lot worse things than dying," murmured Astrid.

"Why do you still help him?" probed Ani, her expression curious. "Xander told us what he did to you, do you do it out of fear, is that it?"

"He's my father and I love him," she admitted, her shoulders sagging. She saw the baffled expression on each of their faces and snarled back, "I don't expect any of you to understand."

Xander crouched next to Astrid and looked deeply into her eyes, holding her stare with a mournful look of his own. "You know I understand better than anyone. But if he got hold of the Perrero gem he'd be master of the worlds of the living, the dead and in between. He'd be able to ferry whoever he wants across those worlds. No one should have that power."

"No, not one person. He'd share it with me," she explained.

"How naïve are you?" exclaimed Evelyn, shaking her head as she blew out her cheeks. "Let's just get on with this."

"Yes, let's," echoed Crista, a wicked smile stretching across her face.

Ani quickly fired an arrow, but Crista clicked her fingers, snapping it before it reached her face. Ani reloaded and dived out of the way as Crista threw a flaming ball of fire at her. The fire hurtled into the trunk of the tree behind them bringing the tree crashing down. Evelyn skidded underneath the falling tree and threw one of her knives at Crista and then another. Crista leapt out of the way and clicking her fingers cracked the earth beneath them. Evelyn yelped as she fell into one of the chasms, she clung to a tree root sprouting from the side.

Xander waved his hands and hurled Crista across the frozen spring. She slid across the ice and then swiftly stood back up. She clicked her fingers, snapping the icicles from the rock's edge and threw them back at Xander. He raced towards her, dodging each one, until a large chunk of ice hit him squarely in the head, knocking him unconscious.

"Stay here," yelled Hesper as she left Astrid on the ground and ran after Xander.

Hesper shattered the icicles and pulled the rocks down from behind Crista. Crista's eyes widened, and she held out her hands struggling to hold the rocks with her magic. Hesper jogged towards Crista, her dagger in hand. Crista clicked her fingers and blasted the rocks. She turned, and Hesper screamed, dropping the dagger as it seared her hand.

With a cackle, Crista clicked her fingers and cracked the ice beneath Hesper. Before Hesper could react, the ice collapsed, and she fell into the freezing water, her arms flailing as she gasped for air, taking water in every time. Her body ached, and her muscles weakened as the cold water took its effect. She slowly dropped beneath the surface, her eyes closing as she slipped away.

A hand grabbed her outreached arm and hauled her up to the surface and onto the sheet of ice. Hesper spluttered as Astrid laid her on her side and gently laid her cloak over the top of her. Astrid glanced over her shoulder quickly. Crista was dealing with Ani and avoiding her arrows. Astrid threw Hesper's arm around her shoulder and dragged her off the ice, gently dropping her down next to Xander who still lay unconscious.

"Thank you," trembled Hesper, holding the cloak close around her. She clicked her fingers and the impotens band dropped off Astrid's wrist. "Now we're even."

"Let's go, Astrid," called Crista, swatting Evelyn and Ani as they came at her.

"I'm sorry." Astrid softly squeezed Hesper's shivering hand and then ran back towards Crista. She clicked her fingers, pulling Ani's crossbow apart and throwing it into the chasm. With a wave of her hands, a tree branch barrelled into Evelyn and Ani knocking them off their feet.

"Little pests," muttered Crista, spinning the golden globe on the floor. The purple flame burst from the casing and they both quickly walked through.

The two witches stepped out of the purple flame portal and into Vincentrio's bed chamber. Crisp new sheets laid across his bed and Vincentrio sat at his desk, a heavy bound book open in front of him. He summoned his staff and turned to face the intruders. He smiled and relaxed at the sight of Astrid and Crista, propping his staff against his desk he stood up and sauntered towards his daughter.

"Well?" He gently placed the palm of his hands on her arms and stared down at his daughter.

Astrid forced a smile and held out the gem that she'd snagged from Hesper when she'd pulled her out of the water. "Easy enough."

CHAPTER 15

Vincentrio had kept himself concealed in his chambers for the past few days now, only the gems and Crista for company. Astrid had gone to his chamber for an audience with him every day, but each day she was met with a closed door. He'd make her wait outside where she had to stand and endure the cries and moans that seemed to go on far too long. Then, once he was done with her, Crista would emerge from his chamber, wearing only a silk robe, to tell Astrid he was too busy to see her today.

Today would be different, Astrid thought, studying herself in the mirror, ensuring her appearance was pristine. She pulled her best cloak from her wardrobe and fastened it so it covered her stomach. She lifted her shoulders and made her way to her father's chambers.

Astrid held her head high as she marched through the row of prison cells. The prisoners had stopped trying to plead with her when she wandered past them on her morning walk. Those with spirit left had resorted to spiteful insults and petty threats. Astrid had grown so used to them she didn't even waste a second to stop and listen to them any more. *Sticks and stones.* She stopped at Paige's cell, like she'd done every day since her encounter with Hesper and slid an apple through her bars.

"You need to eat," urged Astrid, examining the slender shadow that always stayed curled in the darkness. Every day Astrid had been met with silence, not that she could blame her, but she had to come around at some point. "Starving yourself won't help. Crista won't let you die, she likes you too much.

She'll get the food into you one way or another." Still nothing. "If you won't do it for yourself then do it for your sister. Do it for Hesper."

A bruise-covered arm lunged through the bars, grabbing a handful of Astrid's cloak. The trolls on duty ran to Astrid's aid, but she held up her hand and ushered them away. The bars were lined with neros, a magic suppressing element, enough to keep anyone's magic contained.

"Don't you talk about my sister," hissed Paige, drawing her lips back with a snarl. She'd tied her straw-like hair away from her sunken face and her lip was still swollen from the last beating she'd received. She released Astrid's cloak and retreated back to her standard position, clutching her knees tightly to her chest.

"I saw her. Hesper, I mean," replied Astrid, patting down the creases Paige had made in her cloak.

"You're lying. Trying one of your mind games. Well, I'm not playing," spat Paige.

"Why would I lie about that?" quipped Astrid. "She was with Xander and a group of people. She's trying to do the right thing, as always, but she misses you."

"Please just stop. Leave me alone," whimpered Paige as she rested her head against the stone brick wall.

Astrid crouched against the bars and whispered, "I know you don't think a lot of me, but Hesper is like a sister to me. She let me go. I owe it to her to help you, that includes making sure you eat whether I have to shove it down your throat myself."

"You might lose a finger," smirked Paige. She reluctantly took a bite from the apple Astrid had left her.

"Thank you," murmured Astrid, steadying herself as she stood back to her feet, she'd felt light-headed all morning. She looked up and saw the two guards waiting at Paige's cell. One licked his lips as he waved through the bars. Astrid could see the fear transform Paige's face as the whites of her eyes bulged. Astrid turned to the guards eyeing them both up and down. "Can I help you?" she questioned calmly.

"We've been instructed to take the prisoner for more questioning," replied one of the guards with a repulsive grin plastered on his ugly face.

"I don't think that will be necessary." Astrid planted herself firmly in front of the bars. "This prisoner will not be questioned any more. She's told us everything she knows, and she is not to be taken from this cell. And you, nor any other guard, are to enter her cell," barked Astrid, watching them both cower from her glare. "Do I make myself clear?"

"Yes, Ma'am," muttered the guards.

"And if you have a problem with it, you can take it up with *my father*. Now off you go."

One guard puckered his lips through the bars, but he quickly scurried away with the other guard when he caught a glimpse of Astrid's stern glare.

"This doesn't change anything," remarked Paige bluntly, taking another bite from the apple.

"Of course not," sighed Astrid, it would take a lot more than that to relieve her conscience.

Astrid continued up the steps to her father's chamber. His door was open ajar, but she knew better than to just walk in. She gently knocked on the door and slowly edged it open. Her father stood at his glass window with his arms wrapped around Crista's waist as he watched all that was below. Astrid coughed to announce herself and waited in the doorway, diverting her eyes elsewhere when Crista turned around. Crista grabbed her silk robe that she'd dropped on the floor and pressed a supple kiss to Vincentrio's hand before leaving.

Vincentrio turned around, his chest bare, and picked up the shirt Crista had ripped off of him earlier that morning. He traced his hand across the map that traipsed over his desk and ushered his daughter over. Astrid saw he'd marked the territories he'd successfully claimed, only Hirtshelm remained independent. There wasn't much more to gain there than forests and wild animals, Vincentrio probably thought it was more effort than it was worth.

"Father, I wanted to discuss something with you," explained Astrid.

"Take a look at what we've accomplished, Astrid," commanded Vincentrio, laying an arm across her shoulder. "It's tiny compared to what we'll achieve with the Perrero gem. The gem *you* procured for me. Something I'll never forget."

Vincentrio waved his hand across the map and Astrid watched as the map unfurled; a map of the human world to the east, the land of the dead to the north of the Alsek mountains and the land in between to the west of the Hirtshelm forests.

"Once I can get my gem and the Perrero gem to work together I'll be able to create portals. I'll be able to walk between each world and bring back who I please. Just think of the powerful creatures banished in these worlds. Imagine what I could do with their power," rambled Vincentrio, his eyes gleaming at the very thought of all the possibilities as he wandered around his map.

Astrid could tell he hadn't slept for the past few days. He'd been working tirelessly to forge the Perrero gem into his staff and yet it stood on the cabinet below where his staff hung on the wall, mocking him, refusing to bend to his will. He rubbed the bags beneath his eyes and then turned his attention back to his daughter.

"I'm sorry. What was it you wanted to discuss?" questioned Vincentrio, regaining his composure as he buttoned up his shirt.

Astrid looked at her father worryingly. "When was the last time you slept?"

"That's irrelevant. Sleeping won't help me harness the gem's power," he replied.

"But fooling around with Crista will," remarked Astrid. She flinched as Vincentrio raised his hand to strike her.

"Do not forget your place," growled Vincentrio, dropping his hand. He turned back to the gem, drawn by its light.

"Forgive me, Father."

"Forgiven," he muttered, picking up the gem and holding it in the palm of his hand. "She has an important role to play in all of this."

"But I thought I—"

"What did you want to discuss? I'm a busy man. I have work to be doing and prisoners to interrogate," snapped Vincentrio. He propped the gem back on the cabinet and removed his staff from the wall.

"That's actually what I wanted to speak to you about," explained Astrid, preserving her tenacity. "Is there really any need to continue torturing the prisoners now that you have the gem? The cells are practically full, and I don't think holding onto the prisoners will encourage people to follow you."

Vincentrio's eyes narrowed. "Do you think I concern myself with the opinions of lesser creatures?"

"The forces that are rising against you are not to be underestimated. Their numbers are growing and they're a serious threat to what we're trying to achieve," argued Astrid.

"A group of rebels made up of elves, shapeshifters and magic users who are, quite frankly, a disgrace to our kind. Associating with a lesser creature makes you exactly that."

"How can you say that? Your mother was a shapeshifter."

"My parentage is inconsequential. She wasn't powerful enough to protect herself. We have the power to take these worlds and that is what we're doing. Other creatures are simply here to serve a purpose and it's about time that they came to terms with their place in *our* world."

Astrid was taken aback, at a loss for words. She'd always known her father felt superior to others because of his power, that it was his right to rule over the worlds, but this was something else. This was Crista's influence, whispering in his ear her pure blood ideals. That world of union she'd once imagined under her father's reign, a world where they'd have freedom to choose, was quickly fading. They were the dreams of an idealistic child. She cursed her foolishness. Her father had her fealty, her loyalty and her love, something that wouldn't change.

"Nevertheless, it would work in your favour to release the prisoners, an act of goodwill. Give the forces that rise against you more of a reason to follow you," suggested Astrid.

Vincentrio pressed his lips together. "How about a mass execution? That would send a message," replied Vincentrio as a nefarious grin spanned from ear to ear.

"That's something Crista would suggest. You're fierce and powerful, but you're not cruel. Please, Father. Show them the man that I see, the man that I've idolised for most of my life, the man that my mother fell in love with," she pleaded, taking his hand tightly. She was desperate for her father to prove people wrong.

Vincentrio snatched his hand away and struck Astrid across the face with the end of his staff. She dropped to the floor clutching the side of her face. She pulled her hand away and blinked hard at the blood that soaked her palm.

He crouched down next to his daughter and she flinched as he tenderly stroked his thumb across her cheek. "You're my daughter and I love you, but your sentimentality makes you weak. Go clean yourself up."

Vincentrio trailed his cloak in the small puddle of Astrid's blood and shut the door to his chamber behind him, leaving Astrid to her own thoughts. Her thoughts that were now rattled by the fierce blow to her head. She slowly stood herself up, steadying herself on the edge of her father's desk as she waivered. The room had stopped spinning and Astrid paused for a second staring at the golden globe still sitting on the corner of the desk, tempting her. *You could take it, leave and never look back.* But she couldn't do that, she couldn't leave Caius here unprotected.

Astrid pushed the thought out of her mind and found a flannel in her father's bathroom to clean up the gash he'd left on her head. Her hands trembled as she tentatively dabbed at her head, cleaning the worst of it. *That will do*. She left the bloodied flannel in the sink for her father to see and then left back down the steps.

Astrid stopped still at the row of prison cells. Her feet refusing to move forward, they felt as heavy as two cinder blocks as she forced them onwards. Astrid paused when she reached Caius' cell. He wasn't standing at the bars, but that didn't mean he wasn't awake. She'd hoped he'd be asleep and she could just watch him for a couple of minutes. He was such a peaceful sleeper. Watching his chest rise and fall with each rhythmic breath always relaxed her.

Astrid took a deep breath and edged closer. She pressed her hands to the bars and peered through, scanning the darkness of his cell for some movement. A large shadow emerged from the back. Stepping into the light, Caius reached out entwining his fingers in Astrid's. Her knees buckled, and she dropped to the floor squeezing his hands in desperation. He pressed a hand against her cheek and she closed her eyes leaning into the touch she'd been craving. He ran his thumb gently across her cheek wiping the tears that filled her bloodshot eyes. She opened her eyes to look upon his face, a beat-up face that was still beautiful to her. They'd shaved off half his hair and the tatty rags he wore were soiled and falling off his still muscled body, but she'd expected much worse. He barely winced as Astrid traced her fingertips over the branding he now had on the side of his neck, the burn had just started to scar.

"I'm okay, Astrid," Caius murmured, pressing his head against hers through the bars.

The words choked in Astrid's throat as her whole body trembled at the sound of his voice again. "I'm so so… sor… sorry," she stuttered through the tears. Her shoulders heaved with the weight of the guilt she'd been carrying.

"It's all right, shhh," he sighed, tucking a piece of hair behind her ear. "I was beginning to think you'd forgotten about me."

"I thought I was the last person you'd want to see after everything," she admitted, swallowing back the lump in her throat. "I should have told you before. Who I was, about my father and the things I've done."

"Yeah, you should have," replied Caius, the corner of his lips twitched.

"I told myself it was for your sake, to keep you safe, but really I was being selfish. I thought if you knew who I really was you wouldn't want me, and I'd lose you. I'd be alone." She could feel the tears fill her eyes again, but this time she held them back. She needed to hold herself together.

"I don't care about any of that stuff, Astrid. I chose you and I love you. I see you for who you really are and that's a *good* person. I just wished you'd trusted me enough to share your burden."

"It wasn't about trust. I loved you too much to give you that burden."

They both closed their eyes and pressed their heads against the bars. Astrid's heart ached as she felt his breath against her neck. All she wanted to do was rip the bars from the ground and sit in Caius' lap. To feel his arms around her, to let him hold her so she could lean her head against his chest and fall asleep in his arms. But she couldn't. Not now. She pulled away and stood back on her feet. Caius held onto her hand and looked up at her desperately.

"I'll come back. I promise. There's just something I need to do first." She gently squeezed his hand and then walked away, making sure she didn't look back.

Astrid briskly marched back to her chamber. She made sure the door was shut firmly behind her and then pulled a duffle bag from beneath her bed and continued to pack it. It was time to leave. Her father was a lost cause, but she was not. No longer would she fall victim to the path set by her father, she'd set her own path and that path led her straight out of Trepidor, with Caius at her side. First there was one other person she needed to help. She had a debt to repay.

Once Astrid had finished packing, she clicked her fingers and shrunk the bag to a more manageable size. She then took out a pen and piece of paper from her desk and frantically scrawled a note to Hesper telling her of her plan to escape with Paige and Caius using the portal opener in her father's chamber. She detailed explicitly where the portal would open and where she'd take them after that. She just hoped Hesper and Xander would be able to find them.

"Peewee," called Astrid.

Peewee emerged from where he'd been comfortably curled up and leapt onto the desk. He sat and watched curiously as Astrid quickly rolled the note into a tight scroll.

"This is really important Peewee, I need you to find Hesper and give this to her," she explained, tucking the note safely into Peewee's paw. He brushed past her arm affectionately and then hopped off the table before he slid out the door and out of sight. She just hoped he hadn't forgotten his natural instincts.

Astrid threw her bag over her shoulder and wrapped her cloak around her, pulling the hood up and close around her face. She briskly made her way to Paige's cell, maintaining her assertive demeanour as she passed the guards. One of the guards she'd cautioned earlier that day was on duty. He eyed her closely as she stopped at Paige's cell. Astrid's glare soon urged him to continue on his way.

"Two visits in one day, a girl could get used to this sort of attention," mocked Paige. She approached the bars and eyed the mark that was starting to bruise on Astrid's forehead. "What did you do this time?"

"I told him something he didn't want to hear," explained Astrid. Astrid clicked her fingers and the impotens band fell from Paige's wrist.

Paige looked down at her bare wrist and gently rubbed it. A small smile escaped her lips as she looked back at Astrid waiting for her through an open doorway. She wasn't sure if it was a trap, but it was a very tempting one.

"I know I haven't given you any reason to trust me, but I'm going to get us both out of here. I just need you to take a leap of faith and come with me."

"Stopped seeing your father through those rose-tinted glasses?" questioned Paige, still apprehensive to follow her.

"Something like that," murmured Astrid.

"Good enough for me," said Paige. Taking Astrid's hand, she stepped out of her cell. She squinted at the blinding light from the fire pits and stumbled as her legs wobbled beneath her. She wasn't as strong as she once was, even with her magic returning.

Astrid took a cloak from her bag and threw it over Paige concealing her identity.

"So, what's next in your great escape plan?" queried Paige, leaning on Astrid's arm as they briskly walked along the row of prisoners.

"There's a portal opener in my father's chamber, it's the only way out of here, but I can't leave without Caius. First we get him and then we get out of here—"

"Tut, tut, tut, tut, did we forget what happened the last time you tried to run away?" cackled Crista, blocking their path with a guard either side. Peewee struggled against her as she held him firmly by the scruff. "I caught this rat on his way out of the cave and he was carrying a rather *interesting* note." A wicked smile flicked across Crista's face as she held the scroll up in her other hand. "I can't wait to see what your father has in store for you this time."

"Run," exclaimed Astrid. She shoved her bag into Paige's hand and then pushed her towards the steps.

Crista nodded to the guards and they sprang into action, drawing their club from its sheath. Astrid waved her hands and wrenched the prison bars from the floor of the closest cell. She threw her hand forward and impaled one of the guards. She swung another at the other guard, but he was too fast and swerved out of the way. With a heavy swing of his club, he knocked Astrid onto the floor. The back of her head smacked the concrete.

Astrid opened her eyes, blinking hard. The room was spinning. The guard had a shackle round her ankle and was dragging her along the floor back to Crista. She waved her hands and burst the shackle. The guard dropped to the floor howling in pain at the shards that had splintered into his leg.

Peewee slipped from Crista's grasp and leapt onto her other hand, sinking his teeth deep into her fingers he grabbed the note. Crista shrieked and hurled Peewee across the floor. She clutched her hand that was pouring with blood, her eyes bulging with fury. Peewee bounded towards Astrid, the note securely in his paw. Crista pulled a jagged knife from her cloak and threw it at Peewee. Astrid clicked her fingers and Peewee was gone. The knife clinked as it ricocheted off the floor. Astrid flicked her wrist ensnaring Crista in a ring of fire and then fled. *Caius.*

She came to a sudden halt when she heard the clink of guards' armour and saw her father, his staff in hand, leading the march. *Dammit.* She paused for a second and considered standing her ground, but there were too many. *You're no good to him dead.* Astrid cursed her innate need for self-preservation and fled up the steps towards her father's chamber. She heard their pace quicken as she hurried up the steps, taking the stairs two at a time. She slammed the door behind her as she reached his chamber and ran her hands along the doorway, sealing it with her magic.

Paige was tearing the room apart looking for the portal opener. She held her hands out in defence when she heard someone enter, but she quickly resumed her search when she saw it was Astrid.

"What the hell am I even looking for?" questioned Paige, frantically pulling drawers out.

"This," sighed Astrid, grabbing the globe Paige had so carelessly knocked on the floor in her search. Astrid grasped Paige's hand and span the globe on the floor in front of them, the purple portal flame burst from its gold casing.

"Wait," exclaimed Paige as she snatched her hand back. A flicker of the Perrero gem's compelling light had caught her eye. She grabbed a handkerchief from the side and wrapped the gem before quickly pocketing it.

"We don't have ti—" Astrid's gaze darted to the door. They were forcing their way through. It would be a matter of seconds before her father would break down that door. She looked at the portal and then looked back at Paige. *Hesper would never forgive you.* Astrid turned back to the door and thrust her hands out in front of her, holding the door for a few seconds more.

"Go. Get out of here," yelled Astrid, it was taking all of her magic to hold her father back. The door burst off its hinges and Astrid dispelled the splinters. Her father stood in the doorway, fury surging through his veins, twenty guards at his back. "Now."

"Thank you." Paige stepped through the portal and she was gone. But the portal hadn't closed.

Astrid turned back to her father just as he shot out a blazing flare of magic from his staff. Her eyes widened, and she held out her palms, shielding herself. His power swarmed around her. She felt it force her back as he came closer, but she held his glare. The rage ran red through his narrowed eyes, his jaw taut. It was the same look she'd seen on the Underground all those years ago, but she wasn't that same scared little girl any more. She didn't fear death. She didn't fear him. She pitied him. With that she let go.

"Astrid!" Xander emerged from the portal and leapt in front of her. The flare of Vincentrio's magic tore right through Xander's chest. Astrid opened her eyes and caught Xander as his body dropped in front of her. She fell with him and cradled his head carefully in her lap. He gasped with every heavy breath, he kept his eyes fixed solely on Astrid and smiled. His trembling hand desperately grasped hers and she held it firmly.

"Damn you," she sobbed, her voice shaking as she felt the tears fill her eyes.

"I had… a promise to keep." His hand dropped, and his chest stilled. Astrid bent forward and pulled his warm body close. The tears surged like an unbroken stream, her cries muffled against his body. She rocked his lifeless body back and forth never wanting to let him go.

Astrid's chest tightened, and she dropped onto her hands and knees. Her whole body had gone weak. She looked up and saw her father draining her power force. Her voice cracked when she tried to speak. She reached forward trying to grasp a piece of her father's cloak, but she stumbled to the ground. Her vision blurred and then it went black.

CHAPTER 16

"Let me out. Please. Someone. Just let me out," wailed a young Astrid. She hammered her fists against the wooden sides of the toy chest until her knuckles bled. She kicked. She cried, but no one ever seemed to hear her. The older boys weren't fools; they'd hidden the chest inside their closet. Some days they'd lock her in there for hours. Other days they'd stick around to listen to Astrid crying and she would hear their sniggers through the cracks in the wood.

Usually once they'd had their fun, they'd let her out, but the boys had gotten worse recently. Meaner. Astrid had just been sent back from her third foster family in three months. Another *accident* that she couldn't explain. Sometimes she'd try to tell them about her magic, but that only backfired. The foster family would look at her worryingly and send her back like damaged goods. "We didn't sign up for this trouble," they'd say as they'd hand her back to her tired case worker.

Astrid heard a door open and then the click of the padlock as it unlocked. The chest creaked open and she squinted, adjusting her eyes to the sudden light. She eyed the outstretched hand warily. It belonged to a boy similar in age to the boys that had locked her in. She didn't recognise him, but there were so many kids coming and going in the home, it was difficult to keep track. He was a bit taller than the other boys and wore a pair of old-style aviator goggles that he pushed up into his scruffy dark hair.

"What are you looking at?" barked Astrid, ignoring his hand as she made her own way out of the box. She eyed the unlocked padlock lying on the floor with no key in it. She couldn't see a key in his hand either. "How did you open that?" she queried less curtly.

The boy shrugged and pocketed the lock in his dark trousers. He turned and walked away without saying a word.

"Hey! It's rude to not speak when spoken to." Foster family number two had taught her that.

"And it's rude to not say thank you," he replied. Astrid tugged at his arm and he sighed. "You wouldn't believe me if I told you."

"Try me," challenged Astrid, crossing her arms across her small body.

The boy turned around holding the padlock in the palm of his hand, he waved his hand over it. Astrid's eyes widened. His hand was empty, and the lock was gone.

"You have magic," she whispered. The lonesome feeling that had haunted her for the past couple of years suddenly lifted. So many people had told her she was crazy, a liar, so much so that she'd started to believe them. Maybe she had imagined her life before care. Believing in magic made the gloom of her life more bearable, but now she'd found someone else. Someone, like her.

"And now you're looking at me like I'm crazy," the boy mumbled.

"No, no." Astrid tugged again at his jumper. She clicked her fingers and the padlock appeared in her hand.

A smile broadened across the boy's face, a dimple appearing beneath one eye.

"I can't really control it," admitted Astrid, scrunching her face when the padlock disappeared again. She huffed and planted her bottom on the toy chest lid, dropping her chin on her hand.

"If I could, maybe those boys would leave me alone. Maybe families would stop bringing me back."

The boy sighed and sat next to Astrid, his feet almost reached the ground as he dangled his legs over the edge. "Foster families aren't equipped for dealing with kids like me and you. You'll realise that pretty quickly."

"Where's your real family?"

"I don't have one. I've been here for as long as I can remember, you?"

"My dad did some… bad stuff and he had to leave me behind."

"What a guy. At least you've got someone." The boy's smile had faded, and he gazed blankly downwards.

"And now so have you." Astrid hopped off the chest and held out her pinkie finger. The boy chuckled and took her finger with his.

"I, Astrid Harper, swear to annoy you and laugh at you and make fun of you and be the best little sister you could have."

"And I, Xander Black, promise to tease you and be cooler than you and to protect you like any good big brother would."

Astrid shot awake. She wiped the tear from her cheek and looked around frantically. She was in her bed chamber, lying on her canopy bed. She glanced at Peewee's empty bed, and the drawers and cupboards that had been ransacked. She expected to feel a shackle around her wrist or an impotens band, but she pulled back her sleeve and there was nothing. Just the scars that felt as fresh as when Crista had given them to her. *Oh.* The memories of what had happened right before she'd blacked out flooded back. Paige getting away. Her father taking her magic. Xander. Her gut wrenched, and she swallowed back the lump in her throat. The mind was a cruel thing tormenting her with memories, reminding her how she'd failed the only real family she had. *It should have been you.*

Astrid took a deep breath and stood up out of bed, grabbing the bedpost as her legs buckled beneath her. The room was spinning, and her vision was blurred. She tried to steady herself and walk to her dresser, but she fell onto her hands and knees. She was weak without her magic. Her chest felt heavy, yet empty, like a part of her soul was missing.

The door swung open and Crista strutted in with a definite spring to her step. She glanced at Astrid on the floor and then continued to her dresser. Crista picked out an outfit from what was left and laid it carefully on Astrid's unmade bed. She turned back to Astrid and offered her hand fidgeting her fingers exuberantly. Astrid spotted the silver ring Crista was showing off on one of her fingers. A band of purple glistened around its edge. Astrid could feel its draw, it was whispering to her.

"You bitch," spat Astrid. The ring contained her magic, that's what she could hear. Astrid limply lunged her hand forward, but Crista snatched her fingers away.

A gleeful grin stretched from ear to ear as Crista watched Astrid struggle on the floor. "Your father said I could try it out." Crista clicked her fingers and clenched her fist.

Astrid clutched at her chest as it tightened, and her breathing became laboured. She tried to grab a piece of Crista's cloak in desperation, but she fell onto her back wheezing. Her chest getting tighter and tighter. Then Crista stopped. Astrid laid on the floor panting.

"Oh, it's really got that extra kick to it," jeered Crista, clapping her hands together. "It's quite addictive. I can see why you're so weak without it."

"Why don't you just kill me?" murmured Astrid achingly. *Death would be better.*

"What was that?" Crista crouched next to Astrid.

"I said why don't you just kill me," she repeated, glaring sharply at Crista.

"Kill you? Ha! Where's the fun in that?" Crista stood back up and threw the clothes at Astrid. "Get dressed. You've been sleeping for the past few days and your father's invited you for dinner. He's got a few things he wants to discuss with you."

"Well, you can tell *Daddy* that I have nothing more to say to him." Astrid pulled herself up, her knees wobbled as she straightened herself and removed her hand from the bedpost she'd been leaning on. "So, run along little errand girl—"

Crista threw Astrid against the wall holding her firmly with her magic. Astrid's face remained blank.

"Do you think you scare me?" laughed Astrid. "I don't think you quite understand. I'm done. I've lost. I've accepted my fate."

"And what about Caius?" Crista saw Astrid's eyes twitch and continued gloatingly, "Are you willing to seal his fate too?" Crista glanced at Astrid's stomach. "See I don't think you quite realise how much you still have left to lose. Now get dressed." Crista released Astrid gently and left Astrid to tidy herself up, closing the door firmly behind her.

Astrid heaved a heavy sigh and reached for the outfit Crista had thrown at her. She paused for a minute when she caught a glance of herself in her floor-length mirror. She lifted her top slightly and rubbed her stomach wistfully. *Could she be right, could I be-no! She's playing with you.* Crista liked her mind games and that's all that was. Astrid dropped her shirt and quickly changed. Her whole body ached. She winced as she pulled her tight jeans up. Astrid perched on the edge of her bed and carefully plaited her hair. It had been a while since she'd had to do it by hand.

Once Astrid had finished her hair, she slowly stood back up and studied her face in the mirror. She ran her finger along the bags beneath her eyes, empty eyes she barely recognised. She couldn't do much about those. It would have to do. She thought it ironic that Crista had chosen an outfit that covered all her scars, her father always spoke of how scars were an important reminder.

The door opened, and Crista was stood waiting patiently on the other side. Three guards stood behind her, not that she needed them. Astrid imagined it was for show more than anything.

"Ready?" Crista held out her arm and she lifted a brow. "You'd be wise to take it." She was right. Astrid was still tired and weak, and there were a lot of steps up to her father's chamber. She reluctantly took hold and the guards led the way past the prison cells. The prisoners had gone quiet. They were all at the front of their cells, leaning against the bars. They were watching intently, almost respectfully.

"Astrid." Her heart quickened when she heard Caius' voice, his hand reached through the bars desperately. She wanted to run to him, see what she'd earn by relinquishing what remained of her soul.

"Keep moving," hissed Crista, nudging Astrid onwards and up the steps.

They reached the door to Vincentrio's chamber and it opened before Crista could knock. She instructed the guards to wait outside and then led Astrid in. His desk had been replaced by a long mahogany table, silver platters breaming with food were scattered along its length and a grand candelabra stood in the centre. A place setting was laid at either end of the table and Vincentrio was sat at one end patiently waiting for his daughter to join him. He forced a doting smile when Astrid walked through the door and he quickly got up to help his daughter to her seat. Astrid flinched as he rested a hand on her arm, but she let him help. She sighed with relief when she sat in the chair. She was so tired.

"You may go, Crista," instructed Vincentrio, holding the door for her to leave through. Crista bowed her head in respect and reluctantly obeyed. As she left, Vincentrio's eyes narrowed on the power ring she wore on her finger. She quickly removed it and placed it carefully in his open palm. "I'll speak to you about that later," he warned and then firmly closed the door behind her. Vincentrio took his seat and placed the ring on the table out of the way.

"I'm sorry about that. You know I hate taking away anyone's magic, let alone yours, but you'd given me no choice," he explained earnestly.

"It's never pleasant when you're left with no choice," Astrid murmured tartly. She'd noticed where her father was sitting. His chair was positioned in the exact spot where she'd cradled Xander as he breathed his last breath. No doubt it wasn't just a coincidence.

Vincentrio pursed his lips. "I'm aware that there's bound to be some animosity between us after everything that's happened."

"Very perceptive," remarked Astrid. She fidgeted slightly under his icy glare.

"I don't appreciate your snide remarks, Astrid. I think it's about time you showed me some gratitude." He still spoke softly, though Astrid could see his patience was wearing thin.

"Gratitude?" snorted Astrid. "Gratitude for what exactly? For taking my magic? Murdering my best friend? Torturing me?

Corrupting me and convincing me to do your bidding? Poisoning my life? Killing my mother?"

"Astrid," cautioned Vincentrio, his eyes darkened.

"You invited me here to discuss things. So, let's discuss. Why don't we start with you telling me why I should be so grateful?" suggested Astrid flatly.

"That's enough," he snapped, slamming his fist on the table. "You betrayed me, Astrid. You helped a prisoner steal the Perrero gem from me, putting everything that I've worked for at risk. You helped this prisoner escape and planned to escape with her, but when that plan fell through you turned on me. Your own father. I can't tell you which bit hurts me more." Astrid scoffed. She went to respond, but her father held her lips closed tightly with his magic. "I'm not done yet." He released her and calmly continued, "You did all these things and here I am offering you a second chance. A chance to redeem yourself. To earn back my trust and your magic."

"And do tell what's involved in this story of redemption?"

"I simply want back what was stolen from me. You know these people and I think you know where they'd hide, whether you choose to *willingly* share that information is up to you. I'll get it from you either way. How much is your magic worth to you?" He balanced the ring carefully on his fingertips. He could see she was tempted.

"And what would you do with the people who stole it from you?" questioned Astrid. She knew she'd need her magic to protect Caius from Crista and she'd need it if she had any hope of trying to escape with him.

Vincentrio smirked and tucked into the roast beef steaming on his plate. "Let's not quibble over details. One could lose their appetite."

Astrid wasn't all that hungry, she just wanted to go back to bed and the smell of the red wine marinade was starting to make her feel queasy. She could feel her father's eyes fixed carefully on her, so she picked up her knife and fork and reluctantly began grazing on the array of vegetables filling her plate. Every mouthful made her stomach churn.

Vincentrio polished off the last morsel on his plate and dabbed his mouth with the napkin. He leant back in his chair and breathed a content sigh, a glass of red wine in hand. "You know your mother was a vegetarian. I pretended to be one at first to impress her, but she always knew. She cooked me a steak on our first anniversary." He laughed fondly and the creases that often plagued his forehead faded away. His lips curved with an earnest smile. "She was such a great cook. You were her greatest challenge there. So fussy. You knew what you liked and that was that, oh you were stubborn. So much like her."

Astrid's heart ached, he seemed so much like his old self when he was like this. It had been a long time since he'd spoken about her mother like that. She was surprised he still allowed himself to remember.

Astrid rubbed her tired eyes, her brows knitted. "*This* is what makes you so cruel. Every now and then you show me a glimpse of the father I loved and pined for all those years, and that's it. The work of a master manipulator."

"I do love you," he sobered, setting his glass on the table. "Everything I do, everything I've ever done is for you. Everything I'm building here is for you. All of it."

Astrid sighed. "No, it's not. That's what you tell yourself to make you feel better. I'm not sure if you really believe that, but I once did. Do you want me to be honest?" The corners of his eyes crinkled, and he waited for her to continue as he listened intently. "I had put you on this pedestal for so long and you used that, manipulated these childish ideals I had of you to your own advantage. And the worst part is, after everything you've done, there's still a small part of me that holds onto the hope that you're still a good man." The tears stung her eyes and she quickly wiped them away, cursing the foolish fantasy.

"Astrid," Vincentrio murmured softly. He stood from his chair and gently pulled Astrid to her feet. He wrapped his arms around her and held her close, stroking his fingers tenderly through the back of her hair as she rested her chin on his shoulder. She didn't shudder against him. She just closed her eyes.

"I'll always remember you this way," she whispered in his ear.

She grabbed the steak knife from the table behind him and jabbed it into his neck. His eyes widened, and blood spluttered from his mouth as he fell back against the table. His arms flailing looking for something to stop the bleeding. For his staff. Astrid pulled the knife from his neck and with a painful cry plunged it into his chest. He staggered towards Astrid, his eyes bulging, his hands reaching out for her to hold him whilst he died, but she stood back. Her jaw clenched. She made herself watch, watch as he choked on his own blood.

Astrid winced as her father's body hit the ground. His eyes were open and glassy, the blood slowly pooling around his lifeless corpse. She dropped onto her knees next to him, a stifled sob escaped her throat. She looked frenetically at the warm blood soaking around her and the sudden comprehension of what she'd done overwhelmed her. She clasped at her chest as it heaved with every pitiful cry. *There was no other way.*

"Is everything okay in there, Sir?" asked one of the guards as he knocked on the door.

Astrid ran her blood-soaked hands nervously through her hair and then glanced at the power ring on the table. The knocks became more urgent. She quickly grabbed the ring, but before she could do anything with it, a purple flame burst in front of her and Paige and Hesper stepped out from it.

"Now where's that son of a—" Hesper stopped as she heard the squelch of her boot in Vincentrio's still warm blood. Her mouth dropped slightly and then she spotted Astrid in the corner, her clothes stained with her father's blood and her eyes wet with regret.

"He's definitely dead," remarked Paige coldly, nudging his body with the tip of her shoe. "I'm just disappointed we missed it."

"I… had to," murmured Astrid numbly. Her brows knitted, and she stared blankly through Hesper like her mind had gone elsewhere, adrift from her body. Not even the heavy knocks at the door woke her.

"Come on, Hesp, there's no point us sticking around to see what happens next." Paige threw the globe back on the ground and waited for her sister to follow her through the portal.

Hesper paused. "She didn't leave you."

Paige rolled her eyes, but even she couldn't argue, without Astrid she'd have never made it back to Hesper.

"You need to come with us," said Hesper soothingly. She held her hand out to Astrid, but Astrid didn't move.

"We need to go," exclaimed Paige urgently. The guards would be through the door any second.

Hesper dismissed her sister's pleas and gingerly edged towards Astrid trying to catch her hollow gaze. She slowly took Astrid's hand with hers and led her to the portal. Astrid followed blindly. She glanced back at her father's cold body and blinked. The door burst open as Crista crashed through. The corner of Astrid's lips tweaked, and she stepped through the portal.